D0247117

We hope you enjoy this book. Please renew it by the due date.

You can renew it at www.norfolk.gov.uk/libraries or by using our free library app.

Otherwise you can phone 0344 800 8020 - please have your library card and PIN ready.

You can sign up for email reminders too.

NORFOLK ITEM

30129 085 966 449

NORFOLK COUNTY COUNCIL
LIBRARY AND INFORMATION SERVICE

'Funny and original' *SUN*

'Keenly observed, drily funny . . .
Delight after delight from first page to last' *RED*

RiCHARD OSMAN

The Thursday MURDER Club

PENGUIN BOOKS

PENGUIN BOOKS

UK | USA | Canada | Ireland | Australia
India | New Zealand | South Africa

Penguin Books is part of the Penguin Random House group of companies
whose addresses can be found at global.penguinrandomhouse.com.

First published by Viking 2020
Published in Penguin Books 2021
001

Copyright © Richard Osman, 2020, 2021

The moral right of the author has been asserted

Typeset by Jouve (UK), Milton Keynes
Printed and bound in Great Britain by Clays Ltd, Elcograf S.p.A.

The authorized representative in the EEA is Penguin Random House Ireland,
Morrison Chambers, 32 Nassau Street, Dublin D02 YH68

A CIP catalogue record for this book is available from the British Library

ISBN: 978-0-241-98826-8

www.greenpenguin.co.uk

To my mum, 'the last surviving Brenda', with love

Killing someone is easy. Hiding the body, now that's usually the hard part. That's how you get caught.

I was lucky enough to stumble upon the right place, though. The perfect place, really.

I come back from time to time, just to make sure everything is still safe and sound. It always is, and I suppose it always will be.

Sometimes I'll have a cigarette, which I know I shouldn't, but it's my only vice.

PART ONE

Meet New People
and
Try New Things

1

Joyce

Well, let's start with Elizabeth, shall we? And see where that gets us?

I knew who she was, of course; everybody here knows Elizabeth. She has one of the three-bed flats in Larkin Court. It's the one on the corner, with the decking? Also, I was once on a quiz team with Stephen, who, for a number of reasons, is Elizabeth's third husband.

I was at lunch, this is two or three months ago, and it must have been a Monday, because it was shepherd's pie. Elizabeth said she could see that I was eating, but wanted to ask me a question about knife wounds, if it wasn't inconvenient?

I said, 'Not at all, of course, please,' or words to that effect. I won't always remember everything exactly, I might as well tell you that now. So she opened a manila folder, and I saw some typed sheets and the edges of what looked like old photographs. Then she was straight into it.

Elizabeth asked me to imagine that a girl had been stabbed with a knife. I asked what sort of knife she had been stabbed with, and Elizabeth said probably just a normal kitchen knife. John Lewis. She didn't say that, but that was what I pictured. Then she asked me to imagine this girl had been stabbed, three or four times, just under the breastbone. In and out, in and out, very nasty, but without severing an artery. She was fairly quiet about the whole thing, because people were eating, and she does have some boundaries.

So there I was, imagining stab wounds, and Elizabeth asked me how long it would take the girl to bleed to death.

By the way, I realize I should have mentioned that I was a nurse for many years, otherwise none of this will make sense to you. Elizabeth would have known that from somewhere, because Elizabeth knows everything. Anyway, that's why she was asking me. You must have wondered what I was on about. I will get the hang of writing this, I promise.

I remember dabbing at my mouth before I answered, like you see on television sometimes. It makes you look cleverer, try it. I asked what the girl had weighed.

Elizabeth found the information in her folder, followed her finger and read out that the girl had been forty-six kilos. Which threw us both, because neither of us was sure what forty-six kilos was in real money. In my head I was thinking it must be about twenty-three stone? Two to one was my thinking. Even as I thought that, though, I suspected I was getting mixed up with inches and centimetres.

Elizabeth let me know the girl definitely wasn't twenty-three stone, as she had a picture of her corpse in the folder. She tapped the folder at me, before turning her attention back to the room, and said, 'Will somebody ask Bernard what forty-six kilos is?'

Bernard always sits by himself, on one of the smaller tables nearest the patio. It is Table 8. You don't need to know that, but I will tell you a bit about Bernard.

Bernard Cottle was very kind to me when I first arrived at Coopers Chase. He brought me a clematis cutting and explained the recycling timetable. They have four different coloured bins here. Four! Thanks to Bernard, I know that green is for glass, and blue is cardboard and paper. As for red and black, though, your guess is still as good as mine. I've seen all sorts as I've wandered about. Someone once put a fax machine in one.

Bernard had been a professor, something in science, and had worked all around the world, including going to Dubai before anyone had heard of it. True to form, he was wearing a suit and tie to lunch, but was, nevertheless, reading the *Daily Express*. Mary from Ruskin Court, who was at the next table, got his attention and asked how much forty-six kilos was when it was at home.

Bernard nodded and called over to Elizabeth, 'Seven stone three and a bit.'

And that's Bernard for you.

Elizabeth thanked him and said that sounded about right, and Bernard returned to his crossword. I looked up centimetres and inches afterwards, and at least I was right about that.

Elizabeth went back to her question. How long would the girl stabbed with the kitchen knife have to live? I guessed that, unattended, she would probably die in around forty-five minutes.

'Well, quite, Joyce,' she said, and then had another question. What if the girl had had medical assistance? Not a doctor, but someone who could patch up a wound. Someone who'd been in the army, perhaps. Someone like that.

I have seen a lot of stab wounds in my time. My job wasn't all sprained ankles. So I said then, well, she wouldn't die at all. Which she wouldn't. It wouldn't have been fun for her, but it would have been easy to patch up.

Elizabeth was nodding away, and said that was precisely what she had told Ibrahim, although I didn't know Ibrahim at that time. As I say, this was a couple of months ago.

It hadn't seemed at all right to Elizabeth, and her view was that the boyfriend had killed her. I know this is still often the case. You read about it.

I think before I moved in I might have found this whole conversation unusual, but it is pretty par for the course once you get to know everyone here. Last week I met the man who invented Mint Choc Chip ice cream, or so he tells it. I don't really have any way of checking.

I was glad to have helped Elizabeth in my small way, so decided I might ask a favour. I asked if there was any way I could take a look at the picture of the corpse. Just out of professional interest.

Elizabeth beamed, the way people around here beam when you ask to look at pictures of their grandchildren graduating. She slipped an A4 photocopy out of her folder, laid it, face down, in front of me and told me to keep it, as they all had copies.

I told her that was very kind of her, and she said not at all, but she wondered if she could ask me one final question.

'Of course,' I said.

Then she said, 'Are you ever free on Thursdays?'

And, that, believe it or not, was the first I had heard of Thursdays.

2

PC Donna De Freitas would like to have a gun. She would like to be chasing serial killers into abandoned warehouses, grimly getting the job done, despite a fresh bullet wound in her shoulder. Perhaps developing a taste for whisky and having an affair with her partner.

But for now, twenty-six years old, and sitting down for lunch at 11.45 in the morning, with four pensioners she has only just met, Donna understands that she will have to work her way up to all that. And besides, she has to admit that the last hour or so has been rather fun.

Donna has given her talk 'Practical Tips for Home Security' many times. And today there was the usual audience of older people, blankets across knees, free biscuits, and a few happy snoozers at the back. She gives the same advice each time. The absolute, paramount importance of installing window locks, checking ID cards and never giving out personal information to cold callers. More than anything, she is supposed to be a reassuring presence in a terrifying world. Donna understands that, and it also gets her out of both the station and paperwork, so she volunteers. Fairhaven Police Station is sleepier than Donna is used to.

Today, however, she had found herself at Coopers Chase Retirement Village. It seemed innocuous enough. Lush, untroubled, sedate, and on her drive in she had spotted a nice pub for lunch on the way home. So getting serial killers in headlocks on speedboats would have to wait.

'Security,' Donna had begun, though she was really

7

thinking about whether she should get a tattoo. A dolphin on her lower back? Or would that be too much of a cliché? And would it be painful? Probably, but she was supposed to be a police officer, wasn't she? 'What do we mean when we say the word "security"? Well, I think that word means different things to different . . .'

A hand shot up in the front row. Which was not normally how this went, but in for a penny. An immaculately dressed woman in her eighties had a point to make.

'Dear, I think we're all hoping this won't be a talk about window locks.' The woman looked around her, picking up murmured support.

A gentleman hemmed in by a walking frame in the second row was next. 'And no ID cards please, we know about ID cards. Are you really from the Gas Board, or are you a burglar? We've got it, I promise.'

A free-for-all had commenced.

'It's not the Gas Board any more. It's Centrica,' said a man in a very good three-piece suit.

The man sitting next to him, wearing shorts, flip-flops and a West Ham United shirt, took this opportunity to stand up and stab a finger in no particular direction, 'It's thanks to Thatcher that, Ibrahim. We used to own it.'

'Oh do sit down, Ron,' the smartly dressed woman had said. Then looked at Donna and added, 'Sorry about Ron,' with a slow shake of her head. The comments had continued to fly.

'And what criminal wouldn't be able to forge an ID document?'

'I've got cataracts. You could show me a library card and I'd let you in.'

'They don't even check the meter now. It's all on the web.'

'It's on the cloud, dear.'

'I'd welcome a burglar. It would be nice to have a visitor.'

There had been the briefest of lulls. An atonal symphony of whistles began as some hearing aids were turned up, while others were switched off. The woman in the front row had taken charge again.

'So . . . and I'm Elizabeth, by the way . . . no window locks, please, and no ID cards, and no need to tell us we mustn't give our PIN number to Nigerians over the phone. If I am still allowed to say Nigerians.'

Donna De Freitas had regrouped, but was aware she was no longer thinking about pub lunches or tattoos – now she was thinking about a riot training course back in the good, old days in south London.

'Well, what shall we talk about then?' Donna had asked. 'I have to do at least forty-five minutes or I don't get the time off in lieu.'

'Institutional sexism in the police force?' said Elizabeth.

'I'd like to talk about the illegal shooting of Mark Duggan, sanctioned by the state and –'

'Sit down, Ron!'

So it went on, enjoyably and agreeably, until the hour was up, whereupon Donna had been warmly thanked, shown pictures of grandchildren and then invited to stay for lunch.

And so here she is, picking at her salad, in what the menu describes as a 'contemporary upscale restaurant'. A quarter to twelve is a little early for her to have lunch, but it wouldn't have been polite to refuse the invitation. She notes that her four hosts are not only tucking in to full lunches, but have also cracked open a bottle of red wine.

'That really was wonderful, Donna', says Elizabeth. 'We enjoyed it tremendously.' Elizabeth looks to Donna like the sort of teacher who terrifies you all year but then gets you a grade A and cries when you leave. Perhaps it's the tweed jacket.

'It was blinding, Donna,' says Ron. 'Can I call you Donna, love?'

'You can call me Donna, but maybe don't call me love,' says Donna.

'Quite right, darling,' agrees Ron. 'Noted. That story about the Ukrainian with the parking ticket and the chainsaw, though? You should do after-dinner speaking, there's money in it. I know someone, if you'd like a number?'

The salad is delicious, thinks Donna, and it's not often she thinks that.

'I would have made a terrific heroin smuggler, I think.' This was Ibrahim, who had earlier raised the point about Centrica. 'It's just logistics, isn't it? There's all the weighing too, which I would enjoy, very precise. And they have machines to count money. All the mod cons. Have you ever captured a heroin dealer, PC De Freitas?'

'No,' admits Donna. 'It's on my list, though.'

'But I'm right that they have machines to count money?' asks Ibrahim.

'They do, yes,' says Donna.

'Wonderful,' says Ibrahim, and downs his glass of wine.

'We bore easily,' adds Elizabeth, also polishing off a glass. 'God save us from window locks, WPC De Freitas.'

'It's just PC now,' says Donna.

'I see,' says Elizabeth, lips pursing. 'And what happens if I still choose to say WPC? Will there be a warrant for my arrest?'

'No, but I'll think a bit less of you,' says Donna. 'Because it's a really simple thing to do, and it's more respectful to me.'

'Damn! Checkmate. OK,' says Elizabeth, and unpurses her lips.

'Thank you,' says Donna.

'Guess how old I am?' challenges Ibrahim.

Donna hesitates. Ibrahim has a nice suit, and he has great

skin. He smells wonderful. A handkerchief is artfully folded in his breast pocket. Hair thinning, but still there. No paunch, and just the one chin. And yet underneath it all? Hmmm. Donna looks at Ibrahim's hands. Always the giveaway.

'Eighty?' she ventures.

She sees the wind depart Ibrahim's sails. 'Yes, spot on, but I look younger. I look about seventy-four. Everyone agrees. The secret is Pilates.'

'And what's your story, Joyce?' asks Donna to the fourth member of the group, a small, white-haired woman in a lavender blouse and mauve cardigan. She is sitting very happily, taking it all in. Mouth closed, but eyes bright. Like a quiet bird, constantly on the lookout for something sparkling in the sunshine.

'Me?' says Joyce. 'No story at all. I was a nurse, and then a mum, and then a nurse again. Nothing to see here I'm afraid.'

Elizabeth gives a short snort. 'Don't be taken in by Joyce, PC De Freitas. She is the type who "gets things done".'

'I'm just organized,' says Joyce. 'It's out of fashion. If I say I'm going to Zumba, I go to Zumba. That's just me. My daughter is the interesting one in the family. She runs a hedge fund, if you know what one is?'

'Not really,' admits Donna.

'No,' agrees Joyce.

'Zumba is before Pilates,' says Ibrahim. 'I don't like to do both. It's counter-intuitive to your major muscle groups.'

A question has been nagging at Donna throughout lunch. 'So, if you don't mind me asking, I know you all live at Coopers Chase, but how did the four of you become friends?'

'Friends?' Elizabeth seems amused. 'Oh, we're not friends, dear.'

Ron is chuckling. 'Christ, love, no, we're not friends. Do you need a top-up, Liz?'

Elizabeth nods and Ron pours. They are on a second bottle. It is 12.15.

Ibrahim agrees. 'I don't think friends is the word. We wouldn't choose to socialize, we have very different interests. I like Ron, I suppose, but he can be very difficult.'

Ron nods, 'I'm very difficult.'

'And Elizabeth's manner is off-putting.'

Elizabeth nods, 'There it is I'm afraid. I've always been an acquired taste. Since school.'

'I like Joyce, I suppose. I think we all like Joyce,' says Ibrahim.

Ron and Elizabeth nod their agreement again.

'Thank you, I'm sure,' says Joyce, chasing peas around her plate. 'Don't you think someone should invent flat peas?'

Donna tries to clear up her confusion.

'So if you aren't friends, then what are you?'

Donna sees Joyce look up and shake her head at the others, this unlikely gang. 'Well,' says Joyce. 'Firstly, we *are* friends, of course; this lot are just a little slow catching on. And secondly, if it didn't say on your invitation, PC De Freitas, then it was my oversight. We're the Thursday Murder Club.'

Elizabeth is going glassy-eyed with red wine, Ron is scratching at a 'West Ham' tattoo on his neck and Ibrahim is polishing an already-polished cufflink.

The restaurant is filling up around them, and Donna is not the first visitor to Coopers Chase to think this wouldn't be the worst place to live. She would kill for a glass of wine and an afternoon off.

'Also, I swim every day,' concludes Ibrahim. 'It keeps the skin tight.'

What *is* this place?

3

If you are ever minded to take the A21 out of Fairhaven, and head into the heart of the Kentish Weald, you will eventually pass an old phone box, still working, on a sharp left-hand bend. Continue for around a hundred yards until you see the sign for 'Whitechurch, Abbots Hatch and Lents Hill', and then take a right. Head through Lents Hill, past the Blue Dragon and the little farm shop with the big egg outside, until you reach the small stone bridge over the Robertsmere. Officially the Robertsmere is a river, but don't get confused and expect anything grand.

Take the single-track right turn just past the bridge. You will think you are headed the wrong way, but this is quicker than the way the official brochure takes you, and also picturesque if you like dappled hedgerows. Eventually the road widens out and, peeking between tall trees, you will begin to see signs of life rising on the hilly land up to your left. Up ahead you will see a tiny, wood-clad bus stop, also still working, if one bus in either direction a day counts as working. Just before you reach the bus stop you will see the entrance sign for Coopers Chase on your left.

They began work on Coopers Chase about ten years ago, when the Catholic Church sold the land. The first residents, Ron, for one, had moved in three years later. It was billed as 'Britain's First Luxury Retirement Village', though according to Ibrahim, who has checked, it was actually the seventh. There are currently around 300 residents. You can't move here until you're over sixty-five, and the Waitrose delivery vans clink with wine and repeat prescriptions every time they pass over the cattle grid.

The old convent dominates Coopers Chase, with three modern residential developments spiralling out from this central point. For over a hundred years the convent was a hushed building, filled with the dry bustle of habits and the quiet certainty of prayers offered and answered. Tapping along its dark corridors you would have found some women comfortable in their serenity, some women frightened of a speeding world, some women hiding, some women proving a vague, long-forgotten point and some women taking joy in serving a higher purpose. You would have found single beds, arranged in dorms; long, low tables for eating; a chapel so dark and quiet you would swear you heard God breathing. In short, you would find the Sisters of the Holy Church, an army which would never give you up, which would feed you and clothe you and continue to need and value you. All it required in return was a lifetime of devotion, and, given there will always be someone requiring that, there were always volunteers. And then one day you would take the short trip up the hill, through the tunnel of trees, to the Garden of Eternal Rest – the iron gates and low stone walls of the Garden looking over the convent and the endless beauty of the Kentish High Weald beyond, your body in another single bed, under a simple stone, alongside the Sister Margarets and Sister Marys of the generations before you. If you had once had dreams they could now play over the green hills, and if you had secrets then they were kept safe inside the four walls of the convent for ever.

Well, more accurately, three walls, as the west-facing side of the convent is now entirely glazed to accommodate the residents' swimming-pool complex. It looks out over the bowling green, and then further down to the visitors' car park, the permits for which are rationed to such an extent that the Parking Committee is the single most powerful cabal within Coopers Chase.

Beside the swimming pool is a small 'arthritis therapy pool', which looks like a Jacuzzi, largely for the reason that it is a Jacuzzi. Anyone given the grand tour by the owner, Ian Ventham, would then be shown the sauna. Ian would always open the door a crack and say, 'Blimey, it's like a sauna in there.' That was Ian.

Take the lift up to the recreation rooms next. The gym, and the exercise studio, where residents could happily Zumba among the ghosts of the single beds. Then there's the Jigsaw Room for gentler activities and associations. There's the library, and the lounge for the bigger and more controversial committee meetings, or for football on the flat-screen TV. Then down again to the ground floor, where the long low tables of the convent refectory are now the 'contemporary upscale restaurant'.

At the very heart of the village, attached to the convent, is the original chapel. Its pale cream stucco exterior makes it look almost Mediterranean against the fierce, Gothic darkness of the convent. The chapel remains intact and unchanged, one of the few covenants insisted upon by the executors of the Sisters of the Holy Church when they had sold out ten years ago. The residents like to use the chapel. This is where the ghosts are, where the habits still bustle and where the whispers have sunk into the stone. It is a place to make you feel part of something slower and something gentler. Ian Ventham is looking into contractual loopholes that might allow him to redevelop the chapel into eight more flats.

Attached to the other side of the convent – the very reason for the convent – is Willows. Willows is now the nursing home for the village. It had been established by the Sisters in

1841 as a voluntary hospital, charitably tending to the sick and broken when no other option existed. In the latter part of the last century it had become a care home, until legislation in the 1980s led to the doors finally closing. The convent then simply became a waiting room, and when the last nun passed away in 2005, the Church wasted no time in cashing in and selling it as a job lot.

The development sits in twelve acres of woodland and beautiful open hillside. There are two small lakes, one real, and one created by Ian Ventham's builder, Tony Curran, and his gang. The many ducks and geese that also call Coopers Chase home seem to much prefer the artificial one. There are still sheep farmed at the very top of the hill, where the woodland breaks, and in the pastures by the lake is a herd of twenty llamas. Ian Ventham had bought two to look quirky in sales photos and it had got out of hand, as these things do.

That, in a nutshell, is what this place is.

4

Joyce

I first kept a diary many years ago, but I've looked back at it, and I don't think it would be of any interest to you. Unless you're interested in Haywards Heath in the 1970s, which I am going to assume you're not. That is no offence to either Haywards Heath or the 1970s, both of which I enjoyed at the time.

But a couple of days ago, after meeting Elizabeth, I went to my first ever meeting of the Thursday Murder Club, and I have been thinking that perhaps it might be interesting to write about. Like whoever wrote that diary about Holmes and Watson? People love a murder, whatever they might say in public, so I will give it a go.

I knew the Thursday Murder Club was going to be Elizabeth, Ibrahim Arif, who lives in Wordsworth, with a wraparound balcony, and Ron Ritchie. Yes, *that* Ron Ritchie. So that was something else exciting. Now I know him a bit better, the shine has worn off a little, but even so.

Penny Gray also used to be part of it, but she is now in Willows, that's the nursing home. Thinking about it now, I fitted right in. I suppose there had been a vacancy, and I was the new Penny.

I was nervous at the time, though. I remember that. I took along a nice bottle of wine (£8.99, to give you an idea), and as I walked in, the three of them were already there in the Jigsaw Room, laying out photographs on the table.

Elizabeth had formed the Thursday Murder Club with Penny. Penny had been an inspector in the Kent Police for many years, and she would bring along the files of unsolved murder cases. She wasn't really supposed to have the files, but who was to know? After a certain age, you can pretty much do whatever takes your fancy. No one tells you off, except for your doctors and your children.

I'm not supposed to say what Elizabeth used to do for a living, even though she does go on about it herself at times. Suffice to say though, that murders and investigations and what have you wouldn't be unfamiliar work for her.

Elizabeth and Penny would go through every file, line by line, study every photograph, read every witness statement, just looking for anything that had been missed. They didn't like to think there were guilty people still happily going about their business. Sitting in their gardens, doing a sudoku, knowing they had got away with murder.

Also, I think that Penny and Elizabeth just thoroughly enjoyed it. A few glasses of wine and a mystery. Very social, but also gory. It is good fun.

They would meet every Thursday (that's how they came up with the name). It was Thursday because there was a two-hour slot free in the Jigsaw Room, between Art History and Conversational French. It was booked, and still is booked, under the name Japanese Opera – A Discussion, which ensured they were always left in peace.

There were certain favours both of them could call upon, for different reasons, and all sorts of people had been called in for a friendly chat over the years. Forensics officers, accountants and judges, tree surgeons, horse-breeders, glass-blowers – they'd all been to the Jigsaw Room. Whomever Elizabeth and Penny thought might help them with some query or other.

Ibrahim had soon joined them. He used to play bridge with Penny, and had helped them out once or twice with bits and bobs. He's a psychiatrist. Or was a psychiatrist. Or still is, I'm not quite sure. When you first meet him you can't see that at all, but once you get to know him it makes a sort of sense. I would never have therapy, because who wants to unravel all that knitting? Not worth the risk, thank you. My daughter, Joanna, has a therapist, although you'd be hard pushed to know why if you saw the size of her house. Either way, Ibrahim no longer plays bridge, which I think is a shame.

Ron had all but invited himself, which won't surprise you. He wasn't buying Japanese Opera for a second and walked into the Jigsaw Room one Thursday, wanting to know what was afoot. Elizabeth admires suspicion above all else and invited Ron to flick through the file of a scoutmaster found burned to death in 1982, in woodland just off the A27. She soon spotted Ron's key strength, namely, he never believes a single word anyone ever tells him. Elizabeth now says that reading police files in the certain knowledge that the police are lying to you is surprisingly effective.

It is called the Jigsaw Room, by the way, because this is where the bigger jigsaws are completed, on a gently sloping wooden table in the centre of the room. When I first walked in, there was a 2,000-piecer of Whitstable harbour, missing a letterbox of sky. I once went to Whitstable, just for the day, but I couldn't really see what the fuss was all about. Once you've done the oysters, there's no real shopping to speak of.

Anyway, Ibrahim had put a thick perspex screen over the jigsaw, and this is where he, Elizabeth and Ron were laying out the autopsy photos of the poor girl. The one who Elizabeth thought had been killed by her boyfriend. This particular boyfriend was bitter at being invalided out from the army, but there's always something, isn't there?

We all have a sob story, but we don't all go around killing people.

Elizabeth told me to shut the door behind me and come and take a look at some pictures.

Ibrahim introduced himself, shook my hand and told me there were biscuits. He explained that there were two layers, but they tried to finish the top layer before they started the bottom layer. I told him he was preaching to the converted there.

Ron took my wine and put it by the biscuits. He nodded at the label and commented that it was a white. He then gave me a kiss on the cheek, which gave me pause for thought.

I know you might think that a kiss on the cheek is normal, but from men in their seventies it isn't. The only men who kiss you on the cheek are sons-in-law or people like that. So I had Ron down as a quick worker straight away.

I found out that the famous trade union leader Ron Ritchie lived in the village when he and Penny's husband, John, nursed an injured fox back to health and called it Scargill. The story had featured in the village newsletter when I first arrived. Given that John had been a vet and Ron was, well, Ron, I suspected that John had done the nursing and Ron had simply been on naming duties.

The newsletter, by the way, is called *Cut to the Chase*, which is a pun.

We all crowded around the autopsy photos. The poor girl, and that wound that should never have killed her, even back in those days. The boyfriend had bolted from Penny's squad car on the way to a police interview and hadn't been seen since. He had given Penny a belt for her troubles too. No surprises there. If you hit women, you hit women.

Even if he hadn't run off, I suppose he would have got away with it. I know you still read about these things all the time, but it was even worse back then.

The Thursday Murder Club wasn't about to magically bring him to justice; I think everyone knew that. Penny and Elizabeth had solved all sorts of cases to their own satisfaction, but that was as far as they could go.

So I suppose you could say that Penny and Elizabeth never really got their wish. All those murderers remained unpunished, all still out there, listening to the shipping forecast somewhere. They had got away with it, as some people do, I'm afraid. The older you get, the more you have to come to terms with that.

Anyway, that's just me being philosophical, which will get us nowhere.

Last Thursday was the first time it was the four of us. Elizabeth, Ibrahim, Ron and me. And, as I say, it seemed very natural. As if I was completing their jigsaw again.

I will leave the diary there for now. There is a big meeting in the village tomorrow. I help to put the chairs out for these sorts of things. I volunteer, because (a) it makes me look helpful and (b) it gives me first dibs at the refreshments.

The meeting is a consultation about a new development at Coopers Chase. Ian Ventham, the big boss, is coming to talk to us about it. I try to be honest where I can, so I hope you don't mind me saying I don't like him. He's all the things that can go wrong with a man if you leave him to his own devices.

There has been a fearsome hoo-ha about the new development, because they're chopping down trees and uprooting a graveyard, and there's a rumour of wind turbines. Ron is looking forward to causing a bit of trouble, and I am looking forward to watching him do that.

From now on I promise to try to write something every day. I will keep my fingers crossed that something happens.

5

The Waitrose in Tunbridge Wells has a café. Ian Ventham parks his Range Rover in the last empty disabled bay outside, not because he's disabled but because it's nearest to the door.

Walking in, he spots Bogdan by the window. Ian owes Bogdan £4,000. He has been stalling for a while, in the hope that Bogdan is thrown out of the country, but thus far, no luck. Anyway, he now has a real job for him, so it's all worked out OK. He gives the Pole a wave and approaches the counter. He scans the chalkboard, looking for a coffee.

'Is all your coffee fair trade?'

'Yes, all fair trade,' smiles the young woman serving.

'Shame,' says Ian. He doesn't want to pay an extra fifteen pence to help someone he'll never meet in a country he'll never go to. 'Cup of tea please. Almond milk.'

Bogdan isn't Ian's biggest worry that day. If he ends up having to pay him, then so be it. Ian's biggest worry is being killed by Tony Curran.

Ian takes his tea over to the table, spotting anyone over sixty as he goes. Over sixty, and with Waitrose money? Give them ten years, he thinks. He wishes he'd brought some brochures.

Ian will deal with Tony Curran as and when, but right now he has to deal with Bogdan. The good news is that Bogdan doesn't want to kill him. Ian sits down.

'What's all this about two grand, Bogdan?' Ian asks.

Bogdan is drinking from a two-litre bottle of Lilt he has

smuggled in. 'Four thousand. Is pretty cheap to retile a swimming pool. I don't know if you know that?'

'Only cheap if you do a good job, Bogdan,' says Ian. 'The grouting's discoloured. Look. I asked for coral white.'

Ian takes out his phone, scrolls through to a photo of his new pool and shows it to Bogdan.

'No, that is filter, let's take off filter.' Bogdan presses a button and the image immediately brightens. 'Coral white. You know it.'

Ian nods. Worth a try though. Sometimes you have to know when to pay up.

Ian takes an envelope out of his pocket. 'All right, Bogdan, fair's fair. Here's three grand. That do you?'

Bogdan looks weary. 'Three grand, sure.'

Ian hands it over 'It's actually two thousand eight hundred, but that's near enough between friends. Now, I wanted to ask you about something.'

'Sure,' says Bogdan, pocketing the money.

'You seem a bright lad, Bogdan?'

Bogdan shrugs. 'Well, I speak fluent Polish.'

'Whenever I ask you to do something, it gets done, and it gets done pretty well, and pretty cheap,' says Ian.

'Thank you,' says Bogdan.

'So I'm just wondering. You ready for something bigger, you think?'

'Sure,' says Bogdan.

'A lot bigger, though?' says Ian.

'Sure,' says Bogdan. 'Big is the same as small. There's just more of it.'

'Good lad,' says Ian, and drains the last of his tea. 'I'm on my way to fire Tony Curran. And I need someone to step up and take his place. You fancy that?'

Bogdan gives a low whistle.

'Too much for you?' asks Ian.

Bogdan shakes his head. 'No, not too much for me, I can do the job. I just think that if you fire Tony, maybe he kills you.'

Ian nods. 'I know. But you let me worry about that. And tomorrow the job's all yours.'

'If you're alive, sure,' says Bogdan.

Time to go. Ian shakes Bogdan's hand and turns his mind to telling Tony Curran the bad news.

There's a consultation meeting down at Coopers Chase, and he has to listen to what all the old people have to say. Nod politely, wear a tie, call them by their first names. People lap that sort of thing up. He's invited Tony along, so he can fire him straight afterwards. Out in the open air, with witnesses nearby.

There is a ten per cent chance that Tony will kill him on the spot. But that means there is a ninety per cent chance that he won't, and, given how much money it will make Ian, he is comfortable with those odds. Risk and reward.

As Ian gets outside, he hears beeping and sees a woman on a mobility scooter furiously pointing at his Range Rover with a cane.

I was there first, love, thinks Ian, as he steps into the car. What is wrong with some people?

As he drives, Ian listens to a motivational audiobook called *Kill or Be Killed – Using the Lessons of the Battlefield in the Boardroom.* Apparently it was written by someone in the Israeli Special Forces, and it had been recommended to him by one of the personal trainers at the Virgin Active in Tunbridge Wells. Ian isn't certain if the personal trainer himself is Israeli, but he looks like he's from there or thereabouts.

As the midday sun fails to force its way through the illegally tinted windows of the Range Rover, Ian starts to think about Tony Curran again. They've been very good for each other over the years, Ian and Tony. Ian would buy up tattered and tired old houses, big ones. Tony would gut them, divide them up, put in the ramps and the handrails, and on they'd go to the next one. The care-home business boomed, and Ian built his fortune. He kept a few, he sold a few, he bought a few more.

Ian takes a smoothie from the Range Rover's ice box. The ice box had not come as standard. A mechanic in Faversham had fitted it for him, while he was gold-plating the glove box. It is Ian's regular smoothie. A punnet of raspberries, a fistful of spinach, Icelandic yoghurt (Finnish, if they are out of Icelandic), spirulina, wheatgrass, acerola cherry powder, chlorella, kelp, acai extract, cocoa nibs, zinc, beetroot essence, chia seeds, mango zest and ginger. It is his own invention, and he calls it Keep It Simple.

He checks his watch. About ten minutes until he gets to Coopers Chase. Get the meeting done, then break the news to Tony. This morning he had googled 'stab-proof vests', but the same-day delivery option had been unavailable. Amazon Prime? They must think he's a mug.

He's sure it will be fine, though. And great news that Bogdan's on board to take over. A seamless transition. And cheaper, of course, which is the whole point.

Ian had worked out very early on that he needed to take his business upmarket if he wanted to make real money. The worst thing was when clients died. There was admin, rooms left earning nothing as new clients were found and, worst of all, you'd have to deal with the families. Now, the richer a client was, by and large the longer they would live. Also, the richer they were, the less often their family would visit, as they tended to live in London, or New York, or Santiago. So Ian moved upmarket, transforming his company, Autumn Sunset Care Homes, into Home from Home Independent

Living, concentrating on fewer, bigger, properties. Tony Curran hadn't blinked an eye. What Tony didn't know he would quickly learn, and no wet room, electronic key card or communal barbecue pit could faze him. It seemed a shame to let him go really, but there it was.

Ian passes the wooden bus stop on his right, and turns into the entrance to Coopers Chase. As so often, he follows a delivery van over the cattle grid, and is stuck behind it all the way up the long driveway. Taking in the view on the way, he shakes his head. So many llamas. You live and learn.

Ian parks up and makes sure his parking permit is correctly and prominently displayed, on the left-hand side of his windscreen, with permit number and expiration date clearly showing. Ian has been in all sorts of scrapes with all sorts of authorities over the years, and the only two that have ever truly rattled him are the Russian Import Tax Investigation Authority and the Coopers Chase Parking Committee. Worth it, though. Whatever money he had made before, Coopers Chase had been in another league entirely. Ian and Tony both knew it. A waterfall of money. Which, of course, was the source of today's problem.

Coopers Chase. Twelve acres of beautiful countryside, with permission to build up to 400 retirement flats. Nothing there but an empty convent, and someone's sheep up on the hill. An old friend of his had bought the land off a priest a few years before, then suddenly needed some quick cash to fight off extradition proceedings due to a misunderstanding. Ian did the sums and realized this was a leap worth taking. But Tony had done the sums too, and decided to make a leap of his own. Which is why Tony Curran now owned twenty-five per cent of everything that he built at Coopers Chase. Ian had felt compelled to agree to the terms because Tony had never been anything but loyal to him, and also because

Tony had made it clear he would break both of Ian's arms if he refused. Ian had seen Tony break people's arms before, and so they were now partners.

Not for long, though. Surely Tony knew it couldn't last? Anyone can build a luxury apartment really – strip to the waist, listen to Magic FM, dig out some foundations or shout at a bricklayer. Easy work. But not everyone has the vision to *oversee* someone building luxury apartments. With the new development about to start, what better time for Tony to learn his true value?

Ian Ventham feels emboldened. Kill or be killed.

Ian gets out of the car, and as he blinks into the sudden glare of the sun, he just catches the aftertaste of beetroot essence that was one of the key obstacles to him launching Keep It Simple as a commercial proposition. He could leave the beetroot essence out, but it was essential to pancreatic health.

Sunglasses on. And so to business. Ian is not planning on dying today.

6

Ron Ritchie is, as so often, having none of it. He is jabbing a practised finger at a copy of his lease. He knows it looks good, it always does, but Ron can feel his finger shaking, and the lease shaking. He waves the lease in the air to hide the shakes. His voice has lost none of its power, though.

'Now here's a quote. And it's your words, Mr Ventham, not my words. "Coopers Chase Holding Investments reserves the right to develop further residential possibilities on the site, in *consultation* with current residents".'

Ron's big frame hints at the physical power he must once have had. The chassis is all still there, like a bull-nosed truck rusting in a field. His face, wide and open, is ready at a second's notice to be outraged or incredulous, or whatever else might be required. Whatever might help.

'That's what this is,' says Ian Ventham, as if talking to a child. 'This is the consultation meeting. You're the residents. Consult all you like, for the next twenty minutes.'

Ventham sits at a trestle table at the front of the Residents' Lounge. He is teak-tanned, relaxed and has his sunglasses pushed up over his 1980s catalogue-model hair. He is wearing an expensive polo shirt, and a watch so large it might as well be a clock. He looks like he smells great, but you wouldn't really want to get close enough to find out for certain.

Ventham is flanked by a woman around fifteen years his junior and a tattooed man in a sleeveless vest, scrolling through his phone. The woman is the development architect; the tattooed man is Tony Curran. Ron has seen Curran around, has heard about him too. Ibrahim is writing down every word that's said as Ron continues to jab in Ventham's direction.

'I'm not falling for that old bull, Ventham. This ain't a consultation, it's an ambush.'

Joyce decides to chip in. 'You tell him, Ron.'

Ron fully intends to.

'Thanks, Joyce. You're calling it "The Woodlands", even though you're cutting down all the trees. That's rich, old son. You've got your nice little computer pictures, all done up, sun shining, fluffy clouds, little ducks swimming on ponds. You can prove anything with computers, son; we wanted to see a proper scale model. With model trees and little people.'

This gets a ripple of applause. A lot of people had wanted to see a scale model, but according to Ian Ventham it wasn't the done thing these days. Ron continues.

'And you've chosen, deliberately chosen, a woman architect, so I won't be allowed to shout.'

'You are shouting though, Ron,' says Elizabeth, who is two seats away, reading a newspaper.

'Don't you tell me when I'm shouting, Elizabeth,' shouts Ron. 'This geezer'll know when I'm shouting. Look at him, dressed up like Tony Blair. Why don't you bomb the Iraqis while you're at it, Ventham?'

Good line, thinks Ron, as Ibrahim dutifully writes it down for the record.

Back in the days when he was in the papers, they called him 'Red Ron', though everyone was 'Red' something in those days. Ron's picture was rarely in the papers without the caption 'talks between the two sides collapsed late last night'. A veteran of picket lines and police cells, of blacklegs, blacklists and bust-ups, of slow-downs and sit-ins, of wildcats and walkouts, Ron had been there, warming his hands over a brazier, with the old gang at British Leyland. Ron had seen, first-hand, the demise of the dockers. Ron had picketed Wapping as he witnessed the victory of Rupert Murdoch and the collapse of the printers. Ron had led the Kent miners up the A1 and had been arrested at Orgreave as the final resistance of the coal industry was crushed. In fact, a man less indefatigable than Ron might have considered himself a jinx. But that's the fate of the underdog, and Ron simply loved to be the underdog. If he ever found himself in a situation where he wasn't the underdog, he would twist and turn and shake that situation until he had convinced everyone that he was. But Ron had always practised what he had preached. He had always quietly helped anyone who had needed a leg-up, needed a few extra quid at Christmas, needed a suit or a solicitor for court. Anyone who, for any reason, had needed a champion, had always been safe in Ron's tattooed arms.

The tattoos are fading now, the hands are shaking, but the fire still burns.

'You know where you can shove this lease, don't you, Ventham?'

'Feel free to enlighten me,' says Ian Ventham.

Ron then starts to make a point about David Cameron and the EU referendum, but loses his thread. Ibrahim places a hand on his elbow. Ron nods the nod of a man whose work here is done and he sits, knees cracking like gunshots.

He's happy. And he notices his shakes have stopped, just for the moment. Back in the fight. There was nothing like it.

7

As Father Matthew Mackie slips in at the back of the lounge, a large man in a West Ham shirt is shouting about Tony Blair. There is a big turnout, as he had hoped. That's useful, plenty of objections to the Woodlands development. There had been no buffet service on the train from Bexhill, and so he is glad to see there are biscuits.

He grabs a handful when no one is looking, takes a blue plastic seat in the back row and settles himself in. The man in the tightly fitting football top is running out of steam now and, as he sits down, other hands go up. Hopefully this was a wasted trip, but it is far better to be safe than sorry. Father Mackie is aware that he is nervous. He adjusts his dog collar, runs a hand through his shock of snowy-white hair and dips into his pocket for a shortbread finger. If someone doesn't ask about the cemetery, perhaps he should. Just be brave. Remember he has a job to do.

How peculiar to be in this room! He shivers. Probably just the cold.

8

The consultation over, Ron is sitting with Joyce beside the bowling green, cold beers glinting in the sunshine. He is currently being distracted by a retired, one-armed jeweller from Ruskin Court, called Dennis Edmonds.

Dennis, to whom Ron has never spoken before, wants to congratulate Ron on the very salient points he made during the consultation meeting. 'Thought-provoking, Ron, thought-provoking. Plenty to chew on there.'

Ron thanks Dennis for his kind words, and waits for the move that he knows is coming. The move that always comes.

'And this must be your son?' says Dennis, turning towards Jason Ritchie, also cradling a beer. 'The champ!'

Jason smiles and nods, as polite as always. Dennis extends his arm. 'Dennis. I'm a friend of your dad's.'

Jason shakes the man's hand. 'Jason. How do you do, Dennis.'

Dennis stares for a beat, waiting for Jason to start a conversation, then nods enthusiastically. 'Well, a pleasure to meet you, I'm a huge fan, seen all your fights. We'll see you soon again, I hope?'

Jason nods politely again and Dennis ambles off, forgetting even to pretend to say goodbye to Ron. Father and son, well used to these interruptions, resume their conversation with Joyce.

'Yeah, it's called *Famous Family Trees*,' says Jason. 'They've researched the family history and they want to take me round various places, tell me a bit about, you know, family history. Great-granny's a prostitute and all that.'

'I ain't seen it,' says Ron. 'What is it, BBC?'

'It's ITV; it's really very good, Ron,' says Joyce. 'I saw one recently, did you see it Jason, with the actor? He's the doctor from *Holby City*, but I've also seen him in a *Poirot*.'

'I didn't see it, Joyce,' says Jason.

'It was very interesting. His grandfather, it turns out, had murdered his lover. A gay lover as well. His face was a picture. Oh, you should do it, Jason.' Joyce claps. 'Imagine if Ron had a gay granddad. I'd enjoy that.'

Jason nods. 'They'd want to talk to you too, Dad. On camera. They asked if you'd be up for it, and I told them good luck shutting you up.'

Ron laughs. 'But are you really doing that *Celebrity Ice Dance* thing as well?'

'I thought it might be fun.'

'Oh, I agree,' says Joyce, finishing her beer and reaching for another.

'You're doing a lot at the moment, Son,' says Ron. 'Joyce says she saw you on *MasterChef*.'

Jason shrugs. 'You're right, Dad. I should go back to boxing.'

'I can't believe you'd never made a macaroon before, Jason,' says Joyce.

Ron knocks back some of his beer, then motions over to his left with the bottle.

'Over by the BMW, Jase – don't look now – that's Ventham, the one I was telling you about. I ran rings around him, didn't I, Joyce?'

'He didn't know if he was coming or going, Ron,' agrees Joyce.

Jason leans back and stretches, a casual look to his left as he does so. Joyce moves her chair to get a better view.

'Yeah, nice and subtle, Joyce,' says Ron. 'That's Curran with him, Jase, the builder. You ever come across him in town?'

'Once or twice,' says Jason.

Ron looks over again. The conversation between the men looks tense. Talking fast and low, hands aggressive and defensive, but contained.

'They having a little barney, you think?' he asks.

Jason sips his beer and scans across to the car park again, taking the men in.

'They're like a couple out on a date, pretending they're not having an argument,' says Joyce. 'In a Pizza Express.'

'You've nailed it there, Joyce,' agrees Jason, turning back to his dad and finishing his beer.

'Game of snooker this afternoon, Son?' says Ron. 'Or are you shooting off?'

'Love to, Dad, but I've got a little errand.'

'Anything I can help with?'

Jason shakes his head. 'Boring one, won't take long.' He stands and stretches. 'You haven't had any journalists ringing you up today, have you?'

'Should I have?' asks Ron. 'Something up?'

'Nah, you know journalists. But no calls, no mail or anything?'

'I had a catalogue for walk-in baths,' says Ron. 'You want to tell me why you're asking?'

'You know me, Dad, they're always after something.'

'How exciting!' says Joyce.

'See you both,' says Jason. 'Don't get drunk and smash the place up.'

Jason leaves. Joyce turns her face up to the sun and closes her eyes. 'Well, isn't this lovely, Ron? I never knew I liked beer. Imagine if I'd died at seventy? I never would have known.'

'Cheers to that, Joyce,' says Ron, and polishes off his drink. 'What do you reckon's up with Jason?'

'Probably a woman,' says Joyce. 'You know what we're like.'

Ron nods. 'Probably, yeah.'

He watches his son depart into the distance. He's worried. But then there's never been a day with Jason, whether in the ring, or out, when Ron hasn't worried.

9

The consultation went well. Ian Ventham is no longer worried about The Woodlands; it's a done deal. The loud guy from the meeting? He'd met his type before. Let him blow himself out. He'd also seen a priest at the back of the room. What was that? The cemetery, he guessed, but it was all above board, he had all the permits. Let them try and stop him.

And sacking Tony Curran? Well, he hadn't been happy, but he hadn't killed him either. Advantage Ian.

So, Ian Ventham is already thinking ahead. After The Woodlands is up and running there will be another, final phase of the development, Hillcrest. He has driven the five minutes up a rough track from Coopers Chase and is now sitting in the country kitchen of Karen Playfair. Her father, Gordon, owns the farmland at the top of the hill, adjoining Coopers Chase, and he seems in no mood to sell. No matter, Ian has his ways.

'I'm afraid nothing has changed, Ian,' says Karen Playfair. 'My dad won't sell, and I can't make him.'

'I hear you,' says Ian. 'More money.'

'No, I think –' says Karen, 'and I think you know this already – I think he just doesn't like you.'

Gordon Playfair had taken one look at Ian Ventham and disappeared upstairs. Ian could hear him stomping about, proving whatever point he was proving. Who cared? Sometimes people didn't like Ian. He has never quite worked out why, but over the years has learned to live with it. Certainly, it was their problem. Gordon Playfair was just another in a long line of people who didn't get him.

'But listen, leave it with me,' says Karen. 'I'll find a way. It'll work for everyone.'

Karen Playfair gets him. He has been talking her through the sort of money she could expect if she persuades her dad to sell up. Her sister and brother-in-law have their own business, organic raisins in Brighton, and Ian has already tried this line on them, and failed. Karen Playfair is a much better bet. She lives alone in a cottage on the land and she works in IT, which you can tell just by looking at her. She is wearing make-up, but in a subtle, understated way that Ian honestly can't see the point of.

Ian wonders exactly when Karen had given up on life and started wearing trainers and long, baggy jumpers. And you'd think, given that she works in IT, she could have googled 'Botox'. She must be fifty, Ian thinks, same age as him. Different for women, though.

Ian is on a lot of dating apps, and sets a strict upper age limit of twenty-five. He finds the dating apps useful, because it can be hard to meet exactly the right kind of women these days. They need to understand that his time is limited and his work demanding, and that commitment is hard for him. Women over twenty-five don't seem to get that, in his experience. What happens to them, he wonders. He tries to imagine why someone would choose to date Karen Playfair, but draws a blank. Conversation? That runs out soon enough, doesn't it? She'll be rich soon, of course, when Ian buys the land. That will help her.

Hillcrest will be a real life-changer for Ian, too. It will eventually double the size of Coopers Chase, and so double Ian's profits. Profits he will no longer have to share with Tony Curran. If that meant having to flirt with a fifty-year-old for a couple of weeks then so be it.

On dates, Ian has his tried-and-tested material. He'll impress young women with pictures of his pool, and the time he was interviewed on *Kent Tonight*. He had already shown Karen a picture of his pool, because you never knew, but she had simply smiled politely and nodded. No wonder she was single.

He could do business with her, though. She knew the upsides here, and she knew the obstacles, and they end their conversation with a handshake and a plan of action. As he shakes Karen's hand, Ian thinks that using a bit of hand cream every now and again wouldn't kill her. Fifty! He wouldn't wish it on anyone.

The thought briefly occurs to Ian that the only woman over twenty-five he spends any time with at all is his wife.

Oh well, time to go. Things to do.

10

Tony Curran has made up his mind. He brings his BMW X7 to a halt on his heated driveway. There is a gun buried under the sycamore in the back garden. Or is it under the beech? It's one or the other, but that's something he can think about with a nice cup of tea. And he can try to remember where his spade is, while he's at it.

Tony Curran is going to kill Ian Ventham, that's a given now. Surely Ian knows it too? You can only take so many liberties before even the most calm and rational man snaps.

Tony whistles a tune from an advert and heads indoors.

He moved in about eighteen months ago, on the first real profits from Coopers Chase. It was the type of house he had always dreamed of. A house built on hard work, on making the right choices, cutting the right corners and backing his own talent. A monument to what he had achieved, in brick, glass and tempered walnut.

Tony lets himself in and sets to work switching off the alarm. Ventham had got some of his gang to fit it last week. Polish, the lot of them, but then who isn't these days? Tony gets the four-digit code right on the third attempt. A new record.

Tony Curran has always taken his security very seriously. For many years Tony's building company had really just been a front for his drugs business. A way to explain away his income. A way to wash his dirty money. But it slowly got bigger, took up more of his time, brought in more and more money. If you'd told young Tony he would end up living in this house, he wouldn't have been at all surprised. If you'd told him he'd be buying it with money earned legally, he'd have keeled over there and then.

His wife, Debbie, is not back, but that suits him fine for now. Gives him time to concentrate, really think it all through.

Tony rewinds to the row with Ian Ventham, and his fury rises again.

Ian was cutting him out of The Woodlands? Just like that? A conversation on the way to his car? Outdoors, just in case Tony felt like swinging a punch. He would love to have smacked him there and then, but that was the old Tony. So they'd had a little row, nice and quiet. No one could possibly have noticed, and that's good for Tony. When Ventham turns up dead, no one can say they saw Tony Curran and Ian Ventham having a ding-dong. Keeps it clean.

Tony sits on a bar stool, pulls it up to the island in his vast kitchen and slides open a drawer. He needs to get a plan down on paper.

Tony is not a believer in luck, he's a believer in hard work. If you fail to prepare, you prepare to fail. An old English teacher of Tony's had once told him that, and he'd never forgotten it. The next year he had torched the same teacher's car, following an argument about a football, but Tony still had to hand it to the guy. If you fail to prepare, you prepare to fail.

As it turns out, there is no paper in the drawer, so Tony decides to work out the plan in his head instead.

Nothing needs to be done tonight. Let the world continue for a while, let the birds keep singing in the garden, let Ventham think he has won. And then strike. Why did people ever mess with Tony Curran? When had that ever worked out for anyone?

Tony hears the noise a second too late. He turns to see the spanner as it swings towards him. A big one too, real old-school stuff. There's no way of avoiding the swing and, in the brief moment of realization he has, Tony Curran gets it. You can't win 'em all, Tony. That's fair enough, he thinks, that's fair enough.

The blow catches Tony on the left temple and he collapses to the marble floor. The birds in the garden stop singing for the briefest of moments and then continue their merry tune. High up in the sycamore tree. Or is it the beech?

The killer places a photograph on the worktop, as Tony Curran's fresh blood begins to form a moat around his walnut kitchen island.

11

Coopers Chase always wakes early. As the foxes finish their nightly rounds and the birds begin their roll-call, the first kettles whistle and low lamps start to appear in curtained windows. Morning joints creak into life.

Nobody here is grabbing toast before an early train to the office, or packing a lunchbox before waking the kids, but there is much to do nonetheless. Many years ago, everybody here would wake early because there was a lot to do and only so many hours in the day. Now they wake early because there is a lot to do and only so many days left.

Ibrahim is always up by six. The swimming pool doesn't open until seven, for health-and-safety reasons. He has argued, unsuccessfully, that the risk of drowning while swimming unsupervised is dwarfed by the risk of dying from cardio-vascular disease or respiratory or circulatory illness due to lack of regular exercise. He even produced an algorithm proving that keeping the pool open twenty-four hours a day, would make residents thirty-one point seven per cent safer than closing it overnight. The Leisure & Recreation Amenities Committee remained unmoved. Ibrahim could see that their hands were tied by various directives and so held no grudge. The algorithm was neatly filed away, should it ever be needed again. There was always a lot to do.

'I have a job for you, Ibrahim,' says Elizabeth, sipping a mint tea. 'Well, a job for you and Ron, but I'm putting you in charge.'

'Very wise,' says Ibrahim, nodding. 'If I might say?'

Elizabeth had rung him the night before with the news about Tony Curran. She had heard from Ron, who had heard it from Jason, who had heard it from a source yet to be documented. Dead in his kitchen, blunt force trauma to the head, found by his wife.

Ibrahim usually likes to spend this hour looking through old case notes and sometimes even new ones. He still has a few clients and, if they are ever in need, they will make the trip out to Coopers Chase and sit in the battered chair under the painting of the sailing boat, both of which have followed him around for nearly forty years now. Yesterday, Ibrahim had been reading the notes of an old client of his, a Midland Bank manager from Godalming who took in stray dogs and killed himself one Christmas Day. No such luck this morning, Ibrahim thinks. Elizabeth had arrived with the sunrise. He is finding the break in his routine challenging.

'All I need you to do is to lie to a senior police officer,' says Elizabeth. 'Can I trust you with that?'

'When can you not trust me, Elizabeth?' says Ibrahim. 'When have I let you down?'

'Well, never, Ibrahim,' agrees Elizabeth. 'That's why I like to keep you around. Also, you make very good tea.'

Ibrahim knows he is a safe pair of hands. Over the years he has saved lives and saved souls. He was good at what he did, and that's why, even now, some people will drive for miles, past the old phone box and the farm shop, turning right just after the bridge and left by the wooden bus stop, just to speak to an eighty-year-old psychiatrist, long retired.

Sometimes he fails – who doesn't, in this world? – and those are the files that Ibrahim will reach for in those early mornings. The bank manager who sat in the battered chair and cried and cried and could not be saved.

But this morning there are different priorities, he understands that. This morning the Thursday Murder Club has a real-life case. Not just yellowing pages of smudged type from another age. A real case, a real corpse and, somewhere out there, a real killer.

This morning Ibrahim is needed. Which is what he lives for.

12

PC Donna De Freitas carries a tray of teas into the incident room. A local builder, Tony something, has been murdered, and judging by the size of the assembled team it's a big deal. Donna wonders why. If she takes her time with the teas, maybe she can find out.

DCI Chris Hudson is addressing the team. He always seems nice enough. He once opened some double doors for her without looking like he wanted a medal for it.

'There are cameras at the property, and plenty of them. Get the footage. Tony Curran left Coopers Chase at 2 p.m. and he died at 3.32, according to his Fitbit. That's only a small window to search.'

Donna has placed the tea tray on a desk while she stoops to tie her shoelace. She hears Coopers Chase mentioned, which is interesting.

'There are also cameras on the A214, around 400 metres south of Curran's home, and half a mile north, so let's get hold of that footage too. You know the time frame.' Chris stops for a moment and looks over at where Donna De Freitas is crouching.

'Everything all right, Constable?' he asks.

Donna straightens up. 'Yes, sir, just tying my shoelaces. Wouldn't want to trip with a tray of tea.'

'Very wise,' agrees Chris. 'Thank you for the tea. We'll let you get on now.'

'Thank you, sir,' says Donna, and walks towards the door. She realizes that Chris – a detective of course – has probably spotted that her shoes have no laces. But surely he wouldn't blame a young constable for a bit of healthy curiosity?

As she opens the door to leave she hears Chris Hudson continue.

'Until we get all that, the biggest lead is the photograph the killer left by the body. Let's take a look.'

Donna can't resist turning and sees, projected onto the wall, an old photograph, three men in a pub, laughing and drinking. Their table is covered in banknotes. She only has a moment, but she recognizes one of the men immediately.

Things would be very different when Donna was part of a murder squad; very different. No more visiting primary schools to write serial numbers on bikes in invisible ink. No more politely reminding local shopkeepers that overflowing bins were actually a criminal off–

'Constable?' says Chris, snapping Donna from her train of thought. Donna takes her eyes off the photo and looks at Chris. Firmly, but kindly, he motions that she is free to leave. Donna smiles at Chris and nods. 'Daydreaming. Sorry, sir.'

She opens the door, walks through, back to the boredom. She strains to hear every last word before the door finally swings shut.

'So, three men, all of whom we obviously know very well. Shall we take them one by one?'

The door clunks shut. Donna sighs.

13

Joyce

I hope you will forgive a morning diary entry, but Tony Curran is dead.

Tony Curran is the builder who put this place up. Perhaps he even laid the bricks in my fireplace? Who knows? I mean, probably not. He probably had someone else to do that for him, didn't he? And all the plastering and what have you. He would have just overseen things, I suppose. But I bet his fingerprints are here somewhere. Which is quite a thrill.

Elizabeth rang me last night with the news. I would never describe Elizabeth as breathless, but, honestly, she wasn't far off.

Tony Curran was bludgeoned, of all things, by hand, or hands, unknown. I told her what I'd seen with Ron and Jason, the row between Curran and Ian Ventham. She told me she already knew, so she must have spoken to Ron before she spoke to me, but she was polite enough to listen as I gave my view of it. I asked her if she was taking notes and she said she would remember it.

Anyway, Elizabeth seems to have some sort of plan. She said she is seeing Ibrahim this morning.

I asked her if there was any way I might be able to help and she said that there was. So I asked her what that way might be and she said if I held my horses, I would find out soon enough.

So I suppose I sit and wait for instructions? I'm going to take the minibus into Fairhaven later, but I shall keep my mobile on just in case.

I have become someone who has to keep their mobile on.

47

14

'So who killed Tony Curran, and how do we catch him?' asks Elizabeth. 'Or catch "him or her", I know I should say, but it's probably "him". What kind of woman would bludgeon someone? A Russian woman, but that's about it.'

After giving Ibrahim his instructions for the day, Elizabeth had headed straight over for this chat. She is in her usual chair.

'He absolutely seems the type to have had enemies. Sleeveless vest, big house, more tattoos than Ron, so on and so forth. The police will be making a list of suspects right now and we'll have to get our hands on it. In the absence of their list, though, why don't we look at whether Ian Ventham killed Tony Curran? You remember Ian Ventham? With the after-shave? Ventham and Tony Curran had a little fight. Ron saw them, of course – when does he ever miss a thing? And Joyce said something about Pizza Express, but I knew what she meant.'

Elizabeth tries to mention Joyce more often these days, because why deny it?

'Shall we make some reasonable assumptions? Let's say that Ventham is unhappy with Curran, or Curran is unhappy with Ventham? It doesn't much matter which. They have something to discuss, and yet they meet in public, which is peculiar.'

Elizabeth checks her watch. She is subtle about it, despite everything.

'So, let's say straight after the consultation meeting, Ventham has bad news to break. He fears Curran's reaction so much that he meets him in public view. He hopes to placate him. But in Ron's view he was "unsuccessful". I'm paraphrasing Ron there.'

There is a small sponge cube on a stick next to the bed. Elizabeth places it in a jug of water and wets Penny's dry lips. The metallic chirp of Penny's heart monitor fills the silence.

'So how would Ventham react, in that scenario, Penny? Facing Curran with a grudge? Switch to plan B? Follow Curran to his house? "Let me in, let's just talk about this, perhaps I've been too hasty?" And then, *wallop!*, as simple as that, don't you think? He kills Curran before Curran kills him?'

Elizabeth looks around for her bag. She places her hands on the arms of the chair, ready to leave.

'But why? That's the question I know you'd ask. I'm going to try and take a look at their financial relationship. Chase the money. There's a man in Geneva who owes me a favour, so we should be able to get Ventham's financial records by this evening. Either way, it sounds like fun, doesn't it? An adventure. And I think we'll have a few tricks that the police won't. I'm sure they'd appreciate a bit of help, and that's my task for this morning.'

Elizabeth gets out of her chair and walks to the side of the bed.

'A real murder to investigate, Penny. I promise I won't let you miss a thing.'

She kisses her best friend on the forehead. She turns to the chair on the other side of the bed and gives a small smile.

'How are you, John?'

Penny's husband puts down his book and looks up.

'Oh, you know.'

'I do know. You always know where I am, John.'

The nurses say Penny Gray can hear nothing, but who is to say? John never speaks to Penny while Elizabeth is in the room. He comes into Willows at seven each morning and he leaves at nine each evening, back to the flat that he and Penny had lived in together. Back to the holiday trinkets and the old photos and the memories that he and Penny shared for fifty years. She knows that he talks to Penny when she is not there. And every time she walks in, always after knocking, she notices the fading white prints of John's hand on Penny's. His hand back on his book, though he always seems to be on the same page.

Elizabeth leaves the lovers together.

15

Joyce

Every Wednesday I take the residents' minibus into Fairhaven to do a spot of shopping. On Mondays it goes to Tunbridge Wells, half an hour in the other direction, but I like the younger feel of Fairhaven. I like to see what people are wearing and I like to hear the seagulls. The driver's name is Carlito and he is generally understood to be Spanish, but I have chatted to him a number of times now and it turns out he is Portuguese. He is very good about it though.

There is a vegan café, just off the seafront, that I found a few months ago and I am already looking forward to a nice mint tea and an almond-flour brownie. I am not a vegan and have no intention of ever becoming one, but I still feel like it's something that should be encouraged. I read that if mankind doesn't stop eating meat, there will be mass starvation by 2050. With respect, I am nearly eighty and so this won't be my problem, but I do hope they sort it out. My daughter Joanna is vegetarian and one day I will take her there. We'll just drop in, as if me visiting a vegan café is the most natural thing in the world.

The usual crowd are always on the bus. There are the regulars, Peter and Carol, a nice couple from Ruskin, who take the minibus down to visit their daughter who lives on the front. I know there are no grandkids, but nonetheless she seems to be at home during the day. There will be a story there. There's Sir Nicholas, who just goes for a mooch now they won't let him drive any more. There's Naomi with her hip that they can't get to the bottom of and a woman from Wordsworth whose name I have never quite caught and am now too embarrassed to ask. She is friendly enough though. (Elaine?)

I know that Bernard will be in his customary position at the back. I always feel like I would like to sit next to him, he is jolly company when he turns his mind to it. But I know he visits Fairhaven for his late wife, so I leave him in peace. That's where they met and that's where they lived before they moved in here. He told me that since she died he would go to the Adelphi Hotel where she used to work and polish off a couple of glasses of wine, overlooking the sea. That's how I first found out about the minibus, if I'm honest, so silver linings. They turned the Adelphi into a Travelodge last year, so now Bernard sits on the pier. That is less desolate than it sounds, as they recently revamped it and it has won a number of awards.

Perhaps I will just sit next to him at the back of the bus one day, what am I waiting for?

I'm looking forward to my tea and brownie, but I'm also looking forward to a bit of peace and quiet. The whole of Coopers Chase is still gossiping about poor Tony Curran. We are around death a lot here, but even so. Not everyone is bludgeoned, are they?

Right, that's me. If anything happens, I will report back.

16

As the minibus is about to leave, the doors slide open for a final time and Elizabeth steps in. She takes the seat next to Joyce.

'Good morning, Joyce,' she says, smiling.

'Well, this is a first,' says Joyce. 'How lovely!'

'I've brought a book, if you don't want to talk on the journey,' says Elizabeth.

'Ooh no, let's talk,' says Joyce.

Carlito pulls away with his customary care.

'Splendid!' says Elizabeth. 'I haven't really brought a book.'

Elizabeth and Joyce settle into conversation. They are very careful not to talk about the Tony Curran case. One of the first things you learn at Coopers Chase is that some people can still actually hear. Instead, Elizabeth tells Joyce about the last time she went to Fairhaven, which was sometime in the 1960s and whose purpose concerned a piece of equipment that had washed up on the beach. Elizabeth refuses to be drawn into details, but tells Joyce it was almost certainly now a matter of public record and she could presumably look it up somewhere if she was interested. The journey passes very pleasantly. The sun is up, the skies are blue and murder is in the air.

As always, Carlito stops the minibus outside Ryman's. Everyone knows to meet back here in three hours' time. Carlito has done this job for two years now and not a single person has ever been late. Except for Malcolm Weekes, who, as it turned out, had died in the lightbulb aisle in Robert Dyas.

Joyce and Elizabeth let the others out first, allowing their assault course of ramps and sticks and frames to disperse. Bernard doffs his hat to the ladies as he exits and they watch as he shuffles towards the seafront, his *Daily Express* tucked under his arm.

As they step down from the bus and Elizabeth thanks Carlito for his considerate driving in perfect Portuguese, Joyce thinks to ask for the first time what Elizabeth is planning to do in Fairhaven.

'Same as you, dear. Shall we?' Elizabeth starts walking away from the seafront and Joyce chooses to follow, keen for adventure, but still hopeful she might have time for her tea and brownie.

A short walk away is Western Road and the broad stone steps of Fairhaven Police Station. Elizabeth turns back to Joyce, as the automatic doors open in front of her.

'Here's the way I see it, Joyce. If we are going to investigate this murder . . .'

'We're going to investigate the murder?' asks Joyce.

'Of course we are, Joyce,' says Elizabeth. 'Who better than us? But we have no access to any case files, any witness statements, any forensics, and we are going to have to change that. Which is why we're here. I know I don't need to say this, Joyce, but just back me up, whatever happens.'

Joyce nods, of course, of course. They walk in.

Once inside, the two ladies are buzzed through a security door into a public reception area. Joyce has never been inside a police station before, though has watched every ITV documentary going and is disappointed that no one is being wrestled to the ground and dragged to a cell, their obscenities thrillingly bleeped out. Instead there is just a young desk sergeant, pretending he isn't playing patience on his Home Office computer.

'How can I help you, ladies?' he asks.

Elizabeth starts to cry. Joyce manages to control her double-take.

'Someone just stole my bag. Outside Holland & Barrett,' weeps Elizabeth.

So that's why she didn't have a bag with her, thinks Joyce. That had been bugging her in the minibus. Joyce puts her arm around her friend's shoulders. 'It was awful.'

'Let me get an officer to take a statement from you and we'll see what we can do.' The desk sergeant presses a buzzer on the wall to his left and within seconds a young constable enters through a further security door behind him.

'Mark, this lady has just had her handbag stolen on Queens Road. Can you take a statement? I'll make a cuppa for everyone.'

'Certainly. Madam, if you'll follow me?'

Elizabeth stands her ground and refuses to move. She is shaking her head, cheeks wet with tears now.

'I want to talk to a female police constable.'

'I'm sure Mark can sort this out for you,' says the desk sergeant.

'Please!' cries Elizabeth.

Joyce decides the time has come to help her friend out.

'My friend is a nun, Sergeant.'

'A nun?' says the desk sergeant.

'Yes, a nun,' says Joyce. 'And I'm sure I don't need to tell you what that entails?'

The desk sergeant sees that this is a discussion that could end badly in so many ways and chooses an easy life.

'If you'll give me a moment, madam, I will find someone for you.'

He follows Mark back through the security door and Elizabeth and Joyce are alone for a minute. Elizabeth stops the waterworks and looks over at Joyce.

'A nun? That was very good.'

'I didn't have much time to think,' says Joyce.

'If pushed, I was going to say someone had touched me,' says Elizabeth. 'You know how hot they are on that these days. But a nun is much more fun.'

'Why do you want to see a female officer?' Joyce has a number of other questions now, but this is first in the queue. 'And well done on not saying WPC, by the way. I'm proud of you.'

'Thank you, Joyce. I just thought that, as the bus was going into Fairhaven anyway, we should pop in and see PC De Freitas.'

Joyce nods slowly. In Elizabeth's world that is absolutely the sort of thing that makes sense. 'But what if she's not on shift? Or what if she is, but there are other female constables?'

'Would I have brought you here if I hadn't already checked that, Joyce?'

'How did you check th—'

The security door opens and Donna De Freitas steps through. 'Now, ladies, how can I –' Donna registers who is in front of her. She looks from Elizabeth to Joyce and back again, '– help you?'

17

DCI Chris Hudson has been given a file on Tony Curran so thick it makes a pleasing thud if you drop it on a desk. Which is what he has just done.

Chris takes a swig of Diet Coke. He sometimes worries he is addicted to it. He had read a headline about Diet Coke once, which was so worrying he had chosen not to read the article.

He opens the file. Most of Tony Curran's dealings with Kent Police were from before Chris's time in Fairhaven. Charges for assault in his twenties, minor drug convictions, dangerous driving, dangerous dog, possession of an illegal weapon. A tax disc misdemeanour. Public urination.

Then comes the real story. Chris opens an indeterminate sandwich from the garage. There are transcripts of a number of interviews held with Tony Curran over the years, with the last one being after a shooting in the Black Bridge pub, which left a young drug dealer dead. A witness recognized Tony Curran as firing the fatal shot and Fairhaven CID called Curran in for questioning.

Tony Curran had been in the middle of everything back then. Ask around and anyone would tell you. Tony ran the drugs trade in Fairhaven, and plenty more besides. Made a lot of money.

Chris reads the depressingly familiar stream of 'no comments' on the Black Bridge transcript. He reads that the witness, a local taxi driver, had disappeared soon after. Scared away, or worse. Tony Curran, local builder, walked away scot-free.

So what was that? One death? Two? The drug dealer shot at the Black Bridge and, perhaps, the poor taxi driver who witnessed it?

Since 2000 though, nothing. A speeding ticket, promptly paid, in 2009.

He looks at the photograph the killer had left by the body. Three men. Tony Curran, now dead. With his arm around Tony was a local dealer from back in the day, Bobby Tanner. Hired as muscle. Whereabouts currently unknown, but they would track him down soon enough. And the third man, whereabouts very much known. The ex-boxer Jason Ritchie. Chris wonders what the newspapers would pay for this photo. He has heard of officers doing this. The lowest of the low, as far as Chris is concerned. He looks at the smiles, the banknotes and the beers. It was probably sometime around 2000, when the boy was shot in the Black Bridge. Funny to think of the year 2000 as ancient history.

Chris opens a Twix as he studies the photo. He has his annual medical in two months and every Monday he convinces himself that this is finally the week he gets back into shape, finally shifts the stone or so that holds him back. The stone or so that gives him cramp. The stone or so that stops him buying new clothes, just in case, and that stops him dating, because who would want this? The stone or so that stands between him and the world. Two stone if he's really honest.

Those Mondays are usually good. Chris doesn't take the lift on Mondays. Chris brings food from home on Mondays. Chris does sit-ups in bed on Mondays. But by Tuesday, or, in a good week, Wednesday, the world creeps back in, the stairs seem too daunting and Chris loses faith in the project. He's aware that the project is himself, and that drags him further down still. So out come the pasties and the crisps, the petrol-station lunch, the quick drink after work, the take-away on the way home from work, the chocolate on the way home from the takeaway. The eating, the numbing, the release, the shame and then repeat.

But there was always next Monday and one of these Mondays there would be salvation. That stone would drop off, followed by the other stone that was lurking. He'd barely break sweat at the medical, he'd be the athlete he always secretly knew he was. Text a thumbs-up to the new girlfriend he'd have met online.

He finishes the Twix and looks around for his crisps.

Chris Hudson guesses that the Black Bridge shooting was the wake-up call that Tony Curran had needed. That was certainly how it looked. He had started working with a local property developer called Ian Ventham around this time, and perhaps he decided life would be simpler if he turned legit. There was good money in it, even if it was not what he had grown used to. Tony must have known he couldn't keep riding his luck.

Chris opens his crisps and looks at his watch. He has an appointment and he should probably head off. Someone saw Tony Curran having a row just before he died, and that someone is insisting on talking to him personally. It's not a long trip. The retirement community Curran had been working at.

Chris looks at the photo again. The three men, that happy gang. Tony Curran and Bobby Tanner, arms around each other. And, off to the side, a bottle in his hand and that handsome broken nose, maybe a couple of years past the height of his powers, Jason Ritchie.

Three friends, drinking beer, at a table covered with money. Why leave the photo by the body? A warning from Bobby Tanner or Jason Ritchie? A warning *to* them? You're next? More likely a red herring, or a misdirect. No one would be so stupid.

Either way, Chris will need to have a chat with Jason Ritchie. And, hopefully, his team will find their missing man, Bobby Tanner.

Actually, their missing men, thinks Chris, tipping the last of his crisps into his mouth.

Because, who took the photograph in the first place?

18

Donna motions for her two visitors to sit. They are in Interview Suite B, a boxy, windowless room, with a wooden table bolted to the floor. Joyce looks around her with the excitement of a tourist. Elizabeth looks at home. Donna has her eyes on the heavy door, waiting for it to swing shut. The moment it clicks into place she looks straight at Elizabeth.

'So you're a nun now, Elizabeth?'

Elizabeth nods quickly, raising a finger to acknowledge that this is a good question. 'Donna, like any modern woman, I am any number of things, as and when the need arises. We have to be chameleons, don't we?' She takes a notepad and pen from an inside coat pocket and places them on the table. 'But Joyce takes the credit for that one.'

Joyce is still staring around the room. 'This is exactly like you see on television, PC De Freitas. How wonderful! It must be so much fun to work here.'

Donna is not sharing in the sense of awe. 'So, Elizabeth. Have you had a bag stolen?'

'No, dear,' says Elizabeth. 'Good luck to anyone trying to steal my bag. Can you imagine?'

'Then can I ask what the two of you are doing here? I have work that needs finishing.'

Elizabeth nods. 'Of course, that's very reasonable. Well, I'm here because I wanted to talk to you about something. And Joyce was here for shopping, I presume. Joyce? I realize I haven't asked.'

'I like to go to Anything with a Pulse, the vegan café, if you know it?'

Donna looks at her watch, then leans forward. 'Well, here I am. If you want to talk, go ahead. I'll give you two minutes before I go back to catching criminals.'

Elizabeth gives a light clap of the hands. 'Excellent! Well, first I will say this. Stop pretending you are not pleased to see us again, because I know that you are. And we're pleased to see you again. This will be so much more fun if we can all just accept that.'

Donna does not reply. Joyce leans in to the tape recorder sitting on the table. 'For the purposes of the tape, PC De Freitas refuses to answer, but is attempting to hide a slight smile.'

'Secondly, but connected to that,' continues Elizabeth, 'whatever it is we are keeping you from, I know one thing for certain, it isn't catching criminals. It is something boring.'

'No comment,' deadpans Donna.

'Where are you from, Donna? May I call you Donna?'

'You may. I'm from south London.'

'Transferred from the Met?'

Donna nods. Elizabeth makes a note in her book.

'You're taking notes?' asks Donna.

Elizabeth nods. 'Why so? And why to Fairhaven?'

'That's a story for another day. You have one more question before I leave the room. Fun though this is.'

'Of course,' replies Elizabeth. She shuts her notebook and adjusts her glasses. 'Well, I have a statement really, but I promise it ends with a question.'

Donna turns up her palms, inviting Elizabeth to continue.

'This is what I see, and I know you'll stop me if I misspeak. You are in your mid twenties, you give the impression of being clever and intuitive. You also give the impression of being very kind, yet very handy should a fight erupt. For reasons we will get to the bottom of, almost certainly a doomed relationship, you have left London, where I would have thought the life and the work would have suited you to a T. You find yourself here, in Fairhaven, where the crime is minor and the criminals are petty. And you are pounding the streets. Maybe a junkie steals a bicycle, Donna; maybe someone drives off from a petrol station without paying, or maybe there's a fight, over a girl, in a pub. Goodness me, what a bore. For reasons that are not of importance, I once worked in a bar in the former Yugoslavia for three months and my brain was screaming out for excitement, for stimulation, for something extraordinary to happen. Does that sound familiar? You are single, you are living in a rented flat, you have not found it easy to make friends in the town. Most of your colleagues in the station are a bit old for you. I'm sure that young PC, Mark, has asked you out, but there's no way he could handle a south London girl, so you had to say no. You both still find it awkward. That poor boy. Your pride won't allow you to go back to the Met for a good while and so you're stuck here for the time being. You're still the new girl, so promotion is a pretty distant prospect, added to the fact you're not all that popular because, deep down, everyone can tell you've made a mistake and you resent being here. You can't even quit. Why throw away these years on the force, the tough years, just because of a wrong turn? So you strap on the uniform and you turn up, shift after shift, teeth gritted, just waiting for something extraordinary to happen. Like, perhaps, a woman who isn't a nun, pretending her bag has been stolen.'

Elizabeth raises an eyebrow at Donna, looking for a response. Donna is utterly impassive, utterly unimpressed. 'I'm still waiting for the question, Elizabeth.'

Elizabeth nods, and opens her notebook again. 'My question is this. Wouldn't you like to be investigating the Tony Curran murder?'

There is silence as Donna slowly weaves her hands together and rests her chin on them. She considers Elizabeth very carefully before speaking.

'There is already a team investigating the Tony Curran murder, Elizabeth. A highly qualified murder squad. I recently delivered tea to it. They don't really have a vacancy for a PC who tuts every time she gets asked to do the photo-copying. Have you ever thought it's possible you don't really understand how the police works?'

Elizabeth notes this down and talks as she writes. 'Mmm, that is possible. How complicated it all must be. But a lot of fun, I imagine?'

'I imagine too,' agrees Donna.

'They say he was bludgeoned,' says Elizabeth. 'With a large spanner. Could you confirm that?'

'No comment, Elizabeth,' says Donna.

Elizabeth stops writing and looks up again. 'Wouldn't you like to be part of it, Donna?'

Donna starts to drum her fingers on the desk. 'OK. Let's just suppose I would like to be involved in the murder investigation . . .'

'Yes, quite, let's suppose that. Let's start there and see where we get to.'

'You do understand how CID works, Elizabeth? I can't simply ask to be assigned to a particular investigation.'

Elizabeth smiles. 'Oh goodness, don't you worry about that, Donna; we can take care of it all.'

'You can take care of it?'

'I should have thought so, yes.'

'How?' asks Donna.

'Well, there's always a way, isn't there? But you would be interested? If we could make it happen?'

Donna looks back to the heavy door, safely shut. 'When could you make that happen, Elizabeth?'

Elizabeth looks at her watch and gives a small shrug. 'An hour, perhaps?'

'And this conversation never leaves this room?'

Elizabeth puts a finger to her lips.

'Then I would. Yes, please.' Donna holds up her hands, open and honest. 'I would really, really like to chase murderers.'

Elizabeth smiles and puts her notebook back in her pocket. 'Well, this is smashing. I thought I had read the situation correctly.'

'What's in it for you?' asks Donna.

'Nothing, other than a favour to a new friend. And we might have the odd question here or there, about the investigation. Just to satisfy our curiosity.'

'You know I couldn't tell you anything confidential? That's not a deal I can agree to.'

'Nothing unprofessional, I promise you.' Elizabeth crosses herself. 'As a woman of God.'

'And in an hour you say?'

Elizabeth looks at her watch. 'I'd say about an hour. Depending on the traffic.'

Donna nods, as if this makes complete sense. 'About your little speech, though, Elizabeth. I don't know if it was designed to impress me, or to show off in front of Joyce, but it was pretty obvious stuff.'

Elizabeth concedes the point. 'Obvious, but right, dear.'

'Almost right, but you're not quite, Miss Marple. Is she, Joyce?'

Joyce pipes up. 'Oh yes, that boy Mark is gay, Elizabeth. You'd have to be fairly blind to miss that.'

Donna smiles. 'Lucky you have your friend with you, Sister.' She likes that Elizabeth is attempting to hide a smile of her own.

'I'll need your mobile number, by the way, Donna,' says Elizabeth. 'I don't really want to fake a crime every time I need to see you.'

Donna slides a card over the table.

'I hope that's a personal number and not an official one,' says Elizabeth. 'It would be nice to have some privacy.'

Donna looks at Elizabeth, shakes her head and sighs. She writes down another number on the card.

'Lovely,' says Elizabeth. 'I suspect between us we can find whoever killed Tony Curran. It can't be beyond the wit of man. Or rather woman.'

Donna stands. 'Should I ask how you can get me on the investigating team, Elizabeth, or don't I want to know?'

Elizabeth checks her watch. 'Nothing you need to concern yourself with. Ron and Ibrahim should be taking care of it about now.'

Joyce waits for Elizabeth to stand too, then leans into the tape recorder once again. 'Interview terminated, 12.47 p.m.'

19

DCI Chris Hudson swings his Ford Focus onto the long, broad driveway leading up to Coopers Chase. The traffic hasn't been at all bad and he is hoping this won't take too long.

As he checks out his surroundings, Chris wonders why this place needs quite so many llamas. There are no spaces in the visitors' car park, so he eases the Focus onto a verge and steps out into the Kent sun.

Chris has been to retirement communities before and this is not at all what he had been expecting. This is a whole village. He wanders past a bowls match, wine chilling in coolers at each end. One of the players is an extremely elderly woman smoking a pipe. He follows a meandering path through a perfect English garden, flanked by three storeys of flats. There are people gossiping on patios and balconies, enjoying the sunshine. Friends sit on benches, bees buzz round bushes, light breezes play tunes with ice cubes. Chris finds the whole thing deeply infuriating. He's a wind-and-rain guy, a turn-up-the-collar-on-your-overcoat man. If Chris had his way he would hibernate for the summer. He has not worn shorts since 1987.

Chris crosses a residents' car park, past a red postbox looking picture-book perfect, annoying him further, and finds Wordsworth Court.

He rings the buzzer for flat 11: *Mr Ibrahim Arif.*

After being buzzed up and walking across a lushly carpeted hallway and up a lushly carpeted staircase and knocking on a solid oak door, Chris finds himself in that flat of Ibrahim

Arif, sitting opposite the man himself and also opposite Ron Ritchie.

Ron Ritchie. Well, wasn't that quite the thing? Chris had been taken aback the moment they had been introduced. The father of a man Chris was investigating – what was that? Luck? Something more sinister? Chris decides he will just let it play out. He trusts that, if there is an angle, he will spot it.

Strange that this is where 'Red Ron' ended up, though. The scourge of the bosses, the Beast of British Leyland, and British Steel, and British whatever else you'd care to mention? Amidst the honeysuckle and Audis of Coopers Chase? Chris would have barely recognized him, to be honest. Ron Ritchie is wearing mismatched pyjamas, an unzipped tracksuit top and dress shoes. He is looking around vacantly, mouth open. He is a mess and Chris feels awkward, as if he is imposing on a private scene.

Ibrahim is explaining the situation to DCI Chris Hudson.

'It can be very stressful for elderly people to talk to police officers. You mustn't think that's your fault. This is why I suggested you conduct the interview here.'

Chris nods gently, because he has done the training. 'I can assure you that Mr Ritchie is not in trouble, but if, as you say, he has information, I will need to ask him a couple of questions.'

Ibrahim turns to Ron.

'Ron, he just wants to ask you about the argument you saw. Remember, we talked about it?' Ibrahim looks back to Chris. 'He forgets things. He's very old, Detective Chief Inspector. A very, very old man.'

'All right, Ibrahim,' says Ron.

Ibrahim pats Ron's hand and speaks to him slowly.

'I think it's quite safe, Ron. We've seen this gentleman's warrant card. I rang the number on it, then I googled him. Remember?'

'I just . . . I just don't think I can,' says Ron. 'I don't want to get into any trouble.'

'There won't be any trouble, Mr Ritchie,' says Chris. 'I guarantee it. It's just that you might have important information.' 'Red Ron' is a shadow of his former self and Chris is very aware that he must play this carefully. Certainly don't mention Jason yet. The possibility of a pub lunch is also rapidly vanishing. 'Mr Arif is right, you can tell me anything.'

Ron looks at Chris, then back to Ibrahim for signs of reassurance. Ibrahim squeezes his friend's arm and Ron looks at Chris again, then leans forward.

'I think I'd be happier talking to the lady.'

Chris is taking his first sip of the mint tea Ibrahim has made for him. 'The lady?' He looks at Ron and then at Ibrahim. Ibrahim helps him out.

'Which lady, Ron?'

'The lady, Ib. The one who comes and talks to us. The woman copper.'

'Oh yes!' says Ibrahim. 'PC De Freitas! She often comes to talk to us, Detective Chief Inspector. Window locks. Do you know her?'

'Of course. Yes, she is one of my team.' Chris is trying to remember if the young PC with the non-existent shoelaces was Donna De Freitas. He was fairly sure she was. She'd come from the Met and no one knew why. 'We work very closely together.'

'So she is part of the investigation? This is excellent news.' Ibrahim beams. 'We love PC De Freitas here.'

'Well, she's not officially part of the investigation team, Mr Arif,' says Chris. 'She's on other important duties. Catching criminals and . . . so on.'

Ron and Ibrahim don't say a word, they just look expectantly at Chris.

'But it is a terrific idea. I would love her to be on the team,' says Chris, trying to work out who he would need to speak to. Surely someone owed him a favour?

'She is a fine officer,' says Ibrahim. 'She does you credit.'

Ibrahim becomes serious again and turns to Ron.

'So, if the handsome detective here and our friend PC De Freitas came to talk to you together? Would you be happy, Ron?'

Ron takes his first sip of tea.

'That'd be perfect, Ib. I'd like that. I'll talk to Jason too.'

'Jason?' asks Chris, on alert.

'Do you like boxing, son?' asks Ron.

Chris nods. 'Very much, Mr Ritchie.'

'My boy is a boxer. Jason.'

'I know, sir,' says Chris. 'You must be very proud.'

'Only, he was with me, so he should be here. He saw the row too.'

Chris nods. Well, that was very interesting. The trip has not been wasted. 'Well, I'm sure I can come back and talk to you both.'

'And you'll bring PC De Freitas with you? How wonderful!' says Ibrahim.

'Of course,' says Chris. 'Whatever gets us to the truth.'

20

Joyce

So it seems we are investigating a murder. And, better still, I have been in a police interview room. This diary is bringing me luck.

It was interesting watching Elizabeth in action. She is very impressive. Very calm. I wonder if we would have got along if we'd met thirty years ago? Probably not, we are from different worlds. But this place brings people together.

I do hope I'll be of some help to Elizabeth in the investigation. Help to catch Tony Curran's killer. Perhaps I will, in my own way.

I think that if I have a special skill, it is that I am often overlooked. Is that the word? Underestimated perhaps?

Coopers Chase is full of the great and the good, people who have done something or other with their lives. It's really a lot of fun. There's someone who helped design the Channel Tunnel, someone who has a disease named after them and someone who was the ambassador to Paraguay or Uruguay. You know the type.

And me? Joyce Meadowcroft? What do they make of me, I wonder. Harmless, certainly. Chatty? Guilty, I'm afraid. But I think they know, deep down, that I'm not one of them. A nurse, not a doctor, not that anyone would say that to my face. They know that Joanna bought my flat here. Joanna is one of them. Me, not so much.

And yet, if there's a row at Catering Committee, or if

there's a problem with the lake pumps, or if, as happened very recently, one resident's dog impregnates another and all hell breaks loose, then who is there to fix it? Joyce Meadowcroft.

I am very happy to listen to the grandstanding, watch the chests puffing out, hear the furious threats of legal action and wait for them to blow themselves out. Then I step in and suggest that maybe there's a way through, and perhaps there is a compromise to be reached, and perhaps dogs will be dogs. Nobody here feels threatened by me, nobody sees me as a rival, I'm just Joyce, gentle, chatty Joyce, always has her nose in everything.

So everyone calms down through me. Quiet, sensible, Joyce. There is no more shouting and the problem is fixed, more often than not in a way that advantages me. Which is something no one ever seems to notice.

So I am very happy to be overlooked and always have been. And I do think perhaps that will be helpful in this investigation. Everyone can look at Elizabeth and I'll just get on with being me.

The 'Meadowcroft', by the way, is from my late husband, Gerry, and I have always liked it. I had many reasons to marry Gerry and his surname was another to add to a long list. A friend of mine from nursing married a Bumstead. Barbara Bumstead. I think I might have found an excuse and called it off.

What a day! I think I'll watch an old *Prime Suspect* and then bed.

Whatever Elizabeth needs me to do next, I'll be ready.

21

It is another beautiful morning.

Bogdan Jankowski is sitting on a swing chair on Ian Ventham's patio and is taking some time to think things through.

Tony Curran has been murdered. Someone broke into his home and killed him. There were plenty of suspects and Bogdan is going over a few of them in his head. Thinking about reasons they might have for wanting Tony Curran dead.

Everyone seems shocked by Tony's death, but nothing surprises Bogdan. People died all the time of all sorts of things. His father had fallen from a dam, near Krakow, when Bogdan was a child. Or jumped, or was pushed, it didn't matter. It didn't change the fact that he had died. Something will always get you in the end.

Ian's garden is not to Bogdan's taste. The lawn, which stretches down to a line of trees in the far distance, is orderly and English and striped. Down towards the trees, off to the left, there is a pond. Ian Ventham calls it a lake, but Bogdan knows lakes. It has a small wooden bridge crossing its far end as it narrows. Children would love it, but Bogdan has never seen children in this garden.

Ian had bought a family of ducks, but foxes killed the ducks and then a guy Bogdan knew from the pub had killed the foxes. Ian didn't buy any more ducks after that, because what would be the point? There will always be foxes. Sometimes wild ducks still visited. Good luck to them, was Bogdan's view.

The swimming pool is directly on Bogdan's right. You could take a few steps down from the patio and dive straight in. Bogdan had tiled the swimming pool. Bogdan had painted the little bridge duck-egg blue and Bogdan had laid the patio he was sitting on.

Ian had come good on his offer and had asked him to oversee the building of the Woodlands development. So he was taking over from Tony, which some people might now see as bad luck, a jinx perhaps. But to Bogdan it was just something that was happening, and he would do it as well as he was able. Good money. The money doesn't really interest Bogdan, but the challenge does. And he likes being around the village, he likes the people.

Bogdan had seen all the plans now, studied everything. They were complicated at first but, once you'd seen the patterns, simple enough. Bogdan had enjoyed working on smaller jobs for Ian Ventham, he had liked the order of it, but he understands that things change and that he needs to step up.

Bogdan's mother had died when he was nineteen. She had come into some money when Bogdan's father had died. From somewhere, it hadn't been a time for details. The money paid for Bogdan to take up a place at the Technical University in Krakow, to study engineering. And that's where he had been when his mother suffered a stroke and collapsed at home. If he had still been at home then he would have saved her, but he wasn't, and so he didn't.

Bogdan came home, buried his mother and left for England the next day. Nearly twenty years later he is looking at a stupid lawn.

Bogdan is thinking that he will maybe close his eyes for a moment when, from the other side of the house, comes the deep sound of the front-door chimes. A rare visitor to this big, quiet house, and the reason Ian has asked Bogdan to be here today. Ian slides back the patio door of his study.

'Bogdan. Door.'

'Yes, of course.' Bogdan gets to his feet. He goes in via the conservatory he designed, through the music room he'd soundproofed and into the hallway he had once sanded in his underpants on the hottest day of the year.

Whatever you needed him to do.

Father Matthew Mackie is regretting asking his cabbie to drop him at the bottom of the drive. It had been quite the walk from the front gates to the front door. He fans himself a little with his file, then, quickly using the camera on his phone to check his dog collar is straight, rings the bell. He is relieved to hear noises from within the house, because you never know, even when you've made arrangements. He was happy to meet here, it makes things easier all round.

He hears footsteps on a wooden floor and the door is opened by a broad, shaven-headed man. He wears a tight, white T-shirt and he has a cross tattooed on one forearm and three names on the other.

'Father,' says the man. Good news, a Catholic. And, judging by the accent, Polish.

'Dzień dobry,' says Father Mackie.

The man smiles back, 'Dzień dobry, dzień dobry.'

'I have an appointment to see Mr Ventham. Matthew Mackie.'

The man takes his hand and shakes it. 'Bogdan Jankowski. Come in please, Father.'

'We understand, believe me, that you have no legal imperative to help us,' says Father Matthew Mackie. 'We disagree with the council's ruling, of course, but we must accept it.'

Mike Griffin from the Planning Committee had done his job well, thinks Ian. Feel free to dig up the graveyard, Ian, he'd said, be our guest. Mike Griffin is addicted to online casinos and long may that continue.

'However, I do think you have a moral obligation to leave the Garden of Eternal Rest, the graveyard, exactly where it is,' continues Father Mackie. 'And I wanted to meet you face to face, man to man and see if we can come to a compromise.'

Ian Ventham listens closely, but, in honesty, is really thinking about how clever he is. He is the cleverest person he knows, that's for certain. That's how he gets what he wants. It feels almost unfair sometimes. He's not even one step ahead of you, he's on an entirely different path.

Karen Playfair had been an easy one. If he can't persuade Gordon Playfair to sell his land, then he knows she will. Dads and daughters. And she'd see a chunk of the money, surely? An old man can only turn down a seven-figure sum for a big hill for so long. Ian would always find a way.

But Father Mackie is trickier than Karen Playfair, he sees that. Priests weren't like divorcees in their early fifties who could stand to lose a few pounds, were they? You had to pretend to have some respect, and maybe you actually should have some respect. After all, what if they were right? Open mind. Which was another example of cleverness being useful.

That's why Ian has asked Bogdan to join them. He knows this lot like to stick together, and quite right, who doesn't? He realizes he should probably speak.

'We're only moving the bodies, Father,' says Ian. 'It will be done with the greatest of care and the greatest of respect.'

Ian knows that this is not strictly true. Legally he had had to put the job out for public tender. Three bids had come in. One was from the University of Kent Forensic Anthropology Department, who would certainly do the job with the greatest care and respect. One was from a firm of 'Cemetery Special-ists' in Rye, who had recently moved thirty graves from the site of a new Pets at Home and included pictures of solemn men and women in dark blue overalls, digging out graves by hand. The last was from a company set up two months ago by Ian himself, with a funeral director from Brighton he had met playing golf and Sue Banbury from Ian's village, who rented out diggers. That final pitch was extremely competi-tive and had won the business. Ian had looked into the excavation of cemeteries online and it wasn't rocket science.

'Some of these graves are nearly one hundred and fifty years old, Mr Ventham,' says Father Mackie.

'Call me Ian,' says Ian.

Ian hadn't strictly needed to have this meeting, but he feels it's better to be safe than sorry. A lot of the residents can get quite 'churchy' when it suits them and he wouldn't want Father Mackie stirring up trouble. People get funny about corpses. So hear the man out, reassure him, send him hap-pily on his way. Donate to something? There's a thought to keep in the back pocket.

'The company you've employed to relocate the cemetery,' Mackie looks at his file, 'Angels in Transit – the Cremoval Specialists, they know what they're going to find, I hope? There won't be many intact coffins, Ian, just bones. And not skeletons; loose bones, broken down, scattered, half-rotted, sunk through the earth. And every single fragment of every bone, in every single grave, needs to be found, needs to be documented and needs to be respected. That's basic decency, but don't forget that it is also the law.'

Ian nods, though he is actually wondering if it is possible to paint a digger black. Sue will know.

'I am here today,' continues Father Mackie, 'to ask you to think again, to leave these ladies where they are, to leave them in peace. Man to man. I don't know what it would cost you to do that, that's your business. But you have to understand, as a man of God, that it's my business too. I don't want these women moved.'

'Matthew, I appreciate you coming to see us,' says Ian. 'And I see what you're saying about angels. Souls in torment et cetera, if I'm reading you right? But you said it yourself, all we'll find now is bones. That's all there is. And you can choose to be superstitious, or religious in your case, I see that, but I can choose not to be. Now, we'll take care of the bones, and I'm happy for you to be there and watch the lot if that's what floats your boat. But I want to move the cemetery, I'm allowed to move the cemetery and I'm going to move the cemetery. If that makes me whatever I am then so be it. Bones don't mind where they are.'

'If I can't change your mind then I will make this as difficult as I possibly can for you. I need you to know that,' says Father Mackie.

'Join the queue, Father,' says Ian. 'I've got the RSPCA up in arms about badgers. I've got the Kent Forestry Something banging on about protected trees. With you, it's nuns. I've got to comply with EU regulations on heat emissions, on light pollution, on bathroom fittings and a hundred other things, even though I seem to remember we voted to leave. I've got residents bleating about benches, I've got English Heritage telling me my bricks don't qualify as sustainable and the cheapest cement guy in the entire south of England has just gone to prison for VAT fraud. You are not my biggest problem, Father, not even close.'

Ian finally draws breath.

'Also, Tony died, so is difficult time for everyone,' adds Bogdan, crossing himself.

'Yeah, yep. Also, Tony died. Difficult time,' agrees Ian.

Father Mackie turns to Bogdan, now he has broken his silence.

'And what do you think, my son? About moving the Garden of Eternal Rest? You don't think we're disturbing souls? You don't think there will be penance for this?'

'Father, I think God watches over everything and judges everything,' says Bogdan. 'But I think bones is bones.'

22

Joyce is having her hair cut.

Anthony comes in every Thursday and Friday and appointments at his mobile salon are like gold dust. Joyce always books the first appointment, because that's when you get the best stories.

Elizabeth knows this and so is sitting outside by the open doorway. Waiting and listening. She could just walk in, but waiting and listening are old habits she can't break. In a lifetime of listening you pick up all sorts. She looks at her watch. If Joyce isn't out in five minutes she will make her presence known.

'One day I'm just going to dye the whole thing, Joyce,' says Anthony. 'Send you out of here bright pink.'

Joyce giggles.

'You'd look like Nicki Minaj. You know Nicki Minaj, Joyce?'

'No, but I like the sound of her,' says Joyce.

'What do we think about this fella they killed?' asks Anthony. 'Curran? I've seen him round here.'

'Well, it's very sad, obviously,' says Joyce.

'They shot him, that's what I heard,' says Anthony. 'I wonder what he'd done?'

'I think he was bludgeoned to death, Anthony,' says Joyce.

'Bludgeoned, was he? You really do have lovely hair, Joyce. You have to promise you'll leave it to me in your will.'

Outside, Elizabeth rolls her eyes.

'I heard they gunned him down on the seafront,' says Anthony. 'Three guys on motorbikes.'

'No, just bludgeoned in his kitchen, apparently,' says Joyce. 'No motorbikes.'

'Who'd do that?' says Anthony. 'Bludgeon someone in their kitchen?'

Who indeed? thinks Elizabeth, and looks at her watch again.

'I bet he had a lovely kitchen too,' says Anthony. 'What a shame. I always had a bit of a thing for him. Like you could tell he was a wrong 'un, but you still would?'

'Well, we're agreed there, Anthony,' says Joyce.

'I hope they catch whoever did it.'

'I'm sure they will,' says Joyce, and takes a sip of her tea.

Elizabeth decides enough is enough, stands and walks into the room. Anthony turns and sees her.

'Ooh, here she is. Dusty Springfield.'

'Good morning, Anthony. I'm afraid you're going to have to release Joyce. I need her.'

Joyce claps her hands.

23

Joyce

So that was a day I wasn't expecting when I was having my muesli this morning. First the nun business and now this.

If you think I have muesli every morning you've got the wrong idea, but this morning I did and, as things turned out, I was glad of the energy. It has gone 10 p.m. now and I have only just put my things down. At least I had a snooze on the train home.

I was having my hair cut this morning, with Anthony. We were nearly done and were just having a lovely gossip when who should arrive but Elizabeth. With a tote bag and a flask, both of which were out of character. She told me a taxi was on its way and to get ready for a day out. I have learned to be spontaneous since I moved to Coopers Chase, so I didn't bat an eyelid. I asked her where we were going, so I would have an idea about the weather etc., and she said London, which surprised me, but explained the flask. I know exactly how cold London can be, so I popped home and put on a nice coat. And thank goodness I did!

We still use the Robertsbridge taxis, even though they once took Ron's granddaughter to the wrong station, and to their credit they have got better. The driver, Hamed, was Somalian, and Somalia sounds very beautiful. Surprise, surprise, Elizabeth has been there and they had a right old chat. Hamed has six children and the eldest is a GP in Chislehurst, if you know it? I once went to a car boot there, so was at least able to chip in.

All this time Elizabeth was waiting for me to ask where we were going, but I didn't crack. She likes to be in charge and, don't get me wrong, I like her to be in charge too, but it doesn't harm to make your presence felt every now and again. I think she rubs off on me, and in a good way. I have never really thought that I was a pushover, but the more time I spend with Elizabeth, the more I think I probably am. Maybe if I'd had Elizabeth's spirit then I would have been to Somalia too? That's just an example of what I mean.

We got on the train at Robertsbridge (the 9.51 stopper) and she'd cracked by Tunbridge Wells and let me in on it. We were off to see Joanna.

Joanna! My little girl! You can imagine my questions. Elizabeth had me back exactly where she wanted me.

So why were we going to see Joanna? Well, this is what it seems had transpired.

Elizabeth explained, in that way she has that makes every-thing sound so reasonable, that we knew as much as the police did about many things in this case, which was a good thing for everyone. However, it would also be good if there were areas where we knew more than the police. In case we needed to 'trade' at any point. This might be useful, accord-ing to Elizabeth, because Donna is, unfortunately, a bit too canny to tell us everything. After all, who are we?

The big gap, the way Elizabeth would have it, was the financial records of Ian Ventham's companies. Might there be a useful connection between Ventham and Tony Curran there? A reason for their row? A motive for murder? It was important we found out.

To this end, Elizabeth had, of course, acquired detailed financial records of Ian Ventham's companies. By hook or, more likely, by crook. It was all in a big, blue file, hence the tote bag, which she put on the empty seat beside her. I haven't mentioned it yet, but we were travelling First Class. I kept hoping someone would ask to see my ticket, but no one did.

Elizabeth had taken a look through all the financial bumf and couldn't make head or tail of it. She needed someone to take a look and tell her what was what. Was there anything out of the ordinary? Anything we might poke our noses into when we had a spare moment? Hidden in the records would be leads, of that Elizabeth was sure. But hidden where?

I asked if the same person who had found her the records in the first place might be the man for the job. Elizabeth had said that unfortunately this person had owed her one favour, not two. She also said she was surprised I had said 'man' for the job, given my politics. She was right, it was not best practice, but I told her that I bet it was a man all the same and she confirmed that it was.

Somewhere around Orpington I in turn cracked and asked why Joanna? Well, Elizabeth gave her reasons. We needed someone up to speed on modern business accounting and who knows how to value companies, both of which Joanna, apparently, is. Was Ventham in trouble? Did he owe money? Are there any further property developments on the horizon? Are they funded? We needed someone we could trust absolutely and Elizabeth was spot on about Joanna here. Joanna is many things, but she won't let you down over a secret. Finally, we needed someone we could have quick access to and who owed us a favour. I asked Elizabeth what favour Joanna owed us and she said the universal guilt of a child who doesn't see their mum often enough. She had Joanna pegged there too.

It boiled down, Elizabeth said, to needing someone 'forensic, loyal and nearby'.

Anyway, she had emailed Joanna and not taken no for an

answer. She told Joanna not to discuss it with me, so it would be a nice surprise, and here we were.

This all looks convincing written down, but then Elizabeth always has the knack of sounding convincing. I didn't buy it for a moment, though. I don't doubt she could have found many better people for the job. You want the truth? I think Elizabeth just wanted to meet Joanna.

Which, by the way, was fine by me. It was a chance to see Joanna and a chance to show her off to Elizabeth. And all without the embarrassment of trying to arrange it myself. One way or another, if I arrange it, I always get something wrong and Joanna gets exasperated.

Also, today I wouldn't be talking to Joanna about her job, or her new boyfriend or the new house (in Putney; I haven't been, but she's sent me pictures and there is talk of Christmas). I would be talking about a murder. Try acting like a cool teenager when someone has been murdered. Good luck, darling, as they say.

We arrived at Charing Cross fourteen minutes late due to 'the slow running of this service', which Elizabeth had a good mutter about. I didn't need the loo on the train, which was a blessing. Last time I had been in London was for *Jersey Boys* with the gang, which was a while ago now. We used to go three or four times a year if we could. There were four of us. We would do a matinee and be back on the train before rush hour. In Marks they do a gin and tonic in a can, if you've ever had it? We would drink them on the train home and giggle ourselves silly. The gang has all gone now. Two cancers and a stroke. We hadn't known that *Jersey Boys* would be our last trip. You always know when it's your first time, don't you? But you rarely know when it's your final time. Anyway, I wish I had kept the programme.

We took a black cab (what else?) and off we set to Mayfair.

When we were on Curzon Street, Elizabeth pointed out an office where she used to work. It had been closed down in the 1980s for efficiencies.

I have been to Joanna's offices before, when they first moved in, but they have redecorated since then. There is a table tennis table and you can just help yourself to drinks. There is also a lift where you just say the number, instead of pressing a button. Not for me, but very swish all the same.

I know I sometimes go on about her, but really, it was so lovely to see Joanna. She even gave me a proper hug, because we were in company. Elizabeth then excused herself to use the bathroom (I had gone at Charing Cross, in case you were thinking I was superhuman). The second she was out of earshot, Joanna beamed.

'Mum! A murder?' she said. Or words to that effect. She looked like the child I remembered from long ago.

'He was bludgeoned, JoJo. Of all things,' I replied. These were my exact words and I think the fact she didn't immediately screw up her face and tell me not to call her 'JoJo' speaks volumes. (On a side note, I could feel and see that she was a bit too thin, so I don't think her new man is good for her. I almost took advantage and said something, but I thought, don't push your luck, Joyce.)

We were in a boardroom and the table was made out of the wing of an aeroplane. I knew not to make a thing of it in front of Joanna, but it was really something. I sat there as if I saw aeroplane tables every day of the week.

Elizabeth had emailed all the files over and Joanna had given them all to Cornelius, who works for her. Cornelius is American, by the way, in case you were wondering about his name. He asked Elizabeth where she had got all the documents and she said 'Companies House', and he said these are not the sort of documents you can get at Companies House and she said that, well, she wouldn't know about that sort of thing, she was just a seventy-six-year-old woman.

I've gone on too long. The long and short was that Ventham's companies were in very good shape. He knew what he was doing. Though Cornelius had found out two very interesting things, which we'll be telling the police about when they come and visit. They've added it all to Elizabeth's big blue file.

Joanna was funny and bright and engaging and all the things I had worried that she'd lost. There they all were. Perhaps she had just lost them with me?

I have talked to Elizabeth about Joanna before. How I feel we're not as close as we should be, as other mothers and daughters seem to be. Elizabeth has a way of making you want to tell the truth. She knew I had been a bit sad. I hadn't thought about it until now, but I wonder if the whole trip hadn't been for my benefit. Really, an awful lot of people could have told us what Cornelius told us. So, perhaps? I don't know.

As we left, Joanna said she would have to come down next weekend for a proper gossip. I told her I would like that very much and that we could do a trip into Fairhaven, which she said she would love. I asked if the new man might come down with her and she gave a little laugh and said no. That's my girl.

We could have got another black cab straight back to the station, but Elizabeth wanted to have a stroll and so we did. I don't know if you know Mayfair – there are no shops you would actually buy anything in, but it was very pleasant. We stopped for coffee in a Costa. It was in a beautiful building, which Elizabeth said used to be a pub where she and a lot of her colleagues would drink. We stayed there for a while and talked about what we'd learned.

If today was anything to go by, this whole murder investigation is going to be the most enormous fun. It has been a long day, and whether it has got us any closer to catching Tony Curran's killer, I'll let you decide.

I think Joanna saw a different side to me today. Or maybe I saw a different side to myself through her eyes. Either way, it was very pleasant. Also, next time I'll tell you about Cornelius, who we liked.

The village is nearly dark now. In life you have to learn to count the good days. You have to tuck them in your pocket and carry them around with you. So I'm putting today in my pocket and I'm off to bed.

I will just finish by saying that, back at Charing Cross, I nipped into Marks and bought a couple of gin and tonics in a can. Elizabeth and I drank them on the train home.

24

With the lights of the village turning out, Elizabeth opens up her appointments diary and attempts today's question.

'WHAT WAS THE REGISTRATION NUMBER OF GWEN TALBOT'S DAUGHTER-IN-LAW'S NEW CAR?'

She approves of this question. Not the make of the car, that was too easy. Not the colour, that could be guessed, and guessing proved nothing, but the registration number. Something that required genuine recall.

As she has done so often before, in a different life, usually in a different country and a different century, Elizabeth shuts her eyes and zooms in. She sees it immediately, or does she hear it? It is both, her brain is telling her what she sees.

JL17 BCH

She traces a finger down the page and reads the correct answer. She is spot on. Elizabeth shuts the diary. She'll write the next question later, she already has a nice idea.

For the record, the car was a blue Lexus, Gwen Talbot's daughter-in-law having done well for herself in bespoke yacht insurance. As for the daughter-in-law's name, well, that remained a mystery. Elizabeth had only been introduced to her once and had not quite caught it. She was confident that it was just a hearing issue and not a memory issue.

Memory was the bogeyman that stalked Coopers Chase. Forgetfulness, absent-mindedness, muddling up names.

What did I come in here for? The grandchildren would giggle at you. The sons and daughters would joke too, but keep a watchful eye. Every so often you would wake at night in cold dread. Of all the things to lose, to lose one's mind? Let them take a leg or a lung, let them take anything before they take that. Before you became 'Poor Rosemary', or 'Poor Frank', catching the last glimpses of the sun and seeing them for what they were. Before there were no more trips, no more games, no more Murder Clubs. Before there was no more you.

Almost certainly you mixed up your daughter's and granddaughter's names because you were thinking about the potatoes, but who knows? That was the tightrope.

So every day Elizabeth opens her diary to a date two weeks ahead and writes herself a question. And every day she answers a question she set herself two weeks ago. This is her early warning system. This is her team of scientists poring over seismology graphs. If there is going to be an earthquake, Elizabeth will be the first to know about it.

Elizabeth walks into the living room. A number plate, from a fortnight ago, is a real test and she is pleased with herself. Stephen is on the sofa, lost in concentration. This morning, before her trip to London with Joyce, they had been talking about Stephen's daughter, Emily. Stephen is worried about her and thinks she is getting too thin. Elizabeth disagreed, but, all the same, Stephen wished Emily would visit more often, just so they could keep an eye on her. Elizabeth agreed that was reasonable and said she'd talk to Emily.

However, Emily is not Stephen's daughter. Stephen has no children. Emily was Stephen's first wife and had died nearly twenty-five years ago.

Stephen is an expert in Middle-Eastern Art. Perhaps *the* expert if you were talking about British academics. He had lived in Tehran and Beirut in the sixties and seventies and many years later would go back, to track down looted masterpieces for once-wealthy west-London exiles. Elizabeth had briefly been in Beirut in the early seventies, but their paths had not actually crossed until 2004, when Stephen had picked up a glove she had dropped outside a bookshop in Chipping Norton. Six months later they were married.

Elizabeth knocks the kettle on. Stephen still writes every day, sometimes for hours. He has an academic agent in London, whom he says he must get up to see soon. Stephen keeps his work safely locked up, but, of course, nothing is safely locked up from Elizabeth and she reads it from time to time. Sometimes it is just a piece copied from his newspaper, repeated over and over, but most often it is stories about Emily, or for Emily. All in the most beautiful handwriting.

There will be no more trains up to London for Stephen, to have lunch with his agent or to see exhibitions, or just look up a little something at the British Library. Stephen is on the brink. He is over the brink, if Elizabeth is honest with herself. She is choosing to manage the situation. She medicates him as best she can. Sedation, to be truthful. With her pills and his, Stephen never wakes in the night.

The kettle now boiled, Elizabeth makes two cups of tea. PC De Freitas and her DCI are coming to see them soon. That had all worked out very nicely, but she still has some thinking to do. After today's trip with Joyce, she now has some information to hand to the police and she would like their information in return. They are really going to have to do a number on Donna and her boss, though. She has a few thoughts.

Stephen never cooks, so Elizabeth knows the place won't burn down while she's out. He never goes to the shop, or the restaurant, or the pool, so there won't be an incident. Sometimes she will come home to evidence of a poorly concealed flood and sometimes there is emergency washing, but no matter.

Elizabeth is keeping Stephen to herself for as long as she can. At some point he will have a fall, or cough up blood, and he will be exposed to a doctor who won't be fooled, and that will be that, and off he will go.

Elizabeth grinds the temazepam into Stephen's tea. Then adds milk. Her mother would have had rules on the etiquette of that. Temazepam before milk, or milk before temazepam? She smiles, this is a joke Stephen would have enjoyed. Would Ibrahim like it? Joyce? She supposed no one would.

Sometimes they still play chess. Elizabeth once spent a month in a safe house somewhere near the Polish–East German border, babysitting the Russian chess grandmaster and later defector, Yuri Tsetovich. She remembers him crying tears of joy when he saw how well she played. Elizabeth had lost none of her skill, but Stephen beats her every time, and with an elegance that makes her swoon. Though they are playing less and less now she realizes. Perhaps they have played their last game? Has Stephen toppled his last king? Please, no.

Elizabeth gives Stephen his tea and kisses him on the forehead. He thanks her.

Elizabeth returns to her notebook and flicks forward two weeks to write today's question, a fact she learned from Joanna and Cornelius today.

HOW MUCH MONEY DID IAN VENTHAM MAKE FROM THE DEATH OF TONY CURRAN?

She writes the answer further down the page, £12.25 MILLION, and closes her appointments diary for another day.

25

PC Donna De Freitas had got the news the previous morning. Report to CID. Elizabeth was a quick worker.

She had been assigned to the Tony Curran case as Chris Hudson's 'shadow'. A new Kent Police initiative. Something to do with inclusivity, or mentoring, or diversity, or whatever the guy from HR in Maidstone had said when he rang her. Whatever it was, it meant she was sitting on a bench, overlooking the English Channel, while DCI Chris Hudson ate an ice cream.

Chris had given her the Tony Curran file to get her up to speed. She couldn't believe her luck. Donna had enjoyed the file a great deal at first. It felt like some proper police work. It brought back all the things she loved about south London. Murder, drugs, someone who carried off a 'no comment' with a bit of panache. As she read, she felt sure she would stumble across a tiny clue that would crack open some decades-old case. She had role-played it in her head. 'Sir, I did some digging and it turns out that 29 May 1997 was a bank holiday, which rather blows Tony Curran's alibi don't you think?' Chris Hudson would look dubious, no way has this rookie cracked the case and she would raise an eyebrow and say 'I ran his handwriting through forensics, sir, and guess what?' Chris would feign a lack of interest, but she would know she had him. 'It turns out that Tony Curran was actually left-handed all along.' Chris would blow out his cheeks. He would have to hand it to her.

None of this happened. Donna simply read exactly what

Chris had read, a potted history of a man getting away with murder and then being murdered in his turn. No smoking guns, no inconsistencies, nothing to peel back. But she had enjoyed it nonetheless.

'That's something you don't get in south London, eh?' says Chris, pointing to the sea with his ice cream cone.

'The sea?' asks Donna, making sure.

'The sea,' agrees Chris.

'Well, you're right there, sir. There's Streatham ponds, but it's not the same.'

Chris Hudson is treating her with a kindness she senses is genuine and with a respect that could only come with being good at his job. If she was ever to work for Chris permanently, she would have to do something about the way he dressed, but that was a bridge that could be crossed in good time. He really took the expression 'plain clothes' seriously. Where does someone even buy shoes like that? Was there a catalogue?

'Fancy a trip out to see Ian Ventham?' says Chris now. 'Have a little chat about his argument with Tony Curran?'

Elizabeth had come good again. She had rung Donna and given a few more details about the row that Ron, Joyce and Jason had witnessed. They would still have to go and visit in person, but it was something to be going on with.

'Yes please,' says Donna. 'Is it uncool to say "please" in CID?'

Chris shrugs. 'I'm not really the person to ask whether something is cool, PC De Freitas.'

'Can we fast forward to the bit where you start calling me Donna,' says Donna.

Chris looks at her, then nods. 'OK, I'll try, but I can't promise anything.'

'What are we looking for with Ventham?' asks Donna. 'Motive?'

'Exactly. He won't give it to us on a plate, but if we just watch and listen, we'll pick a couple of things up. Let me ask the questions though.'

'Of course,' says Donna.

Chris finishes off his cone. 'Unless you really want to ask a question.'

'OK,' says Donna, nodding. 'I probably will want to ask one. Just to warn you.'

'Fair enough.' Chris nods, then stands. 'Shall we?'

26

Joyce

'Nothing ventured, nothing gained.' That's what they say isn't it? That's why I invited Bernard for lunch.

I cooked lamb with rice. The lamb was Waitrose, but the rice was Lidl. That's the way I do it, you honestly don't notice the difference with the basics. You see more and more Lidl vans here these days as people catch on.

Bernard's not the sort to notice the difference anyway. I know he eats in the restaurant every day. What he has for breakfast I don't know, but who really knows what anyone has for breakfast? I usually have tea and toast with the local radio. I know some people have fruit, don't they? I don't know when that came into being, but it's not for me.

It wasn't a date with Bernard, don't think that, but I asked Elizabeth not to tell Ron and Ibrahim anyway, because they would have a field day. If it had been a date, which it wasn't, I will say this. This is a man who likes to talk about his late wife a lot. I don't mind that, and I do understand it, but I'd gone to quite an effort. Anyway, not something I should complain about, I know.

Perhaps I feel guilty because I don't really talk about Gerry. I suppose it's just not how I deal with things. I keep Gerry in a tight little ball just for me. I think if I let him loose here, it would overwhelm me, and I worry he might just blow away. I do know that's silly. Gerry would have enjoyed Coopers Chase. All the committees. It feels unfair that he missed out.

Anyway, this is exactly my point, I feel the tears prickling, and this isn't the time or the place. I'm supposed to be writing.

Bernard's wife was Indian, which must have been very unusual back then, and they were married for forty-seven years. They moved in here together, but she had a stroke and was in Willows within six months. She died about eighteen months ago, before I'd arrived. From the sound of her, I do wish I'd met her.

They have one daughter, called Sudhi. Not Sophie. She lives in Vancouver with her partner and they come over a couple of times a year. I wonder what would happen if Joanna moved to Vancouver. I absolutely wouldn't put it past her.

We talked about other things too, I don't want to give you the wrong impression. We discussed poor Tony Curran. I told Bernard how excited I was that Tony Curran had been murdered. He looked at me askance, in a way that reminded me I can't talk to everyone in the same way I talk to Elizabeth, Ibrahim and Ron. But, between you and me and the gatepost, Bernard looks rather handsome with an askance look on his face.

He talked a little about his work, though I am still none the wiser, to be honest. If you know what a chemical engineer is, then you are a better woman than me. Don't get me wrong, I know what an engineer is and I know what chemicals are, but I can't join the dots. I talked a little bit about my work and told some funny stories about patients. He laughed and, when I told a story about a junior doctor who'd got his bits trapped in a hoover nozzle, I saw a little twinkle in his eye, which gave me cause for optimism. It was nice, I wouldn't go further than that, but I sensed there was more to learn about Bernard, a gap that needs to be crossed. I know the difference between alone and lonely, and Bernard is lonely. There is a cure for that.

I am drawn to strays. Gerry was a stray; I knew it from the moment I met him. Always joking, always clever, but always a stray, needing a home. Which is what I gave him and he gave me back so much more in return. Oh, Joyce, this place would have suited that lovely man down to the ground.

I'm banging on like Bernard, aren't I? Do shut up, Joyce. There are silly, proper tears now. I'll let them fall. If you don't cry sometimes, you'll end up crying all the time.

Elizabeth is inviting Donna and her DCI to come to see us later. She is planning to give them the information we found out from Joanna and Cornelius and to see what we might get in return.

Because it isn't Thursday, Elizabeth asked if we can use my front room to meet them. I told her it would be too small for all of us and she said that was perfect for her purposes. Make the DCI uncomfortable and maybe he'll give something away. That's her plan. She says it's an old work trick of hers, though she no longer has access to all the equipment that she used to have. Her express instruction was: 'No one leaves the room until we've made DCI Hudson tell us something we can use.'

She has asked me to bake. I am doing a lemon drizzle, but also a coffee and walnut, because you never know. I have used almond flour because they are so good with it at Anything with a Pulse and I have been looking for an opportunity. I can tell that Ibrahim is tempted by the idea of being gluten-intolerant and this will head him off at the pass.

I wonder if I should have a nap? It is 3.15 and my cut-off point for a nap is usually 3 p.m., otherwise I struggle to sleep later. But it has been a busy few days, so perhaps I have earned a bit of rule-breaking?

Either way, I will just add that coffee and walnut is Bernard's favourite, but you mustn't read anything into that.

27

Donna looks out of the window of the Ford Focus. What do people see in trees? There are just so many of them. Trunk, branches, leaves, trunk, branches, leaves, we get it. Her mind wanders.

Chris has shown her the photograph left by the body. Surely it's a red herring though? It must be. If you're Jason Ritchie, or Bobby Tanner, or whoever took the photo, it's asking for too much trouble. It would be idiocy for any of the men to have left the photograph by the body. A hundred different people might have murdered Tony Curran; why do the police's job for them and narrow it down to three?

So someone else must have got hold of a copy of the photograph? But how?

Perhaps Tony Curran had had a copy? That would make sense. And perhaps Ian Ventham had seen it one day? Tony showing off? Ian had clocked it and tucked it away for future use? A bit of misdirection to confuse the bungling cops? From what Donna has read, he seems the type who might try to do that.

They are passing through a village, which is a respite from the trees, but there is still not enough concrete for Donna. Maybe she'll grow to love it? Maybe there was more to life than south London?

'What are you thinking?' asks Chris, eyes off to the left, trying to find the right road sign.

'I'm thinking of Atlanta Fried Chicken on Balham High

Road. And I'm thinking we should show the photo to Ian Ventham,' says Donna. 'Ask him if he's ever seen it before.'

'Look him in the eye when he tells us he hasn't?' says Chris, indicates left and turns onto a narrow country road. 'Good plan.'

'I'm also thinking, why don't you ever iron your shirts?' says Donna.

'So this is what it's like to have a shadow?' says Chris. 'Well, I used to iron just the front bit, because the rest was always under a jacket. And then I thought, well I'm wearing a tie too, so why bother at all? Does anyone really notice?'

'Of course they notice,' says Donna. 'I notice.'

'Well, you're a police officer, Donna,' says Chris. 'I'll start ironing shirts when I get a girlfriend.'

'You won't get a girlfriend until you start ironing your shirts,' says Donna.

'It's a real Catch 22 for sure,' says Chris and turns onto a long driveway. 'Anyway, I've always found that shirts sort of iron themselves while you're wearing them.'

'Have you now?' says Donna, as they pull up in front of Ian Ventham's house.

28

'You can hold your breath for three minutes if you really put your mind to it,' says Ian Ventham. 'It's all about controlling your diaphragm. The body doesn't need as much oxygen as they say. Look at mountain goats, if you need proof.'

'That makes sense, Mr Ventham,' says Chris. 'But perhaps we can get back to the photograph?'

Ian Ventham looks at the photograph again, and shakes his head again. 'No, I'm certain, I've never seen it. I recognize Tony, of course, God rest his soul, and that's the boxer, isn't it?'

'Jason Ritchie,' says Chris.

'My boxing trainer says I could have turned pro,' says Ian. 'Physique plus mentality. There's some stuff you can't teach.'

Chris nods again. Donna looks around Ian Ventham's living room. One of the more extraordinary rooms she has ever seen. There is a bright red grand piano, with golden keys. The piano stool is ebony and zebra-skin.

'I don't suppose you and Tony had a falling out, Mr Ventham?' says Chris. 'Before he died?'

'A falling out?' asks Ian.

'Mmm,' says Chris.

'Me and Tony?' asks Ian.

'Mmm,' repeats Chris.

'We never argued,' says Ian. 'Arguing is very bad for your wellbeing. You look at the science of it, it thins the blood. Thinner blood, less energy. Less energy, slippery slope.'

Donna is listening to every word, just taking it all in, but her eyes continue to scan the room. There is a large oil painting in a huge gold frame above the fireplace. It is a painting of Ian, carrying a sword. There is a stuffed eagle in front of it. Wings outstretched.

'Well, we can all agree with that,' says Chris. 'But what if I told you I've got three witnesses who saw the two of you arguing before he was killed?'

Donna watches as Ian leans forward slowly, puts his elbows on his thighs and rests his chin on his clasped hands. He is giving every impression of pretending to think.

'Well, listen,' says Ian, taking his elbows off his thighs and spreading his hands. 'We had an argument, sure, sometimes you have to, don't you? Just to release the toxins. I guess that would explain what they saw.'

'OK, yes, that would explain it,' agrees Chris. 'But I wonder if I could ask what the argument was about?'

'Of course, sure,' says Ian. 'It's a valid question and I appreciate you asking it, because, when all's said and done, Tony died.'

'Tony was murdered, actually. Shortly after the argument,' says Donna, looking at an emerald-encrusted skull and getting bored of being quiet.

Ian nods at her. 'Accurate, yep, he was. You have a bright future. Well, listen, how much do you know about automatic sprinkler systems?'

'As much as the next man,' says Chris.

'I want to fit them to all the new flats; Tony didn't want the expense. To me – and listen, this is just me, just how I do business – the safety of my clients is paramount. And I mean paramount. So I said this to Tony, and he's more laissez-faire about the whole thing, not my style and we, I'm not going to say "argued", I'm going to say we "bickered".'

'And that was that?' asks Chris.

'And that was that,' says Ian. 'Just sprinklers. If you want to find me guilty of something, find me guilty of going above and beyond as regards building safety.'

Chris nods, then turns to Donna. 'I think that's us done for now, Mr Ventham. Unless my colleague has any questions?'

Donna wants to ask why Ventham is lying about the row, but that's probably a bit much. What should she ask? What would Chris want her to ask?

'Just one question, Ian,' says Donna. She doesn't want to call him Mr Ventham. 'Where did you go when you left Coopers Chase that day? Did you come home? Perhaps you visited Tony Curran? To continue discussing the sprinklers?'

'I did neither,' says Ian, and seems on solid ground. 'I drove up the hill and met with Karen and Gordon Playfair, they own the land up there. They'll vouch for me, I'm sure. At least Karen will.'

Chris looks at her and nods. Her question was OK.

'You're very beautiful, by the way,' says Ian to Donna. 'For a police officer.'

'You'll see how beautiful I am if I ever have to arrest you,' says Donna, remembering, a moment too late, that rolling her eyes was probably unprofessional.

'Well, not beautiful,' adds Ian. 'But attractive enough for round here.'

'Thank you for your time, Mr Ventham,' says Chris, standing. 'If there's anything else we'll be in touch. And if you ever need to tell me that *I'm* beautiful, you have my number.'

As Donna stands, she takes a final look around the room. The last thing she notices is Ian Ventham's aquarium. At the bottom of the tank is an exact scale replica of Ian Ventham's house. A clownfish emerges from an upstairs window as Donna and Chris make their way out.

Donna's phone pings as she and Chris reach the car.

A text from Elizabeth. Which doesn't seem right to Donna at all. Surely a message from Elizabeth should be delivered in Morse code, or by an intricate series of flags?

Donna smiles to herself and opens the text. 'The Thursday Murder Club, asking if we could come over to Coopers Chase, sir? They have some information.'

'The Thursday Murder Club?' asks Chris.

'That's what they call themselves. There's four of them, a little gang.'

Chris nods. 'I've met Ibrahim and poor old Ron Ritchie. Are they in this gang?'

Donna nods. She has no idea why he said 'poor' Ron Ritchie, but no doubt Elizabeth will be behind that, somehow. 'Shall we go and see them? Elizabeth says Jason Ritchie will be there.'

'Elizabeth?' says Chris.

'She's their . . .' Donna thinks. 'I don't know what you'd say. Whatever Marlon Brando was in *The Godfather.*'

'Last time I went to Coopers Chase someone clamped the Ford Focus,' says Chris. 'I was charged £150 to release it, by a pensioner with a high-vis jacket and an adjustable spanner. You reply to Elizabeth and you tell her we'll visit when we decide, not when she decides. We're the police.'

'I'm not sure that Elizabeth will take no for an answer,' says Donna.

'Well, she's going to have to, Donna,' says Chris. 'I've been in this job for nearly thirty years and I'm not going to be pushed around by four pensioners.'

'OK,' says Donna. 'I'll let her know.'

29

It turned out that Chris had been wrong and Donna had been right.

Chris Hudson finds himself jammed uncomfortably on a sofa, with Ibrahim, whom he has met before, on one side, and tiny, chirpy, white-haired Joyce on the other. It is clearly a two-and-a-half-seater sofa and when Chris had been shown to it, his assumption was that he would be sharing it with only one other person. Then, with a grace and swiftness he hadn't expected from two people deep into their pensionable years, Ibrahim and Joyce had slid in one either side of him and so here he was. If he had known, he would have declined the invitation and taken one of the armchairs, now occupied by Ron Ritchie, looking sprightlier than when they last met, and the terrifying Elizabeth. Who really doesn't take no for an answer.

More to the point, he could have taken that cosy-looking IKEA recliner that Donna is virtually curled up in, feet tucked underneath her, without a care in the world.

Could he move? There is another seat, a hard-backed chair, but Joyce and Ibrahim would surely take offence? They seem oblivious to his discomfort and the last thing he wants to do is seem churlish. He is sitting where he is sitting because of their kindness and because he is to be the centre of attention. He understands and appreciates that. There is a psychology to seating arrangements that any good police officer picks up over the years. He knows they have tried their best to make him feel important and they would be horrified to know that the effect is actually the complete opposite.

Chris has just been given a cup of tea on a saucer, yet he is so hemmed in that he fears any attempt to drink it might be physically impossible. So here he is, stuck, but like a professional, he will make the best of it. Look at Donna though, she's even got a side table for her tea. Unbelievable. They couldn't have made this more awkward for him if they'd tried. Still, stay professional.

'Shall we begin?' says Chris. He attempts to shift his weight forward, but, without realizing it, Ibrahim has his elbow nestling against Chris's hip and Chris is forced to settle back again. His teacup is too full to safely hold in one hand and too hot to sip. He would feel annoyance, but the kindly, attentive looks on the faces of the four residents make annoyance impossible.

'As you know, myself and PC De Freitas, over there in the chair, making herself comfortable, are investigating the murder of Tony Curran. He's a man I believe you all have some knowledge of, a local builder and property developer. As you also know, Mr Curran tragically passed away last week, and we have certain questions pertaining to this event.'

Chris looks at his audience. They are nodding with such innocence, taking it all in. It makes him glad he's adopted a slightly more formal way of speaking. Saying 'pertaining' had been a good call. He attempts a sip at the tea, but it is still scalding hot and any blowing would send a wave over the brim. It would also suggest to whoever made the tea that he would have preferred it to be less scalding, which would look rude.

Joyce has more bad news for him. 'We have forgotten our manners, Detective Chief Inspector. We haven't offered you any cake.' She produces a lemon drizzle, already cut into slices and offers it across.

Chris, unable to raise a hand to say no thank you, says 'I won't, I had a big lunch.' No such luck.

'Just try a slice. I made it specially,' says Joyce, in a voice so proud that Chris has no choice.

'Go on then,' he says, and Joyce balances a slice of the cake on his saucer.

'So perhaps you have a suspect by now?' asks Elizabeth. 'Or are you only looking at Ventham?'

'Ibrahim says it's better than M&S lemon drizzle,' says Joyce.

'He will have a number of suspects,' says Ibrahim. 'If I know DCI Hudson. He is very thorough.'

'If you notice anything unusual, that's the almond flour,' says Joyce.

'Is that right, son? You got any suspects?' Ron asks Chris.

'Well, it wouldn't be . . .'

'Narrowing it all down. Bet you got forensics?' says Ron Ritchie. 'I always watch *CSI* with Jason. He'll love all this. What you got? Fingerprints? DNA?'

Chris remembers Ron as being more confused than this the other day. 'Well, that's why I'm here, as you know. I know you and Joyce were having a drink with your son, Mr Ritchie, and I think he may be joining us? It would be good to talk to him too.'

'He just texted,' says Ron. 'He'll be ten minutes.'

'I bet he'd love to know the circumstances,' says Elizabeth.

'He'd love that,' confirms Ron.

'Well, again, it's not really in my . . .' says Chris.

'M&S lemon drizzle cake is oversugared, Inspector, that's my opinion,' interrupts Ibrahim. 'Not just my opinion either, if you look at the discussion boards.'

Chris is struggling further now, because the slice of cake is slightly too big for the gap between the bottom of the cup and the edge of the saucer and it is taking all his efforts to keep it balanced. Still, he has had a career of interviewing killers, psychopaths, con artists and liars of every sort, so he ploughs on.

'We really just need to talk to Mr Ritchie and his son – and Joyce, I think you also saw . . .'

'*CSI* is too American for me,' interrupts Joyce. '*Lewis* is my favourite. It's ITV3. I've got them backing up on my Sky Plus. I think I'm the only one in the village who can work Sky Plus.'

'I like the Rebus books,' adds Ibrahim. 'If you know them? Rebus is from Scotland and, goodness me, he has a terrible time of it.'

'Patricia Highsmith for me,' says Elizabeth.

'They'll never top *The Sweeney* though and I've read all the Mark Billinghams,' says Ron Ritchie, again with more confidence than Chris remembers.

Elizabeth, meanwhile, has opened a bottle of wine and fills up the glasses that have suddenly appeared in her friends' hands.

Chris cannot even attempt to sip his tea now, as lifting it to his lips would unbalance the cake and lifting the cup off the saucer would tip the cake in the saucer's centre and make it impossible to put the cup back down again. He feels sweat start to trickle down his back, reminding him of the time he interviewed a twenty-five-stone Hell's Angels enforcer with 'I KILL COPPERS' tattooed around his neck.

Fortunately, Elizabeth is on hand to help him out. 'You look a little hemmed-in on that sofa, Detective Chief Inspector.'

'We normally meet in the Jigsaw Room, you see,' says Joyce. 'But it's not Thursday and the Jigsaw Room is being used by Chat and Crochet.'

'Chat and Crochet is a fairly new group, Detective Chief

Inspector,' says Ibrahim. 'Formed by members who had become disillusioned with Knit and Natter. Too much nattering and not enough knitting, apparently.'

'And the main lounge is off limits,' says Ron. 'The Bowls Club have got a disciplinary hearing.'

'To do with Colin Clemence and his defence of medicinal marijuana,' says Joyce.

'So why don't we sit you on the upright,' says Elizabeth, 'and you can talk us through the whole thing?'

'Ooh yes,' says Joyce. 'Talk slowly because it's not really our area, but that would be lovely. And there's some coffee and walnut where the lemon drizzle came from.'

Chris looks over at Donna. She simply shrugs and holds out her palms.

30

Father Matthew Mackie walks slowly up the hill, through the avenue of trees.

He had hoped Tony Curran's death might be the end of all this. No need for any further action on his behalf. But he had visited Ian Ventham to put his case and he had been disappointed. The Woodlands was continuing as planned. The cemetery was to go.

Time to conjure up a plan B. And quickly.

As the path curves to the left, then straightens, the Garden of Eternal Rest comes into view, further and higher up the path. From here Father Mackie can see the iron gates, wide enough for a vehicle, set into the red-brick wall. The gates look old, the wall looks new. In front of the gates is a turning circle, once for hearses and now for maintenance vehicles.

He reaches the gates and pushes them open. There is a central path, leading to a large statue of Christ on the cross at the very far end. He walks silently towards Christ, through the sea of souls. Beyond the statue, beyond the Garden, are tall beech trees, reaching further up the hill to the open farmland. Father Mackie crosses himself, by the plinth at Christ's feet. No kneeling for him these days though, arthritis and Catholicism being an uneasy mix.

Matthew Mackie turns and looks back across the Garden, squinting into the sun. Either side of the path are the gravestones, neat, ordered, symmetrical, stretching forward in time towards the iron gates. The oldest graves are nearest to

Christ, with the newest joining the line when their time had come. There are around 200 bodies high on the hill, a spot so beautiful, so peaceful, so perfect, Mackie thinks it could almost make him believe in God.

The first grave is dated 1874, a Sister Margaret Bernadette and this is where Mackie eventually turns and starts his slow walk back.

The older gravestones are more ornate, more showy. The dates of death flick slowly forward as he walks. There are the Victorians all neatly in a line, probably furious about Palmerston or the Boers. Then it's the women who sat in the convent and heard about the Wright brothers for the first time. Then the women who nursed the blind and the broken who flooded through their gates, as they prayed for brothers to return safely from Europe. Then there were doctors and voters and drivers, women who had seen both wars and still kept the faith, the inscriptions getting easier to read now. Then television, rock and roll, supermarkets, motorways and moon landings. Father Mackie steps off the path sometime around the 1970s, the headstones clear and simple now. He walks along the row, looking at the names. The world was changing in the most extraordinary ways, but the rows are still neat and orderly and the names are still the same. He reaches the side wall of the Garden, waist height and much older than the wall at the front. He takes in the view that hasn't changed since 1874. Trees, fields, birds, things that were permanent and unbroken. He walks back to the path, clearing a leaf off one of the headstones as he passes.

Father Mackie continues to walk, until he reaches the final gravestone. Sister Mary Byrne, dated 14 July 2005. What a lot Mary Byrne could tell Sister Margaret Bernadette, just a hundred yards up the path. So much had changed, yet, here at least, so much had stayed the same.

Behind Sister Mary Byrne there is room for many more graves, but they had not been needed. Sister Mary was the last of the line. So here they all lay, this sisterhood, with the walls still around them, the blue skies above them and the leaves still falling on the headstones.

What could he do?

Exiting through the gates, Mackie turns back for a final look. He then begins the walk downhill, back through the avenue of trees towards Coopers Chase.

A man in a suit and tie is sitting on a bench set just off the path, enjoying the same view that Father Mackie had been enjoying. The view that never changed. Through wars and deaths and cars and planes, to Wi-Fi and whatever was in the papers this morning. There was something to be said for it.

'Father,' acknowledges the man, a folded copy of the *Daily Express* by his side. Matthew Mackie nods back, keeps walking and keeps thinking.

31

Chris has his own chair and his own side table and he now feels like the King of the World. He sometimes forgets the impact a police officer can have on members of the public. The gang in front of him are looking at him with something approaching awe. It's nice to be taken seriously once in a while and he is happily giving them the benefit of his wisdom.

'The whole house is wired up with cameras, pretty state-of-the-art stuff too, but we got nothing. On the blink. They often are.'

Elizabeth is nodding with interest. 'Anyone you were expecting to see, though? Any suspects?' asks Elizabeth.

'Well, listen, that's not something I can really share,' says Chris.

'So you do have a suspect? How wonderful! What do you make of the coffee and walnut?' says Joyce.

Chris lifts a slice of coffee-and-walnut cake to his mouth and takes a bite. Also better than M&S. Joyce, you wizard! Also, it was a well known fact that there were no calories in home-made cakes.

'It's delicious, and look, I didn't say we had a suspect, but we have persons of interest and that's normal.'

'"Persons of interest",' says Joyce. 'I love it when they say that.'

'More than one, then?' asks Elizabeth. 'So not just Ian Ventham? I suppose you couldn't possibly say?'

'He couldn't say, you're quite right,' says Donna, deciding enough is enough. 'Now leave the poor man alone, Elizabeth.'

Chris laughs. 'I don't think I need protecting here, Donna.'

Ibrahim turns to Donna. 'DCI Hudson is a fine investigator, PC De Freitas. You are lucky to have such a good boss.'

'Oh, he's a pro,' agrees Donna.

Elizabeth claps her hands. 'Well, it feels like this meeting has been all give and no take. You've been very kind, Chris. If I can call you Chris?'

'Well, I've possibly shared more than I was intending, but I'm glad it's been interesting,' says Chris.

'It has. And I think we owe you a favour in return. You might like to take a look at this.' Elizabeth hands Chris a bright blue binder about a foot thick. 'It's a few financials on Ian Ventham. Details of this place, details of his relationship with Tony Curran. Probably all nonsense, but I'll let you be the judge.'

There is a buzz on Joyce's intercom and she heads off to answer it, while Chris weighs up the binder.

'Well, we can certainly take a look through this . . .'

'I'll look through it, don't panic,' says Donna, and gives Elizabeth a reassuring look.

The door swings open and Joyce walks in with Jason Ritchie himself. The tattoos, that nose, those forearms.

'Mr Ritchie,' says Chris. 'We meet at last.'

32

Chris had asked Jason if he wouldn't mind stepping outside for a photograph, to make use of the natural light.

Donna is taking the photo. The two men are smiling happily, arms around each other's shoulders, leaning against a decorative fountain shaped like a dolphin.

Poor Chris, they had really done a number on him. Donna wonders if Chris truly understands that he's one of the gang now.

It had been useful though. They had talked to Ron and Jason, and to Joyce, about what they saw. It had been a row, that much was clear. None of them could shed a light on what the row was about, but they had all thought it significant, and as Ron and Jason were fighting men, Chris and Donna had listened.

Ron was very proud of his boy, that much was clear. It was natural, of course, but something to be careful about. Just in case the photo left by the body hadn't been a red herring.

Donna tells Chris to move to his left a little.

'This is very kind of you, Jason, you must have to do it a lot,' Chris says, moving to his left a little.

'Price of whassname, innit?' agrees Jason.

Donna has been doing her homework on Jason Ritchie. Hadn't needed much, to be honest, her dad had been a boxing fan.

Jason has been famous since the late eighties and would now, it seemed, be famous for ever. He had been the hero, sometimes the villain, of a series of iconic fights that captivated the whole country. Nigel Benn, Chris Eubank, Michael Watson, Steve Collins and Jason Ritchie. It was boxing as soap opera. Sometimes Jason was J. R. Ewing and other times he was Bobby.

The public loved Jason Ritchie. The brawler, the bruiser, tattoos running up and down each arm, long before that was a mandatory requirement for a professional sportsman. He was charming, he was conventionally handsome, becoming more and more unconventionally handsome as his career took its toll. And, of course, he had his famous firebrand dad, 'Red Ron', always good for a quote. The chat shows loved Jason too. He accidentally knocked out Terry Wogan while showing him how he'd knocked out Steve Collins. Donna had read that that clip still brought him in steady royalties.

It never got better than the third Benn v Ritchie fight. The body slowed a little, the reflexes dulled. This didn't matter while he was still fighting the guys who were ageing alongside him, but one by one they started retiring. Jason had found out, many years later, that he'd made less money than the lot of them. Problems with his manager. To this day, a lot of his money was in Estonia. The opponents got younger, the paydays smaller and the training harder, until an Atlantic City night in 1998, fighting a last-minute Venezuelan stand-in, Jason Ritchie hit the canvas for the final time.

A few years in the wilderness followed. A few years that were never mentioned in the profiles Donna had read in the papers. A few years where Jason made his money in a very different way. When he was being photographed with Tony Curran and Bobby Tanner. The years that Donna and Chris were interested in.

The wilderness years didn't last, though. As a new century dawned, there was almost endless demand for a man who exuded menace and charm in equal parts. From the lad mags to the mockney film directors to the reality shows and the adverts for gambling companies, Jason started making more money than he ever had in the ring. He came third in *I'm a Celebrity*, he dated Alice Watts from *EastEnders*, he starred in a film alongside John Travolta as a washed-up fighter and one alongside Scarlett Johansson, also as a washed-up fighter.

This new career fairly quickly followed the same trajectory as his boxing career, however. You only had so many days top of the bill. These days there were no films, fewer adverts, and you'd see him turning up on all sorts of things.

But no matter, Jason Ritchie was now famous for ever and he appears to be grateful too. His smile, in front of the fountain shaped like a dolphin, seems, to Donna, entirely genuine.

Donna puts down the big blue file Elizabeth has given her and holds up her phone for the photo. 'Say cheese, or whatever two men are comfortable saying.'

Jason starts, 'I duck and I dive,' and then Chris joins him for the shouted, 'and I always survive!'

The two men both instinctively punch the air with their free arm and Donna takes the photo.

'That was his catchphrase,' Chris explains to Donna. 'I duck and I dive and I always survive!'

Donna pockets her phone. 'Everyone always survives until they die. It's meaningless.' She thought of adding that Rodolfo Mendoza had knocked Jason out in the third round on the East Coast, so he hadn't exactly survived then. But why upset two middle-aged men unnecessarily?

'They'll love that at Fairhaven, Jason; thanks, mate.'

'No problem. Hope the old man was useful.'

Donna knows Chris will never show the photo to any of his colleagues. He already has a much more interesting photograph of Jason Ritchie.

'Very useful,' says Chris. 'Anyway, what's your thinking, Jason? About Tony Curran? You must have known him a bit, from around Fairhaven?'

'A bit, yeah. I knew of him. Not really, though. He had plenty of enemies.'

Chris nods, then steals a glance at Donna. Donna steps up and offers Jason her hand.

'Thank you so much, Mr Ritchie,' she says.

Jason shakes Donna's hand, 'My pleasure. Could you send me a copy of the photo? It looked a nice one.' Jason writes down his number for Donna. 'I'll head back up and see Pops.'

'Before you head up,' says Donna, taking Jason's number. 'You knew Tony Curran a little better than you've suggested, didn't you, Jason?'

'Tony Curran? Nah. Seen him in the pub, know people who know him. Heard gossip.'

'You ever drink in the Black Bridge, Jason?' asks Chris.

Jason misses just the slightest beat, as if a punch has slipped through, but won't again.

'Near the station? Once or twice. Years ago.'

'Twenty-odd years, I'm guessing,' says Donna.

'Maybe,' nods Jason. 'Who remembers, though?'

'You had no dealings with Tony Curran back then?' asks Chris.

Jason shrugs, 'If I remember something I'll tell you. I'll get up to Dad; nice to meet you both.'

'I saw a photo recently, Jason,' says Chris. 'Group of friends in the Black Bridge. Bobby Tanner, Tony Curran. Nice one of you. All very friendly.'

'Lot of weirdos ask me for photos, mate,' says Jason. 'No offence.'

'You'd recognize it. Table covered in money. You don't have a copy of it, by any chance?' asks Chris.

Jason smiles. 'Never seen it.'

'You wouldn't know who took it?' asks Donna.

'A photo I've never seen? Nope.'

'And we're having trouble tracking down Bobby Tanner, Jason,' says Chris. 'I don't suppose you know where he is these days?'

Jason Ritchie purses his lips for the briefest of moments, then shakes his head, turns and waves over his shoulder as he goes back inside to join his dad. Chris and Donna watch as the automatic doors slide shut behind him. Chris looks at his watch then motions towards the car. He walks and Donna walks alongside him, a smile on her lips.

'That entire conversation was the most Cockney I've ever heard you sound, sir.'

'Guilty,' admits Chris, finally pronouncing a 't'. 'Why does Jason want a copy of that photo of us? What's that? To blackmail me if he ever needs to?'

'Simpler than that, sir,' says Donna. 'It's to get my number. Classic move.'

'Either way,' says Chris.

'Don't worry,' says Donna. 'He won't be getting the photo, or my number.'

'Good-looking fella,' says Chris.

'He's like forty-six or something,' says Donna. 'No thanks.'

Chris nods. 'Heaven forbid! You'd have to say he didn't look too worried, though. But he's definitely lying about not knowing Tony Curran.'

'Could be lots of reasons,' says Donna.

'Could be,' agrees Chris.

Hearing footsteps behind them, they turn to see Elizabeth and Joyce hurrying after them. Joyce has a Tupperware container with her.

'I forgot to give you this,' says Joyce, handing over her

Tupperware. 'It's the last of the lemon drizzle. I'm afraid the coffee and walnut already has someone else's name on it.'

Chris takes the cake. 'Thank you, Joyce, that will go to a good home.'

'And Donna,' says Elizabeth, gesturing to the blue file. 'Do call me if your bedtime reading gets complicated.'

'Thank you, Elizabeth,' says Donna. 'I'm sure I'll struggle through.'

'Here, you should probably have my number too,' says Elizabeth, and hands Chris her card. 'We'll have lots to chat about in the weeks ahead. Thank you for coming to see us, we do love visitors.'

Donna smiles as Chris virtually bows to Elizabeth and Joyce.

'It really was an education,' says Joyce, with a smile. 'And you should probably let Donna drive, DCI Hudson. There was an awful lot of vodka in those cakes.'

33

Elizabeth had come straight over to Willows after meeting with the police. She makes sure that Penny has a wash and a set once a week. Anthony, the hairdresser, comes to Willows at the end of his appointments and always insists on doing it for free.

One day, if Anthony ever gets into any sort of trouble, or ever needs help, he will discover how grateful Elizabeth is for this kindness.

'Mafia, I heard,' says Anthony, gently running a soaped sponge through Penny's hair. 'Tony Curran owed them money, so they cut off his fingers and killed him.'

'That's an interesting theory,' says Elizabeth. She has a hand cupped under Penny's neck and lifts her head. 'And how did the Mafia get into the house?'

'Shot their way in, I suppose,' says Anthony.

'Without leaving bullet holes?' asks Elizabeth. Penny's shampoo smells of rose and jasmine and Elizabeth buys it at the shop on site. They stopped selling it for a while, but Elizabeth paid them a visit and they changed their mind.

'Well, that's the Mafia for you, Elizabeth,' says Anthony.

'And without tripping any alarms, Anthony?' says John Gray, from his usual chair.

'Have you seen *Goodfellas*, John?' says Anthony.

'If that's a film then I won't have,' says John.

'There you are then,' says Anthony. He is now combing Penny's hair. 'You're going to need a little trim next week, Penny darling. Get you disco-ready.'

'No bullet holes, Anthony,' says Elizabeth. 'No alarms, nothing broken, no sign of a struggle. What does that suggest to you?'

'Triads?' Anthony is unplugging his curling tongs. 'One of these days I'm going to unplug you by mistake, Penny.'

'As Penny would be the first to tell you,' says Elizabeth. 'It suggests that he let his killer in. So it must have been someone he knew.'

'Oh I love that,' says Anthony. 'Someone he knew. Of course. You ever killed someone, Elizabeth?'

Elizabeth shrugs.

'I can just picture it,' says Anthony, putting on his jacket. 'There you go, Penny. I'd kiss you, but not with John in the room. Look at those forearms.'

Elizabeth stands and hugs him. 'Thank you, darling.'

'She looks gorgeous,' says Anthony. 'If I say so myself. See you next week, Elizabeth. Bye, Penny; bye, handsome John.'

'Obliged, Anthony,' says John.

As Anthony leaves, Elizabeth sits by Penny again. 'Here's another thing though, Pen. They took young Jason out for a photo afterwards. I know he gets that a lot, but something didn't seem right. It felt off. Why go outside? Joyce has one of those big picture windows. You know, the ones in Wordsworth? That would be a lovely photo.'

Mentioning Joyce again. Easier every time.

'Do you think they were asking Jason about something? Are we missing something? We passed him on the stairs coming back up and he was his usual charming self, but who knows?'

Elizabeth sips some water and feels grateful. Then feels guilty for feeling grateful. Then feels weak for feeling guilty. So she carries on talking to Penny. To Penny, or to herself? Who knew?

'Perhaps it wasn't Ventham at all? Perhaps we're just being blinded by what's in that file? By the twelve million. I mean, where was he when Curran was killed? Do we even know? Could he have done it? Do the timings work?'

'Elizabeth, forgive me,' says John. 'But have you ever watched *Escape to the Country*?'

Elizabeth is still not really used to John speaking, but he does seem to be coming out of his shell recently. 'I don't believe I have, John, no.'

John is fidgeting a little. Something is clearly on his mind. 'I mean, it's rather good. I'm sure it's nonsense, but even so. There will be a couple on and they will be looking for a new home.'

'In the country, John?'

'In the country, as you say. And a chap, well sometimes it's a woman, will show them around some houses. I watch it with the sound down, because it's not really Penny's sort of thing. You can really see in the eyes of the couple which one wants to move and which one is just going along with it. For a quiet life, you know?'

'John,' says Elizabeth, leaning forward and staring straight into his eyes. 'I've never known you utter a sentence without a reason. Where is this heading?'

'Well, it's only heading here, I suppose,' says John. 'I was watching *Escape to the Country*, you see, on the day that Curran was killed and they'd just got to the end, where they decide whether to buy the house or not. They never do, but that's half the fun. I got up and wandered out to get a Luco-zade Sport from the machine and I looked out of the window, the one at the front, and saw Ventham's car driving off.'

'The Range Rover?' asks Elizabeth.

'Yes, the Range Rover,' says John. 'Coming down the track from the top of the hill. And I just thought I would mention it to you, as *Escape to the Country* is on straight after *Doctors* and it finishes at three on the dot.'

'I see,' says Elizabeth.

'And I thought that perhaps if you knew exactly when Ventham left Coopers Chase and you knew exactly when Curran had been killed, it might be useful? For the investigation?'

'Three p.m.?' asks Elizabeth.

'Mmm. On the dot.'

'Thank you, John. I think I need to send a text message.' Elizabeth takes out her phone.

'I don't think you're supposed to use your mobile telephone in here, Elizabeth,' says John.

Elizabeth gives a kindly shrug. 'Well, imagine if we only ever did what we were supposed to, John?'

'You have a point there, Elizabeth,' agrees John, and goes back to his book.

34

Donna is getting ready to go out when her phone pings. A message from Elizabeth. She only left her a few hours ago. It will be trouble, for sure, but she likes seeing the name pop up.

What time was Tony Curran killed?

Well, that was short and to the point. Donna smiles and composes a reply.

Maybe ask how I am, share a bit of gossip, before asking for a favour? And sign off with a kiss. Soften me up a bit x

Donna sees the speech bubble, showing that Elizabeth is replying. She is taking her time, so what will it be? A lecture? A reminder of why Donna is investigating a murder, instead of measuring the depth of tyre treads in the car park at Halfords, which is what Mark was doing today? Perhaps it would be something in Latin? There is a ping.

How are you Donna? Mary Lennox has just had a new great grand-daughter, but she is worried that her granddaughter has been having an affair, because the husband has a very prominent chin and it is nowhere to be seen. What time was Tony Curran killed? X

Donna is choosing between lipsticks. She wants something that doesn't look too obvious, while at the same time looking obvious. She replies.

I can't tell you that. I'm a professional.

There is an immediate ping back.

LOL!

LOL? Where had Elizabeth got that from? Two can play at that game.

WTF?

This has clearly foxed Elizabeth and Donna has time to look in the mirror and check her interested face, her laughing face and her quietly seductive face before the next ping.

I'm afraid I don't know WTF. I only discovered LOL from Joyce last week. I'm going to assume that it doesn't refer to the Warsaw Transit Facility, as that was shut down in 1981 when the Russians came sniffing.

Donna sends back an emoji of big eyes and an emoji of the Russian flag and then starts to floss. Even though they say you don't need to floss any more. *Ping!*

That's the Chinese flag, Donna. Just let me know the time of death. You know we won't tell a soul and you also know we might just come up with something useful.

Donna smiles. What harm could it do, really?

3.32. His Fitbit broke when he fell.

There is another ping.

Well, I don't know what a Fitbit is either, but thank you. X

35

Joyce

The police came over today and at first I had to feel sorry for DCI Hudson, but I think he rather enjoyed himself by the end. Anyway, Elizabeth gave him and Donna the file, so we'll see what they make of it. Joanna's name is not on the file anywhere, which Elizabeth reassured me helps with 'plausible deniability' just in case anything we're doing is against the law. Which I assume it is.

I asked Elizabeth to repeat the phrase 'plausible deniability' and I wrote it down. She asked me why I was writing it down and I said it was because I'm writing a diary and she rolled her eyes. Though she then asked if she was in the diary and I said of course she was and she then asked if I was using her real name. Which I said I was, though I've thought about it since and who knows with Elizabeth? Perhaps she's really a Jacqueline? We tend to accept what people tell us they're called. No questions asked.

But I've been thinking. You must think I'm murder obsessed, it's all I've written about since I started this diary. So perhaps I should tell you some other things. Let's talk about a few things that aren't murder. What can I tell you?

When I was putting the hoover round after the police had gone, Elizabeth said she thought I would get on with a Dyson. But I said I didn't think so, not at my age. But perhaps I should take the plunge?

And after the hoovering we had a glass of wine. It was a

screw top, but you don't notice these days, do you? It's just as good.

When Elizabeth went home, I asked her to give my love to Stephen and she said she would. Then I said they should both come to dinner one night and she said that would be lovely. But all is not right, there. She will tell me when she's ready.

What else that isn't murder?

Mary Lennox's granddaughter has just had a baby. He's called River, which has raised a few eyebrows, but I rather like it. The woman who works in the shop is getting divorced and they've started stocking chocolate digestives. Karen Playfair, from up on the hill, is coming to give us a 'Coopers Chase Breakfast Masterclass' talk on computers. The last newsletter said she's coming to give a talk about tablets and that caused some confusion, so they had to print an explanation this week.

Apart from that, and the murder, all is peace and quiet.

Anyway, I see that it's getting late, so I will wish you a good night. While I have been writing, Elizabeth has sent me a message. We are off on a road trip tomorrow. No idea when and no idea why, but I shall look forward to it very much.

36

Donna can't believe she is already in bed at 9.45. She had gone on the date because, frankly, it was about time. A man called Gregor had taken her to Zizzi's, where he had nibbled at a salad and talked her through his protein-shake regime for ninety minutes.

At one point Donna had asked him who his favourite author was. For Donna an acceptable answer would be Harlan Coben, Kurt Vonnegut, or any woman. Gregor had sagely replied that he 'didn't believe in books' and that 'you only learn in this life through having experiences and keeping your mind open'. When she then raised the thorny philosophical dilemma of whether you could both 'keep your mind open' and 'not believe in books' he had replied, 'Well, I think you rather prove my point there, Diana,' and sipped his water in a manner that suggested great wisdom.

Close to tears through boredom, Donna had wondered where Carl was this evening. Donna has recently taken to scrolling through the Instagram feed of her ex-boyfriend and the Instagram feed of his new girlfriend, who appeared to be called Toyota. It has become such a habit now, she will sort of miss it when Carl and Toyota split up. Which they will, because Carl is an idiot and he's not going to keep a hold of a girlfriend with eyebrows that great.

Does Donna still love Carl? No. Did she ever, if she's being honest? Probably not, now she's had time to think about it. Does she still feel belittled by his rejection? Yes, that's showing no signs of going away. It's sitting like a stone just under her heart. She had arrested a shoplifter in Fairhaven last week, and when he had struggled, she had brought him down with a baton behind the knees. She was aware she had hit him much harder than she should. Sometimes you just had to hit things.

Was it a mistake to get as far away from Carl as she could? To transfer to Fairhaven in a frightened huff? Of course it was a mistake. It was stupid. Donna has always been headstrong, always acted quickly and decisively. Which is a fine quality when you are right, but a liability when you are wrong. It's great to be the fastest runner, but not when you're running in the wrong direction. Meeting the Thursday Murder Club was the first good thing that had happened to Donna in a long time. That and Tony Curran being murdered.

Donna had taken a photo of herself and Gregor just after he'd finished his superfood salad. She posted it to Instagram with the caption 'This is what you get when you date a personal trainer!' and added not one but two wink emojis. The only thing men were ever jealous of was good looks, and Carl wasn't to know that Donna had spent much of the evening surveying the dinner table, idly wondering how she would murder Gregor, if she absolutely had to. She had settled on injecting a dough ball with cyanide. Although she later realized that there was no way she could have got Gregor to eat a carb.

Talking of Gregor, she hears the toilet flush. She slips her clothes back on and, as he comes back out of the bathroom, she gives him a peck on the cheek. There is no way she's staying overnight in the room of a twenty-eight-year-old man who has two posters on his bedroom wall, one of the Dalai Lama and one of a Ferrari. It is still not 10 p.m. and she wonders if she is allowed to text Chris Hudson and see if he fancies a quick drink. Have a little chat about Elizabeth's file, the bits of it that she had understood. Also, she has finally just watched *Narcos* on Netflix and wants to discuss it with someone. Gregor had not seen it. Gregor didn't watch television, due to a long reason that Donna had quickly lost interest in.

Maybe she should just head home and ring Elizabeth instead? Talk through what she'd read in the folder? Would 10 p.m. be too late? Who knew with that lot? They had lunch at half eleven.

So, it's either Chris, her boss, or Elizabeth, her . . . well what exactly was Elizabeth? The word that came to Donna's mind first was 'friend', but surely that wasn't right.

37

'Not too late at all, PC De Freitas,' says Elizabeth, nearly dropping the phone receiver in the darkness and blindly struggling to switch on the bedside light. 'I was just watching a *Morse*.'

Elizabeth manages to flick the light on, sees the gentle rise and fall of Stephen's ribcage. His faithful heart beating on.

'And why are you up at this hour, Donna?'

Donna sneaks a look at her watch. 'Well, it's quarter past ten. Sometimes I just stay up this late. Now, Elizabeth, the folder was a bit long and a bit complicated, but I think I got some of it.'

'Excellent,' replies Elizabeth. 'I wanted it to be long and complicated enough for you to need to ring me to talk about it.'

'I see,' says Donna.

'It keeps me involved, you see, and it reminds you that we can be useful. I wouldn't want you to feel like we were interfering, Donna, but at the same time I do want to interfere.'

Donna smiles. 'Why don't you take me through it?'

'Well, firstly, just to note, there are documents in that folder that would take you weeks to track down. You'd need warrants and all sorts. Ventham wouldn't let you anywhere near some of them. So, I'm not blowing my own trumpet, but even so.'

'Feel free to let me know how you got hold of them.'

'Ron found them in a skip. Amazing what you can find, a lucky break for us all. Now, do you want the headlines before bed? You want to know why Ian Ventham might have murdered Tony Curran?'

Donna lies back on her pillow, remembering her mum reading her bedtime stories. She is aware that this shouldn't feel similar, but it does. 'Mmm hmm,' she assents.

'Now, Ventham's business is very profitable, very well run. But here's the first headline that's of interest to us. We discover that Tony Curran owns twenty-five per cent of Coopers Chase.'

'I see,' says Donna.

'But then we discover that Curran is not a partner in the new company Ventham is using for The Woodlands.'

'The new development? OK. And?'

'There is an appendix in your folder – 4c, I think. The Woodlands was due to be exactly the same as the rest of Coopers Chase, seventy-five per cent Ian Ventham, twenty-five per cent Tony Curran, until Ventham changed his mind and cut Curran out entirely. Now you know what question to ask next?'

'When did Ventham change his mind?'

'Precisely. Well, Ventham signed the papers to cut Curran out of the deal the day before the consultation meeting. Which was, of course, the day before their mysterious row. And the day before someone murdered Tony Curran.'

'So Curran misses out on The Woodlands,' says Donna. 'What would that have cost him?'

'Millions,' says Elizabeth. 'There are huge projections in the folder. Curran would have been counting on an enormous payday before Ventham cut him out of the deal. That's the news he received from Ian Ventham the day he was murdered.'

'Certainly enough for him to threaten Ventham. Is that your thinking?' asks Donna. 'So Curran threatens Ventham.

Ventham gets scared and kills Curran? Gets his retaliation in first?'

'Exactly. And it would get even worse after the next phase of the development, Hillcrest. That's what our expert says.'

'Hillcrest?' asks Donna.

'The real golden goose. Buying the farmland on top of the hill. Doubling the size of the development.'

'And when will Hillcrest happen?' asks Donna.

'Well that's a sticking point for Ventham. He doesn't even own the land yet,' says Elizabeth. 'It is still owned by the farmer, Gordon Playfair.'

'This is too complicated for me now, Elizabeth,' admits Donna.

'Forget Hillcrest for now, and forget Gordon Playfair, they're red herrings. What that folder tells you are two key things. Firstly, Ventham double-crossed Tony Curran, on the day Curran died.'

'Agreed.'

'And secondly – listen carefully to this – Tony Curran's shares have all reverted to Ian Ventham.'

'Tony Curran's shares pass back to Ian Ventham?'

'They do,' confirms Elizabeth. 'If you want to put a figure on it, something simple to tell Chris Hudson, our expert says Tony Curran's death just earned Ian Ventham around twelve and a quarter million pounds.'

Donna gives a low whistle.

'Which sounds an awful lot like a motive to me,' continues Elizabeth. 'So I hope this is helpful?'

'It is helpful, Elizabeth. I'll let Chris know.'

'Chris, is it?' says Elizabeth.

'I'll let you get back to sleep now, Elizabeth; sorry for ringing so late. And I'm grateful for what you've done. And it's cute you keep saying "our expert" instead of "Joyce's daughter". Very loyal. I promise we'll look into it.'

'Thank you, Donna, and no comment. When you're over next, I would like you to meet my friend Penny.'

'Thank you, Elizabeth, I'll look forward to it. Can I ask why you wanted to know what time Tony Curran died?'

'Just idle curiosity. I think Penny will like you very much. Night, night, dear.'

38

The morning sun is rising in the Kent sky.

'Ibrahim, if you keep driving at twenty-nine miles per hour, this whole exercise will be moot,' says Elizabeth, her fingers drumming on the glove box.

'And if I crash on a sharp bend, the exercise will also be moot,' says Ibrahim, eyes fixed on the road and intending to remain steadfast.

'Would anyone like a Mini Cheddar?' asks Joyce.

Ibrahim was tempted, but he liked to have both hands on the wheel at all times. Ten and two.

Ron was the only one of them who had a car, but there had still been an argument about who was going to drive. Joyce hadn't held a licence for thirty years and so was out immediately. Ron had put up a token fight, but Ibrahim knew he had lost his confidence on right-hand turns and would be secretly delighted to be voted down. Elizabeth put up more spirited opposition, mentioning that she still held a fully valid tank licence. She really could play fast and loose with the Official Secrets Act at times. But, in the end it all came down to this: Ibrahim was the only one who understood how the satnav worked.

It had been Elizabeth's idea, he was happy to grant her that. They knew, somehow, that Ian Ventham had left Coopers Chase at exactly 3 p.m. and they knew that Tony Curran had been murdered at 3.32. Ibrahim had had to explain to everyone what a Fitbit was. And so here they were, timing the journey in Ron's Daihatsu. Ibrahim knew they could have just plotted the journey on the satnav, but he also knew no one else realized that and he had fancied the drive. It had been a long time.

So Ibrahim is behind the wheel. Joyce and Ron are happily sharing their Mini Cheddars in the back seat, Elizabeth has stopped drumming her fingers and is now texting someone on her phone and everyone had been to the toilet before they left, as per his instructions.

Could Ian Ventham have made it from Coopers Chase to Tony Curran's house in time to kill him? If he couldn't, then they were barking up the wrong tree. They were about to find out.

39

'OK, folks, I'll show you mine if you show me yours.'

Another early morning and Chris Hudson's murder squad is assembled, in various stages of dishevelment. Chris has brought in Krispy Kremes from the garage and they are doing brisk business. Chris goes through what he'd discovered from the Thursday Murder Club and what Donna had told him about the file, after she'd buzzed on his door at 11 p.m. They'd talked about it over and over and then watched the first episode of *Narcos* season two with a bottle of red. Donna had invited herself over and Chris had wondered if this was just what constables were like in London these days. You had to hand it to her, she knew how to make a quick impression.

'Ian Ventham, Tony Curran's business partner, broke some bad news to Curran less than two hours before the murder. He was cutting him out of a development that would extend Coopers Chase, a retirement village out near Robertsbridge. This would have cost Curran a lot of money, and his death has made Ventham even more money. Over twelve million. The two men were seen having an argument shortly before Curran returned home. Did he threaten Ventham? Did Ventham decide it was better to be safe than sorry and send someone round? We know that Curran was killed at 3.32 last Tuesday, but when did Ventham leave Coopers Chase that day?'

'Where's this info from?' asks a young DI, Kate something.

'Sources,' says Chris. 'Where are we on traffic cameras, Terry? You've got Ventham's reg number?'

Donna's phone buzzes and she looks down at a message.

Good luck at the briefing this morning. Love, Elizabeth x.

Donna shakes her head.

'Got the number, but nothing yet. Still looking,' says DI Terry Hallet, shaven-headed, muscles bulging from underneath a white T-shirt. 'There's a lot of traffic. It's a fun job.'

'That's why you get doughnuts, Terry,' says Chris. 'Keep it up. And where are we on our other friend in the photograph, Bobby Tanner?'

'They've talked to the police in Amsterdam,' says Kate something. 'Bobby was working for some Scousers there after he did a runner. It didn't end well, as far as we can tell, and no one's heard of him since. No records, no bank details, nothing. We're still asking around, to see if he's come back under a different name, but it was a long time ago, there's not many of the old faces left.'

'It'd be nice to chat to him, rule him out at least. Anyone with anything positive for me?'

A junior DS puts up her hand. She's been sent over from Brighton and is eating carrot sticks instead of a doughnut.

'Yes, DS Grant,' says Chris, taking a punt on her name.

'DS Granger,' says DS Granger.

So close, thinks Chris. There are too many officers on this team.

'I've been looking at Tony Curran's phone records. He gets three calls on the morning of the murder, all from the same number, doesn't pick them up. A mobile, untraceable, probably a burner.'

Chris nods. 'OK, good work DS Granger, email me everything you've got and get on to the phone company, in case they can help. I know they won't, but one of these days they will.'

'Of course, sir,' says DS Granger and treats herself to a carrot baton.

Donna's phone buzzes again.

> We are having a little Thursday Murder Club road trip, in case there was anything you wanted to pass on?

'OK, gang, let's get back to it. Terry, anything from the traffic cams, let me know straight away. Kate, can I team you up with DS Granger and see what you can learn about the phone calls? And keep tracing Bobby Tanner, wherever he is, alive or dead, someone must know. Anyone who feels they've got nothing to do, come and knock at my door and I'll find something boring for you. One way or another, let's get Ventham.'

There is a final buzz on Donna's phone.

> PS, my sources saw Chris buying doughnuts this morning. You lucky thing. Also, Joyce says hello xx

Bernard Cottle finishes the Codeword puzzle in the *Express* and puts his pen back in the pocket of his jacket. It is beautiful up here this morning. On the bench, on the hill. Too beautiful, a cruel trick, played on those not still here to see it.

He had seen Joyce and her friends driving off somewhere this morning. How happy they had looked! But, then, Joyce seems to make everyone happy.

Bernard knows he has gone too far inside himself. Knows he is out of reach, even to Joyce. Bernard is not going to be saved and he doesn't deserve to be saved.

Still, what he wouldn't give to be in that car right now. Looking out at the view, as Joyce nattered away, perhaps picking the loose thread from the cuff of his jacket.

But instead he will stay here, on the hill, where he sits every day, and waits for what's to come.

Ibrahim had wanted to drive the Daihatsu right up to Tony Curran's front gate, just for the purposes of absolute accuracy. Elizabeth had told him that this was poor fieldcraft, however, and so they are now in a lay-by, about 300 metres from Tony Curran's house. It will do, he supposes.

Ibrahim has his notebook open on the bonnet and is showing some calculations to Joyce and Elizabeth. Ron is urinating in the woods.

'So it took us thirty-seven minutes at an average speed of twenty-seven and a half miles per hour, give or take. There was no traffic, because I am very efficient at plotting routes. I have a sixth sense. Other people would have hit traffic, I assure you.'

'I will recommend you for a gallantry honour,' says Elizabeth. 'As soon as we get back. Now, what does this mean for Ventham?'

'Would you like the detailed answer, or the simple answer?' asks Ibrahim.

'The simple answer please, Ibrahim,' says Elizabeth without hesitation.

Ibrahim pauses. Perhaps he had phrased his question poorly? 'But I have prepared a detailed answer, Elizabeth.'

Ibrahim lets this hang in the air, until Joyce says, 'Well, let's all enjoy the detailed answer shall we?'

'As you wish, Joyce.' Ibrahim claps his hands and turns over a page in his notebook. 'Now, Ventham could have taken one of three routes. He might have taken our route, but I doubt it; I don't think he has my insight for road networks. Route two, along the A21, looks the most obvious on the map, it's the straightest line, but here our friend temporary roadworks come into play. I spoke yesterday to a very interesting man at Kent County Council, who says the roadworks are to do with fibre optics. Would you like me to elaborate further on fibre optics, Joyce?'

'I think I'm OK, if Elizabeth is,' says Joyce.

Ibrahim nods. 'Another time. So route three, you could take the London Road, down past Battle Abbey, cut across and then down the B2159. Now, I know what you're thinking. You're thinking that seems slower, surely?'

'I was certainly thinking something, but it wasn't that,' says Elizabeth. Ibrahim could swear he senses impatience, but he is going as quickly as he can.

'So, we take our speed, which you will remember was . . . ?'

'I've forgotten, Ibrahim, forgive me,' says Joyce.

'Approximately twenty-seven point five miles per hour, Joyce,' says Ibrahim, with his trademark patience.

'Of course,' nods Joyce.

'And we will allow an extra three miles per hour for Ian Ventham's average speed. I was being careful, as you know.' Ibrahim looks at both Elizabeth and Joyce and is gratified by their quick nods. 'So, I then took the liberty of aggregating his three possible routes, dividing the answer by his average speed and subtracting a margin of error. I have calculated the margin of error in a rather elegant way. Take a look at my notebook and you'll see the maths. We take the average speed of route A and then we . . .'

Ibrahim stops as a noise comes from the woods. It is Ron, emerging and zipping himself up without a care in the world.

'Better out than in,' says Ron.

'Ron!' says Elizabeth, as if greeting her oldest friend in the world. 'We were about to enjoy Ibrahim showing us some maths, but I imagine you'd have little patience with that?'

'No maths, Ibrahim old son,' says Ron. 'Could Ventham have got here on time?'

'Well, I can show . . .'

Ron waves this away. 'Ibrahim, I'm seventy-five, mate. Could he have done it?'

Ian Ventham is on his treadmill, listening to the audiobook of Richard Branson's *Screw It, Let's Do It: Lessons in Life and Business*. Ian doesn't agree with Branson's politics, far from it, but you have to admire the guy. Admire what he's achieved. One day Ian will write a book. He just needs a title that rhymes and then he'll get to work.

As Ian runs, he is thinking about the graveyard and he's thinking about Father Mackie. He wouldn't want anything to get out of hand there. In the good old days he could have sent Tony Curran round to have a quiet word with him. But Tony's gone and Ian is not going to dwell on that any more than Richard Branson would. Branson would move on and so will Ian.

The diggers are due to start in a week. Get the graveyard done first, that's the tough bit, like eating your vegetables. Everything else will be a breeze.

The diggers are ready to go, the permits are signed off, Bogdan's lined up a couple of drivers.

In fact, thinks Ian, in fact, what is he waiting for? What would Branson do? What would the one guy he likes on *Dragons' Den* do?

They'd get on with it. Screw it, let's do it.

Ian switches off the audiobook and, without breaking stride, rings Bogdan.

Joyce

So, could Ian Ventham have killed Tony Curran? That was today's big question.

Well, according to Ibrahim, and I do trust him in the area of attention to detail, Ian Ventham would have been cutting it very fine, but it would have been possible. If he had left Coopers Chase at 3 p.m., he would have arrived at Tony Curran's house (big, and a bit tacky, but still nice) at 3.29. That would have given him two minutes to get out of his car, get into the house and hit Tony Curran with a large object.

So, Ron said that if Ian Ventham had killed Tony Curran, then he'd done it very quickly and Elizabeth had said that that was always the best way to kill someone and that there was never any point faffing around.

I asked Ibrahim if he was certain of the timings and he told me that of course he was and that he had tried to show me his workings, but that he'd been interrupted by Ron returning from urinating. I told him that was a shame and he perked up a bit and suggested that perhaps he could show me the workings later. I told him that I would like that very much, because a white lie harms no one.

So, we had a lot of fun today and it seems that Ian Ventham really could have killed Tony Curran. He had the motive and he had the opportunity and I suppose where bludgeoning is concerned, the means is just something big and heavy, so that wouldn't be beyond him either. Lewis would have him bang to rights.

What if they arrest Ventham though? And the fun stops? Let's see what tomorrow brings.

Ian Ventham is having an early night. He sets his alarm for 5 a.m. Tomorrow is the big day. He puts on his blackout goggles and his noise-cancelling headphones and happily drifts off.

Ron shuts his eyes. He liked it the other day, the police coming to see them, and he liked shouting at Ventham in the meeting. In truth he misses the limelight a bit. He misses people listening when he talks. Put him on *Question Time*. They wouldn't dare. He'd tell them a thing or two. Thump the table, blame the Tories, raise the roof, like the good old days. Or would he? Maybe not. He's drifting now. Maybe they'd see through him, maybe his tricks were yesterday's tricks? He has certainly lost a yard of pace. What if they asked about Syria? Is it Syria? Libya? What if Dimbleby looks him in the eye and says, 'Mr Ritchie, tell us what you saw.' But that was the copper wasn't it? And it's Fiona Bruce now isn't it? He likes Fiona Bruce. Who killed Tony Curran though? Ventham. Typical Blairite. Unless he was missing something. Was he missing something?

Across the path, Ibrahim is learning the countries of the world, just to keep his left brain ticking over. He is letting his right brain get on with the job of thinking about who killed Tony Curran. Somewhere between Denmark and Djibouti, he falls asleep.

*

In her three-bed, in Larkin, the one with the decking, Elizabeth cannot sleep. She is getting used to that these days.

Her arm is around her Stephen in the darkness. Can he feel it? Does Penny hear her? Have they both already disappeared? Or are they only real for as long as she chooses to believe they're real? Elizabeth clings on a little tighter and holds on to the day for as long as she is able.

Bernard Cottle is online. His daughter, Sudhi, had bought him an iPad last Christmas. He had asked for slippers, but Sudhi hadn't considered slippers a proper present, so he'd had to buy himself some in Fairhaven in the sales. He hadn't known how to use the iPad, but Joyce had told him not to be so silly and had taken it out of the drawer and shown him. By his side, Bernard has a large glass of whisky and the last slice of Joyce's coffee and walnut cake. A pale, blue glow illuminates his face, as he looks at the plans for The Woodlands for what must be the hundredth time.

One by one, the lights of the village switch off. The only remaining illumination comes from behind the thick hospital blinds of Willows. The business of dying keeping different hours from the business of living.

45

Ellidge had seen them first.

Every morning, Edwin Ellidge wakes at 6 a.m. and walks slowly, but with purpose, to the bottom of the drive at Coopers Chase. Once across the cattle grid and onto the main road, he looks both ways, looks again for good measure, then turns and walks slowly back up the drive. Job done, he is back in his flat by 6.30 a.m., whereupon he is not seen for the rest of the day.

Coopers Chase being Coopers Chase, no one has ever asked him why. After all, a woman in Tennyson walks a dog she doesn't have. Whatever gets you out of bed.

Elizabeth, being Elizabeth, once decided to casually intercept him on his walk back. As she approached him, the early mist, her frozen breath and the trudging figure of a man in an overcoat all reminded her of happy times in East Germany. He raised his gaze to meet hers, gave a reassuring shake of the head and said, 'No need, I've already checked.' Elizabeth replied 'Thank you, Mr Ellidge.' She turned back and the two of them walked together up the drive in a very pleasant silence.

Ibrahim says Ellidge was once a head teacher and latterly a beekeeper, and Elizabeth had detected a buried hint of Norfolk in his voice, but that was all the information they had on file for Mr Edwin Ellidge.

Ian Ventham's Range Rover was first. This was at 6 a.m. Ellidge saw it veer off the road before it reached him, taking the track which led up the hill to the Playfair farm. The diggers passed Ellidge at around 6.20 a.m., as he was walking home. He didn't even give them a glance. Evidently these were not the vehicles he had been looking for. They were set, nose to nose, on a low-loader that slowly ground its way up the drive.

A dawn raid is all well and good for catching drug dealers, or armed gangs, but at Coopers Chase it is next to useless. If such things were logged, the first phone call would have been recorded at 6.21. Diggers are here, coming up the drive, two of them. I mean I don't know, do you? That beacon lit, the news was across the whole village by 6.45 a.m. at the very latest, the news spread by landline alone – Ibrahim had tried to set up a WhatsApp group in February, but it hadn't caught on. Residents began to emerge and discuss what could be done.

At 7.30 a.m. Ian Ventham comes back down the hill and turns into the drive to discover the whole village is out. Except for Edwin Ellidge, who has had enough excitement for one day. Karen Playfair is in Ian Ventham's passenger seat. She has a breakfast lecture to give at Coopers Chase this morning.

The low-loader has continued its slow growl up the drive and is now being carefully driven through the car park. Bogdan jumps from the passenger seat and unbolts the heavy wooden gate, so the journey can continue upwards on the narrow path towards the Garden of Eternal Rest.

'Hold up, son.' Ron approaches Bogdan and shakes his hand. 'Ron. Ron Ritchie. What's all this?'

Bogdan shrugs. 'Diggers.'

'I'll give you diggers, son. What are they doing?' says Ron, quickly adding, 'Don't say digging.'

More residents have reached the gate now and they begin to crowd around Ron, all waiting for an answer.

'Well, son? What are they for?' asks Ron.

Bogdan sighs. 'You said to not say digging. I don't have other answer.' He looks at his watch.

'Son, you just opened this gate and this gate only leads one place.' Ron sees he has a crowd and this is an opportunity he is not going to waste. He turns towards the gathering. He spies his gang among them. Ibrahim has his swimming stuff under one arm, Joyce has just arrived with a flask and is looking out for someone. Bernard, no doubt. Elizabeth is at the back and there's a rare sighting of Stephen by her side. He's in a dressing gown, but he's not the only one. Ron feels a pang of guilt as he sees Penny's husband, John, in his suit, as ever, stopped on his way over to Willows. Ron hasn't visited Penny in a long time and knows he must put that right before the chance is gone. It frightens him, though.

Ron clambers onto the first bar of the gate to address his crowd. He then almost loses his balance, thinks the better of it and returns to solid ground. No matter, he's in business here.

'Well, this is nice. Just us, a couple of Polish lads and some diggers. All enjoying the morning air. Ventham's little gang. Crawling in at six thirty in the morning to dig up our nuns. No warning, no consultation. Coming into our village and digging up our nuns.' He turns to Bogdan. 'That's your game, is it, son?'

'Yes, that's our game,' concedes Bogdan.

Ventham's Range Rover pulls up alongside the low-loader and he steps out. He looks at the crowd and then at Bogdan, who shrugs. Karen Playfair steps out too and smiles at the scene before her.

'And here's the man himself,' says Ron as he spots Ventham walking over.

'Mr Ritchie,' says Ventham.

'Sorry to disturb your morning, Mr Ventham,' says Ron.

'Not at all. Carry on, make a speech,' replies Ventham. 'Pretend it's the fifties, or whenever you were around. But when you're done I'm going to need to access that path to do some digging.'

'Not today, old son, afraid not,' says Ron, turning back to the crowd. 'We're all weak, Mr Ventham, you can see that, right? Look at us, give us a nudge and we'd topple over. That's the last you'd see of us. We're feeble, the lot of us, we're a pushover. A pushover, eh? Should be easy. But, you know, there's a few people here who've done a few things in their life. Am I right?'

Cheers.

'There's a few people here who've seen off, and no disrespect, better men than you.' Ron pauses and looks around at his audience. 'We got soldiers here, one or two. We got teachers, we got doctors, we got people who could take you apart and people who could put you back together again. We got people who crawled through deserts, people who built rockets, people who locked up killers.'

'And insurance underwriters!' shouts Colin Clemence from Ruskin, to happy applause.

'In short, Mr Ventham,' says Ron, his arm sweeping, 'we got fighters. And you, with your diggers at half seven in the morning, have picked a fight.'

Ian waits to make certain Ron has finished, that the bolt has been shot, then steps forward to talk to the same crowd.

'Thanks, Ron. All rubbish, but thank you. There's no fight here. You've had your consultation, you've made your objections, they were all overturned. You've got lawyers here, right? Alongside the people you're telling me have crawled through deserts? You've got barristers? Solicitors? Jesus, you've got judges here! That was your fight. In court. It was a fair fight and you lost it. So if I want to drive onto land that I own at eight a.m. and carry out work that I've planned and that I'm paying for and that, also no disrespect, will keep your service charge at the reasonable level it currently is, then I will. I will and I am.'

The term 'service charge' has a noticeable effect on the softer element in the crowd. They might well have four hours to kill until lunch and be looking forward to a show, but this fella does have a point.

Joyce and Bernard, who had slipped away together during Ron's grandstanding, are now returning with garden chairs under their arms. They walk through the crowd and open them out on the path.

It is Joyce's turn to address the crowd. 'Radio Kent says it's going to be lovely all morning, if some of you would like to join us? We could make a day of it if anyone's got a picnic table they're not using?'

Ron turns to the crowd. 'Who's up for a nice sit down and a cup of tea?'

The crowd gets to business, chairs and tables to be collected, kettle on, see what's in the cupboard, too early for a drink, but let's see if we can string it out. If nothing else this should be fun. Though, again, he does make a very good point about the service charge.

Ibrahim stands by the cab of the low-loader, talking to the driver. He had estimated, by eye, that it was thirteen point five metres in length and is gratified to learn that it is thirteen point three. Not bad, Ibrahim, still got it.

Elizabeth leads Stephen home, unscathed. Make him a coffee and she can head back out.

46

The call from Ian Ventham comes through to Fairhaven Police Station at around 7.30 a.m. Donna is drinking a litre carton of cranberry juice as she overhears the words 'Coopers Chase'. She volunteers her services and sends Chris Hudson a text. He's off this morning, but he won't want to miss this.

At 7 a.m. Father Matthew Mackie receives a call from a Maureen Gadd. By 7.30 he is up and dressed, dog collar front and centre and waiting for a cab to the station.

In front of the gate that leads to the Garden of Eternal Rest there are now twenty chairs. Mainly sun loungers, but also one dining chair because of Miriam's back.

As a barricade it is unorthodox, but effective. Trees crowd in on either side of the gate, so the only way up to the Garden of Eternal Rest is now through a phalanx of pensioners, some of whom are taking the opportunity to stretch out in the morning sun and have a well-earned nap. The diggers are not getting past for a while.

Ian Ventham is back in his car, watching the scene. Karen Playfair has stepped outside and is merrily vaping away on an apple and cinnamon e-cigarette.

Ian sees picnic tables, ice-coolers and parasols. Tea is being fetched and carried on padded trays. Photographs of grandchildren are being swapped. The Garden of Eternal Rest is a sideshow, for most of the residents this is just a street party in the midsummer sun. No need for Ian to get involved, they will fold like their loungers the moment the police arrive and they'll wander off to do whatever they do.

Ian is sure this little display will blow over, but he hopes the police show up soon. With the amount of tax he hypothetically pays, it's really not too much to ask.

Elizabeth is not at the scene. Instead, after dropping Stephen at home, she has taken a route up through Blunts Wood and, as she clears the treeline, she steps onto the broad path leading up to the Garden of Eternal Rest. She walks up the path until she reaches the wooden bench, Bernard Cottle's bench, where she sits and waits.

She looks down towards Coopers Chase. The path curves towards the bottom, so the barricade is out of sight, but she can hear the polite disturbance at the bottom of the hill. Always look where the action isn't, because that's where the action is. A part of her is surprised that Joyce hasn't made the walk up the hill too. Perhaps she lacks some of Elizabeth's instincts after all.

Elizabeth hears a rustling coming from the trees about twenty metres down on the other side of the path and that rustling very soon turns into the figure of Bogdan emerging from the trees, with a shovel over his shoulder.

He heads up the path, nodding to Elizabeth as he passes.

'Missus,' he says, nodding to her. If he had a cap, Elizabeth felt sure he would doff it.

'Bogdan,' she replies. 'I know you have work to do, but I wonder if I might ask you a question?'

Bogdan stops his walk, lowers the shovel from his shoulder and rests his weight on the handle. 'Please,' he replies.

Elizabeth had been thinking things through last night. Really – Ventham arrives, gets inside, makes his way to the kitchen and then kills Tony Curran within two minutes?

She'd seen it done before, but not by an amateur. So what was she missing?

'Did Mr Ventham tell you he wanted Tony Curran murdered?' asks Elizabeth. 'After their row? Perhaps he asked you to help? Perhaps you did help?'

Bogdan considers her for a moment. Not fazed.

'I know that's three questions, forgive an old woman,' adds Elizabeth.

'Well, is only one answer, so is OK,' begins Bogdan. 'No, he didn't tell me and no he didn't ask, so no I didn't help.'

Elizabeth gives this her consideration. 'All the same, it's worked out nicely for you. You have a lucrative new job, don't you?'

'Yes,' agrees Bogdan, nodding.

'Can I ask if you fitted Tony Curran's alarm system?'

Bogdan nods. 'Sure, Ian gets me to do all that stuff for people.'

'So you could have got in, very easily? Waited for him?'

'Sure. Would have been simple.'

Elizabeth hears more cars pulling up at the bottom of the path.

'I know I'm being rude in asking, but if Ian Ventham had wanted Tony Curran dead, might he have asked you to do it? Is that the sort of relationship you have?'

'He trust me,' says Bogdan, thinking. 'So I think maybe he would ask me, yes.'

'And what might you have said? If he had asked you?'

'There are some jobs I do, like fix alarms, tile swimming pools, and there are some jobs I don't do, like kill people. So, if he ask, I say, "Listen, maybe you have good reason, but I would say kill him yourself, Ian." You know?'

'Well, I agree,' says Elizabeth, nodding. 'You're absolutely sure you didn't kill Tony Curran though?'

Bogdan laughs, 'I am absolutely sure. I would remember.'

'This has turned into a lot of questions, Bogdan, I'm sorry,' says Elizabeth.

'Is OK,' says Bogdan, looking at his watch. 'Is still early and I like to talk.'

'Where are you from, Bogdan?'

'Poland.'

'Yes, I'd got that. Which part?'

'Near Krakow. You heard of Krakow?'

Elizabeth certainly has heard of Krakow. 'I have, yes, it's a very beautiful city. In fact I went there, many years ago.'

It was in 1968 to be exact, to conduct an informal interview, on trade delegation business, with a young Polish army colonel. The Polish army colonel later very happily went on to run a bookmaker's in Coulsdon and had an MBE for services to the British State, which stayed in a locked drawer until the day he died.

Bogdan looks out over the Kent hills. He then holds out a hand. 'I should work. It is nice to meet you.'

'It is nice to meet you too. My name is Marina,' says Elizabeth, as she shakes his huge hand.

'Marina?' repeats Bogdan. His smile returns, once again, like a baby deer attempting to walk. 'Marina was my mother's name.'

'How lovely!' says Elizabeth. She's not proud of herself, but you never know when this sort of thing could come in handy. And really, if someone is going to have so much personal information tattooed on his body, what is she expected to do? 'I hope to see you again, Bogdan.'

'I hope to see you too, Marina.'

Elizabeth watches as he continues up the path, swings open the heavy iron gates and takes his shovel into the Garden of Eternal Rest.

There is more than one type of digger, thinks Elizabeth, as she starts to walk back down the hill. She thinks of another question she should have asked. Does Ian Ventham have the same alarm system as Tony Curran? If so, it would have been an easy job for him to get into Tony Curran's house. Had he needed to. She would bet he does. She will ask Bogdan the next time she sees him.

When Elizabeth reaches the barricade, she finds that the gate has been padlocked and that the padlock is being guarded by three women, including Maureen Gadd, who plays bridge with Derek Archer. Very badly, in Elizabeth's view.

Elizabeth climbs the gate and makes the small jump on the other side back into the heart of the action. How many more years of that? Three or four? She spies Ian Ventham climbing out of his car as Chris Hudson and Donna De Freitas approach. Time to join in the fun, she thinks, and taps Joyce on the shoulder. Bernard is asleep in the chair next to her, which at least explains why Joyce hadn't come snooping.

In theory, she approves of chasing after men, if that's what you wanted to do, but surely Joyce must find it exhausting?

49

Joyce

When Elizabeth arrived, Bernard had already fallen asleep, which I think was a blessing, because he does get worked up. He had looked tired when I had knocked for him this morning. I don't think he's sleeping at night.

Elizabeth and I went to see Donna and Chris, collecting Ron on the way. He was looking in the pink, which was nice to see. While it is still fresh, this is everything I remember after that.

Donna does something with her eye shadow and I always mean to ask what it is, but I haven't yet. Anyway, it was DCI Hudson doing the talking and he was quite impressive in his way. He was saying such and such to Ian Ventham. Ian Ventham said he wanted us all out of the way and had the paperwork to back it up. Which seemed fair.

DCI Hudson said he wanted to talk to the residents and Ron told him to talk to him (Ron) instead. Ron also said that Ian Ventham could stick his paperwork up the proverbial. Which is par for the course for Ron, as you know. Donna then suggested that DCI Hudson perhaps should talk to me. As a level head, of all things.

So DCI Hudson explained the legal niceties to me and warned that he would be forced to arrest anyone who blocked the diggers. I said that I was sure he wouldn't actually arrest anyone and he agreed that this was true. So there we were, back to square one.

Ron then asked DCI Hudson if he was proud of himself and DCI Hudson replied that he was an overweight, fifty-one-year-old divorcee and so, by and large, no, he wasn't. This made Donna smile. She likes him, not like that, but she likes him. I do too. I was going to say to him that he wasn't overweight, but he actually is a bit and, as a nurse, it's best to never sugar-coat things, even when your instinct is to be protective. Instead I told him he should never eat after 6 p.m., that's the key if you don't want diabetes and he thanked me.

That's when Ibrahim joined us and suggested that DCI Hudson might try Pilates and Donna said that was something she would pay to see. Ian Ventham didn't want to join in the fun and told Donna and DCI Hudson that he paid their wages. Donna said in that case could she ask him about a pay rise and that's when Ian Ventham started shouting the odds about this, that and the other. People without a sense of humour will never forgive you for being funny. But that's an aside.

Anyway, Ibrahim, who is very good with this sort of thing, conflict and inadequate men and stalemates and so on, stepped in and offered to 'thin the crowd out' to give everyone a bit of breathing space. It was agreed that this was the thing to do.

Ibrahim walked over to the barricade picnic, which was in full swing, and suggested that anyone who didn't want to be arrested should perhaps move their chairs off the path. This shifted a few of the fairweathers. Colin Clemence led the charge. When Ibrahim reassured the rest that they only had to clear the path and were very welcome to stay out and watch the action, there was a proper exodus. Though not a quick exodus, because you know that getting out of a garden chair at our age is a military operation. Once you are in one, you can be in it for the day.

Eventually the scene was as follows. The barricade, with the gate firmly locked behind it, was the stage and the crowd, happily back in their chairs, was the audience. And who was on the stage? There was Maureen Gadd, who plays bridge with Derek Archer (and not just bridge, in my opinion, but that's not to be repeated), Barbara Kelly from Ruskin who once walked out of Waitrose with a whole salmon and pleaded dementia (my foot, but it worked) and Bronagh something, who is new and on whom I have no further information. I have seen all three of them on their way to the Catholic Mass on Sundays, then hours later, trudging back. They were padlocked to the gate like bikes on railings.

And in front of them? The barricade had disappeared and left just one man. Awake now, sitting to attention, unmoved, unbowed, terrific posture: Bernard. Unlike him, I suppose, but he must feel strongly about the graveyard. You should have seen him. The last guard, like Henry Fonda, or Martin Luther King, or King Midas. This was too much for Ron, who grabbed a chair and sat right next to him. Whether out of solidarity or a desire for attention, who knows? But I was glad that he did. I was very proud of them both, my stubborn boys.

(I don't mean King Midas by the way, I mean King Canute.)

Ventham had gone back to his car, for the time being, with Donna and Chris.

I poured Bernard and Ron cups of tea and settled down myself, assuming the fun was about to end.

Which was when the taxi arrived and the fun really began.

Forgive me, my doorbell is ringing, I'll be back in a moment.

50

Father Matthew Mackie always likes to chat to taxi drivers. These days they are often Muslim, even in Kent, and their kinship makes him feel very comfortable. They also react well to the dog collar. But today he has been silent.

He is relieved to see that the gate up to the Garden is still locked and guarded and that the diggers are idling on their trailer. He had left a phone number on the noticeboard outside the chapel for just this eventuality and that was the number Maureen Gadd had phoned this morning, promising also that she would 'alert the troops'.

Mackie took those 'troops' to be the three women in black standing stock-still by the gate. In front of them are a woman and two men in chairs, who didn't seem quite the type. In fact, now he looks closer, he is sure that one is the gentleman with the opinions from the public meeting. And the man in the middle, is he the man from the bench the other morning? Well, whoever they are, and whatever their motive, all are welcome in this particular flock. To the side of the gate is a crowd of around fifty residents, sitting, watching and waiting for a show. Fine, he will give them a show. He supposes this might be his last and only chance.

Stepping out of the taxi and giving the driver a large tip, Father Mackie sees Ventham is in a Ford Focus, talking to two police officers. One of them is a large man looking too hot in a jacket, the other a young, black woman in uniform. No sign of Bogdan, not even in the cab of the trailer. He will be somewhere nearby, surely?

Mackie wanders over to the gate; Ventham has yet to spot him. He takes a moment to speak to, and bless, the three guards. One of them, the mysterious Maureen Gadd, asks if there is the chance of a cup of tea and Mackie says he will see what he can do. Before heading over to confront Ventham, he stops, to introduce himself to the seated figures.

51

Joyce

Sorry, the ring at the door was a parcel for upstairs and we always sign for each other, so that's where I've been. Sometimes, if I know Joanna is sending me flowers, I pretend not to be in, just so a neighbour picks them up and sees them. Terrible of me, really, but I'm sure people do worse.

Anyway, Bernard was saying that he wouldn't take orders from the police. Bernard was staying put and that was that.

Ron said that he'd once been chained to a pit shaft in Glasshoughton for forty-eight hours and they'd had to defecate into sandwich bags, though he didn't say 'defecate', and that was when Father Mackie introduced himself.

I had seen him at the meeting. He had sat at the back, quiet as you please and slipped biscuits into his pocket when he thought no one was looking. As I've said, no one ever realizes I'm watching. I just have one of those faces.

I have to say he was very polite and he thanked us for protecting the Garden. Bernard told him the Garden was only the start of it and once you give someone an inch, then we all know what they'd take. Ron then had to have his say and told Father Mackie that 'his lot' (the Catholics) had not always been squeaky clean when it came to graveyards, but that a liberty is still a liberty and he didn't like to see one being taken. Father Mackie said that 'wouldn't happen on my watch' and it all got a bit cowboy film, which was fine by me. I like to see men being men, up to a point.

This is when Ventham must have caught sight of Father Mackie, because over he rushes, with Chris, Donna and Ibrahim chasing behind. And so, the stage was now set.

52

Bogdan has been digging for a long time. Why not? Might as well be getting something done. He started at the very top of the Garden of Eternal Rest, where the earliest graves are now permanently under the shadow of the wide branches of the trees behind the wall. The ground is softer, with no sunlight in many years, and Bogdan knows that the older, grander coffins here will be intact. They will be solid oak. They won't be split or rotten. There will be no skulls staring up at him, hollow and eaten and hopeful.

He hears the odd bit of excitement from down the hill, but still no rumble of the low-loader, and so he keeps digging. One of the machines could uncover a whole row of graves in minutes, especially if not much care is taken, which Bogdan knows will be the case. So he chooses to be neat and tidy, for as long as it is just him and his shovel.

The next grave he chooses to tackle is tucked tightly in the top corner of the graveyard. As he digs, he is thinking about Marina, the woman he met on his way up here. He has seen her before in the village, but mainly people don't talk to him, they don't even notice him, and that's OK. He doesn't suppose you are allowed to visit people here, but maybe one day if he bumped into her again, then that would be OK. He misses his mother some days.

Bogdan's shovel finally strikes something solid, but it is not the lid of the coffin. There are many stones and tree roots, which make the job harder, but more fun, for Bogdan. He reaches down and clears thick earth off the obstruction.

It is pure white. Beautiful, in fact, thinks Bogdan, in the moment before he realizes what it is.

This was not part of Bogdan's plan. The very point of digging here was that there would be no rotten coffins and no bones. And yet here they were. So even 150 years ago they were cutting corners? Cheap coffins, who would ever find out?

Should he just fill the grave back in? Pretend it never happened and wait for the diggers? Something about that makes him feel uncomfortable. Bogdan has uncovered a bone and that makes him the guardian. He has no smaller tool than the shovel with him, so kneels down on the compacted earth and starts to work with his hands alone. He is as gentle as he can be. He shifts his kneeling weight to get a better angle to clear away more dirt, and as he does so he realizes he is not kneeling on compacted dirt but on something much more solid. He realizes that he is kneeling on the solid oak lid of the solid oak coffin. Which can't be. A body can't escape from a coffin. Bogdan tries to force out a horrific thought. Had someone been buried alive? Had they managed to somehow clamber out of the coffin, but no further?

Bogdan works quickly, with no room for ceremony or superstition. There are many bones and then a skull, though he tries not to disturb it. He uncovers enough of the coffin to jam the blade of his shovel under the lid. After considerable effort he breaks open the lower third. Inside is another skeleton.

Two skeletons. One inside the coffin and one outside. One small, one big. One grey and yellow, one cloud-white.

What to do? Somebody should take a look at it, that was fairly certain. Though that would take a long time. They would dig with tiny trowels, Bogdan had seen it on TV. And they wouldn't just be digging into this grave, they would be digging into all of them. And Bogdan knows it will end up being nothing. It will just be how they used to bury people in this country, or one year there was a disease and they buried people together, or a million other possibilities. Meanwhile the development will be delayed and he will be waiting to work. So, the question remains. What to do?

Bogdan needs thinking time, but unfortunately he doesn't have that luxury. In the distance, Bogdan hears a siren. He waits a moment and the siren comes closer. It sounds like an ambulance to Bogdan, but he knows, logically, that it must be the police. Which means the barricade will be clear soon enough and the circus will begin. Bogdan hauls himself out of the grave and starts to fill it in once more.

Ian will tell me what to do, he thinks, as the sirens reach the bottom of the path.

53

Ian Ventham, exiting the police car, is calm, happy even.

The police have had a placatory chat with him. He'll come back tomorrow. The graves aren't going anywhere. Perhaps sending in the diggers so early was a mistake. But it was a cool thing to do, so a mistake worth making. It was a statement, and making statements is important, whatever they are.

He doesn't mind the residents being up in arms, they'll soon lose interest. He can just give them something else to complain about. Sack one of the waiting staff that they like, or ban grandkids from the pool on health-and-safety grounds. Then they'll be all 'what graveyard?' He has to laugh, really, and so he does.

But, at that very moment, he sees Father Matthew Mackie.

Standing there in his frock and little white collar, like he owns the place. As bold as you like.

This is Ian's land, for Christ's sake! It's Ian's property! He storms towards the barricade, and has his finger in Father Mackie's face in seconds.

'If you weren't a vicar I would knock you out.' The crowd starts to surround them, like a fight in a pub car park. 'Get off my property, or I'll get you thrown off.'

Ian aims a shove at Mackie's shoulder, knocking the older man backwards. Mackie reaches out for balance, grabbing Ian's T-shirt, and the two men lose their balance and fall to the ground together. Donna, with the help of a horrified-looking Karen Playfair, pulls Ian up and off the priest. A group of residents, including Joyce, Ron and Bernard, then surround and restrain Ian Ventham while a group of residents on the other side form a guard around Father Mackie, now sitting, dazed, on the ground. School playground really, but he looks shaken.

'Calm it, Mr Ventham, calm down,' yells Donna.

'Arrest him! Trespass!' yells Ian, now being pulled away from the scene by a group of determined septuagenarians, octogenarians and even one nonagenarian, who had missed Second World War call-up by a day and has regretted it ever since.

Joyce finds herself in the scrum. How strong these men must have been in their time, Ron, Bernard, John, Ibrahim. And how diminished they were now. The spirit was still willing at least, but only Chris Hudson was really able to hold Ventham back. The testosterone was lovely while it lasted though.

'I'm protecting sacred ground. Peacefully and lawfully,' says Father Mackie.

Donna helps Father Mackie to his feet, dusting him down and feeling the frailty of the old man beneath the loose black cassock.

Chris pulls Ian Ventham from the scrum of bodies surrounding him. He can see the adrenaline surging through Ventham's body, the sort of thing he's seen a thousand times before, in the late-night drunks of too many towns. The veins riding the muscles that poke out from his T-shirt, a giveaway of steroid abuse.

'Home now, Mr Ventham,' orders Chris Hudson, 'before I arrest you.'

'I didn't touch him,' protests Ian Ventham.

Chris remains quiet, to keep the conversation private. 'He stumbled, Mr Ventham, I saw that, but he stumbled after you made contact with him, however light. So if I want to arrest you I will. And, allow a policeman a hunch, there might be one or two witnesses to help me in court. So, if you don't want to be charged with assaulting a priest, which wouldn't look good in your brochures, then you get in your car and you drive away. Understand?'

Ian Ventham nods, but without conviction, his brain already somewhere else, making some other calculation. He then shakes his head, slowly and sadly, at Chris Hudson.

'Something's not right here. Something's up.'

'Well, whatever's up will still be up tomorrow,' says Chris. 'So get yourself home, calm yourself down and mop your brow. Be a man and take a defeat.'

Ian turns and walks towards his car. Defeat? As if. As he passes the low-loader he bangs twice on the cab door and cocks his thumb towards the exit.

He walks slowly, thinking. Where's Bogdan? Bogdan is a good guy. He's Polish. He needs to get Bogdan to tile his swimming pool. He's too lazy, they all are. He'll talk to Tony Curran. Tony will know what to do. But did Tony lose his phone? Something about Tony.

Ian reaches the Range Rover. The car has been clamped! His dad will be furious, he's only borrowed it. He'll have to get the bus from town and his dad will be waiting for him. Ian is frightened and starts to cry. Don't cry, Ian, he'll see. Ian doesn't want to go home.

He searches his pockets for change, then stumbles and topples backwards. He reaches out for something to hold on to, but, to his surprise, there is only air.

Ian Ventham is dead before he hits the ground.

PART TWO

Everyone here has a Story to Tell

54

Joyce

I tripped over a loose paving slab in Fairhaven a few weeks ago. I didn't mention it in my diary because of murders and trips to London and my pursuit of Bernard. But it was a nasty tumble and I dropped my bag and my things went everywhere. Keys, glasses case, pills, phone.

Now, here's the thing. Every single person who saw me fall came over to help. Every single one of them. A cyclist helped me to my feet, a traffic warden picked up my things and dusted down my bag, a lady with a pushchair sat with me at a pavement table until I'd got my breath back. The woman who ran the café came out with a cup of tea and offered to drive me around to her GP.

Perhaps they only came to help because I look old. I look frail and helpless. But I don't think so. I think I would have helped if I saw a fit youngster take the tumble I did. I think you would too. I think I would have sat with him, I think the traffic warden would have picked up his laptop and I think the woman in the café would still have offered to drive him to her GP.

That's who we are as human beings. For the most part, we are kind.

However, I still remember a consultant I once worked with, at Brighton General, up on the hill. A very rude, very cruel, very unhappy man, and he made our lives a misery. He would shout and would blame us for mistakes he made.

Now, if that consultant had dropped dead in front of my eyes I would have danced a jig.

You mustn't speak ill of the dead, I know, but there are exceptions to every rule and Ian Ventham was of the same type as this consultant. Come to think of it, he was called Ian too, so that's something to look out for.

You know those people. People who feel the world is theirs alone? They say you see it more and more these days, this selfishness, but some people were always awful. Not many, that's what I'm saying, but always a few.

All of which is to say that, in one way, I'm sorry that Ian Ventham is dead, but there is another way to look at it.

On any given day lots of people die. I don't know the statistics, but it must be thousands. So somebody was going to die yesterday and I'm just saying that I would rather it was Ian Ventham who died in front of me than, say, the cyclist or the traffic warden, or the mum with the pushchair, or the woman who ran the café.

I would rather it was Ian Ventham the paramedics failed to save, than that it was Joanna, or Elizabeth. Or Ron, or Ibrahim, or Bernard. Without wanting to sound selfish about it, I would rather it was Ian Ventham who was zipped into a bag and wheeled into a coroner's van, than me.

For Ian Ventham, though, yesterday was the day. We will all have one and yesterday was his. Elizabeth says he was killed, and if Elizabeth says he was killed then I expect he was. I don't suppose he expected that when he woke up yesterday morning.

I hope I don't sound callous, it's just that I have seen a lot of people die and I have shed so many tears. But I have shed none for Ian Ventham and I just wanted you to know why. It is sad that he is dead, but it hasn't made me sad.

And now, if you'll excuse me, I have to go and help solve his murder.

55

'Well, here's the big headline.' Chris Hudson is standing at the front of the briefing room, his team spread out in front of him. 'Ian Ventham was murdered.'

Donna De Freitas looks around at the murder squad. There are a few new faces. She simply cannot believe her luck. Two murders and here she is, right in the middle of it all. She had to hand it to Elizabeth. She definitely owed her a drink, or whatever else Elizabeth might prefer. A scarf? Who knew what Elizabeth would like? A gun, probably.

Chris opens a folder. 'Ian Ventham's death was caused by fentanyl poisoning. A massive overdose, delivered into the muscle of his upper arm. Almost certainly in the moments leading up to his collapse. You'll tell by the speed that this is not official; this is me calling in a favour, OK? And they see enough fentanyl overdoses at the path lab these days to know one when they see one. We're the only people who have that piece of information at present, so let's keep it that way as long as we can, please. No press, no friends and family.'

He gives Donna the briefest of looks.

56

'So, we were all witnesses to a murder,' says Elizabeth. 'Which, needless to say, is wonderful.'

Fifteen winding miles away, the Thursday Murder Club is in extraordinary session. Elizabeth is laying out a series of full-colour photos of the corpse of Ian Ventham, alongside every conceivable angle of the scene. She had taken them on her phone while pretending she was calling for an ambulance. She then had them privately printed by a chemist in Robertsbridge who owed her a favour, due to her keeping quiet about a criminal conviction from the 1970s that she had managed to uncover.

'Tragic too, in its way, if we wanted to be traditional about our emotions,' adds Ibrahim.

'Yes, if we wanted to be melodramatic, Ibrahim,' says Elizabeth.

'First question, then,' says Ron. 'How do you know it was a murder? Looked like a heart attack to me.'

'And you're a doctor, Ron?' asks Elizabeth.

'As much as you are, Liz,' says Ron.

Elizabeth opens a folder and takes out a sheet of paper. 'Well, Ron, I've already been over this with Ibrahim, because I had a job for him, but listen carefully. The cause of death was an overdose of fentanyl, administered very shortly before death. This information is straight from a man who has access to the email correspondence of the Kent Police Forensic Service, but it hasn't yet been confirmed by Donna, even though I have texted her repeatedly. Happy, Ron?'

Ron nods. 'Yeah, I'll give you that. What's fentanyl? That's a new one on me.'

'It's an opioid, Ron, like heroin,' says Joyce. 'They use it in anaesthesia, pain relief, all sorts of things. Very effective, patients rave about it.'

'Also you can mix it with cocaine,' says Ibrahim. 'If you were a drug addict, say.'

'And the Russian security services use it for all sorts of things,' says Elizabeth.

Ron nods, satisfied.

Ibrahim says, 'And, as it must've been administered very shortly before his death, then we are all suspects in his murder.'

Joyce claps her hands. 'Splendid. I'm not sure how any of us would have got hold of fentanyl, but splendid.' She is arranging Viennese whirls on a plate commemorating Prince Andrew and Sarah Ferguson's wedding, something Joanna had assumed she would like many years ago.

Ron is nodding, looking at the photos of the scene. Looking at the faces of the residents craning for a better view of Ian Ventham's slumped body. 'So, someone at Coopers Chase killed him? Someone in these pictures?'

'And we are all in the pictures,' says Ibrahim.

'Except for Elizabeth, of course,' says Joyce. 'Because she was taking the photos. But she would still be a suspect for any half-decent investigation.'

'I would hope so,' agrees Elizabeth.

Ibrahim walks over to a flip chart. 'Elizabeth asked me to make a few calculations.'

Elizabeth, Joyce and Ron settle into the Jigsaw Room chairs. Ron takes a Viennese whirl, to the relief of Joyce, who now feels able to do the same. They are own-brand, but there had been a Gregg Wallace programme which had said they were made in the same factory as the proper ones.

Ibrahim begins. 'Somebody in that crowd administered an injection to Ian Ventham which killed him, almost certainly within a minute. There was a puncture wound found on his upper arm. I asked you all to compile a list of everybody you remembered seeing, which you kindly did, although not all of your lists were alphabetized in the way I had asked.'

Ibrahim looks at Ron. Ron shrugs. 'Honestly, I get mixed up somewhere around F, H and G and then I give up.'

Ibrahim continues. 'If we combine those lists – an easy job if you know your way around an Excel spreadsheet – then in total there were sixty-four residents at the scene, ourselves included. Then we add DCI Hudson and PC De Freitas, the builder Bogdan, who went missing . . .'

'He was up on the hill,' says Elizabeth.

'Thank you, Elizabeth,' says Ibrahim. 'We add the driver of the low-loader whose name was Marie, another Pole if that is of interest. She also teaches yoga, but that's by the by. Karen Playfair, the lady who lives at the top of the hill, was there, as she was supposed to teach us about computers yesterday. And then, of course, Father Matthew Mackie.'

'That makes seventy, Ibrahim,' says Ron, now onto his second biscuit, whatever diabetes might say.

'And Ian Ventham makes seventy-one,' explains Ibrahim.

'So you think he might have driven up, started a ruck, then killed himself? All right, Poirot,' says Ron.

'This isn't thinking, Ron,' says Ibrahim. 'This is just a list. So no impatience please.'

'Impatience is all I got,' says Ron. 'It's my superpower. You know Arthur Scargill once told me to be patient? Arthur Scargill!'

'So one of these seventy people killed Ian Ventham. Now

these are nicer odds than the Thursday Murder Club usually faces, but can we narrow down the field still further?'

'It would have to be someone with access to needles and drugs,' suggests Joyce.

'That's everyone here, Joyce,' says Elizabeth.

'Quite so, Elizabeth,' agrees Ibrahim. 'If I might be permitted a visual image, that would be like looking for a needle in a haystack made entirely of needles.'

Ibrahim pauses, under the assumption there might be applause at this point. In its absence, he continues.

'Now, the injection would be the work of a split second to anyone experienced in intramuscular injections, which, again, is all of us. But the drug would need to be administered at very close quarters. So, I have deleted the names of anyone we know, for a fact, was never in close proximity to Ian Ventham. That loses a lot of the supporting cast. The fact that many of the crowd suffer from severe mobility issues has played into our hands here, as we know they couldn't have managed a quick dash when none of us were looking.'

'No Zimmers,' agrees Ron.

'We lose eight names on Zimmer frames alone,' agrees Ibrahim. 'Mobility scooters are also our friends here, as are cataracts. There are also many people, such as Stephen, I hope you agree, Elizabeth, who never found themselves close to Ian Ventham on that morning. They are struck from the list. Also, three residents were padlocked to the gate until someone thought to call the fire brigade, sometime later in the day. And so here we find ourselves.'

Ibrahim turns over the top sheet of the flip chart to reveal a list of names.

'Thirty names. Ourselves included. And one of them is the killer. I pause only to note that, alphabetically, by surname, I am first on the list.'

'Well done, Ibrahim,' says Joyce.

'So that's the list,' says Elizabeth. 'And I'm guessing it's now time for the thinking?'

'Yes, I think between us we can trim down the list a little further,' says Ibrahim.

'Who wanted him dead?' says Ron. 'Who gained? Did the same person kill Curran and Ventham?'

'Funny to think, isn't it?' says Joyce, wiping crumbs from the front of her blouse. 'That we know a murderer? I mean, we don't know who it is, but we know we definitely know one.'

'It's brilliant,' agrees Ron. He is considering biscuit three, but knows there's no way he would get away with it.

'Well, we had better get started,' says Ibrahim. 'Conversational French are due in at twelve.'

57

'Which means,' says Chris Hudson, 'that the fentanyl must have been administered by someone who was there that morning. So, one way or another, we already know our killer. Today, we work on a full list of everyone who was there, which won't be easy, but the sooner we have it, the sooner we'll have the killer. And who knows, maybe Tony Curran's killer too. Unless Ventham killed Curran and this was retaliation.'

Donna chances a quick peek out of the briefing-room window. Her uniformed colleague, Mark, is putting on a bicycle helmet, perfectly complementing his morose expression. Donna sips her tea – murder squad tea – and thinks about suspects. She thinks about Father Mackie. What do they really know about him? Then she thinks about the Thursday Murder Club. They were all there. All surrounding Ventham at one point or another. She could imagine them each, in their own particular way, being a murderer. Hypothetically, anyway. But actually? She couldn't see it. They would certainly have a view, though. Donna should probably head over and see them.

'In the meantime,' continues Chris, opening another folder, 'I have some other fun jobs for you. Ian Ventham was not a popular man. His business dealings were complicated and wide-reaching and his phone has revealed a list of affairs, which must have been pretty tiring for him. Tell your loved ones they won't be seeing much of you for a while.'

Loved ones. Donna thinks about her ex, Carl, then realizes

she hasn't thought about Carl for a good forty-eight hours, which is a new record. Though she has thought about him now, which spoils it a little. She realizes, though, that soon she won't think about him for ninety-six hours, and then a week, and before you know it Carl will just seem like a character from a book she once read. Really, why had she left London? What happens when these murders are solved and she's back in uniform?

'And the rest of you, no let-up on the Tony Curran case. The two could be connected, we can't rule it out. We still need the speed-camera info. I particularly want to know if Ian Ventham's car was on that road that afternoon. I need to know where Bobby Tanner is and I need to know who took that photograph. And I still need the information on the phone number that called Curran.'

Which reminds Donna of a little hunch she has been meaning to check.

58

Elizabeth is back in Willows, sitting in her low chair in Penny's room. She is filling Penny in on the drama.

'Simply everyone was there, Penny. You would have been in your element, swinging your truncheon and arresting everyone in sight, no doubt.'

Elizabeth looks over at John, in the chair where he spends most of his waking hours. 'I'm guessing you filled Penny in on the details, John?'

John nods. 'I may have overstated my own bravery a little, but other than that, it was chapter and verse.'

Elizabeth, satisfied, pulls a notepad and ballpoint from her handbag. She taps a page of the notepad with her pen, like a conductor giving notice to her orchestra, and begins.

'So, where are we, Penny? Tony Curran is bludgeoned to death, by person, or persons, unknown. As a side note, I will never tire of saying "bludgeoned". I bet you used to say that a lot in the police, you lucky thing. Now Ian Ventham, meanwhile, dies within seconds of being injected with a huge dose of fentanyl. You know fentanyl, John?'

'Of course,' says John. 'Used it all the time. Anaesthetic, mainly.'

John the vet. Elizabeth remembers the fox that John nursed back to health with Ron. Once healthy, it had gone on to murder Elaine McCausland's chickens. Not proven, but there were no other suspects. Ron had taken a lot of grief for it at the time, which had pleased him enormously.

'How easy would it be to get hold of it?' asks Elizabeth.

'For someone here?' John starts. 'Well, not easy, but not impossible. Pharmacies would have it. You could break in here, I suppose, but you'd have to be very determined, or very lucky. And you can get it on the internet.'

'Goodness,' says Elizabeth. 'Can you?'

'The dark web. I read about it in *The Lancet*. You can get all sorts. A rocket launcher, if you really wanted one.'

Elizabeth nods. 'And how would one go about getting on the dark web?'

John shrugs. 'Well, I'm guessing, but if it were me, the first thing I would do would be to buy a computer. Perhaps go from there?'

'Mmm,' says Elizabeth. 'Might be worth checking who has a computer.'

'You never know,' agrees John. 'It would certainly narrow it down.'

Elizabeth turns back to Penny. How unfair to see her lying there. 'One man bludgeoned, Penny, the other poisoned. But by whom? If Ventham was killed straight away, then somebody out there this morning killed him. Me or John. Or Ron or Ibrahim? Or . . . who knows? Ibrahim has a list of thirty names on a spreadsheet, to start us off.'

Elizabeth looks at her friend again. She wants to walk out of the door with her right now, arm in arm. Share a bottle of white, listen to her swear like a docker about some imagined slight and sway home happy and tipsy. But that will never happen again.

'I always find it peculiar that Ibrahim doesn't come and visit you, Penny.'

'Oh, he does,' says John.

'Ibrahim visits?' says Elizabeth. 'He's never said.'

'Like clockwork, Elizabeth. Every day he brings a magazine and solves bridge puzzles with her. He talks them through. They solve a puzzle, he kisses her hand and off he pops half an hour later.'

'And Ron?' asks Elizabeth. 'Does he visit?'

'Never,' says John. 'I suppose it's not for everyone, Elizabeth.'

Elizabeth nods. She supposes so too. Back to business. 'So, Penny, who wants to kill Ian Ventham? And why at the very moment digging was about to start? I suspect your question might be, who loses what if the development goes ahead? Wouldn't you think? I want to talk to you about Bernard Cottle at some point. Do you remember him? With the *Daily Express* and the nice wife? I feel like there is a motive there, waiting to be winkled out.'

Elizabeth stands, ready to leave.

'Who loses what, Penny? That's the question, isn't it?'

59

Chris Hudson has his own office, a little bolthole where he can pretend to work. There is a space on his desk where a family photograph might ordinarily sit and he feels a prick of shame every time he notes its absence. Perhaps he should have a photo of his niece? How old was she now? Twelve? Or maybe fourteen? His brother would know.

So who killed Ventham? Chris was right there when it happened. One way or another, he actually watched him being killed. Who had he seen? The Thursday Murder Club, they were all there, the priest. The attractive woman in the jumper and trainers. Now who was she? Was she single? Now's not the time, Chris. Concentrate.

Had the same person murdered Ventham and Tony Curran? It made sense. Solve one, solve the other?

Who were the three calls to Tony Curran's phone from? Almost certainly someone trying to sell him life insurance, but you never knew. Chris is sure that Tony Curran's phone could tell all sorts of tales. Human rights are all well and good, but Chris would love to tap the phone of every single person in Fairhaven who looked even a bit suspicious. Like they do in prison.

He remembers an armed robber called Bernie Scullion who ran out of money in Parkhurst, but wanted to buy himself a PlayStation, so phoned his uncle and told him where he'd buried half a million pounds. The police had the money and the uncle within the hour and Bernie never got his PlayStation.

There is a knock at the door and Chris has the brief, disturbing, realization that he hopes it's Donna.

'Come.'

The door opens. It's DI Terry Hallet. Terrifyingly efficient, handsome in that Royal Marine way that everyone seemed to like, but also, annoyingly, a nice guy. Chris would never be able to wear a T-shirt that tight. One day Terry will have this office. Terry has four kids and a happy marriage. Imagine the photographs he will have on the desk. Chris wishes he was Terry, but who really knew what went on at home? Perhaps Terry had a hidden sadness, perhaps he cried himself to sleep? Chris doubts it, but at least it's something to cling to.

'I can come back?' says Terry and Chris realizes he has been staring at him for a beat too long.

'No, no, sorry, Terry, miles away.'

'Thinking about Ian Ventham?'

'Yep,' lies Chris. 'What have you got?'

'Sorry to drag you back to Tony Curran, but I've got something I think you're going to like,' says Terry. 'I've got a car that took twelve minutes to travel the half mile between the two speed cameras either side of Tony Curran's house. Exactly the right time frame too.'

Chris looks at the details. 'So it stopped somewhere between the two? Nice little ten-minute break for something or other?'

Terry Hallet nods.

'Anything else around there except Tony Curran's house? Somewhere you'd stop?'

'There's a lay-by. If you needed a slash. But . . .'

'Long slash,' agrees Chris. 'We've all had them, but even so. And you've run the number plate?'

Terry nods again. Then smiles.

'I like that smile, Terry. What have you got?'

'You won't believe the registered owner, Guv.'

Terry slides another piece of paper onto Chris's desk. Chris takes it in.

'Well, this is very good news. Are you sure about these timings?'

Terry Hallet nods and drums his fingers on Chris's desk. 'That's our killer, surely?'

Chris has to agree. Time to go and have a chat.

Bogdan has seen where Marina lives, and now is as good a time as any. She will know what to do about the bones; he sensed that as soon as he met her. He has brought her flowers. Not from the shop but from the wood, tied the way his mother used to tie them.

Flat 8. He presses the buzzer and a man's voice answers. This surprises Bogdan. He has kept a close eye on her for a while and not seen a man.

The external door to the flats swings open. 'I am here for Marina? To see Marina?' he says as he walks through. The first door off the carpeted hallway swings open and he sees an elderly man in pyjamas running a comb through his thick, grey hair. Maybe he has got this wrong? Either way, the man will know Marina and can point him in the right direction.

'I come looking for Marina?' says Bogdan. 'I think maybe she live here, but maybe another flat?'

'Marina? Of course, of course, come in, let's get the kettle on shall we? Never too early, is it?' says Stephen.

With an arm around his shoulder, the man ushers Bogdan in. Bogdan is relieved to see a picture of Marina, a younger Marina, on the hallway table. It's the right flat.

'I don't know where she is, old chap, but she won't be long,' says Stephen. 'Probably at the shops or round at her mother's. Sit yourself down and let's make the most of the peace and quiet, eh? You play chess at all?'

Chris Hudson is pulling his coat over his jacket as he leaves the station. He turns as a voice behind him calls out, 'Sir?'

It is Donna De Freitas. She catches up with him.

'Wherever you're going, I think I've got a change of plan for you,' says Donna.

'I doubt it, PC De Freitas,' says Chris. He still calls her PC De Freitas at work. 'I'm off to have a little chat with someone.'

'Only, I was looking through the call logs,' says Donna. 'And I recognized the number.'

'The mobile that called Tony Curran?'

Donna nods, then takes out a scrap of paper for Chris to see. 'Remember this? Jason Ritchie's number. He's the one who phoned Tony three times on the morning of the murder. Is this worth a change of plan?'

Chris holds up a finger to silence her and takes the piece of paper Terry Hallet had handed him from his jacket pocket. He passes it to Donna. 'Vehicle records, from the day of the murder.'

Donna reads and then looks up at Chris.

'Jason Ritchie's car?'

Chris nods.

'Jason rings Tony Curran that morning. Jason's car is outside Tony's house when he dies. So we're going to see Jason?'

'Maybe just me this time,' says Chris.

'I don't think so,' says Donna. 'Firstly, I'm your shadow, which is a sacred bond of trust et cetera, et cetera. And secondly, I just solved the crime.'

Neither Chris nor Donna had known that Maidstone had an ice rink. Why on earth did Maidstone have an ice rink? That had been a large part of the conversation on the drive there. This was after Donna had asked Chris to turn off his compilation of early Oasis B-sides.

Bit by bit, Donna was intent on dragging Chris from his century into hers.

The mystery had not been solved when they pulled up outside Ice-Spectacular. How was anyone making money out of an ice rink, just off a ring road, sandwiched between a tile warehouse and a Carpetright?

Chris would often tell friends that if there was a business in their neighbourhood that didn't make any sense, which had no customers, then it was a front for a drugs business. Always. No real customers needed, no real profit needed, just a way of washing money. Every town had one, tucked away somewhere on a little row of shops, or in the railway arches, or sat next to a Carpetright. Whether it was a waxing parlour, or a party lights hire shop or an ice rink with a neon sign that last lit up in 2011.

Always a front, always drugs, thought Chris as he closed the passenger door of his Focus. Which seemed apt, given who Chris and Donna were here to see.

They walk through the front doors, across the sticky, carpeted foyer and into the arena. At this time of day it is mostly empty, except for an elderly man hoovering up popcorn from rows of plastic seats and two figures out on the ice.

She waves Jason's phone number at him.

Chris waves the vehicle records at her. 'I solved it first, Donna. So I'm just going to pay him a quick visit at home, alone, and see if he wouldn't mind answering a couple of questions. Very low key.'

Donna nods. 'Good idea. He's not at home, though, I checked already.'

'Then where is he?'

'If you take me along, I'll show you,' says Donna.

'And what if I ordered you to tell me where he was?' asks Chris.

'Well, you can try,' says Donna. 'See where it gets you?'

Chris shakes his head. 'Come on, then, you can drive.'

Anyone who had seen Jason Ritchie in his prime would tell you the same. He had a fluid strength, his feet simply gliding around the ring. Those powerful arms arcing through the air, or flicking forwards in rib-rattling jabs. His tiny feints and dips, eyes never leaving his opponent, his whole body ready to pounce and strike. He wasn't a slugger, a big plank of wood, a zombie. He was an athlete, strong and brave, a magnificent, flowing machine, everything given, nothing wasted. With his grace and his poise and his movement, Jason Ritchie was beautiful to watch.

However, as Chris and Donna sip on coffees, watching, it becomes apparent that Jason Ritchie cannot ice dance.

The session seems to be over, as Jason is gingerly skating towards the side of the rink, his elbow being supported by a small woman in a purple leotard. Even so, about a metre from the sweet safety of the side, Jason's left skate disappears from underneath him, slices into his right skate and his tumbling weight is too much for the lady in the leotard to save. The big man is down again. Chris and Donna have been watching for only a matter of minutes, but have already lost count of his falls.

Chris leans over the board and offers a hand. It is the first time Jason clocks the two officers. He has been preoccupied. He looks Chris in the eye as he takes the proffered hand and finally reaches dry land.

'Have you got five minutes, Jason?' asks Chris. 'We've come ever such a long way.'

'Are you OK, Jason?' asks the lady in the leotard.

Jason nods and gestures for her to go on ahead. 'Yeah, couple of mates. I'm going to stop for a chat.'

'Well, look, I'm going to write this all up and send it to the producers,' says the skater. 'You're not a lost cause, I promise!'

'Darling, you're a superstar, thanks for putting up with me and picking me up off my arse.'

'Hopefully see you on the show!' says the skater and waves as she disappears up the steep stairs on her narrow blades.

Jason collapses onto a moulded plastic chair, which bends a little under his weight. He starts to unlace his skates.

'Thought I might see the two of you again. You got another photo for me?'

'Well, shall we dive straight in?' starts Chris. 'What were you doing at Tony Curran's house on the day he was murdered?'

'None of your business,' says Jason. He nearly has the first skate off, though it's a struggle.

'But you agree you were there?' asks Donna.

'Am I under arrest?' asks Jason.

'Not yet,' says Donna.

'Then it's none of your business if I was or I wasn't.' The first skate is finally off. Jason puffs like he's gone three rounds.

'Just so you have the full picture,' says Chris, pulling out his phone from his pocket and swiping it into life. 'We'd been trying to find Ian Ventham's car on the traffic cameras near Tony Curran's house. A nice open-and-shut case. Ian Ventham didn't visit Tony Curran that afternoon, but we found something even more interesting. The first traffic camera catches your car, Jason, about four hundred yards east of Tony's house at three twenty-six and then the next camera, the other side of Tony's house, catches you at three thirty-eight. So either you took twelve minutes to drive half a mile, or you stopped somewhere in between.'

Jason looks at Chris very calmly, then shrugs and starts on his right skate.

'OK, I've got one too,' says Donna. 'The day that Tony Curran was murdered, did you ring him?'

'Don't remember, I'm afraid.' Jason is picking at what seems to be an impossible knot in his laces.

'You'd remember that though, Jason, wouldn't you?' asks Donna. 'Ringing Tony Curran? One of the old gang, wasn't he?'

'Never been in a gang,' says Jason, finally making a breakthrough with the knot.

Chris nods. 'But here's our issue, Jason. A mystery number phones Tony Curran three times on the morning of his death. A number we couldn't trace, thanks to Vodafone and to data protection legislation. But a number that, thankfully, you had personally written down and handed to PC De Freitas. So your number, Jason.'

Jason finally has the second skate off. He nods. 'That was silly of me.'

'And then, that very afternoon, you are driving along the road outside Tony Curran's house, at which point you stop to perform some sort of errand, which takes around ten minutes. At the exact time that Tony Curran was murdered.' Chris looks at Jason for a response.

'Yep. Sounds like you've got yourself a mystery there,' says Jason. 'Now I've got these skates off, I'm going to head back.'

Jason stands. Chris and Donna do too.

'I wonder if you'd like to come in and give us some fingerprints and a bit of DNA?' says Chris. 'Just to eliminate you from our inquiries? We could eliminate you from two murders at once. That would be nice.'

'You should probably ask yourself why you don't have my prints and DNA already,' says Jason. 'Maybe because I've never been arrested for anything?'

'Never been caught, Jason,' says Chris. 'That's different.'

'Be interesting to hear a motive too,' says Jason.

'Robbery?' says Chris. 'Man like that has a lot of money lying around. You got any money worries at the moment?'

'I think time's up here, don't you?' says Jason, starting to climb the stairs to the changing room. Chris and Donna don't follow.

'Or are you doing *Celebrity Ice Dance* for the prestige, Jason?' asks Donna. To which Jason turns and gives a genuine smile. Then raises his middle finger, turns again and continues towards the dressing room.

Chris and Donna see him disappear, then sit back down on their plastic chairs and look out over the empty ice.

'What do you make of that?' asks Chris.

'If he did it, why on earth would he leave a photo with him in it by the body?' asks Donna.

Chris shakes his head. 'Perhaps some people are just stupid?'

'He doesn't seem stupid,' says Donna.

'Agreed,' agrees Chris.

63

From outside, Elizabeth can immediately see that something is wrong. The curtains in Stephen's study are open. They are always closed. Stephen doesn't like the glare of the morning sun when he writes.

Her brain makes all of the necessary calculations in a second. Has Stephen woken and broken his routine? Is he hurt? Lying on the floor? Alive? Dead?

Or has someone broken in? Someone from her past life? It does happen, even now. She has heard of it happening. Or perhaps someone from the messy present has paid her a visit?

Elizabeth circles to the fire door at the back of Larkin Court. It is impossible to open from the outside without a piece of kit available only to the Fire Service. Elizabeth opens it and slides inside.

Her feet make no sound on the carpeted hallway, but they would have made no sound on the concrete walkway of an East German detention centre. She takes out her keys and coats the Yale in lip balm. It makes no noise when she inserts it in the lock and Elizabeth opens the door as quietly as she can. Which is very quietly.

If there is someone in the flat Elizabeth knows her time may be up. Holding her key ring in the palm of her hand, she slides a different key through each of the gaps in her fist.

Stephen has not collapsed in the hallway, that is news at least. His study door is open, morning sun streaming in. She feels a momentary shame at the bright dust dancing in the doorway.

'Checkmate,' says a voice from the living room. An eastern European voice.

'Well I'm damned,' replies Stephen.

Elizabeth slips her keys back into her bag and opens the living-room door. Stephen and Bogdan sit across the chess board from each other. They both smile to see her.

'Elizabeth, look who it is!' says Stephen, gesturing to Bogdan.

Bogdan has a moment of confusion. 'Elizabeth?'

'He calls me that. He gets things wrong.' To Stephen, 'It's Marina, dear, remember.' This doesn't feel wonderful, but needs must.

'Like the man said,' agrees Stephen.

Bogdan has risen from his chair and extends his hand towards Elizabeth. 'I brought you flowers. Your husband has put them somewhere. I'm not sure where.'

Stephen is examining the end-game on the chess board. 'The bugger got me, Elizabeth. Fair and square.'

Elizabeth looks at her husband, crouched over the board, backtracking moves, clearly delighted with the trap in which he has been caught. Life in the old dog yet, then, thinks Elizabeth, and falls in love again for the thousandth time. She repeats. 'It's Marina, darling.'

'I call you Elizabeth. Is OK,' says Bogdan.

'He fixed the light in my study too, dear,' says Stephen. 'We have a marvel on our hands.'

'That's very kind of you, Bogdan. I'm sorry we're not as clean as we might be. We don't get guests, so sometimes . . .'

Bogdan places his hand on Elizabeth's upper arm. 'You have a beautiful home, Elizabeth, and a wonderful husband. I wonder if I can speak to you?'

'Of course, Bogdan,' says Elizabeth.

'I can trust you?' asks Bogdan, staring deep into Elizabeth's eyes.

'You can trust me,' says Elizabeth, her eyes never leaving his.

Bogdan nods. He believes her.

'Can we go for a walk? You and I? This evening?'

'This evening?' asks Elizabeth.

'I have something to show you. Is best to wait till dark.'

Elizabeth studies Bogdan. 'Something to show me? Any clues?'

'Yes. It is something you will be interested to see,' says Bogdan.

'Well, I'll be the judge of that,' says Elizabeth. 'And where will we be walking, Bogdan?'

'To the cemetery,' says Bogdan.

'The cemetery?' A slight shiver runs down Elizabeth's spine. How wonderful the world can be at times!

'I meet you here,' says Bogdan. 'And wear warm clothes, we be there for a while.'

'I think you can count me in,' says Elizabeth.

64

Joyce

Yes, I know Ian Ventham is dead, and we will get to that, I promise. But guess what else? Joanna is here!

We took ourselves down to Fairhaven in her new car (I will check the make in a moment). We stopped at Anything with a Pulse. I was very casual about it, but it was an unqualified success. Not a word of complaint, or, 'No one's a vegan any more, Mum,' or, 'They do better brownies in a Lebanese shop round the corner from mine, Mum.' Green tea, flapjack, macaroon. And I didn't think I'd be saying that.

She has a meeting down this way. Something to do with 'optimization'. If I think back to that girl who would eat her fish fingers and potato waffles, but scream blue murder about eating her peas, I didn't imagine she would ever be having meetings about 'optimization'. Whatever it is.

The boyfriend is history, as we'd guessed. Did you know you can lock your mobile phones these days, so that no one can take a peek? And you can unlock them with your thumbprint? Anyway, he had fallen asleep on the sofa one evening and she had used his thumb to open his phone. One look through his messages and, by the time he woke up, his suitcases were packed and in the hall. That's my girl.

No details of the messages were forthcoming, but Joanna strongly hinted that photographs were involved. I listen to enough *Woman's Hour* to get the gist of that. Excuse my language, but the silly sod.

We had a giggle about it, so I don't think her heart is broken.

I can hear Joanna getting up from a nap, so I'll say bye for now. You wouldn't know it, but I've been typing quietly.

My gorgeous baby, happy and sleeping in my bed, and two murders to solve. Who could ask for more?

Joanna brought a bottle of wine down with her. There is something special about it, but I'm afraid I've forgotten what it is. One day she will realize that she is the something special. Anyway, I invited Elizabeth over to have a drink with us this evening, but she has 'other plans'.

Your guess is as good as mine there. Something to do with the murder though, you can bet on that.

(ADDITIONAL NOTE ADDED LATER: IT IS AN AUDI A4)

65

The path up the hill towards the Garden of Eternal Rest is a pale ribbon in the dusk light. Bogdan offers his arm and Elizabeth takes it.

'Stephen is not well?' says Bogdan.

'No, dear, he's not well.'

'You put something in his coffee I think? When we left?'

'We're all on pills for something, dear.'

Bogdan nods, he understands.

They walk past the bench where Bernard Cottle spends most of his days. Elizabeth has been thinking some more about Bernard, has had to in the circumstances. She always gets the sensation that he is keeping guard for the cemetery. That he's somehow at sentry duty on his bench. He won't go in, but he's never far away. What does Bernard lose if the development goes ahead? She would have to speak to him at some point, or, perhaps better, ask Ron and Ibrahim to speak to him. Which might mean tiptoeing around Joyce.

'He hasn't played chess in a long time, Bogdan. That was nice to see.'

'He is good. He was a tough player for me.'

They have reached the iron gates of the Garden of Eternal Rest. Bogdan pushes one of them open and guides Elizabeth through into the cemetery.

'You must be quite the player yourself?'

'Chess is easy,' says Bogdan, continuing the walk between the lines of graves and now flicking on a torch. 'Just always make the best move.'

'Well, I suppose,' says Elizabeth. 'I've never quite thought about it like that. But what if you don't know what the best move is?'

'Then you lose.' Bogdan leads her on for a few more paces before stopping by an old grave in the top corner.

'You said I can trust you, OK?' says Bogdan.

'Implicitly,' says Elizabeth.

'Even though you are really called Elizabeth, because I see bills in the study?'

'Sorry,' says Elizabeth. 'But, other than that, implicitly.'

'Is OK, whatever you need to do. But if I show you something, you don't tell the police, you don't tell no one?'

'You have my word.'

Bogdan nods. 'You sit while I dig.'

It is a pleasant evening to sit on the steps of a statue of Jesus Christ, and Elizabeth watches very happily as Bogdan, over to her left, starts digging the grave in the faint torchlight. She wonders what he might have uncovered. What secret was he about to reveal? She goes through the possibilities in her head. The most obvious answer was money. There would be a suitcase, or a canvas sports bag, and Bogdan would heave it out and lay it at her feet. Banknotes, gold perhaps, a haul, buried by goodness knows who and goodness knows when. And a big haul too, or why has Bogdan dragged her up here in the middle of the night? Enough for someone to kill for? A couple of thousand and surely Bogdan would just have taken it? Finders keepers, no harm done. But, a suitcase full of fifties, well that would –

'OK, you come see,' says Bogdan, standing in the grave, spade now over his shoulder.

Elizabeth pushes herself up, walks over to the grave and sees what Bogdan saw the morning that Ian Ventham was murdered. She supposes that of all the things to find in a grave, a body should be the least surprising. But as Bogdan's torch plays over the bones and the coffin lid on which they rest, she has to admit this wasn't what she had been expecting.

'You thought money, right?' says Bogdan. 'Maybe I found some money or something and didn't know what to do?'

Elizabeth nods. Money or something. Bogdan is very good.

'I know. Sorry, no money. Would have been good. Instead, bones. Bones inside the coffin. Other bones, different bones, outside the coffin.'

'And you found these yesterday, Bogdan?' asks Elizabeth.

'Just when Ian was killed, yes. I didn't know what to do. I wanted a day to think. Maybe it's nothing, do you think?'

'I'm afraid it's probably something, Bogdan,' says Elizabeth.

'Yes, maybe is something,' agrees Bogdan glumly.

Elizabeth sits now and dangles her feet into the grave. She looks down on the lid of the coffin. 'So you opened the coffin?'

'I thought was best. To check.'

'Quite right,' agrees Elizabeth. 'And you're sure it's a different body in there?'

Bogdan jumps into the grave and pulls away part of the coffin lid, exposing the bones inside. 'Yes. Bones where bones should be. Much older.'

Elizabeth nods and thinks. 'So, two bodies. One where it belongs and another, much newer, where it doesn't belong?'

'Yes. Maybe I should have told police, but I don't know. You know how the police are.'

'I do know, Bogdan. You did the right thing coming to me. At some point we might need to talk to the police, but not yet, I think.'

'So what do we do?'

'Fill it back in, Bogdan, if you wouldn't mind? Just for the time being. Give me some thinking time.'

'I dig, I fill in, I dig, I fill in. Whatever you need, until the job is done, Elizabeth.'

'We are birds of a feather, Bogdan,' says Elizabeth, thinking she must call Austin. He'll know what to do with all this.

She looks down towards the lights of the village. Mostly off now, but Ibrahim's light is shining bright. He'll be working away. Good man.

She looks back at Bogdan, shovelling earth into the grave, covered in dirt and sweat. Sliding a broken coffin lid back over one body while carefully avoiding disturbing another body. She thinks this is absolutely the sort of son she would like to have had.

'They are bang at it all the time,' says Ron. 'Always have been. Whatever it is, the Catholic Church will have a piece of it.'

'Even so,' says Ibrahim.

Ibrahim and Ron are discussing who might have murdered Ian Ventham.

They are working their way through the list of thirty names, weighing up the possibilities. It is just the boys this evening. Joyce has Joanna staying and Elizabeth was nowhere to be found. Which, at this time of the evening, was suspicious, but they have chosen to carry on regardless.

Ron is insisting on marking everyone out of ten, and the more whisky he drinks, the higher his scores are climbing. Maureen from Larkin had just scored a seven, largely because she had once pushed in front of Ron at dinner, which 'spoke a thousand words'.

'Father Mackie's our first ten, Ibbsy, write it down. Top of the list. He'll have something buried up in one of the graves. Guaranteed, nailed on. Gold, or a body, or porn. All three, knowing that lot. He's worried they'll dig it up.'

'Seems unlikely, Ron,' says Ibrahim.

'Well, you know what Sherlock Holmes said, old son. If you don't know who did it, then . . . something or other.'

'Indeed, wise words,' says Ibrahim. 'And Father Mackie wouldn't just have dug it up himself, Ron? At some point? To save himself the worry?'

'Lost his spade, I dunno. Mark my words though,' says Ron, those very words beginning to slur gently and warmly.

Late nights, whisky, something to solve, this was the life. 'It's a ten from me.'

'This is not *Strictly Come Poisoning*, Ron.' Ibrahim strongly disagrees with Ron's marking system, but writes '10' next to Father Mackie's name. As it happens, Ibrahim also strongly disagrees with the *Strictly Come Dancing* scoring system, believing it gives too much weight to the public vote when compared to the judges' scores. He once wrote a letter to this effect to the BBC and received a friendly, but non-committal, reply. He looks at the next name on the list.

'Bernard Cottle, Ron. What do we think there?'

'Another of the big guns for me.' The ice in Ron's whisky chimes as he gestures with his glass. 'See how he was that morning?'

'He has become increasingly agitated, I agree.'

'And we know he sits up there a lot, on that bench, like he's marking his territory,' says Ron. 'Used to sit there with his wife, didn't he? So that's where he gets his peace, innit? You can't take that away from a man, especially our age. Too much change don't sit right.'

Ibrahim nods, 'Too much change, yes. There comes a time when progress is only for other people.'

For Ibrahim one of the beauties of Coopers Chase was that it was so alive. So full of ridiculous committees and ridiculous politics, so full of arguments, of fun and of gossip. All the new arrivals, each one subtly shifting the dynamic. All the farewells too, reminding you that this was a place that could never stay the same. It was a community and, in Ibrahim's opinion, that was how human beings were designed to live. At Coopers Chase, any time you wanted to be alone, you would simply close your front door and any time you wanted to be with people, you would open it up again. If there was a better recipe for happiness than that, then Ibrahim was yet to hear it. But Bernard had lost his wife, and showed no signs of finding a way through his grief. And so he needed to sit on Fairhaven Pier, or on a bench on a hill, and nobody ever needed to ask why.

'Where is your place, Ron?' asks Ibrahim. 'Where do you find your peace?'

Ron purses his lips and chuckles. 'If you'd asked me a question like that a couple of years ago I'd have laughed and left, wouldn't I?'

'You would,' agrees Ibrahim. 'I have successfully changed you.'

'I think,' starts Ron, face alert, eyes alive, 'I think . . .' Ibrahim sees Ron's face relax as he decides to just let the truth come out, rather than think. 'Honestly? I'm flicking through it all in my head, all the things you're supposed to say. But, listen. It might be here in this chair, with my mate, drinking his whisky, dark outside, with something to talk about.'

Ibrahim knots his hands together and lets Ron talk.

'Just think of everyone who isn't here, Ibbsy. Every bugger who didn't make it? And here we are, a boy from Egypt and a boy from Kent, and we made it through it all, and then someone in Scotland made us this whisky. That's something, isn't it? This is the place, isn't it, old son? This is the place.'

Ibrahim nods and agrees. His place of peace is actually the wall of files directly behind him, but he doesn't want to spoil the moment. Ron has stopped speaking, and Ibrahim can see he has gone somewhere very deep inside himself. Lost to memories. Ibrahim knows to keep quiet, to let Ron go where he needs to go. To think what he needs to think. Something Ibrahim has seen so many times over the years, with people in that very armchair. It is his favourite thing about his job. Seeing someone go deep inside themselves to access things they never knew were there. Ron tilts his head up; he is ready to talk again. Ibrahim leans forward, just a touch. Where has Ron just been?

'Do you think Bernard is banging Joyce, Ibbsy?' says Ron.

Ibrahim leans back, just a touch. 'I haven't really thought about it, Ron.'

'Course you have, I know you have. Psychiatrist. I bet he is, lucky sod. All that cake and what have you. Could you still, you know, if you had to?' he asks.

'No, not for a few years now.'

'Same, same. A blessing in some ways. I was a slave to it. Anyway, I'd say he's a nine, wouldn't you? Old Bernard? He was there, you could see he doesn't want the place bulldozed, and he worked in science or something didn't he?'

'Petrochemicals I think.'

'There you are then, fentanyl. Nine.'

Ibrahim is inclined to agree. Bernard does not seem to be living entirely in grace. He writes a '9' next to Bernard Cottle's name.

'Of course, if they are banging, Joyce won't like that nine,' says Ron.

'Joyce has the same information that we have. She will already know he's a nine.'

'She's no fool, that one,' agrees Ron. 'What about that girl from the top of the hill? The farmer's girl with the computers?'

'Karen Playfair,' says Ibrahim.

'She was there, eh?' says Ron. 'Bang in the middle of it. Probably knows a thing or two about drugs. Pretty, too, and that's always trouble.'

'Is it?'

'Always,' says Ron. 'To me, anyway.'

'Motive?' asks Ibrahim.

Ron shrugs. 'Affair? Forget graveyards, it's usually an affair.'

'A seven perhaps?' says Ibrahim. 'Or perhaps a seven with an asterisk and a footnote explaining that the asterisk means "in need of further investigation"?'

'Asterisk seven,' agrees Ron, though with a pronunciation of the word 'asterisk' very much his own. 'And that just leaves the four of us, eh? The only ones left on the list?'

Ibrahim looks down at the list and nods.

'Shall we?' asks Ron.

'You think there is a chance one of us did it?'

'I didn't do it, that's for sure,' says Ron. 'They can redevelop what they like, more the merrier, far as I'm concerned.'

'And yet you led the objections at the public meeting, you lobbied the council and you started the barricade. All designed to stop the redevelopment.'

'Of course,' says Ron, as if his friend has lost his mind. 'No one takes liberties with me. And when else do you get the chance to cause a bit of trouble when you're nearly eighty? But, mate, think of the service charge, the new facilities. Probably won't happen now. No way I'd have killed him, that'd be cutting off my nose. Score me a four.'

Ibrahim shakes his head. 'You get a seven. You are very combative, you are hot-headed, often irrational, you were there at the heart of the scuffle and you are insulin-dependent, so you know how to use a needle. That adds up.'

Ron nods, fair enough. 'All right, let's call me a six.'

Ibrahim taps his pen against his book seven times, before looking up. 'And your son, I think, perhaps knew Tony Curran a little. Which adds up to seven.'

Ron is no longer in his place of peace and his ice cubes now dance a different jig. He remains quiet, if not calm. 'Don't bring Jason into this, Ibrahim. You know better than that.'

Interesting, thinks Ibrahim, but says nothing. 'Are we scoring ourselves, Ron, or are we not scoring ourselves?'

Ron stares at his friend for a long while. 'We are, we are, you're right. Well if I'm a seven then you're a seven too.'

'That's fine,' says Ibrahim and writes it in his book. 'Any reason?'

So many reasons, mate, Ron thinks. He is smiling now, the tension broken. 'Too smart by half, there's one. You might want to write these down. You're a psychopath, or sociopath, whichever one the bad one is. Terrible handwriting, that's a sure sign. You're an immigrant, and we've all read about them. There's some poor British psychiatrist, a white fella, sitting at home without a job because of you. Also, perhaps you're furious that your hair is thinning, people have killed over less.'

'My hair isn't thinning,' says Ibrahim. 'Ask Anthony about my hair. He admires it.'

'You were there, right in the thick of it, as usual. And you're exactly the sort of person in a film who would commit the perfect murder just to see if he could get away with it.'

'That is certainly true,' agrees Ibrahim.

'Played by Omar Sharif,' adds Ron.

'Ah, so we agree I have hair. OK I am a seven. Now, Joyce and Elizabeth.'

Ibrahim relishes the thought of talking late into the night. Once Ron goes, all there will be to do is read, to make more lists, then force himself to lie on his bed waiting for a sleep that always takes too long to come. Too many voices wanting his attention. Too many people still lost in the dark, asking for his help.

Ibrahim knows he is usually the last person awake in Coopers Chase, and tonight he is glad to have the excuse of company. Two old men, fighting against the night.

Ibrahim opens his pad again and looks out of his window towards Joyce's flat. Darkness everywhere. The village is asleep.

Of course, Elizabeth is too much of a professional to let her torch beam show on her walk back down the hill.

67

Jason Ritchie sits at a corner table, finishing his lunch. Monk-fish and pancetta, both locally sourced.

He doesn't know quite what to do.

Jason is surprised by the changes in the Black Bridge. It is now a gastropub called Le Pont Noir, with its name written, black against grey, in minimalist lower-case font. Some of the rough edges have really been knocked off Fairhaven over the years, some of the darker corners have gone.

You and me both, Jason thinks, as he sips his sparkling water.

Jason is thinking about the photograph. He would feel a lot safer with a gun, and twenty years ago that would have been easy. He would have walked into the Black Bridge, talked to Mickey Landsdowne, who would have rung Geoff Goff and, before he'd finished his pint, a kid on a BMX would have delivered a brown parcel to the saloon bar and been given a packet of crisps and twenty B&H for his troubles.

Simpler times.

Now Mickey Landsdowne was in Wandsworth for arson, and for selling fake Viagra at car-boot fairs.

Geoff Goff had tried to buy Fairhaven Town FC, lost his money in a property crash, made another fortune selling stolen copper and had eventually been shot dead on a jet ski.

And did kids even ride BMXs any more?

The photograph lies in front of Jason on the table. Taken in the Black Bridge long ago. In the days before pancetta and sourdough bread.

The gang, just like it was yesterday. Laughing away like trouble wasn't round the next corner.

Ever since he sat down, Jason has been trying to work out exactly where in the pub Tony Curran had shot that drug dealer down from London, trying his luck in sleepy Fairhaven. In about 2000, was it? It was hard because they had moved a wall, but he thinks perhaps it was by the reclaimed fireplace, with the locally sourced logs.

'Coffee, sir?' The waitress. Jason orders a flat white.

Jason remembers that the bullet had gone through the guy's stomach, straight through the paper-thin wall and out into the car park, where it went through the front wing of Turkish Johnny's Cosworth RS500. Johnny was gutted, you could see it, but it was Tony, so what could he do?

Turkish Johnny. Jason has been thinking about him a lot. He is sure Johnny had taken the photograph which had been left by the body. Always had that camera with him. Did the police know? Had Johnny come back to town? Had Bobby Tanner come back? Was Jason next on their list?

The boy Tony shot had died in the end. They had often come down from London in those days. Sometimes south London, sometimes north; gangs looking to expand, to find soft new markets.

The waitress brings his flat white. With an almond biscotto.

Jason still remembers the boy Tony had shot. He was only a kid. He'd offered a wrap of coke to Steve Ercan, in the Oak on the seafront. Steve Ercan was a Cypriot lad, used to hang around on the fringes of the gang, never liked to get involved, but was loyal. Owned a gym now. Steve Ercan had set him up, told the young drug dealer to try his luck at the Black Bridge. Which the boy had done, before quickly realizing his luck was out.

He was bleeding a lot, Jason remembers that, and it wasn't

fun, he remembers that too. Thinking back, the kid must have been about seventeen, which seems young now, but didn't at the time. Someone put him in Bobby Tanner's old British Telecom van, and a cabbie Tony liked to use in this sort of situation drove him out to the 'Welcome to Fairhaven' sign on the A2102 and dumped him there. That's where they found him the next morning. Too late for the boy, he was long dead, but he'd known the risks. The cabbie got shot too, because Tony thought you could never be too careful.

That had been the end of things for Jason. The end of it for all of them, really. It was no longer young men making money, friends having fun, pretending to be Robin Hood, or whatever he had thought it was at the time. It was bullets and dead bodies and police and grieving parents. He'd been an idiot. He'd spotted it all too late.

Bobby Tanner left soon after. His younger brother, Troy, had died on a boat in the Channel. Bringing drugs in? Jason never found out. Johnny did a runner too, straight after the cabbie was shot. And that was that. Just like that, with one bullet, those days were gone. And good riddance to them.

They say two brothers from St Leonards now run things in Fairhaven. Good luck to them, thinks Jason. Still keeping it locally sourced.

He walks over to the fireplace, then crouches. Yep, this was the place all right. He runs his finger across the reproduction antique tiles. Take them off, keep scraping and you'd find a little hole Mickey Landsdowne had filled in and painted over, twenty-odd years ago. The one bullet that changed everything.

There was nothing left here now, in the Black Bridge, with its memories and with its green tea with ginseng. All the gang gone. Tony Curran, Mickey Landsdowne, Geoff Goff.

Where's that Cosworth with a hole, now? Rusting some-where in a field? And where was Bobby Tanner? Where was Johnny? How could he find them before they found him?

Jason sits back down and sips his flat white. Well, he sup-poses, he probably knows the answer to that. Has known it all along.

Jason sighs, dips his biscotto into his flat white and calls his dad.

68

'I got the photo on the Tuesday morning,' says Jason Ritchie. 'Hand-delivered, through the letter box.'

Father and son are drinking from bottles of beer on Ron's balcony.

'And you recognized it?' asks Ron.

'Well, not the photo, I'd never seen the photo before. But I recognized what it was, where it was, all that,' says Jason.

'And what was it? And where was it? And all that,' asks his dad.

Jason takes out the photograph and shows it to Ron.

'Here you are. It's Tony Curran, Bobby Tanner and me. The three of us around the table in the Black Bridge, that's where we used to drink. Remember, I took you there once, when you came down?'

Ron nods and looks at the photo. In front of the little gang, the table is covered in cash. Thousands, twenty-five grand maybe, all in notes, just scattered about. And the boys all looking pleased about it.

'And where was the money from?' asks Ron.

'That time? No idea, it was one evening out of many.'

'But drugs?' asks his dad.

'Drugs. Always, in those days,' confirms Jason. 'That's where I put my money. To keep it safe.'

Ron nods and Jason holds out his palms, no defence.

'And the police have got the photo?' asks Ron.

'Yep, they've got plenty more on me too.'

'You know I've got to ask, Jason? Did you kill Tony Curran?'

Jason shakes his head. 'I didn't, Dad, and I'd tell you if I did, because you know there'd have been a good reason if I had.'

Ron nods. 'Can you prove you didn't do it?'

'If I can find Bobby Tanner or Johnny, then I reckon. It's one of them. I can understand someone else leaving the photo by the body, you know, red herring for the cops to find. But why send it to me too? Unless Bobby or Johnny want me to know they did it?'

'And you're not talking to the police?'

'You know me. I thought I'd find them myself.'

'And how's that going?'

Well, that's why I'm here, isn't it, Dad?'

Ron nods. 'I'll call Elizabeth.'

69

Donna and Chris are in Fairhaven Police Station. Interview Suite B.

Not so long ago Donna had been sitting in this interview room talking to someone pretending to be a nun. She now sat in front of a man pretending to be a priest. The parallel was not lost on her.

Donna herself had made the breakthrough. Just a few background checks on Father Matthew Mackie. Run him through the computer, see what popped up.

The background checks had taken a couple of days, because nothing at all had popped up. Which had made no sense at all. So Donna had spent a bit of time piecing it together, working out what was what, before taking the information to Chris. And now here they all were.

'At every step of the process, Mr Mackie,' Chris continues. 'At every step, you referred to yourself as "Father"? You introduced yourself as "Father"?'

'Yes,' agrees Matthew Mackie.

'Even now, you're wearing a dog collar, are we agreed?'

'I am, yes.' Mackie fingers the dog collar in confirmation.

'And the rest. The full kit, if you like?'

'The vestments, yes.'

'And yet, when we start looking into you, what do we find, do you think?'

Donna watches and learns. Chris is being gentle with the old man. She wonders if he will turn, given what they know.

'I think . . . well, I think perhaps, possibly, there may have been a misapprehension.' Chris sits back and lets Matthew Mackie talk. Which he does in fits and starts. 'For which I accept my share of the blame, and if you feel I have . . . fallen short, I suppose, in some way, my intentions were not to mislead, but I see that that's how it might look, without all the, uh, facts.'

'The facts, Mr Mackie?' says Chris. 'Excellent! Let's get on to the facts. You are not Father Matthew Mackie, that's a fact. You do not work for the Catholic Church, or any church. That's another one. You are, and this has taken a full fifteen minutes of research with the local NHS Trust, Doctor Michael Matthew Noel Mackie? Can we have that one as a fact too?'

'Yes,' admits Matthew Mackie.

'You retired from private practice as a GP fifteen years ago. You live in a bungalow in Bexhill and, asking around there, you don't even attend Mass.'

Matthew Mackie looks to the floor.

'All facts?'

Mackie nods without looking up. 'All facts.'

'I wonder if you could remove the dog collar for me, Mr Mackie?'

Mackie looks up, and directly at Chris. 'No, I'll keep it on if you don't mind. Unless I'm under arrest, which you haven't mentioned.'

Now Chris nods. He looks over at Donna, then turns back and drums his fingers on the table. Here we go, thinks Donna. It takes a lot to get Chris to drum his fingers on a table.

'A man has just died, Mr Mackie,' says Chris. 'And you and I watched it happen, didn't we? And do you know what I thought I saw? I thought I saw a man pushing a Catholic priest. A Catholic priest protecting a Catholic graveyard. And, as a police officer, that painted things in a certain light for me. You understand?'

Mackie nods. Donna is staying quiet. There is nothing she can think to add. She wonders if Chris would ever drum his fingers on a table at her. She hopes not.

'But what did I actually see? I actually saw a man pushing someone impersonating a priest, for reasons still known only to himself. Pushing a conman, which is what you are. A conman protecting a graveyard?'

'I'm not a conman,' says Matthew Mackie.

Chris holds up a hand to stop him. 'Moments after scuffling with this conman, the first man drops down dead from a lethal injection. Which puts a different complexion on things, especially when we discover the conman is a doctor. But perhaps I've missed something?'

Mackie remains silent.

'I'm just going to ask you again, sir. I wonder if you could remove the dog collar for me?'

'I am not presently a father, I grant you that,' says Mackie with a long sigh. 'But I was, and for many years. And that confers privileges and this collar is one. If I choose to wear it, and if I still choose to call myself Father Mackie, then that is my business.'

'Doctor Mackie,' says Chris, 'this is a murder case. I need you to stop lying to me. PC De Freitas here has been through every record. The Church has been very helpful. Whatever you've said to us, whatever you said to the council, to Ian Ventham, to the ladies who protected the gate, you are not a priest and you never were a priest. There is no record anywhere, no dusty ledger, no old photo. I have no idea why you are lying to us, but we have ourselves a dead body and we're looking for a murderer, so it's probably best that we find out quickly. If I'm missing something important, I need you to tell me.'

Mackie looks at Chris for a moment, thinking. Then shakes his head.

'Only if you arrest me,' replies Mackie. 'Otherwise, I'd like to go home now. And no hard feelings, I know you are doing your job.'

Matthew Mackie crosses himself and stands. Chris stands too.

'I would stay, Doctor Mackie, if I were you.'

'The moment you charge me, I promise I will,' says Mackie. 'But, in the meantime . . .'

Donna stands and opens the interview room door for him and Matthew Mackie takes his leave.

It can be very hard to smoke in a sauna, but Jason Ritchie is giving it his best shot.

'Are you sure you're OK with this, Dad?' he asks, sweat dripping from his brow.

'Just tell them everything,' replies Ron. 'They'll know what to do.'

'And you reckon they'll find them?' asks Jason.

'I should have thought so,' says Ibrahim, stretched out on a lower bench.

The sauna door opens and Elizabeth and Joyce enter, with towels wrapped around swimsuits. Jason puts out his cigarette in a pile of hot ash.

'Well, this is nice,' says Joyce. 'Eucalyptus.'

'Nice to see you, Jason,' says Elizabeth, taking a seat opposite the half-naked boxer. 'I believe you think that we might be of use to you. I must say, I agree.'

That's it for pleasantries. Elizabeth fixes her eyes on Jason. 'So?'

Jason tells Elizabeth and Joyce the same story he told his dad. A copy of the photo is passed around the sauna. Ibrahim has had it laminated.

'I get the photo,' confirms Jason, 'and I'm, like, what's this about? Where's this from? Is this the papers? Is this the front page of the *Sun* tomorrow? That's what I was thinking. But there's no message, nothing. There's no journalist on the phone, and they've got a number for me, so what's up?'

'And what was up?' asks Elizabeth.

'Well, I'm thinking, do I ring my PR? Maybe they've spoken to her. I was in shock, to be fair, this is twenty-odd years ago, this photo, and a world I'd left behind. So I'm ready to deny whatever, or come up with something, stag-do, fancy dress, anything to explain it away.'

'Ooh, that's good,' says Joyce.

'So there I am, still looking at his picture, and something clicks. I think, well maybe this is the game. Maybe Tony's got hold of this photo, famous boxer, surrounded by cash, jailbirds everywhere. He sends me a copy, looking for a bit of money. Give me twenty K, whatever, and I don't go to the papers. Fair enough, really, so I think, yeah, I should just ring him, have a little chat. See if we can work something out.'

'Was Tony Curran the sort of man who might blackmail you?' asks Elizabeth.

'Tony's the sort of man who might do anything, yeah. So, first things first, I get hold of a new phone, cheap one, in town.'

'Afterwards, will you tell me where, because I'm looking for one at the moment,' says Ibrahim.

'Of course, Mr Arif,' says Jason. 'So, I ring him once, and no answer. I ring him again – same; leave it twenty minutes and try again. He's still not picking up.'

'I never pick up if it's a number I don't recognize,' says Joyce. 'I saw that on *Rogue Traders*.'

'Very wise, Joyce,' continues Jason. 'Then I came here for a quick drink with Pops and I saw the man himself, Curran, arguing with Ventham.'

'Keeping all this quiet from me,' says Ron, and Jason raises his hand to acknowledge it.

'So after me and Dad had a couple of beers . . .'

'And me,' says Joyce.

'And Joyce,' agrees Jason. 'After that, I went for a little drive, just to do a bit of thinking. Then I headed down there, Tony's house, lovely place. Now, we're always cautious around each other, me and Tony, too many secrets, but I wouldn't be at his front door without a reason. His car's on the drive, so when there's no answer, I think he's seen me on his security and doesn't fancy a chat. And I didn't blame him, so I rang the bell a few more times and then I left.'

'And this is the day he died?' asks Joyce.

'The day he died. I couldn't hear anything from inside, so I don't know if that was before or after or whatever. Anyway, home I go and a couple of hours later I'm on this WhatsApp group . . .'

'A WhatsApp group?' asks Elizabeth, but Joyce waves her away and Jason continues.

'A few of the old faces, and someone says Tony's been found dead at home. I go cold, you know? I get sent the photo that morning and Tony dies that afternoon. Which leaves me worried. I mean, I can look after myself, but Tony could look after himself too, and see where that got him? So I'm nervous, that's natural, and then the police get wind that I've been to Tony's and they get records saying I'd rung Tony's phone that day too. And they've got a photo of me that was left by the body. You can't blame them, they think that stinks and so would I.'

'But you didn't kill Tony Curran?' asks Elizabeth.

'No, not me,' says Jason. 'But you can see why the police think I did.'

'Their case is compelling,' agrees Ibrahim.

'And you're here to see if we can find your old friend for you?' asks Elizabeth.

'Well,' says Jason, 'the way my dad tells it, however good the police are, you lot are better.'

There are quiet nods all round.

'And it's old friends,' says Jason. 'There's the lad who took the photo too.'

'And who was that?' asks Elizabeth.

'Turkish Johnny, the fourth member of our little gang.'

'And he's Turkish?' asks Joyce.

'No,' says Jason.

Ibrahim notes this down.

'He's Turkish Cypriot and scarpered back there years ago.'

'I know some good operatives in Cyprus,' says Elizabeth.

'Look,' says Jason. 'You owe me nothing. Less than that. I've done nothing good here and Tony never did. But if Bobby or Johnny killed Tony, then they're still out there, and if they're still out there, then why not me next? Again, not your business, I know, but Dad thought it might be up your street, and I'm not going to turn down the help.'

'So . . . what do you reckon?' Ron asks.

'Well,' says Elizabeth. 'Here's my take. The others might disagree, though I suspect they won't. This is a mess of your own making. And a mess that came from greed and from drugs. And those are downsides for me. But there is an upside too. And that is that you are Ron's son. And I believe you are probably right, I believe we can find Bobby Tanner and Turkish Johnny for you. Probably quickly. And whatever you've done, and whatever we might think of that, I would like to catch a murderer. Before that murderer catches you.'

'Agreed,' says Joyce.

'Agreed,' says Ibrahim.

'Thank you,' says Jason.

'Thank you,' adds Ron.

'Not at all,' says Elizabeth, standing. 'Now, I will leave you to your sauna. I have to make a few calls. Ron, I need to see you at the graveyard at ten this evening, if you're free. Joyce and Ibrahim, I'll need you there too.'

'Sounds lovely. Wouldn't miss it,' says Ron. His son gives him a questioning look.

'And Jason?' says Elizabeth.

'Yes?' says Jason.

'If this is a bluff, it's a high-risk one. Because we will catch this murderer. Even if it's you.'

71

'Do you need a hand to get down into the grave?' asks Ibrahim.

'Yes, please,' says Austin, 'that would be terribly kind of you.'

Bogdan has borrowed an arc light and it is trained on the grave he had opened on the morning that Ian Ventham was murdered. The grave that had revealed an extra occupant on top of the coffin. A skeleton, buried where it had no right to be buried.

Austin holds on to Ibrahim's arm and takes a step down into the grave. He is careful not to step on the bones scattered on the lip of the coffin. He looks up at Elizabeth and chuckles. 'This takes me back, Lizzie. Remember Leipzig?'

Elizabeth smiles, she certainly does remember. Joyce also smiles, because she has never heard Elizabeth called Lizzie before. She wonders if the others caught it.

'Whaddaya think, Prof?' asks Ron, sitting happily at the feet of our Lord Jesus Christ, and drinking from a can of Stella.

'Well, I wouldn't ordinarily like to say,' replies Austin, raising his glasses to get a closer look at the femur he is now holding, 'but if I were a gossip, among friends, of course, I would say these have been down here some while.'

'Some while, Austin?' asks Elizabeth.

'I would say so,' considers Austin. 'Just by the colouration.'

'And if you were being more specific?' asks Elizabeth.

'Well, goodness!' says Austin. 'If you want me to be

specific, I would say . . .' He takes a moment to calibrate his thoughts. 'I would say really quite some while indeed.'

'So they could have been buried at the same time as Sister Margaret?' asks Joyce.

'What's the date on the headstone?' asks Austin.

'Eighteen seventy-four,' reads Joyce.

'Not a chance. Thirty, forty, fifty years perhaps, depending on the soil, but not a hundred and fifty.'

'So at some point,' says Ibrahim, 'somebody has dug up this grave, buried another body in it and then filled it in again?'

'Certainly,' agrees Austin. 'You have yourselves a mystery.'

'Another nun, perhaps, Austin?' asks Elizabeth. 'Any jewellery down there? Any fragments of clothing?'

'Not a thing on this one,' says Austin. 'Stripped bare. If it was murder, then someone knew what they were doing. I'm going to take a few bones with me, if you don't mind?' I'll have a little look at them in the morning, just to give you a clearer picture.'

'Absolutely, Austin, take your pick,' says Elizabeth.

Bogdan blows out his cheeks. 'So we got to tell police now?'

'Oh, I think we can probably keep this to ourselves until Austin gets back to us,' replies Elizabeth. 'If everyone agrees?'

Everyone agrees.

'Someone give me a hand out of the grave,' says Austin. 'Bogdan, old chap?'

Bogdan nods, but seems to want to get something clear first. 'Listen, I just need to say one thing. Is OK? In case maybe I go mad. This is not normal? Right? An old man in a grave looking at bones. Someone is murdered maybe, but no one tells the police?'

'Bogdan, you didn't tell the police when you first dug up the bones,' says Joyce.

'Yes, but I am me,' says Bogdan. 'I'm not normal.'

'Well, we're us,' says Joyce, 'and we're not normal either. Although I did use to be.'

'Normal is an illusory concept, Bogdan,' adds Ibrahim.

'Bogdan, trust us,' says Elizabeth. 'We just want to find out whose these remains might be and who buried them, and that will be a lot easier without the police poking their noses in until absolutely necessary. If the police have the bones first, you can bet that will be the last we hear about them. And that seems unfair, after all our hard work.'

'I trust you,' says Bogdan, then screws up his face as a thought occurs. 'Though if it goes wrong I bet it's me sent to prison.'

'I won't let that happen; you're too useful,' says Elizabeth. 'Now, please help Austin out of the grave and grab those bones for me. I suggest we all go back to Joyce's for a nice cup of tea.'

'Splendid!' says Austin, placing his selection of bones on the lip of the grave before reaching out for Bogdan's arms.

'You lead the way, Lizzie,' says Ron and finishes off his can of Stella.

72

Joyce

There was a jolly atmosphere, and I can understand the reasons why. We each of us understand we're in a gang and we understand we are in the middle of something unusual. We understand also, I think, that we are doing something illegal, but we are past the age of caring. Perhaps we are raging against the dying of the light, but that is poetry, not life. There will be other reasons I have missed out, but I know on the walk back down the hill we felt giddy. Like teenagers out too late.

But when Austin laid the pile of bones on my dining table, while we still knew it was an adventure, I think they began to have a sobering effect on all of us. Even Ron.

It is all very well, the Thursday Murder Club and all our derring-do, and the freedom of age and whatever we like to tell ourselves. But someone had died, however long ago it might have happened, so it was right to pause for reflection.

There was no way around it, we couldn't conjure a single good reason why the extra body was there. On closer inspection, fuelled by orange drizzle cake (Nigella), Austin was fairly sure that the body was a man, so it wasn't a nun.

But who was he? And who had killed him? The first step to finding out the answers would be to discover when he had been killed. Thirty years ago? Fifty years ago? There was a big difference.

Austin explained he would take the bones away and do

further tests. After everybody had left, I googled him and it turns out he is a Sir. I can't say I was surprised, he really did know a great deal about bones. Quite what he made of standing in a grave, at ten at night, in his eighties, is his business, but I suppose any friend of Elizabeth is probably used to these things. Three sugars in his tea too, though you wouldn't know by looking at him.

And then the biggest question of all, of course. You'll be ahead of me here. Had the motive been found for one much more recent murder? Did someone else know the bones were hidden there? Was Ian Ventham killed to protect the Garden of Eternal Rest and the secret of those bones?

We talked for around an hour, I suppose. Were we right not to involve the police? We will have to tell them eventually, but the feeling was that this is our story, our graveyard, our home and, just for the time being, we wanted to keep it for ourselves. As soon as we get the results from Austin we will have to tell all, of course.

So we are trying to solve two murders, and possibly three, if the skeleton was murdered. Or, I should say, if the skeleton is of someone who was murdered. Is a skeleton a person? That's a question for greater minds than mine.

I know Elizabeth is keen to track down Bobby and Johnny, but we all agreed the bones have to take precedence for now.

I wonder if Chris and Donna are making any progress? We certainly haven't heard if they are. I do hope they're not keeping anything from us.

73

Chris and Donna are walking the three flights of stairs up to Chris's office. Donna has pretended to be frightened of lifts, to force Chris to walk.

'So, Jason Ritchie for the Tony Curran murder,' says Chris. 'And Matthew Mackie for Ian Ventham?'

'Unless we're missing something,' says Donna.

'I wouldn't put that past us,' says Chris. 'So, let's work it through. We know Matthew Mackie was there and we know he's a liar. He's a doctor, not a priest.'

'So we know he could get hold of fentanyl and he'd know how to use it,' says Donna.

'Agreed,' says Chris. 'I think we've got everything except a motive.'

'Well, he doesn't want the graveyard moved,' says Donna. 'Is that enough?'

'Not enough to arrest him. Unless we find out why he doesn't want it moved.'

'Is impersonating a priest a crime?' asks Donna. 'Someone I met on Tinder once pretended he was a pilot and tried to grope me outside an All Bar One.'

'I bet he regretted that.'

'I punched him in the balls, then called in his reg number and got him breathalysed on the way home.'

They both smile. But the smiles are fleeting. Both know they are in danger of letting Matthew Mackie slip between their fingers. No evidence whatsoever.

'Have you heard anything from your pals in the Thursday Murder Club?' asks Chris.

'Not a peep,' says Donna. 'Which makes me nervous.'

'Me too,' says Chris. 'And I really don't want to be the one to tell them about Jason Ritchie.'

Chris pauses for a moment on the landing. Pretending to think, but really just to catch his breath.

'Perhaps Mackie's got something buried in the graveyard?' says Chris. 'Doesn't want it dug up?'

'Good place to bury something,' agrees Donna.

74

Joyce

Have you ever used Skype?

I hadn't until this morning, and now I have. Ibrahim set it up, and so we had gone round to his. He keeps his flat so clean, and I don't think he has anyone in to do it.

There are files everywhere, but all locked away, so you can see them but not read them. Imagine the stories you must hear if you're a therapist. Who did what to who? Or is it, whom did what to who? Either way, I bet he's heard all sorts.

Austin rang at ten on the dot, as you would expect from a Sir, and told us what he knew. We could see him on screen, and we took it in turns to go in the little box in the corner. It was hard, because the box is very small, but I expect you get used to it if you do it a few times.

The body was a man, which he'd already told us. He had a gunshot wound to the femur. Austin held it up to show us. We all tried to get in the box for that bit. Had that been the wound that killed him? Austin wouldn't like to say for certain, but probably not. A pre-existing injury.

At one point his wife walked past in the background. What must she think? Her husband holding up bones to a computer screen? Perhaps she is used to it.

Now, how much do you know about how to tell how old bones are? I knew nothing, and Austin went through the whole thing in detail. It was fascinating. There was a machine, and there was a special dye, and something to do with carbon. I tried to remember this all the way home so I could write it down, but I'm afraid it's gone. But it was very interesting. He would be very good on *The One Show* if they ever needed it.

He'd taken some soil with him too, and done tests on that, but the soil stuff was less interesting. Back to the bones, please, I had been thinking.

The long and short of it, though, is that Austin had done some maths, and you can't be certain, and there were variables, and no one has all the answers, and all he could really do was make his best guess. At this point Elizabeth told him to stop prattling on and get to it. Elizabeth can get away with that sort of thing, even to a Sir.

So he came out with it. The body was buried sometime in the 1970s, probably earlier rather than later. So fifty-odd years ago, give or take.

We thanked Austin, but then no one knew how to hang up. Ibrahim tried for a while and you could see he was losing face. In the end Austin's wife came to the rescue his end. She seems lovely.

So there we had it. Two potential murders fifty years apart. Plenty to chew on for everyone there. And probably time to tell Chris and Donna what we have done. I hope they don't take it too personally.

Elizabeth then asked if I would like to go to a crematorium in Brighton with her today, on a hunch, but I had already said that I would cook lunch for Bernard, so nothing doing.

I know you can't smell it, but I'm making him steak and kidney. He is getting thin, so I'm just seeing what I can do.

75

Donna and Chris are waiting for their free coffee at the Wild Bean Café inside the BP garage on the A21. Anything to get out of the station for half an hour. To stop looking at the endless files from the Irish passport office. Chris picks up a chocolate bar.

'Chris, you don't need that,' says Donna.

Chris gives her a look.

'Please,' says Donna. 'Let me help, I know it's hard.'

Chris nods and puts the chocolate bar back.

'So, what's in it for Mackie?' asks Donna. 'What's the connection with the graveyard? Why protect it if he's not a priest?'

Chris shrugs. 'Perhaps it's just a way of getting to Ventham? Perhaps there's another connection between them. Have we looked at Doctor Mackie's patient lists? You never know.'

Chris then picks up a cereal bar.

'That's even worse than a chocolate bar,' says Donna. 'Even more sugar.'

Chris puts it back down. He's going to be forced to eat a piece of fruit at this rate.

'He's dodgy as hell,' says Chris. 'All we're missing is his motive.'

Donna's phone buzzes and she reads a message. She purses her lips and looks up at Chris.

'It's Elizabeth. She wonders if we might like to pop over this evening.'

'I think that might have to wait,' says Chris. 'Tell her we're busy solving two murders.'

Donna continues to scroll through the message. 'She says she has something for us. I quote "Please do not read another file until you have seen what we have found. Also there will be sherry. See you at eight."' Donna puts her phone in her pocket and looks at her boss.

'Well?' she asks.

Well? Chris slowly strokes his stubble and considers the Thursday Murder Club. He has to face it, he likes them. He's happy drinking their tea, eating their cake and chatting off the record. He likes their rolling hills and their big sky. Was he being taken advantage of? Well, almost certainly, but, for now, he was getting plenty in return. Would this all look very bad if it came out? Yes, but it won't. And, if it did, why not just take Elizabeth into his disciplinary hearing and let her work her magic?

Eventually he looks up at Donna, who has her eyebrows raised waiting for an answer.

'I'm a reluctant yes.'

76

'Now we can do this one of two ways,' says Elizabeth. 'You can kick up a fuss and curse us to the heavens and we can all waste a lot of time. Or you can just accept what has happened and we can enjoy our sherry and get on with this. Your choice.'

Chris cannot speak for a moment. He looks at the four of them. Then to the air, then to the floor. Looking for words that don't want to come. He holds the flat of a palm in the air in front of him, in an effort to pause reality for the briefest of moments. But no luck.

'You . . . ,' he begins, slowly, 'you . . . dug up a body?'

'Well, technically *we* didn't dig it up,' says Ibrahim.

'But a body was dug up, yes?' says Chris.

Elizabeth and Joyce nod. Elizabeth takes a sip of her sherry.

'That's the long and short of it,' confirms Joyce.

'And you then performed a forensic analysis on the bones?'

'Well, again, not us personally. And only on some of them,' says Ibrahim.

'Oh, that's fine then. Just a few?' Chris's voice is raised, and Donna realizes it's the first time she's experienced this. 'Then I wish you all a good evening. Nothing to see here.'

'I knew you'd get melodramatic,' says Elizabeth. 'Can we just get this over with and move on to business?'

Donna steps in.

'Melodramatic?' she addresses Elizabeth directly. 'Elizabeth, you just dug up a human body and failed to report it to the police. This isn't pretending to be a nun who's had her bag stolen.'

'What nun?' asks Chris.

'Nothing,' says Donna quickly. 'This is a serious crime. Elizabeth, you could all go to jail for this.'

'Nonsense,' says Elizabeth.

'Far from nonsense,' says Chris. 'What on earth are you doing? I need you to think very carefully about what you say next. Why did you dig up a body? Let's take this step by step.'

'Well, as I stated previously, we didn't dig up the body. But our attention was drawn to the fact that a body had been dug up,' says Ibrahim.

'And we were curious, naturally,' says Ron.

'Our attention was grabbed,' agrees Ibrahim.

'What with the murder of Ian Ventham,' adds Joyce, 'it seemed it might be important.'

'You didn't think Donna and me might have been interested at this point?' asks Chris.

'Firstly, Chris, it's "Donna and I",' says Elizabeth. 'And secondly, who knew what the bones were? We didn't want to waste your time until we knew for sure what we were dealing with. What if we'd called you out and they were nothing but cow bones? Wouldn't we have looked silly old fools then?'

'We wouldn't have wanted to waste your time,' agrees Ibrahim. 'We know you are busy with two murders already.'

'But off they went for analysis,' continues Elizabeth. 'And back it comes, human bones, good to have it confirmed, no cost to the taxpayer. Male, died sometime in the 1970s, a gunshot wound to the leg, but no way of telling if that's what killed him. Now to invite Chris and Donna to take a look, and to lead things from here. Get the professionals in. It really feels like you might be thanking us.'

Chris is trying to compose a response. Donna decides that this one might be her responsibility.

'Christ, Elizabeth, just give it a rest for one second. You can drop the act with us. The second you dug up that body you knew they were human bones, because I think you can tell the difference. Joyce, you were a nurse for forty years, do you know the difference between human bones and cow bones?'

'Well, yes,' admits Joyce.

'The second you did that, Elizabeth, you and your whole gang . . .'

'We are not Elizabeth's gang,' interrupts Ibrahim.

Donna raises her eyebrows at Ibrahim, who holds up a hand in concession. She continues. 'The lot of you, from that moment, were in deep, deep trouble. This is not a neat little trick. You might fool the rest of the world, but you don't fool me. You're not plucky underdogs, or helpful amateurs. This is a serious crime. This is bigger than a serious crime. And this doesn't end with us all giggling over a glass of sherry. It ends in a courtroom. How could you be so stupid? The four of you? We're friends, and you treat me like this.'

Elizabeth sighs. 'Well this is exactly what I meant, Donna. I knew you'd both make a fuss.'

'A fuss!' says Donna incredulously.

'Yes, a fuss,' says Elizabeth. 'And I do understand, in the circumstances.'

'Just doing your job,' agrees Ron.

'Admirable, if you want my opinion,' adds Ibrahim.

'But the fuss ends here,' says Elizabeth. 'If you're going to arrest us, arrest us. Take the four of us to the station, question us all night. Get the same answer all night.'

'No comment,' says Ron.

'No comment,' says Ibrahim.

'Like on *24 Hours in Police Custody*,' says Joyce.

'You don't know who dug the body up and you won't hear the answer from any of us,' continues Elizabeth. 'You don't know who took the bones away for analysis and you won't hear that from us either. At the end of the evening you might try and explain to the CPS that four people in their seventies and eighties have failed to report digging up a body. For what reason? With what evidence, other than the inadmissible confession you've taken from us this evening? And with four suspects, all of whom are quite happy to go to court, smile happily and pretend to mistake the judge for their granddaughter and ask why she doesn't visit often enough. The whole process is difficult, costly and time-consuming, and achieves nothing. No one is going to prison, no one is getting a fine, no one's even going to be picking litter by the roadside.'

'Not with my back,' says Ron.

'Or,' continues Elizabeth, 'you can forgive us, and believe us when we say we were trying to help. You can let us apologize for our overenthusiasm, because we did know what we were doing was wrong, but we did it anyway. We know you've spent the last twenty-four hours in the dark and we know we are in your debt. And if you forgive us, then tomorrow morning, on a wild hunch, you can order a search of the Garden of Eternal Rest. You can dig up the body, you can send it to your own forensics team, who will tell you it's a male who was almost certainly buried in the early 1970s, and then we'll all happily be on the same page.'

There is a moment's silence.

'So,' asks Chris, very slowly, 'you've reburied the bones?'

'We thought it was best,' says Joyce. 'To give you the glory.'

'I'd leave the grave in the top right-hand corner till about fourth or fifth, if I were you,' says Ron. 'Don't want to make it too obvious.'

'And in the meantime,' continues Elizabeth, 'we can all have a nice evening and no more shouting. We can tell you everything we know. So you can really hit the ground running in the morning.'

'You could even share a bit of information with us if you thought that was appropriate,' adds Ibrahim.

'How about some information about the custodial sentences you can get for perverting the course of justice? Or disturbing a grave?' says Chris. 'Up to ten years, if you're interested.'

'Oh, we just went through all this, Chris,' sighs Elizabeth. 'Stop grandstanding and swallow your pride. And besides, we're not hampering, we're helping.'

'I didn't notice either of you digging up a body,' adds Ron, to Chris and Donna.

'We have certainly done an awful lot of the work so far,' says Ibrahim.

'So this is how I see it,' confirms Elizabeth. 'Either you arrest us, which we would all understand, and Joyce, in fact, I think would actually enjoy.'

'No comment,' says Joyce, nodding happily.

'Or you don't arrest us and we can spend the rest of the evening talking about exactly why someone buried a body, on this hillside, sometime in the 1970s.'

Chris looks at Donna.

'And we can also discuss whether that same person has just murdered Ian Ventham to keep it secret,' says Elizabeth.

Donna looks at Chris. Chris has a question.

'So you think the same person might have committed two murders? But nearly fifty years apart?'

'It's an interesting question, isn't it?' asks Elizabeth.

'It's an interesting question we could have been asking last night,' says Chris.

'It might have been useful to know we could be looking out for someone who was right here in the 1970s and is still right here now,' adds Donna.

'We really are sorry,' says Joyce. 'But Elizabeth was adamant, and you know Elizabeth.'

'Let's move on,' says Elizabeth. 'Put this behind us.'

'Do we have a choice, Elizabeth?' asks Chris.

'Choice is overrated; you'll learn that as the years fly by,' says Elizabeth. 'Now, to business. What do you make of the priest, I wonder? Father Mackie? Might he have been around when this place was a convent?'

'I take it from that question that you haven't been able to find out anything about Father Mackie?' says Chris. 'Don't tell me I've found a chink in your armour.'

'My inquiries are ongoing,' says Elizabeth.

'No need, Elizabeth, we've cracked that one for you,' says Donna. 'It's Doctor Mackie. Not a priest, never has been, never will be. A doctor in Ireland, moved over here in the nineties.'

'That's very curious,' says Elizabeth. 'Why pretend to be a priest?'

'Told you he was a wrong 'un,' says Ron to Ibrahim.

'So, he might have killed Ian Ventham,' says Donna. 'And he's certainly up to something. But I doubt it's because of your bones.'

'Is it worth my pointing out any more that this is all confidential?' says Chris.

'You are quite safe with us. You know that, don't you? Nothing ever leaves this room,' says Elizabeth. 'Shall we just forget this ever happened, the business with the bones and what have you, and pool our knowledge?'

'I think we've pooled quite enough for one day, Elizabeth,' says Donna.

'Oh really?' says Elizabeth. 'And yet, you haven't even told us about the Tony Curran photograph yet. We had to find that out for ourselves.'

Donna and Chris both look at Elizabeth. Chris lets out a theatrical sigh.

'By way of a peace offering,' says Ibrahim, 'perhaps you would like to know who took the photograph?'

Chris looks up to the heavens. Or Joyce's Artex ceiling. 'I *would* actually like to know that, yes.'

'Lad named Turkish Johnny,' says Ron.

'Although he's not Turkish,' adds Joyce.

'You've seen the photo, Ron?' asks Donna.

Ron nods.

'Nice one of Jason, eh?'

'You want my view, for what it's worth?' says Ron. 'You find Turkish Johnny or Bobby Tanner, you find Tony Curran's killer.'

'Well then, if we're laying all our cards on the table,' says Chris, 'has Jason explained away his phone calls to Tony Curran on the morning of the murder? And has he explained away the presence of his car in the area at the exact moment that Tony Curran was murdered?'

'Yes,' says Elizabeth. 'To our satisfaction.'

'Anything you'd like to share?' asks Donna.

'Listen, I'll get him to give you a bell and explain, don't worry,' says Ron. 'But shall we get on and find this Johnny fella and Bobby Tanner?'

'Just leave that with us, please,' says Chris.

'I think we're unlikely to just leave that with you, Chris,' says Elizabeth. 'I'm ever so sorry.'

'Would you like some sherry?' asks Joyce. 'It's only Sainsbury's, but it's Taste the Difference.'

Chris sinks back into his chair and submits.

'If any of this ever gets back to my superintendent, I will personally arrest you and march you into court myself. I swear, on my life.'

'Chris, no one will ever find out,' says Elizabeth. 'You know how I used to make my living?'

'Well, not really, if I'm honest.'

'Exactly.'

As a complicit silence falls over the room, it seems the evening's drinking can now begin in earnest.

'I am very proud of how we all work together as a team,' says Ibrahim. 'Cheers.'

77

Joyce

I'm glad we told Chris and Donna about the bones. It seems right. Now everyone can keep an eye out. Who was here in the 1970s and is still here today? That should keep them all occupied for a bit.

Everyone knows everything now and that seems fair.

So where are Johnny and Bobby? Now we've dealt with the bones, I know Elizabeth will be thinking about how we track them down. That's right up her street, isn't it? I will get a call in the morning and it will be, 'Joyce, we're going to Reading,' or, 'Joyce, we're going to Inverness, or Timbuktu,' and bit by bit she'll tell me why and before you know it we'll be having a cup of tea with Bobby Tanner, or a café au lait with Turkish Johnny. You wait and see. Tomorrow morning, before 10 a.m. Guaranteed.

The only time I ever use my passport is when I need to pick up a parcel, but I've just checked and it has three years left. I remember when I first got it, wondering if it would be my last ever. The odds on it being renewed are with me now I think. Anyway, that's just to say that if Johnny or Bobby Tanner are abroad somewhere, then I wouldn't put it past Elizabeth to hop on a plane. We're only a drive from Gatwick here.

I could send Joanna a postcard. 'Who, me? Oh, I'm in Cyprus for a couple of days. Tracking down a fugitive. Possibly armed, but you mustn't worry.' Though no one sends postcards any more, do they? Joanna has shown me how to send photos on my phone, but I'm beggared if it's ever worked when I tried. I just get that spinning circle.

Perhaps I could ask Bernard to come along with me. 'A couple of days in the sun? Last-minute thing. We just fancied it.' I think it might frighten the poor man to death.

I don't like to give up on a chase, but Bernard seems to be drifting further and further away from me. He was not a bundle of fun at lunch and there was plenty of steak and kidney left over.

And don't think I don't know what the others think. What they suspect. They'll be checking whether Bernard was here fifty years ago. They haven't spoken to me about it, but you mark my words. Check away, don't mind me.

Timbuktu is a real place by the way. Did you know that? It came up in a quiz once. Ibrahim will remember where it is, but I did think that was interesting.

78

Chris Hudson is cradling a whisky. He likes a real log fire and they have a nice one in Le Pont Noir. He's never eaten here, because who would he eat with, but he likes the bar. The fire has a vintage tile surround, very tasteful. If you'd asked him twenty years ago, he would have imagined this was the sort of place he might live. Leather armchair, whisky on the go, wife reading some sort of book opposite him. Something prize-winning and beyond him, but she'd be turning the pages, smiling wryly. A love story set against the backdrop of the Raj. He could be looking at murder case notes. Slowly solving something.

He is still sure that Mackie is guilty as hell. It added up. But these bones? Did they change things? Had there been two murders, fifty-odd years apart, one to protect the other? If so, then Mackie wasn't their man, they've been through the records, he hadn't left Ireland until the nineties.

His mind drifts back to his dream life. Were there kids sleeping upstairs? In new pyjamas. A boy and a girl, two years apart. Good sleepers. But no, none of that, just a fireplace in a bar that wasn't doing enough business, in a restaurant that he had no one to talk to. Then a walk home, stop at the all-night shop for a Dairy Milk. A proper big one. Then the key fob, the apartment block, the three flights up, the flat that the cleaner kept clean, that no one ever cooked in, the spare room that was never used. If he opened his window he could hear the sea, but couldn't see it. Didn't that just sum it up?

There was a life that Chris hadn't been able to take in his grasp. Families, driveways, trampolines, friends round for dinner, all the stuff you'd see on adverts. Was this for ever now? The lonely flat with the neutral walls and the Sky Sports? Maybe there was a way out, but Chris couldn't immediately spot it. Treading water, getting fatter, laughing less. Chris was out of rocket fuel. It was lucky that Chris loved his job. Was good at his job. Chris always found it easy to get up in the morning. He just found it hard to go to sleep at night.

Leave Mackie be for a minute and focus on Tony Curran's murder. Jason Ritchie had rung him earlier. Told his tale. Explained away the calls and the car. If he was lying, then he'd done a good job of it. But then he would, wouldn't he?

Bobby Tanner was still proving elusive. After Amsterdam, there was no more Bobby Tanner on any official record. But he'd be somewhere. Maybe Brussels, living under some name or other, plenty of gangs could use him out there. He'd be doing what he'd always done. Smuggling, fighting, making himself useful. Not a big enough fish for anyone to worry about. Burned often enough to be careful. They'd catch him coming out of some expat gym one day, put their hand on his shoulder and fly him back for a few questions.

Though, of course, there was a good chance that Bobby Tanner was dead too. Steroids, pub fight, fell off a ferry, so many ways to go and the only way to identify him a false passport. But Chris thinks Bobby is still out there somewhere, and if he's still out there somewhere, then who's to say he hadn't just paid a visit to Tony Curran for some long-forgotten reason? Something to do with his brother drowning with that boat full of drugs? Who knew?

And then the new name, Turkish Johnny. Chris had found plenty on record for him. Johnny Gunduz was his real name. Fled the country in the early 2000s after a tip-off he'd murdered the cabbie in the Black Bridge shooting. Everything kept coming back to that one night. In this very bar.

Had Johnny come back to town?

Chris finishes his whisky and looks at the tiles once again. Beautiful really.

He should probably go home.

79

Joyce

Just two quick things this morning, as I find myself in a hurry.

Firstly, Timbuktu is in Mali. I bumped into Ibrahim on my way back from the post box and I asked him. I also saw Bernard walking, slowly, up the hill. It's every day now, but never mind.

And, as I say, Mali. So now you know.

Secondly, Elizabeth rang at 9.17 and we're off to Folkestone. From the looks of it it's two changes, one at St Leonards and one at Ashford International, so we're setting off nice and early. I haven't been to Ashford International, but I doubt a station would have 'International' in its name and not have an M&S. Maybe even an Oliver Bonas. Fingers crossed.

I promise I will report back later.

80

In many ways, his neighbours owed Peter Ward a debt of thanks and, to be fair, most of them knew it.

Pearson Street had always been a little down at heel. A newsagent with no papers, a mini-mart, with a mountain of cheap alcohol behind the counter, a travel agent with fading posters of the sun, two bookies, a pub on its last legs, a party accessories shop, a nail bar and a boarded-up café.

And then The Flower Mill had moved in. Peter Ward's shop, bursting with colour, a little rainbow explosion on this grey street.

And what flowers! Peter Ward knew his stuff and when you know your stuff in a small town, word soon gets around. People would start making detours from the town centre. And they would tell their friends, who would tell their friends and, before you know it, someone down from London has spotted the boarded-up café and bought the lease and now there were two reasons to visit Pearson Street. Then a bride ordering flowers from Peter and enjoying a latte in the café, sees this little street is on the up and wonders if it might be the place to open a small hardware store? So now The Tool Chest sits next to The Flower Mill, opposite Casa Café. The travel agent suddenly has people walking past, feels the need to change those posters and those people start walking in. Under-thirties mainly, who have no idea what a travel agent might be. The Londoner with the café buys the pub and starts doing food. Terry at the newsagent starts ordering in more papers, more milk, more everything. The nail bar paints more nails, the party shop sells more balloons, the mini-mart starts stocking gin alongside the vodka. John from the butcher's counter at Asda takes the leap and opens a store of his own, taking his customers with him. A local art group hires out a vacant storefront and takes it in turns to buy pieces of each other's art.

All thanks to Peter Ward's orchids and sweet peas and Transvaal daisies.

Pearson Street is just what you want a shopping street to be. Busy, friendly, local and happy. Joyce thinks it's so perfect, that it's surely only six months away from having a Costa and losing what it now has. Which would be sad, but Joyce has to admit that she likes a Costa, so must shoulder some of the blame.

Joyce and Elizabeth are sitting in Casa Café. Peter Ward has just bought them both a cappuccino. Becky from The Tool Chest will keep an eye out for customers while he takes half an hour off. It's that sort of street.

Peter Ward is greying and smiling and has the easy air of a man who has made a series of good decisions in life. A Folkestone florist, whom karma has rewarded for a lifetime of kindness and calmness, a man whose good deeds have delivered him the prize of happiness.

This impression is misleading. As the scar under his right eye and the bulge of the biceps will tell you, Peter Ward is Bobby Tanner. Or perhaps Peter Ward has left Bobby Tanner behind? That is what they have come to find out. Is the fighter still there? The killer perhaps? Has he recently made the short trip along the coast to Fairhaven and bludgeoned to death his former boss? Elizabeth lays the photograph on the table between them and Peter Ward picks it up, smiling.

'The Black Bridge,' says Peter. 'We had a few nights in there. Where'd you get this from?'

'A number of places,' says Elizabeth. 'Well, two places, in fact. One was sent to Jason Ritchie and one was found by the corpse of Tony Curran.'

'I read about Tony,' nods Peter Ward. 'That was about time.'

'You've never seen this photograph before?' asks Elizabeth.

Peter looks again, then says, 'Never have.'

'You weren't sent one?' asks Joyce, and sips her cappuccino.

Peter shakes his head.

'Well, that's either good news for you, or it's good news for us,' says Elizabeth.

Peter Ward raises an inquiring eyebrow.

'Well, it's either good news for you, in that Tony Curran's killer has no idea where you are. Or it's good news for us, in that you killed Tony Curran yourself and we haven't wasted a trip to Folkestone.'

Peter Ward gives a half smile and looks at the photo again.

'Not that the trip would really be wasted,' says Joyce. 'We're having a very nice day.'

'The police have the idea that Jason killed Tony Curran,' starts Elizabeth. 'And perhaps he did. But, for reasons of our own, we would prefer that he didn't. Would you have a view on that, Bobby?'

Peter Ward holds up a hand.

'Peter around here, please.'

'Would you have a view on that, Peter?' asks Elizabeth.

'I don't see it,' says Peter Ward. 'Jason went nowhere near that side of things. He looks mean, but he's a teddy bear.'

Joyce looks up from her notes for a moment. 'A teddy bear who funded a major drugs ring.'

Peter acknowledges this with a nod.

Elizabeth puts the photo back down on the table. 'So, if not Jason, then perhaps you? Or perhaps Turkish Johnny?'

'Turkish Johnny?' says Peter.

'He took the photo.'

Peter Ward thinks for a while. 'Did he now? I don't remember, but that would make sense. I'm guessing you know the story? The boy Tony shot in the Black Bridge? Johnny shooting the taxi driver who got rid of the body?'

'We know that story, yes,' confirms Elizabeth. 'Then Johnny disappears back to Cyprus.'

'Well, it wasn't quite that simple,' says Peter Ward.

'I'm all ears,' says Elizabeth.

'Someone grassed Johnny up to the cops. They raided his flat, but he'd gone already.'

'And who grassed him up?' asks Elizabeth.

'Who knows? Not me.'

'No one likes a grass,' says Joyce.

'It doesn't matter who,' says Peter Ward. 'What matters is that when Johnny legged it, he took a hundred grand of Tony's cash with him.'

'Is that so?'

'Money he had lying around his flat. Tony's money. All disappeared. Tony went mental. A hundred grand was a lot of money to Tony in those days.'

'Did he try and find Johnny?' asks Elizabeth.

'You bet. Went off to Cyprus a couple of times. Didn't find a thing.'

'Not easy when it's not your natural territory,' says Elizabeth.

'So I'm guessing you haven't found Johnny either?' asks Peter Ward.

Elizabeth shakes her head.

'How did you find me, by the way?' he goes on. 'If you don't mind me asking? I don't really want to be found by anyone if Johnny's back in town, leaving photos of me next to bodies.'

Elizabeth takes a sip of her coffee. 'Woodvale Cemetery, where they buried your brother Troy?'

Peter Ward nods.

'I got access to the CCTV, thanks to a mortician whose uncle I once saved on a train,' says Elizabeth. 'That's where I found you.'

Peter Ward looks at Elizabeth.

'Elizabeth, I've been there twice in a year. There's no way you found me from the CCTV. That'd be a needle in a haystack.'

'You went there twice, yes,' agrees Elizabeth. 'But on what days?'

Peter Ward sits back, folds his arms, then nods and smiles. He sees it now.

'Twelfth of March and seventeenth of September,' continues Elizabeth. 'Troy's birthday and the anniversary of his death. I was hoping to see the same car both times, jot down a number plate, get the friend of a friend to run it through a computer somewhere. But on March the twelfth I saw a white van from a Folkestone flower shop, which I thought unusual at a cemetery in Brighton. Not impossible, but noteworthy. And I thought it very, very unusual to see the same van on September the seventeenth. I found that very noteworthy indeed. You see?'

'I do see,' nods Peter Ward. 'And no need for a number plate.'

'Because you had your name, your address and your telephone number signwritten on the side,' says Elizabeth.

Peter can't help but give Elizabeth a quiet round of applause and she responds with a slight bow.

'That's very good, Elizabeth,' says Joyce. 'She's very good, Peter.'

'I see that,' says Peter. 'So no one else knows where I am? No one else can find me?'

'Not unless I tell them where you are,' says Elizabeth.

Peter Ward leans forward. 'And is that something you'd be likely to do?'

Elizabeth leans forward too. 'Not if you come and see us tomorrow, sit down with Jason and the police and tell them what you just told us.'

81

'Would you like a walnut?' asks Ibrahim.

Bernard Cottle looks at him and then down at the open bag of walnuts he is being offered.

'No thank you.'

Ibrahim withdraws the bag. 'Very low carb, walnuts. In moderation, nuts are very healthy. But not cashews, cashews are an exception. Am I disturbing you, Bernard?'

'No, no,' says Bernard.

'Just enjoying the view?' asks Ibrahim. He can sense that Bernard feels uncomfortable sharing his bench.

'Just taking the weight off,' says Bernard.

'What a place to be buried,' says Ibrahim. 'Wouldn't you think?'

'If one has to be buried,' says Bernard.

'Sadly, it comes to the best of us, doesn't it? However many walnuts we might eat.'

'I mean no offence by this, but I'm very happy to sit in silence,' says Bernard.

'That's not unreasonable,' says Ibrahim, nodding. He eats a piece of walnut.

The two men sit, taking in the view. Ibrahim turns, and sees Ron walking up the path, trying to hide his limp. He has a stick, but he won't use it.

'Well, this is nice,' says Ibrahim. 'Here comes Ron.'

Bernard looks, there is the slightest pursing of the lips.

Ron reaches the bench. He sits the other side of Bernard.

'Afternoon, gents,' says Ron.

'Good afternoon, Ron,' says Ibrahim.

'So, Bernard, old son,' says Ron. 'You keeping guard?'

Bernard looks at Ron. 'Keeping guard?'

'Of the graveyard. Sitting here like a gnome, "none shall pass", all that. What's up?'

'Bernard wants to be left in silence, Ron,' says Ibrahim. 'That's what he tells me.'

'Fat chance of that with me around,' says Ron. 'So come on, mate. What are you hiding up here?'

'Hiding?' asks Bernard.

'I don't buy all this grief stuff, son. We all miss our wives, with the greatest respect. Something else is going on here.'

'I think grief affects people in different ways, Ron,' says Ibrahim. 'Bernard's behaviour is not unusual.'

'I don't know, Ib,' says Ron, shaking his head and looking out over the hills. 'Geezer gets killed the other day, when all he wanted to do was dig up the graveyard. Bernard sits here by that same graveyard all day, every day. That changes things for me.'

'Is that what's happening here?' asks Bernard, voice calm and level, refusing to look at Ron. 'You're talking to me about the murder?'

'That's what's happening, Bernard, yeah,' says Ron. 'Someone down there injected the guy and killed him. We all had our hands on him, remember? Any one of us could have done it.'

'We simply need to eliminate some people from our inquiries,' says Ibrahim.

'Maybe you had a good reason?' says Ron.

'Is there ever a good reason to murder someone, Ron?' asks Bernard.

Ron shrugs. 'Maybe you've got something hidden up there in the graveyard. You a diabetic? Good with a needle?'

'We all are, Ron,' says Bernard.

'Where were you in the seventies, mate? Were you local?'

'That's a peculiar question, Ron,' says Bernard. 'If you don't mind me saying.'

'All the same, were you?' says Ron.

'We're just exploring avenues,' says Ibrahim. 'We're asking everyone.'

Bernard turns to Ibrahim. 'Is this the game? Good cop, nasty cop?'

Ibrahim considers this. 'Well, yes, that is the idea. Psychologically, it is often very effective. I have a book you could read if you are interested?'

Bernard lets out a long breath and turns to Ron. 'Ron, you met my wife. You met Asima.'

Ron nods.

'And you were nothing but kind to her. She liked you.'

'Well, I liked her, Bernard. You had a good one there.'

'Everyone liked her, Ron,' says Bernard. 'And yet you still ask me why I sit here? It's nothing to do with the graveyard and it's nothing to do with needles. Or where I lived fifty years ago. I'm just an old man who misses his wife. So spare me.'

Bernard stands.

'Gentlemen, you have spoiled my morning. Shame on you both.'

Ibrahim looks up at Bernard. 'Bernard, I don't believe you, I'm afraid. I want to, but I don't. You have a story you are desperate to tell. So, any time you want to talk, you know where to find me.'

Bernard smiles and shakes his head. 'Talk? To you?'

Ibrahim nods. 'Yes, talk to me, Bernard. Or to Ron. Whatever has happened, the worst thing you could do is to stay silent.'

Bernard tucks his paper under his arm. 'With respect, Ibrahim, Ron, you have no idea what the worst thing I could do is.'

And with that, Bernard starts a slow walk down the hill.

82

Joyce

Well, that was jolly good fun. For starters, I had never been to Folkestone.

Peter Ward is Bobby Tanner's name now, but we are sworn to secrecy. He owns a florist.

I suppose I have two things to write about then. Why was Peter Ward a florist? And, florist or not, who did he think killed Tony Curran?

I might write about Bernard too, but I will leave that to the end, because I want to think about it while I write the rest.

Peter Ward – I will call him Peter – left Fairhaven shortly after his brother died, for reasons you can imagine. He got himself a new passport. It's easily done if you listen to Elizabeth and Peter, but I wouldn't know how to go about it, would you? He ended up in Amsterdam, doing odd jobs. Not odd jobs as we would think about them, like clearing your gutters or painting a fence, but taking cocaine across the Channel on ferries. Or, I suppose, threatening people. You could see that in him, underneath everything.

He fell in with a gang from Liverpool. He wouldn't tell us the name, as if I would have any sway if he had. Their ruse was to smuggle drugs in the backs of those big flower lorries you see coming over from Holland and Belgium. That was their 'angle'.

At first, Peter would do the loading. A driver would be

paid such and such to stop his lorry in a lay-by in Belgium, and Peter and a few cronies would hop in the back and stash what they could, where they could. Over the lorry would go, another stop in Kent and Bob's your uncle. These lorries were back and forth all the time. It's a daily schedule, isn't it? Has to be, because of fresh flowers. So it was perfect.

They just had the odd driver here and there and that's how it worked at first. Until the penny dropped and they bought one of the nurseries. The business ran as usual, but Peter was on hand to 'inspect' every shipment as it went out, and to add that little special something to each one. So now they had three lorries a day travelling through Zeebrugge and they could do what they liked with them. Clever, really.

Peter would spend all his time at the nursery, and the young lad who ran it was paid to turn a blind eye. They'd play cards and chat and whatever else you do all day in Belgium.

(Off-subject for a minute, but there was a notice pinned up the other day about a trip to Bruges and I thought of signing up. Joanna went a few years ago and her verdict was, 'It's too twee, Mum, but you would love it,' so I might take the plunge. Would Elizabeth like it?)

That's by the by, because here's what happened next. There was an error, no one knows how or why, or at least Peter doesn't, but the upshot was that a small florist's shop in Gillingham accidentally took delivery of two kilograms of cocaine alongside their begonias and promptly reported it to the police.

The police, who are no fools at times, didn't rush straight in and arrest the driver, they followed him instead and saw where he headed and what was what. There was a whole team on it eventually, and one by one they worked out who was doing what and arrested everyone they could.

The way Peter told it, he and the young lad running the

nursery had seen the police coming a mile off (Belgium is as flat as Holland, says Peter) and they hid in a field of sunflowers for six hours as the police stripped the place bare. In Amsterdam, one of the Liverpudlians was killed by a Serbian shortly afterwards and that was that.

You can see where it's going, I'm sure. Peter had never really risen through the ranks, he wasn't really the type, but he'd made a bit of money and he had learned an awful lot about flowers. And he saw them at their most beautiful, of course. He described the colours and so on and got quite lyrical. Elizabeth had to hurry him along eventually.

So, now, every day, one of those big lorries pulls up in Pearson Street and Peter gets in the back, like he always used to, but this time he just unloads his flowers and carries them into his shop. And the lorry continues on its rounds and heads back to Belgium, to the nursery run by the young lad he'd played cards with and hidden in a sunflower field with.

So that's a nice story. I bet the Liverpudlians and the Serbians are still shooting each other left, right and centre in Amsterdam, but Peter has his beautiful shop, in that lovely street, where everybody knows his name. Or doesn't know his name, but you take my point. And the benefit of going straight was that no one has ever come looking for him, no one has ever arrested him and taken a closer look at that passport, so Peter Ward had left his past behind and found some peace, which is not easy to do.

Just to satisfy Elizabeth's curiosity, Peter took her to The Flower Mill and showed her the CCTV from the day Tony Curran was murdered. There he was, Peter, I mean, plain to see, behind the till. Which I think rules him out. He is sure that Turkish Johnny is our man. Tony had betrayed him to the police and Johnny had stolen from Tony in turn. That would do it, I suppose.

Elizabeth and I talked about it on the train. And we had half an hour at Ashford International, where, believe it or not, there are no shops. Perhaps there are shops beyond passport control? There must be, surely?

So that's Bobby Tanner. Time for bed, Joyce. I wonder what Ron and Ibrahim were up to today?

I know I was going to say something about Bernard, but it hasn't really formulated, so I won't.

I bought Bernard some freesias from Peter Ward's shop. I wanted to buy something but I couldn't think who to buy them for and I thought perhaps Bernard would like them. Do women give men flowers? Not where I'm from, but perhaps that's not where I am any more. So they're in the sink, and I will take them over tomorrow morning.

Bernard would like Bruges. Don't you think?

83

The path is uneven, but by shining a torch at the ground he is able to make his way up to the allotments without drawing attention to himself. It is late, and everyone will be asleep, but why take a risk? He reaches the shed. There is a padlock, but it's a cheap one and his wife's hatpin soon springs it open.

The shed is shared by all the residents who have an allotment at Coopers Chase. A select band. There are a couple of folding chairs for nice weather and there's a kettle for colder weather. There are bags of fertilizer and mulch along one wall. These are bought from the kitty and Carlito carries them in whenever the minibus comes back from the Garden Centre. Pinned above the fertilizer are the rules of the Coopers Chase Allotment Users Association. They are lengthy and they are enforced with vigour. It is cold, even on a summer's night. The torch continues its circuit. There are no windows, which makes it easier.

The spade rests against the back wall inside the shed.

One look tells him all he needs to know. All he already knew, if he was honest, as he walked up the path. But what to do? You have to try.

He lifts it by the handle, but is quickly beaten by its weight. When did he get so weak? What happened to his body? It was never much to write home about, but to think he could now barely lift a spade? Digging was out of the question.

So what now? Who could help? Who would understand? It was hopeless.

Bernard Cottle sits in a folding chair and weeps for what he has done.

84

Chris and Donna are sitting in the Jigsaw Room, with mugs of tea. Opposite them are Jason Ritchie and Bobby Tanner. Bobby Tanner, whom detectives across eight forces had failed to locate. Elizabeth has repeatedly refused to say where or how she found him.

Elizabeth and Joyce have both seen evidence that Bobby was busy elsewhere when Tony Curran was murdered. Chris had wondered if he might see that evidence and Elizabeth had told him he certainly could, the moment he produced a warrant. Bobby's deal was that he would tell them everything he knew and then slip back into the crowd, never to be seen again.

'A hundred grand, bit more than that,' says Bobby Tanner. 'Johnny had it at his flat, used to keep it safe for Tony.'

'Did he have a nice flat?' asks Joyce.

'Uhh, one of the big ones on the front?' says Bobby.

'Oh yes, with the picture windows,' says Joyce. 'Lovely.'

'And Tony went out to Cyprus looking for him?' asks Chris.

'A couple of times, yeah. Never found a thing. Nothing was the same after that. Jason, you drifted off, didn't you? Started doing telly and all that.'

Jason nods. 'It wasn't for me any more, Bobby.'

Bobby nods. 'I left town a couple of months after, when my brother died. Nothing left for me here then.'

'But someone would have seen Johnny, surely?' asks Donna. 'If he'd come back to town recently? Someone would have seen him, someone would be talking?'

Bobby thinks about this. 'Not too many faces left from those days.'

'Hard to know who Johnny would turn to if he needed a place to stay,' says Jason.

Bobby looks at Jason. 'Unless, Jase . . . ?'

Jason looks back at Bobby, thinks for a moment, then nods. 'Of course, of course. Unless . . .'

Jason starts composing a text.

'Are you going to share this with the group?' asks Elizabeth.

'Just someone me and Bobby need to talk to,' says Jason. 'Someone who'd know for sure. Leave it with us. It's not fair if you get to solve everything, Elizabeth.'

'Perhaps you could share it with the police?' suggests Donna.

'Oh come on,' says Bobby, laughing.

'Worth a try,' says Donna.

Jason's phone pings. He looks down, then turns to Bobby. 'He can meet us at two. That OK for you?'

Bobby nods and Jason starts another message.

'Only one place for it, eh?'

85

Lunch at Le Pont Noir. Just like old times and yet, of course, not like them at all.

'Astronaut?' guesses Jason Ritchie.

Bobby Tanner smiles, and shakes his head.

'Jockey?' guesses Jason.

Bobby Tanner shakes his head again. 'I ain't gonna tell you, even if you guess.'

Fair enough, fair enough.

'You happy though, Bobby?' asks Jason.

Bobby nods his head.

'Good lad,' says Jason. 'You deserve it.'

'We both do,' agrees Bobby Tanner. 'One way or another.'

'Well, we do and we don't,' says Jason.

Bobby Tanner nods. Maybe so.

They are on desserts, still waiting for their guest, and a bottle of Le Pont Noir's finest Malbec has been dispatched.

'I mean, it must have been Johnny, right?' asks Bobby. 'I've always thought he was dead somewhere.'

'I've always thought that you were dead somewhere,' says Jason. 'I'm glad you're not though.'

'Thanks, Jase,' says Bobby.

Jason looks at his watch. 'We'll know for sure soon enough.'

'You reckon he'll know?' asks Bobby.

'If Johnny's been over, then he'll know. That's where he'd have stayed.'

'I can't do lunchtime drinking any more, can you?' asks Bobby.

'We're old men now, Bob,' agrees Jason. 'Time for another bottle though?'

They agree that they do have time for another bottle. And then in walks Steve Ercan.

86

Donna has spent the evening looking through aeroplane passenger lists to and from Cyprus for the last two weeks. As if Johnny Gunduz would be using his own name these days. But you never knew.

Fun though the passenger lists had been, however, Donna is now back on Instagram.

Toyota was history already, but Carl wouldn't wait around. Who was he seeing now? Donna was nothing if not a natural detective. Was he seeing that woman from his work, Poppy? Poppy, whose photo he'd liked on Facebook? Not just liked, but replied to with a wink emoji? Poppy, who seemed incapable of having her photo taken without being shot from the left and pouting? Yes, she was obvious enough for Carl. Donna had run her name through the Home Office computer on the off-chance, but nothing.

Donna knows it is time for bed, but she is still thinking about Penny Gray.

After the Thursday Murder Club meeting, Elizabeth had told her she wanted her to meet someone and had led her into Willows, the nursing home attached to Coopers Chase.

They had walked down quiet beige corridors, with dim strip lighting and seaside watercolours lining the walls. It all carried an appalling weight, and the hopeful sprigs of flowers on cheap MDF side tables were powerless against it. Who brought the flowers in every day? That was a losing battle, but what was the alternative? Donna had gulped for air at one point. Willows was a prison from which no escape was possible. Where release could mean only one thing.

They had walked into the room and Elizabeth had said, 'Constable De Freitas, I'd like you to meet Detective Inspector Penny Gray.'

Penny had been lying in bed, a light sheet covering her to the neck, a blanket further down, folded back. Tubes running from her nose and from her wrists. Donna had once been on a school trip to the Lloyd's Building, where everything that should be on the inside was on the outside. She preferred everything tidied away.

Donna saluted. 'Ma'am.'

'Take a seat, Donna, I thought it would be nice for the two of you to get to know each other. I do think you'll get along.'

Elizabeth had taken Donna through Penny's career. Smart, resilient, opinionated, thwarted at every turn, by her gender and by her temperament. Or rather by the unacceptable combination of them both.

'She's a wrecking ball,' Elizabeth had said. 'I'm a thin blade, you understand. Penny is all brute force. I don't know if you could tell that now.'

Donna looked at Penny and fancied that she could.

'It was fashionable in the police back then,' Elizabeth had gone on. 'A bit of blunt force. Fashionable if you were a man at least, it never helped Penny, she never made it higher than Detective Inspector. Absurd if you knew her. I'm right, John, absurd, wasn't it?'

John had looked up and nodded. 'A waste.'

'She was trouble, Donna,' said Elizabeth. 'And I can think of no finer compliment. That's why Penny enjoyed looking over the old cases. She could finally be in charge. Could finally be the bull in a china shop. She didn't have to be polite and laugh at the jokes and make the tea.'

Donna saw Elizabeth's hand close around Penny's.

Elizabeth looked at her and nodded. 'We fight on though, do we not? Penny took it all, sucked it up, as they say, day after day, without complaint.'

'She complained a lot.' This was John. 'With respect, Elizabeth.'

'Well, yes, she had an impressive temper on her when she wanted to.'

'Very focused,' John had agreed.

As they had left, generations apart, but shoulder to shoulder and in perfect step, Elizabeth had turned to Donna and said, 'You will know better than me, Donna, but I think perhaps not all the battles have been won?'

'I think perhaps too,' Donna had agreed. They had continued, in companionable silence, out through the front doors of Willows, grateful to be breathing the air of the outside world.

Back at home – was this really home now? – Donna is not fully concentrating on Instagram any more. The visit to Penny has made her proud and sad. She would love to have met her. Really met her. There are many reasons why Donna would like to be the one to crack these murders, and she adds making Detective Inspector Penny Gray proud to her list.

Johnny for the Tony Curran murder? Matthew Mackie for Ventham? Elizabeth had told her to look into another of the residents. A Bernard Cottle. She had written the name down.

And the bones? Are they important?

What do you say, Penny Gray?

It would be nice to wrap it all up. A nice tribute to someone who has gone before. She should get back to those passenger lists.

Donna scrolls through some final pictures. Poppy has just been bungee-jumping for Cancer Research. Well of course she has; that was so Poppy.

87

Joyce

I don't often write in the morning, I know. But today I am. I just felt I should. So here I am.

Yesterday was all very interesting, wasn't it? Those boys and all the murders and the drugs and what have you. I bet they had a lot to talk about when they headed off afterwards. I wonder who they were meeting?

Really, it was very interesting to someone like me. Very interesting. Johnny certainly sounds a likely culprit, doesn't he?

I wonder if . . . Oh stop it, Joyce, just stop it. You're putting it off. You don't want to write it.

All right then. So I have had some sad news, and the sad news is this.

I made my 'All's Well' call to Bernard this morning.

Lots of people have an 'All's Well' arrangement. You buddy up with a pal, ring them at 8 a.m., let it ring twice and put the phone down. Then they do the same back. So you each know the other is OK without it costing you a penny. And, of course, you don't have to have a conversation.

So I rang Bernard this morning. Two rings, letting him know I was safe and sound, hadn't had a fall or what have you. But nothing back. I never worry too much, sometimes he forgets and I wander round and ring his buzzer and he shuffles to the window in his dressing gown and gives me a guilty thumbs-up. I always think, 'Oh let me in, you silly old man, let's have some breakfast, I don't mind the dressing gown,' but that's not Bernard.

So over I trotted. Did I know? I suppose I did, but I also didn't, because it's too big a thing to know. But I suppose I did know, because Marjorie Walters saw me on my way over, and said she'd waved but I hadn't seen, just lost in a world of my own, which isn't like me. So, yes, I suppose I knew.

I buzzed and looked up at the window. The curtains were drawn. Perhaps he was asleep? Had a touch of flu and stayed in bed. 'Man flu', someone had said on *This Morning* the other day. It had tickled me and I'd told Joanna, but she said the expression had been around for years and had I really never heard it? Which put me in my place.

I'm stalling, I know. Let's get on to it.

I let myself into the block with the spare key fob, I walked up the flight of stairs and saw an envelope Sellotaped to Bernard's door. On the front of it he had written 'Joyce'.

Sorry, I have to finish there.

There was even a smiley face in the 'O'. You really never knew with Bernard.

88

Joyce opens up the envelope and slips out a handwritten letter. Maybe three or four pages. She is grateful that her friends have come to her flat. She didn't want to go out there again today.

'So, I'll just read it. Not all of it, but the bits of interest. It answers a few questions we had. I know what some of you had been thinking about him. Maybe thought he'd, you know . . . Ian Ventham. Anyway.'

'You take your time,' says Ron, and places his hand on Joyce's for a moment.

Joyce begins to read, with an unfamiliar waver.

'"Dear Joyce, I am sorry for the nuisance. Don't try to come in, I have bolted the door. First time I have used that bolt since I moved here. You will know what I have done, and I suppose it's nothing you haven't seen before a thousand times. I will be lying on the bed, all things being well, and perhaps I will look peaceful, but perhaps I won't. I would rather not take that chance, so I'll leave it to the ambulance men to decide if I look in a fit state for you to say goodbye. That is if you wish to say goodbye."'

Joyce stops reading for a moment. Elizabeth, Ron and Ibrahim are completely silent. She looks up at them. 'They didn't let me see him in the end. I'm sure that's policy, when you're not family. So he got that bit wrong, didn't he? And they were both ambulance women.'

Joyce gives a weak smile and her three friends mirror it. She continues reading.

'"I have the pills by my side and I have a Laphroaig I had been saving for a rainy day. I see the lights turning off around me and it will be my turn next. Next to the bed are the beautiful flowers you bought me. They are in a milk bottle, because you know me and vases. But before I go, I suppose I should tell you the whole thing."'

'The whole thing?' says Elizabeth.

Joyce puts a finger to her lips. Elizabeth does as she is told and Joyce continues reading Bernard's final letter.

'"As you know, Asima" – that's his wife – "died shortly after we moved to Coopers Chase, which was a spanner in the works. I know you don't talk about Gerry very much, Joyce, but I know you understand. Like someone reached in and took out my heart and my lungs and told me to keep living. Keep waking up, keep eating, keep putting one foot in front of the other. For what? I don't think I ever really found an answer to that. You know I would often walk up the hill and sit on the bench Asima and I used to sit on when we first moved here, and you know I felt close to her there. But I had another reason for climbing that hill, a reason for which I feel profound shame. A shame that has become too much for me to bear."'

Joyce pauses for a moment. 'I wonder if I might have some water?'

Ron pours her a glass and hands it to her. Joyce drinks, then returns to the letter.

'"You will know that many Hindus have their ashes scattered on the Ganges. These days, other rivers will do, but for a certain generation it's still the Ganges, if you have the wherewithal. This was Asima's wish many, many years ago, certainly a wish that our daughter Sudhi had grown up hearing about. Asima's funeral is not something I wish to think about or write about, but two days afterwards Sudhi

and Majid – that's the daughter and son-in-law – flew to Vara-
nasi in India and scattered Asima's ashes on the Ganges. But
Joyce – and here's where the pills and the whisky come in,
I'm afraid – they weren't her ashes."'

She pauses and looks up.

'Well. Goodness!' says Ibrahim, and sits forward as Joyce
reads on.

'"I am not a religious man, Joyce, as you are aware. But in
her later years, Asima was not a religious woman either. She
shook off her faith slowly, like the leaves from a tree, until
nothing remained. I loved that woman with everything I
possess and she loved me. The thought of her leaving, being
placed in hand luggage, Joyce, and then floating away from
me. Well, that wasn't something I was able to comprehend
two days after saying goodbye. None of this excuses my
actions, but I hope it might explain them. I had the ashes at
home, for the first night. Sudhi and Majid weren't in my spare
room, they had preferred to stay in a hotel, despite it all.

'"Many years ago Asima and I had been browsing at an
old antique shop and she had picked up a tea caddy in the
shape of a tiger. 'Well, that's you,' I said, and we both laughed.
I called her Little Tiger and she called me Big Tiger, you
know the drill. I went back a week later to buy it for her, as a
surprise Christmas present, but it had already been sold.
Anyway, that Christmas, I opened my present from her, and
there it was. She had obviously gone straight back and bought
it for me. I have kept it ever since. So, I took the urn and
poured the ashes from the urn into the tiger tea caddy, then
placed the caddy back in the cupboard. I filled the urn with
a mixture of sawdust and bonemeal, it's surprisingly convincing, then sealed it shut again. And that's what Sudhi took
to Varanasi and that's what she scattered on the Ganges.
Bear in mind I wasn't thinking straight, Joyce, I was

paralysed with grief. I would have done anything to stop my Asima floating away. I had forgotten, of course, that she was Sudhi's Asima too. The next day, as soon after dark as I dared, I took a spade from the allotment shed and walked up the hill. I cut the turf from underneath the bench, I dug a hole and I buried the tin. Even then I knew it could only be temporary, but I wasn't ready to let her go. The turf settled back in, nobody ever noticed a thing – why would they? – and every day I would go and sit on the bench, say hello when people walked by and talk to Asima when they didn't. I knew then that it was wrong, I knew that I had betrayed my daughter and that I could never make amends. But the pain was so very great."'

'Some people love their children more than they love their partner,' says Ibrahim, 'and some people love their partner more than their children. And no one can ever admit to either thing.'

Joyce nods, absent-mindedly and begins a new page.

'"The immediate pain goes, however much you might want it to stay, and I soon came to understand the enormity of what I had done. The awful selfishness, the entitlement. I started to think of plans and plots, something to put it right. Maybe I would dig the tea caddy up, I would take it on the bus down to Fairhaven, let some of her go and keep some of her with me. I could never tell Sudhi what I had done, but at least her mother would be in the waves, returning to wherever Sudhi imagines we return to. I knew it wasn't enough, but it was the best I could do. Until one morning I climbed the hill to find workmen laying a concrete foundation for the bench. They had dug down, not far enough to find the tin, and filled the hole with cement. They had the job done in half an hour. And that was that, I suppose, so silly when you look at it, but I had no easy way of digging the tea caddy back up. So I would continue to walk up the hill and continue to talk to Asima when no one was listening, telling her my news, telling her how much I loved her and telling her I was sorry. And honestly, Joyce, for your eyes only, I realize that I have run out of whatever it is that we need to carry on. So that's me, I'm afraid.'"

Joyce, finishes, stares down at the letter for another moment, running a finger across the ink. She looks up at her friends and attempts a smile, which turns, in an instant, to tears. The tears turn to shaking sobs and Ron leaves his chair, kneels in front her and takes her in his arms. The thing Ron is so good at. Joyce buries her head in Ron's shoulder and flings her arms around him, weeping for Gerry and for Bernard and for Asima and for the ladies who went to *Jersey Boys* and drank G&Ts out of cans all the way home.

89

It is too late to be in Fairhaven Police Station, but Donna and Chris have nowhere else to be.

Chris kneels and unblocks the paper jam in the photocopier. Chris finds it hard to kneel without cramping up these days. He isn't sure what that is. Too much salt, or not enough salt? It's one or the other.

'Fixed it,' he tells Donna.

Donna presses 'Print' and makes a series of copies of the reports she's been sent by the Cypriot Police Service.

'I'll bind them all together for you,' says Donna. 'It'll take a while, but it'll be easier for you.'

'Very kind, Donna,' says Chris. 'But you're still not coming to Cyprus with me.'

Donna sticks out her tongue.

Chris has a very interesting interview lined up. One that should tell them once and for all where Johnny Gunduz is.

Johnny's name has not appeared on any of the passenger lists that Donna had waded through. No flight, no boat, no train, either into or out of the UK. But Chris supposes that Johnny is unlikely to still be using his old name. Not when the police had been hunting him down for the murder of the young cabbie and Tony Curran had been hunting him down for the £100,000 he had stolen.

But no one could simply disappear. There would be a trace somewhere.

Chris shuts down his computer. He feels sure that Turkish Johnny is their man, he's been around long enough to sense when something fits perfectly. Evidence was another thing, but hopefully the trip to Nicosia will help him out there.

'Shall we call it a night?'

'Quick drink?' says Donna. 'Pont Noir?'

'Six-fifty flight in the morning,' says Chris.

'Don't rub it in,' says Donna.

Chris stands and pulls down his office blinds. Johnny was one thing, but Ian Ventham? That was harder. Was it really connected to a murder from fifty years ago? Surely not? How many people could there be? Chris even had two DIs tracking down nuns in case they could remember anything. Surely some of them had left at some point? Lost their calling and gone out into the real world? What would they be now? Eighty-odd? Records were sketchy though, and he held out little hope. Or were they all missing something simpler?

'Don't crack the case while I'm gone please.'

'I can't promise anything,' says Donna.

Chris picks up his briefcase. Time to go home. Always the worst time. Chris's dream life remains just one stone away. But in his briefcase there is a packet of Salt & Vinegar McCoys, a Wispa and a Diet Coke. Diet Coke? Who did Chris think he was kidding?

Sometimes Chris thinks he should join a dating website. In his mind his perfect date would be a divorced teacher who had a small dog and sang in a choir. But he'd be happy to be proved wrong. Just someone kind and funny really.

Chris holds the door open for Donna, then follows her out.

What kind of woman would want Chris? Did women really mind a bit of extra timber these days? Well, yes, he was sure they did, but even so? He was just about to solve a murder, and surely, somewhere in the whole of Kent, there was someone who might find that attractive?

90

Joyce

Oh, I can't sleep. It's Bernard, Bernard, Bernard, of course. I'm already wondering about the funeral. Will it be here? I do hope so. I know I hadn't known him long, but I'd hate to think of him in Vancouver.

So I'm back here at two in the morning, to give you some news. Don't worry, no one has died this time.

After Ian we had all been wondering what's to become of us here at Coopers Chase. Who was going to take it over? I don't think anyone was too concerned; it seems to be profitable enough, so we knew there would be takers. But who?

You can probably guess who found out.

Elizabeth 'accidentally' bumped into Gemma Ventham, Ian Ventham's unfortunate widow yesterday, at the new deli they've opened in Robertsbridge. It used to be Claire's Hairdressers, until Claire was struck off. Is 'struck off' the correct expression for hairdressers? Either way, the local GP's wife lost the top of an ear and that was that. They say Claire's in Brighton now, and that's probably for the best.

Gemma was with a man, who Elizabeth described as 'a tennis-coach type', though conceded that these days he might have been 'a Pilates-instructor type'. Certainly not a grieving widow, and I think we all agreed that she'd earned a bit of happiness, so good for her.

She has also, it seems, earned an awful lot of money. This is what Elizabeth got out of her. I don't know exactly how, but I do know that at one point she had pretended to faint, because she had actually grazed her elbow in the effort. She always finds a way, that one.

Anyway, Gemma Ventham has sold Coopers Chase Holdings to a company called Bramley Holdings. Of course, we've tried to find out as much as we can about Bramley Holdings, but thus far, no luck. We even called in Joanna and Cornelius, but they've turned up a blank. They promised they would keep looking, although you can hear that Cornelius's patience is beginning to wear a bit thin.

But here's something else keeping me awake. That name.

Bramley Holdings? It is ringing a bell and I can't work out why. Elizabeth says they take names off the shelf, and perhaps she is right, but an alarm is ringing in my brain and I can't switch it off.

Bramley? Where have I heard that before? And I know I'm an old woman, but don't say apples. Something else. Something important.

Anne, who edits *Cut to the Chase*, came to see me today. People will always come and see you when you lose a friend. By now we've all worked out the right things to say. We've said them often enough.

I don't think she is doing it just to be nice, but Anne has asked if I will write a column in *Cut to the Chase*. She knows I like to write and she knows I have my nose in everything, so would I write something about the comings and goings at Coopers Chase? I said yes, of course, and we are going to call it 'Joyce's Choices', which I like. I had suggested 'Joyce's Voices', but Anne had thought that might sound a bit mental health. She wants a picture of me, so I will go through a few tomorrow and pick out a nice one.

We are off to see Gordon Playfair tomorrow as well. The farmer at the top of the hill? He's the only person any of us can think of who was here in the early 1970s and is still here today. He was nowhere near Ventham when he was murdered, so I don't think we can count him as a suspect, but we're hoping he might remember something useful from all those years ago.

I must try and sleep again.

91

'Quaint?' repeats Gordon Playfair, laughing. 'This place? You and I know it's an old house, falling apart, for an old man falling apart.'

'We're all falling apart, Gordon,' says Elizabeth.

The walk to the Playfair farm had taken longer than expected, because a police cordon has been placed around the Garden of Eternal Rest. By all accounts, two police cars and a white van, popularly believed to be a forensics unit, had carefully parked at around 10 a.m. and a number of officers in white body suits had walked up the hill with spades. Martin Sedge has a top-floor flat in Larkin and is training binoculars on the site, but no news yet. 'Just some digging,' was his most recent report.

'This house and me have grown old together. Roof coming off,' says Gordon, and rubs the few strands of hair left on his head. 'Things creak that didn't use to creak. Dodgy plumbing. We're two of a kind.'

'We don't disturb you too much? The village?' asks Elizabeth.

'Never hear a peep,' says Gordon. 'Might as well still be the nuns down there.'

'You should come and visit us sometime,' says Joyce. 'There's a restaurant, there's a pool. There's Zumba.'

'I used to go down a lot in the old days. Just for bits and bobs, have a chat. They were a lively bunch when they weren't praying. Also, if you ever put a nail through your thumb or your ankle down a rabbit hole, they'd fix you up,' says Gordon.

Elizabeth nods, fair enough. 'You met Ian Ventham on the morning he was murdered?'

'Unfortunately, yes. Not my choice.'

'Whose choice?'

'Karen, my youngest. She just wanted me to hear him out. She wants me to sell. Why wouldn't she?'

'And what was discussed?' asks Elizabeth.

'Same old nonsense. Same offer, same manners. I'll put it politely by saying I never took to Ian Ventham. I can be less polite if you'd like?'

'You weren't for turning?'

'They both tried to talk me round. Karen could see it wasn't washing, but Ventham kept on for a bit longer. Trying to make me feel guilty about the kids.'

'But you didn't budge?'

'I rarely do.'

'I'm much the same,' says Elizabeth. 'And how did you leave it?'

'He told me he was going to get my land, one way or another.'

'And what did you say to that?' asks Joyce.

'I said, "Over my dead body," ' says Gordon Playfair.

'Well, quite,' says Elizabeth.

'Anyway,' says Gordon Playfair, 'I've been made another offer. And I'm taking it, now Ventham's out of the picture.'

'Good for you,' says Elizabeth.

'Now, might I ask, is this just a social call?' says Gordon Playfair. 'Or is there something I can help you with?'

'Funny you should ask,' Elizabeth says, nodding. 'We were wondering if you had any memories of this place? From the seventies, say?'

'I certainly have plenty of memories,' says Gordon Play-fair. 'Might even have a few photo albums if they'd help?'

'It wouldn't do any harm to take a look,' says Elizabeth.

'I should warn you now, my photos are mainly of sheep. What is it you're looking for?'

92

Joyce

So we told Gordon Playfair about the body. And we all had a good old chat about who might have buried it there all those years ago. All those years ago, when Coopers Chase was a convent and a young Gordon Playfair sat in the very same house, with his young family, on this very hill.

The offer for his land, by the way? It was from our mysterious friends at Bramley Holdings. That name is still driving me crazy. But it'll come. He was just cutting off his nose to spite his face with Ventham, refusing to sell simply because he couldn't stand him. The moment Ventham was out of the picture, the sale was on.

I asked Gordon what he might do with the money, and it won't surprise you to know that most of it will go to the kids. There's three. We know one of them, of course: Karen, who lives in the small cottage in the next field over and was supposed to be teaching us about computers, until we were so unexpectedly interrupted.

Unmarried, but then so is Joanna. So am I, come to think of it.

So, lucky kids, but Gordon says he has enough left over to buy himself a little place somewhere nice and, you will see where this is going, we're going to give him a guided tour of Coopers Chase in a few days and see if anything takes his fancy. Wouldn't that be fun? Gordon is craggy, rather than conventionally handsome, but has broad, farmer's shoulders.

Anyway, back to the bones. Gordon understood now why we wanted to hear his memories of the 1970s. And why we were studying his photo albums so intently. Just to take a look at any shots he'd taken on those trips down the hill all those years ago. See if anyone rang a bell.

In the end, it was in the second album we looked through. It started with wedding photos, Gordon and Sandra (or Susan, I had glazed over I'm afraid, you know other people's wedding photos), then pictures of a baby, suspiciously shortly afterwards. That will be their eldest. Then, and I'm not making this up, page after page of pictures of sheep and, the way Gordon was telling it, all different. And then, just as the wine and the fire and the sheep were making us drowsy, we reached the final photos in the album. Six in all, black and white. All six photos taken at a Christmas party at the convent. Probably not a party as such, but certainly Christmas.

It was in the fifth photo, a group shot. At first you couldn't really see it. We've all changed a lot over fifty years, I'm sure I wouldn't recognize Elizabeth, or she me. But we all looked and we all looked again. And we all agreed.

And so we have our evidence, and we have a plan. Well, Elizabeth has a plan.

And, speaking of photos, I found a nice one for my column in *Cut to the Chase*. It's an old photo, which I know is vain, but you'd still know it's me. Gerry is also in it, but Anne tells me she can crop him out on the computer. Sorry, love.

93

There is still a confessional stall in the chapel at the heart of Coopers Chase. It is used as storage for the cleaners now. Joyce had helped Elizabeth clear it out, stacking up the boxes of floor polish on the altar, neatly tucked behind Jesus. Elizabeth had given the whole place a spruce up, even polishing the grille. As a final touch, she puts a pair of Orla Kiely cushions on the hard wooden seats.

Elizabeth had conducted many interviews in her time, and brought many people to some kind of justice. If tapes existed of any of these interviews, they had long since been buried, erased or burned. That was Elizabeth's fervent hope at least.

Lawyers? No. Procedure? Certainly not. Just whatever worked quickest.

Nothing physical ever, that wasn't Elizabeth's style. She knew it happened from time to time, but it was never effective. Psychology was key. Always try the unexpected, always approach from an angle, always lean back in your chair, with all the time in the world, and wait for them to tell all. Like the whole process was their idea in the first place. And for that you always needed an angle, something unexpected. Something bespoke.

Like inviting a priest to a confession.

Elizabeth realized she was very fond of Donna and Chris. The Thursday Murder Club had got lucky with those two. Imagine the bores they might have been saddled with. She knew that even Donna and Chris would have limits, though, and that this was way beyond those limits. But if she could work her magic with Matthew Mackie, she knew they would forgive her.

And if she couldn't work her magic? If her magic was just a memory? She had been wrong about Ian Ventham murdering Tony Curran, hadn't she?

But Matthew Mackie was different. Here was a man who had scuffled with Ventham. A man who didn't seem to exist, yet had been in a photo taken in this very chapel. A man who both was a priest and wasn't a priest. A man who had brushed over his footsteps.

Until someone had decided to dig up a graveyard. His graveyard?

And a man who was on his way this very moment. When it would have been easier for him to stay at home. Was he coming to confess? Was he coming to find out what she knew? Or was he coming with a syringe full of fentanyl?

Elizabeth has never been afraid of death, but, all the same, in this moment, she thinks of Stephen.

It is cold in the ageless dark of the chapel and Elizabeth shivers. She buttons her cardigan, then looks at her watch. She would soon find out, one way or another.

94

Chris Hudson is in a small cell, opposite a large man. The small cell is an interview room in the Central Prison of Nicosia and the large man is Demir Gunduz. The father of Johnny Gunduz.

Chris is in a concrete seat, bolted to the floor. The back is ramrod straight. It would be the most uncomfortable chair that Chris had ever sat in, had he not just made the flight to Cyprus on Ryanair.

Chris's trips abroad for work have been few and far between. Many years ago, he had gone to Spain to escort home Billy Gill, a seventy-year-old antiques dealer from Hove who had run a counterfeit pound-coin operation from a garage close to the seafront. It was a lovely little business, running pretty much undetectably for many years, until, with the advent of the two-pound coin, Billy had got greedy. His coins had looked terrific, but the middles kept falling out, and after a lengthy stakeout of a Portslade launderette, Billy's mint was tracked down and Billy had fled for the sun, pockets jangling as he went.

Chris's memory of that trip was a cramped charter flight from Shoreham airport, landing somewhere in Spain beginning with A, being driven for forty-five minutes in searing heat, the van stopping and a handcuffed Billy Gill being shoved alongside him, and waiting seven hours for a flight home, all the while listening to Billy Gill telling him you couldn't get Marmite in Spain.

Then a few years later there had been a compulsory IT

course on the Isle of Wight. And, so far, that had been that for globetrotting.

But Cyprus was a bit more like it. Too hot, obviously, but more like it. He'd been met at Larnaca airport and driven to the capital by Joe Kyprianou, the Cypriot detective who now sat next to him. The prison was nice and cool and, Chris discovered, it's impossible to sweat when sitting on a concrete chair. From the moment the cell doors closed, he had been happy.

Demir Gunduz was, Chris guessed, somewhere in his seventies, but was a lot less chatty than Billy Gill.

'When was the last time you saw Johnny?' asks Chris.

Demir looks straight at him and shrugs.

'Last week? Last year? Does he visit? Come on, Demir.'

Demir looks at his nails. Which, Chris notes, are immaculate for a man in prison.

'Here's the thing, Mr Gunduz. We have records showing that your son arrived back in Cyprus, on 17 May 2000. Landing at Larnaca airport at around two p.m. And from that moment to this, nothing. Not a trace. Why might that be, do you think?'

Demir thinks for a moment. 'Why do you want Johnny? After this time?'

'I would like to speak to him about an offence in the UK. To rule him out.'

'Pretty big offence if you fly here? No?'

'A pretty big offence, Mr Gunduz, yes.'

Demir Gunduz nods slowly. 'And you can't find Johnny?'

'I know where he was at two p.m. on 17 May 2000, and I'm hazy after that,' says Chris. 'Where would he have gone? Who would he have seen?'

'Well,' says Demir, sitting up tall in his chair, 'he would have come to see me.'

'And did he?'

Demir leans forward a little and gives Chris a smile. Then shrugs once again. 'Time up, I think. Good luck to you. Enjoy Cyprus.'

Joe Kyprianou leans forward now, and regards Demir Gunduz.

'Demir and his brother Alper, they used to steal motor-cycles, Chris, here in Nicosia, and ship them off to Turkey. Pretty easy, if you have a guy in each port. They had a little workshop, file off the serial number, change the registration, that's right, Demir, isn't it?'

'A long time ago,' says Demir.

'Then it was cars every now and again. But they could go on the same boats, with the same men turning the same blind eye, so everything is OK for Demir and Alper. The years roll by, bikes and cars, cars and bikes. And the cars mean a bigger workshop, and a bigger lorry, and bigger crates.'

'And bigger money for Demir?' asks Chris, looking at Demir.

'Bigger money, for sure. So all is calm and everyone is happy, and Demir and Alper do very nicely, thank you so much. And then 1974 and Turkey invade. You know the story?'

'Yes,' says Chris. He doesn't, but he really wants a meal before his flight and he can bet the story is a long one. He will look it up on Wikipedia if it becomes important.

'So the Turkish invade, they take over Northern Cyprus. Pretty much. The Greek Cypriots in the north come down south, the Turkish Cypriots in the south go up north. The few that hadn't left in 1963, that is. And that's Demir and Alper.'

'So Demir moved north?'

Joe Kyprianou laughs. 'You moved north, eh Demir? Like three streets north. Nicosia was cut in two, Turkish in the north of the city, Greek in the south. So they just moved north of the Green Line and found themselves in a whole new world.'

Google 'Green Line', thinks Chris.

'And Demir, you sensed opportunity in this new world, eh? Started a new business.'

'Drugs?' asks Chris. 'Naughty Demir.'

Demir shrugs.

'Drugs,' confirms Joe Kyprianou. 'They paid the right people. Drugs from Turkey come into Northern Cyprus. Then from Northern Cyprus on to wherever, whoever. Huge business very, very quickly, and all protected. Frontier country, you know? Ten years on, the brothers run everything, they're Kings of the North. Untouchable, Chris, the whole family. They pay charities, open schools, the whole match. Gunduz. You just say the name in Northern Cyprus and see what you see.'

Chris nods, he gets it. 'When Johnny landed back here in 2000, he disappeared, never to be seen again. There was a warrant, we had officers fly over, the Cypriot police searched, but found nothing.'

Joe nods. 'It's simple, Chris, really. If Johnny has to get out of England quick, he just calls his dad. He lands at the airport, Demir sends people to pick him up, burn the passport, new one straight away. New guy, new name, back up to Northern Cyprus, back to business. Next day, back to business, I guarantee. Is that what happened, Demir?'

'Nothing happened,' says Demir.

'And the search?' asks Chris. 'Our guys? Your guys?'

'No chance. No chance at all,' says Joe. 'I won't say bad things, Chris, because you know how it is. But no way they even looked. Not in the right places. See if your boys wrote it up. They won't have set foot in Northern Cyprus. In 2000,

you can't believe the power Demir had. You owned everything and everyone, eh, brother?'

Joe looks at Demir. Demir nods.

'Still does, even from prison. So, however good a cop you
are, why even try? Johnny could be here, could be Turkey,
could be US or back in the UK. You can see Demir knows
where he is, but he's never going to help you.'

Demir holds out his hands.

'He could have flown into the UK?' says Chris. 'Under
any name, killed Tony Curran and flown back out, and we'd
be none the wiser?'

Joe nods. 'Definitely. Though if he flew to the UK he'd
have had help when he got there. Any Cypriots there who
could help him? Put him up? Anyone who might be scared
of Demir here, and what he can still do?'

Chris shrugs, but tucks this away.

Demir has had enough, and stands. 'Are we done,
gentlemen?'

Chris nods, he is out of ammunition. He knows a pro
when he interviews one. Chris takes out his card and puts it
on the table in front of Demir.

'My card, if anything comes back to you.'

Demir looks at the card, then at Chris, then back at the
card and lets out a belly laugh. He looks over at Joe Kyprianou and says something Chris can't catch. Joe Kyprianou
laughs too. Demir looks back at Chris for a final time and
shakes his head, firmly, but not unkindly.

Chris gives Demir a shrug of his own. He is a pro too.

Chris had googled it earlier and there is a Starbucks and a
Burger King at Larnaca airport. You saw fewer and fewer
Burger Kings these days. Time to make tracks. He stands.

'What did they get you for, Demir?' asks Chris. 'In the
end?'

Demir gives a small smile. 'I bought a Harley-Davidson, from the US, had it shipped over. Forgot to pay the duty.'

'You're kidding? And they gave you life?'

Demir Gunduz shakes his head. 'Sentenced to two weeks and then I killed a prison guard.'

Chris nods. 'Quite a family.'

95

Matthew Mackie had been surprised to get the call from Elizabeth. Asking if he was available for a confession. He had been gardening and thinking. The police interview had upset him, thrown him off balance. Life had been so simple a few months ago. His life wasn't happy, exactly, he hadn't been happy for many years, but was he at peace perhaps? Had he found some contentment? As much as he was ever going to, he supposed.

He had his house, his garden, his pension. He had nice neighbours who would look in on him. A young family had recently moved in opposite, and the kids would play on their bikes on the pavement. He could hear bells and laughter if he kept the windows open. He could walk down to the sea in five minutes. He could sit and watch the gulls and read the paper, when it wasn't too windy. People knew him, and would smile and ask how he was keeping and, if he wasn't too busy, could they tell him about their nose bleeds, or their hip, or their sleepless nights? It was a life, it had a rhythm and a routine and it kept the ghosts at bay. What more could you ask, really?

But now? Brawls, police interviews, non-stop worry. Would he ever get his peace back? Would this blow over? He knew it wouldn't. Whatever they say about time healing, some things in life just break and can never be fixed. For now, Matthew Mackie was keeping his windows shut. There were no bells and there was no laughter, and he was old enough to know there might never be again.

It seemed that every bit of news he had received in the last month had been bad. So what to make of the phone call? What was this to be?

Did he know the confessional stall at St Michael's Chapel, she had asked. Did he know it? He would still dream of it now, the darkness, the dull echo, the walls closing in on him. The place where his life broke in two, never to be fixed.

Should he go back there? It wasn't a fair question. He had never left. He had known his life would lead him back there one day. God's sense of humour. You had to hand it to him.

He had seen Elizabeth, he was sure. At the consultation meeting and again on the awful day of the murder. She stood out. So what was on Elizabeth's mind? What sin could she no longer hide? And why ask for him? And why there? She must have seen him on the day of the murder, he supposed. Must have seen the dog collar, that usually stuck in people's minds. It often made people want to tell their secrets, to spill all. What had he unlocked in her that made her pick up the phone? And, for that matter, how had she got his number? He wasn't listed. Perhaps it was on the internet? She must have got it somewhere.

And so that was that. Back to St Michael's. Into the confessional, with Elizabeth. Back to where it all began and where it all ended. A macabre coincidence. If only she knew.

Matthew Mackie was already on the platform at Bexhill station when he realized Elizabeth hadn't actually mentioned which of them would be doing the confessing.

He thought about turning straight round. But, by that point, he had already bought a ticket.

She couldn't possibly know? Could she?

96

So that, supposed Chris, was that. Johnny Gunduz had managed to disappear, the prodigal son returned, protected by his powerful family. Now to find out if Johnny had recently taken a flight back to England. A little trip down memory lane. But under what name? And with what face? Johnny could come and go as he pleased.

Chris had got to the airport with plenty of time to spare and was enjoying a triple chocolate muffin from Starbucks. He shouldn't, of course, just empty calories, but he could think about that when he'd finished the muffin. He hears an English voice.

'This seat taken?'

Chris motions that the seat is free, without looking up. Until his brain registers that the voice is familiar to him. But of course. Of *course*. Chris looks up, and nods.

'Good afternoon, Ron.'

'Afternoon, Chris,' says Ron, sitting down. 'Four hundred and fifty calories in one muffin, you know.'

'Are you following me, Ron?' asks Chris. 'Seeing what there is to see?'

'No, we got here yesterday, old son,' says Ron.

'We?' says Chris.

Ibrahim arrives with a tray. He nods at Chris. 'How lovely to bump into you, Detective Chief Inspector! We heard you were here. Ron, I didn't really know how to ask for just an instant coffee, so I got us Caramel Frappuccinos.'

'Thanks Ib,' says Ron, and takes his drink.

'I wonder if it's worth my while asking what you two are doing here,' asks Chris. 'Assuming it is just the two of you? Perhaps Joyce is stocking up in Duty Free?'

'Just us boys,' says Ron. 'Little jolly to Cyprus.'

'Quite bonding, in fact,' says Ibrahim. 'I have never had many close male friends. Or close female friends. Or been to Cyprus.'

'Elizabeth sent us over with instructions,' says Ron. 'She knew someone who knew someone who knew someone, so here we are. Probably finding out the same as you.'

'A very powerful family,' says Ibrahim. 'Very easy for Johnny to go missing. To change his identity. No trace of him anywhere.'

'A ghost,' says Ron.

'A ghost with a grudge,' agrees Chris. He has given up on the muffin. He has already eaten half, so what was that? Two hundred and twenty calories? If the gate was a good walk from Starbucks, he would work some of that off. Then nothing on the plane.

'We heard you've been to see Johnny's dad,' says Ron. 'You get anything?'

'Who did you hear that from?' asks Chris.

'Does it matter?' asks Ron.

Chris supposes it doesn't. 'He knows where Johnny is. But even Elizabeth wouldn't be able to get it out of him.'

The men nod.

'Joyce, maybe,' adds Chris, and they all nod again, smiling this time.

'You don't smile very often, Detective Chief Inspector,' says Ibrahim. 'If you don't mind me saying so? That's just an observation.'

'If I can make an observation of my own?' says Chris, realizing that Ibrahim is right and not wanting to think about it right here, right now. 'If Elizabeth knows someone who knows someone who knows someone, then why isn't she here? Why send Starsky and Hutch when Cagney and Lacey could have come and done the job?'

'Starsky and Hutch, very good,' says Ibrahim. 'I would be Hutch, more methodical.'

There is a boarding announcement, and the three men gather their belongings. Chris sees that Ron has a walking stick with him.

'First time I've seen you using a stick, Ron.'

Ron shrugs. 'If you've got a stick they let you on the plane first.'

'So where are Elizabeth and Joyce?' asks Chris. 'Or don't I want to know?'

'You don't want to know,' says Ibrahim.

'Oh great!' says Chris.

97

Candlelight is flickering in the chapel. Elizabeth and Matthew Mackie are inches apart, in the confessional.

'I see no point in dressing it up. And I don't want forgiveness, yours or the Lord's. I just want it on record, I want someone to bear witness, before I die and it's all dust. I know there are rules, even in the confessional, so you must do whatever you need to do with this information. I killed a man. This was a lifetime ago, and for what it's worth, he attacked me and I defended myself. But I killed him.'

'Go on.'

'I was living in digs in Fairhaven. I don't know if you're the type to judge me, but I had invited him home. Stupid, perhaps, but you were probably stupid back then too. That's where he attacked me. The details are grisly, but that's not an excuse. I fought back and I killed him. I was so frightened, I knew exactly how it looked. No one had seen what happened, so who would believe me? They were different times, you know that, you remember that?'

'I remember.'

'I wrapped the body in a curtain. I dragged it to my car. And that's where I left it while I thought what to do. This had all happened very quickly, that's what you have to understand. That morning I had woken like everybody else and now here I was. It seemed so absurd.'

'How did you kill him? Can I ask?'

'I shot him. In the leg. I hadn't thought he would die, but he bled and he bled and he bled. So much blood, so quickly.

Perhaps if he'd made a noise it would have been different. But he just whimpered. In shock, I suppose. And I watched him die, as close as I am to you now.'

Silence in the confessional. Silence in the chapel. Elizabeth has locked and bolted the door. No one is going to come in. And, of course, no one is going to get out. If that was the way this was going to end.

'Then . . . well, then I sat and I wept, because what else was there to do? I waited for the hand on my shoulder, for someone to take me away. It was so monstrous. But as I sat there and I sat there and I sat there, nothing much happened. No one knocked, no one screamed. There was no lightning. So I made myself a cup of tea. And the kettle still boiled and the steam rose, and I still had a body, wrapped in a curtain, in the boot of my car. It was a summer evening, so I turned on the wireless and I waited until dark. And then I drove here.'

'Here?'

'St Michael's, yes. I worked here for a time. I don't know if you knew that?'

'I didn't.'

'So I drove through the gates, and I switched off my lights as I drove up the hill. The Sisters would always sleep early. I kept driving, past St Michael's, past the hospital and up the lane to the Garden of Eternal Rest. You know it?'

'I know it.'

'Of course. And I took my spade, and I don't want these walls to crumble around us, but I chose a grave, of one of the Sisters. It was right at the top, where the earth was soft, and I dug. I dug until I hit the wood of a coffin. Then I walked back to my car. I tipped the body out of the boot and out of the curtain. I hadn't had to remove any clothes, because he was naked when he attacked me, you understand. And so I dragged the body up the path, through the headstones. It was hard going, I remember that. At one point I cursed, and then I apologized for cursing. I got the body up to the hole and tipped it into the grave. On top of the coffin. Then I took my spade again, I filled in the grave and I said a prayer. Then I walked back to my car, I put the spade in the boot and I drove home. That's as plain as I can tell it.'

'I understand.'

'And the knock at the door never came. Which, I suppose, is why I'm telling you all this now. Because no one knocked at my door and surely someone should have? In my dreams they knock every night. There have to be consequences. So, what do you think? Please, just be honest with me.'

'Be honest with you?' Matthew Mackie lets out a long, slow, sigh. 'I'll be honest. I don't believe a word of it, Elizabeth.'

'Not a word?' queries Elizabeth. 'There was a lot of detail, Father Mackie. The date, the gunshot to the leg, that very particular grave. What a peculiar thing for me to make up.'

'Elizabeth, you didn't work here in 1970.'

'Mmm. *You* did, though. I've seen the pictures.'

'I did, yes. I've sat here before. And I've sat where you are too.'

Elizabeth decides to start turning the screw.

'You sound like a man who wants to talk? Anything I've said triggered any memories? Convinced you I might just know something?'

Matthew Mackie gives a sad laugh. Elizabeth keeps at him.

'If you don't mind me saying, Father Mackie, you gave quite the little jump when I mentioned the Garden of Eternal Rest?'

'I do mind you saying that, Elizabeth, but I suppose I would like to talk. I've always wanted to. And since we're both here, why don't you play your real cards and see where that gets you?'

'You're sure?'

'I'm at home here, Elizabeth. In God's house. Let's talk awhile, shall we? Two old fools? You just start somewhere and I'll join in where I can.'

'Shall we start with Ian Ventham? Shall we talk awhile about him?'

'Ian Ventham?'

'Well, let's start there at least. We can always work backwards. I might start with a question, Father Mackie, if you don't mind?'

'Ask away. And call me Matthew, please.'

'Thank you, I will. So, first things first, Matthew. Why did you kill Ian Ventham?'

Joyce

I have been given express instructions, and Elizabeth has been gone too long. I wish Ron and Ibrahim were with me. I'm writing this down while I wait for Donna to arrive, which I hope will be very soon.

It's beginning to feel like this isn't all some jolly lark. An adventure where everything resolves itself and we all come back for more of the same next week. Elizabeth said two hours and she has now been gone two hours. A bit more than two hours. What had I been thinking when I agreed to this in the first place? There have been lots of things we had kept from Chris and Donna, but this is by far the most dangerous. I am not one of nature's liars. I can keep my secrets to myself, right up until the time someone asks me about them.

So I made the call to Donna and I told her where Elizabeth had gone and I told her she hadn't returned.

Donna was very angry, and I understand that. I told her I was sorry for lying and she said that Elizabeth had been the liar, I had simply been a coward. She then called me something which I wouldn't want to repeat, but which, I have to admit, was fair comment.

I am so keen for people to like me that I chose that moment to say how much I had always liked her eye shadow and to ask her where it was from. But she had already put the phone down.

Donna is on her way. I know she is very worried and so am I. I have always thought Elizabeth was indestructible. I hope I'm not wrong.

Elizabeth has made this walk many times before, along the curving path, through the avenue of trees and up to the Garden of Eternal Rest. She can feel Matthew Mackie's hand in the small of her back, guiding her forward.

It is always quiet, but she can never remember it being this quiet. Even the birds are silent. What do they know? It looks like rain. The sun is doing what it can to pierce the cloud cover, but she still shivers. There had been police crime tape here until a matter of days ago. A fragment has been left tied to a sapling and flaps its blue and white tail in the wind.

They pass Bernard's bench. It looks absurdly empty.

Bernard would have wanted to know what the two of them were doing, Elizabeth and the priest, walking slowly up the hill, faces set in stone. Bernard would have looked up from his newspaper, wished them a good day and kept them in sight for the rest of the walk. But Bernard has gone. Like so many before him. Time's up, that's it. No return. An empty bench on a silent hill.

They reach the gates and Matthew Mackie pushes them open. He ushers Elizabeth inside, hand still at her back, and she hears the hinges squeal shut behind them.

Matthew Mackie does not walk her all the way to the top right-hand corner of the Garden of Eternal Rest, to where the older graves hold their secrets. Instead, he takes his hand from her back, steps off the path and walks between two rows of newer headstones, cleaner and whiter. The route he always takes. Elizabeth follows him this time and they stop in front of a headstone. Elizabeth looks at the inscription.

Sister Margaret Anne

Margaret Farrell, 1948–1971

Elizabeth takes Matthew Mackie's hand and interlaces her fingers with his.

'It's a beautiful place, Elizabeth,' he says.

Elizabeth looks out, beyond the wall, to the rolling fields, the hills, the trees, the birds. It really is a beautiful place. The peace is broken by a commotion further down the hill, the sound of footsteps running. Elizabeth looks at her watch.

'That'll be my rescue party,' she says. 'I told them if I wasn't out in two hours, they were to break down the door. Come in shooting.'

'Two hours?' asks Mackie. 'Were we really two hours?'

Elizabeth nods. 'There was a great deal to say, Matthew.'

He nods too.

'You'll probably have to go through it again when this lot finally get up the hill.'

Elizabeth can see Chris Hudson now, fresh off the plane she guessed, running as best he can. She gives him a friendly wave and sees the relief on his face. Both that she is still alive and that he can now stop running.

100

There had been a schism in the Cryptic Crossword Club. Colin Clemence's weekly solving challenge had been won by Irene Dougherty for the third week running. Frank Carpenter had made an accusation of impropriety and the accusation had gained some momentum. The following day a profane crossword clue had been pinned to Colin Clemence's door, and, the moment he had solved it, all hell had broken loose.

The upshot of all this was that Cryptic Crossword Club had been postponed this week, to let all parties cool down, and so the Jigsaw Room was unexpectedly free. The Thursday Murder Club are in their regular seats and Chris and Donna have brought through a couple of stacking chairs from the lounge. Matthew Mackie sits in an armchair in the corner. The focus of attention.

'I was not long over from Ireland. I'd only left for adventure, really. In those days they could send you all sorts of places, Africa or Peru, but that's not for me, converting and what have you. So this place came up and I sailed over in 1967, sight unseen. It was what you see now, really. Very beautiful, very quiet, a hundred Sisters, but quiet enough you wouldn't know it. They'd pad about. There was peace, here, in the convent, but it was also a place of work, and the hospital was always busy. So I'd stroll about the place. I'd give sermons and take confessions. I'd smile when people were happy and I'd cry with them when they were sad, and that was my job. Twenty-five years old, without a thought in my head and without a bone of wisdom in my body. But I was a man, and that seemed to be the only thing that counted.'

'And you lived here?' Chris asks the question. Elizabeth had suggested that Chris and Donna take charge of any questioning, as she was aware she would probably need a few Brownie points by the time today was done.

'There was a gatehouse back then and I had rooms there. Nice enough, certainly nicer than the Sisters' rooms. No visitors, of course. That was the rule, at least.'

'A rule you followed?' asks Donna.

'At first, of course. I was eager to do well, eager to please, didn't want to be sent home. All of that.'

'But . . . things change?' asks Chris.

'Things change, yes. Things do change. I'd met Maggie very early on. She would clean the chapel. There were four of them cleaning.'

'But only one Maggie?' says Donna.

'Only one Maggie,' smiles Matthew Mackie. 'You know when you look into someone's eyes for the first time and the whole world breaks apart? And you just think, "Of course, of course, this is what I've been waiting for all this time"?' That was Maggie, all right. And at first it would be, "Good morning, Sister Margaret," and, "Good morning, Father," and so on, and she'd get on with her work and I'd get on with mine. Such as it was. But I would smile, and she would smile, and sooner or later it would be, "A fine morning, Sister Margaret, we're blessed with this sunshine," and "You're right, Father, how blessed we are." And then it would be, "What's that you're using on the floor, Sister Margaret?" and, "It's floor polish, Father." This wasn't immediate; this would be a few weeks in.'

Ron leans forward to say something, but Elizabeth shoots him a look and he doesn't.

'Anyway, let's say I had been there a month or so, when Maggie came in for confession. There we both were. And neither of us said so much as a word. We sat there and we sat there, our bodies inches apart, just the wood between them. I can hear her breathing and I can hear my heart thumping. It's trying to jump clean out of my chest. Don't ask me how long it was, I wouldn't have the first clue, but eventually I say, "You've probably work to be getting on with, Sister Margaret," and she says, "Thank you, Father," and that was that. That was the whole thing clinched and we both knew it. We both knew the confession was the sin and it wouldn't be the last.'

'Would you like a top-up?' asks Joyce, tipping her flask of tea. Mackie lifts his fingers to say no thank you.

'We would meet in private, which goes without saying, I know. I would see her every morning, but obviously we couldn't speak with others around. So I would take her confession and we would talk. And on those two wooden seats we fell in love. Maggie and Matthew. Matthew and Maggie. Speaking through a grille. Can you imagine a love so doomed?'

'And, forgive me, but just for the record, Maggie is Sister Margaret Anne?' asks Chris.

'She is.'

'Nineteen forty-eight to nineteen seventy-one?'

Matthew Mackie nods. 'I knew we had to get out. It would be easy enough. I'd find a job, I had all my exams, Maggie would nurse, we'd buy a place on the coast. We both grew up by the sea.'

'You were going to quit the priesthood?'

'Of course. Let me ask you. Why did you join the police, DCI Hudson?'

Chris thinks for a moment. 'Honestly? I'd finished my A

levels, my mum told me I had to get a job, and that night we were watching *Juliet Bravo*.'

'Well, isn't that just it?' says Matthew Mackie. 'In a different town, in a different country, I'd have been a pilot or a greengrocer, but for no good reason other than circumstance, I was a priest. In truth, I'm not a great believer and never have been. It was a job, and a roof, and a passage away from home.'

'And Maggie?' asks Donna. 'She was going to quit too?'

'It was harder for Maggie. She had the religion, it was still in her. But she would have. I think she would, one day. I think she'd be in Bexhill with me now, green eyes blazing. But it was hard for her. Mine was the risk of a young man and hers was the risk of a young woman, and that was a greater risk in those days, wasn't it?'

Joyce reaches over and takes his hand. 'What happened to your Maggie, Matthew?'

'She would visit me. At night, if you get the picture. In the gatehouse. It was easy enough to slip away after lights out. Maggie was no fool, she would have fitted in with you lot, no problem. Tuesdays and Fridays she could see me, those were the safest. I would light a candle for her, in an upstairs room. If there was no candle, it meant I'd been called away, or had guests, and she knew not to come. But if I lit the candle, she would always come. Sometimes straight away and sometimes I'd be waiting and pacing, but she would always come.'

Mackie clears his throat and furrows his brow. Joyce squeezes his hand.

'I haven't told this story in fifty years, and now twice in a day.' He gives a weak smile, then presses on. 'It was a Wednesday, the seventeenth of March, and I had lit the candle and I was waiting and pacing. There was one floorboard in the sitting room that, when you trod on it, would give three little squeaks. And I was back and forth and back and forth and it was "squeak, squeak, squeak", "squeak, squeak, squeak". And I would hear little sounds outside and think, "It's her," and stop and listen some more, but each time, just silence. The wait went on too long and I got worried. Had she been caught sneaking out? Sister Mary was fierce. I knew everything would be fine really, because at that age, everything always was. So I went upstairs, blew out the candle, came down, laced up my boots and headed up to the convent. To see what I could see.'

Matthew Mackie looks to the floor. An old man telling the story of a young man. Elizabeth catches Ron's eye and taps her breast pocket. Ron nods, then reaches into the inside pocket of his jacket and pulls out a small hip flask.

'I'm just going to have a little nip of whisky. I hope you'll keep me company, Matthew?'

Without waiting for an answer, Ron pours whisky into Matthew Mackie's mug. Mackie nods his thanks, eyes still to the floor.

'And what did you see, Father Mackie?' asks Donna.

'Well, the convent was dark, which was good. If she'd been caught sneaking out there'd be a light somewhere. Sister Mary's office, maybe. Or some midnight scrubbing in the chapel. But the only lights were in the infirmary. I just wanted to do a little tour, make sure Maggie was safe and sound. I could think of a hundred good reasons she hadn't come to me that night, but I wanted to ease my mind. I thought I would pick up some papers from the little office I had, off the back of the chapel. You know, if anyone saw me, I was just catching up on some work. I couldn't sleep. Maybe have a wander around. If I could have, I would have had a peek into the dorms, just to see her lying there.'

'This room we're in,' says Joyce, 'this was one of the dorms.'

Matthew Mackie looks around, nodding. His left hand gently pats the arm of his chair and he continues.

'I had the chapel key. You know that door, it's so heavy and the lock was so noisy, but I opened up as quietly as I could, then shut it behind me. The place was pitch black, but I knew my way around, of course. Near the altar I bumped into an old wooden chair that shouldn't have been there, and that clattered across the floor making a terrible racket. I thought I should light one of the lamps, by the altar, just to make me feel a little calmer, a little less like a thief. I lit the lamp and it was a very dim light, you wouldn't have seen it from outside, I don't think, not a bright light at all. Just a dim glow, really. And that's what I would say about the lamp.'

Matthew Mackie picks up his mug and takes a sip. He places the mug back down.

'So, that was the light, the one that I lit. And really all you could see was the altar, just shadows, but enough to see. Enough to see.'

Matthew Mackie rubs his mouth with the back of his hand.

'And there was Maggie. There's a beam above the altar. At least there was. You could hang incense or blessings. It was structural, I think, the beam, but we used it. Anyway, Maggie had looped a length of rope around the beam and hung herself. And not long before I'd got there. Perhaps she did it when I was tying my laces. Or perhaps it was when I blew out the candle? But she was dead, I could see that clearly. That's why she hadn't come.'

There is quiet in the Jigsaw Room. Matthew Mackie takes another sip from his mug.

'Thank you, Ron, for this.'

Ron makes a 'don't mention it' gesture with his hands.

'Was there a note, Father Mackie?' asks Chris.

'No note. I raised the alarm – quietly, of course; this wasn't a scene for all to see. I woke Sister Mary and she told me the story, really.'

'The story?' asks Donna.

Matthew Mackie nods to himself and Elizabeth takes the reins for a moment.

'Maggie was pregnant.'

'Bugger me!' says Ron. Matthew looks up, and continues his tale.

'She'd confided in someone, another of the young nuns. I never found out who. Maggie must have trusted her, whoever she was, but that was a mistake. The nun told Sister Mary and then, about six, after prayers, Sister Mary called Maggie to her room. Sister Mary didn't tell me what was said, but I can guess, and that was Maggie packed and on her way. She was to stay one last night and be collected in the morning, straight back to Ireland. I'd have lit my candle around seven, I suppose. Maggie went back to the dorms, maybe right here where we're sitting. She knew how to slip out, of course, so she slipped out. But that night she didn't come to me. She came to the chapel and she slipped a noose around her neck. And she took her life and the life of our child.'

Matthew Mackie looks up at the six other people in the room.

'And that's my story. So, you see, it wasn't fine, was it now? And nothing was ever fine again.'

'So how is she buried up on the hill?' asks Ron.

'That was the deal I made,' says Mackie. 'I was to leave, which I did, not a word to a soul. Back to Ireland. They found me a job in Kildare, at a teaching hospital. All records destroyed, new records made, the Church could do what it wanted back then. They wanted me out of the way, no trouble, no scandal. Not a soul but me and Sister Mary saw the body hanging. Whatever story they told in the end, I've no idea, but it wasn't the story of a priest and a baby and a suicide. And in return I asked that they allowed her to be buried in the Garden of Eternal Rest. She wouldn't have wanted to go home and St Michael's was the only other place Maggie knew.'

'And Sister Mary agreed?' asks Donna.

'It looked better for her too. There would have been questions otherwise. Me leaving suddenly, Maggie sent away for burial, people would have strung two and two together. So we made the deal, and the next morning the car that was coming to pick up Maggie, picked me up instead. We drove through the day to Holyhead. I went back home, and that's where I stayed until I heard that Sister Mary had died. She's up there in the graveyard too, you'll see the cherubs on her headstone. The day I heard the news I walked out of my job, I packed a case and I came back to stay. As near as I could to Maggie.'

'And that's why you did everything you could to stop the bodies being moved?'

'It was the only thing I could do for her. To find her some final peace. You've all been up there; you all understand. It was all I had, to say sorry and to say, "I still love you." Somewhere so beautiful, for the only love I ever knew, and for our baby boy. Or baby girl, but it's a boy I've always carried in my heart. I called him Patrick, which is silly, I know.'

'Without being indelicate, Father,' says Chris. 'I would say that gives you an extraordinary motive for killing Ian Ventham.'

'It's not a day for being delicate. But I didn't do it. Can

you imagine Maggie ever forgiving me if I'd killed Mr Ventham? You didn't know her, but she'd a temper on her when she wanted. Every step, I did what Maggie would have wanted, and what would have made Patrick proud. I fought in all the ways I knew how, but one day I'll see Maggie again, and I'll meet my little boy, and I intend to do that with a pure heart.'

101

'Do you like Pilates?' asks Ibrahim.

'I couldn't tell you,' says Gordon Playfair. 'What is it?'

His tour of Coopers Chase finished, Gordon Playfair is sitting with Ibrahim, Elizabeth and Joyce, on Ibrahim's balcony. Ibrahim has a brandy, Elizabeth has a G&T and Gordon has a beer. Ibrahim has them in the fridge for Ron, although Ron seems to be drinking wine these days.

Chris and Donna have returned to Fairhaven. Before they left, Chris had told them a little about Cyprus and about Johnny's connections. He was pretty sure they have identified their man.

Donna was clearly still angry at them, but she would get over it. The sun is setting and the day is winding down.

Matthew Mackie has gone home to Bexhill, and to the two candles he keeps lit at all times. Joyce has promised to come down and visit him. She loves Bexhill.

'It is the art of controlled movement,' says Ibrahim.

'Hmmm,' says Gordon Playfair, considering this. 'Is there darts?'

'There is snooker,' says Ibrahim.

Gordon nods. 'That's near enough.'

They look out over Coopers Chase. In the foreground is Larkin Court, curtained windows in Elizabeth's flat. Beyond that is Ruskin Court, Willows and the convent. Then those beautiful hills, rolling to the horizon.

'I could get used to this,' says Gordon. 'There seems to be a lot of drinking involved.'

'Always,' agrees Ibrahim.

The phone rings and Ibrahim gets up to answer it. He talks to Gordon Playfair over his shoulder as he goes.

'I think I've made Pilates sound too boring. It is very good for the core muscles and for flexibility. At any rate, it is every Tuesday.'

Gordon watches some of the residents pass by below and sips his beer. 'You know, I'm not kidding, but I wouldn't know if any of these women had been here back then. Who's to say? All those nuns. I wouldn't know, you know. You could have been one of the nuns, Joyce.'

Joyce laughs. 'It feels like I have been for the last couple of years. Not for the want of trying.'

Elizabeth has been thinking the same as Gordon Playfair. The nuns. Perhaps that was the route they would have to go down next? It was Thursday Murder Club tomorrow. Maybe that's where they should start. She feels the gin beginning to work its magic. Ibrahim returns from his call.

'That was Ron. He would like us to join him for a drink. It seems Jason has gifts for us all.'

102

'Me and Bobby had a little reunion drink in the Black Bridge, after we all left here. In Le Pont Noir, anyway.'

Jason Ritchie takes a swig from his bottle of beer. Ron has a beer too, as he always does if Jason is around. It is important to be a role model.

'You could tell we sort of trusted each other, you know? It felt like we'd both changed for the better over the years. Bobby wouldn't let on what he's up to these days, but he seemed happy, so fair play. I don't suppose anyone wants to tell me what he does now?'

Jason looks expectantly at Elizabeth and Joyce and they both shake their heads.

'Good,' says Jason. 'No one likes a grass. But we still couldn't be sure, you know? Couldn't be certain one of us hadn't done it. Couldn't be sure that it was Johnny, alive and kicking and back for revenge. So I made a call.'

'Ooh, who to?' asks Joyce.

Jason smiles. 'What does no one like, Joyce?'

Joyce nods her defeat. 'A grass, Jason.'

'Let's say I called a friend, someone we all trusted, but someone who Johnny would have trusted too, for different reasons. And he came down – no choice, really, if it's the two of us ringing – and we asked him straight out. Has Johnny been over? You seen him? Just between us and it never goes further?'

'And had he?' asks Elizabeth.

'He had,' says Jason. 'Johnny came over three days before

Tony was murdered and left the day he died. He blamed Tony for grassing him up all those years ago, so he said. Who knows with Johnny?'

Joyce nods sagely and Jason continues.

'Maybe he just felt the time was right. Put the record straight. Some people have long memories.'

'And you trust this source? And Peter trusts him?' asks Elizabeth.

'Peter?' asks Jason.

'Sorry, Bobby,' says Elizabeth. 'That's my age showing. You and Bobby both trust him?'

'With our lives,' Jason says. 'He's the straightest shooter you'll find. And he had his reasons to help Johnny. If your friends in the police don't work out who the guy is, then I promise I'll tell them. But I reckon they're bright enough to work it out.'

'Why did Johnny send you the photograph, Jason?' asks Ibrahim.

Jason shrugs. 'I think he just wanted us to know it was him. Showing off. Johnny was always like that. He could find my address pretty easy too, everyone knows me round here. Whatever Johnny did, he always had to tell you.'

'And did Johnny look the same? What was his new name?' asks Elizabeth.

Jason shakes his head. 'None of our business. We just asked what we asked. We just wanted to know for sure. That was enough.'

'Shame,' says Elizabeth.

'Well, if the police don't track him down, I'm sure you four will,' says Jason. 'And listen, me and Bobby, we just wanted to say thank you. For bringing us together and for helping us get to the truth. None of this would have happened without you. Let's be honest, without you I'd probably be banged up for this. So I got you all a little something, if that's OK?'

That's definitely OK. Jason unzips a sports bag at his feet and pulls out his gifts. He hands a wooden box to Ibrahim.

'Ibrahim, cigars; Cuban, of course.'

'That is the height of urbanity, Jason, thank you,' says Ibrahim.

The next gift goes to Ron.

'Dad, a bottle of wine, and a nice one too. You can stop pretending you still prefer beer in front of me.'

Ron takes his gift. 'Ooh, a drop of white. Thanks, Jase.'

Jason hands Joyce an envelope. 'Joyce, two tickets to come up and see *Celebrity Ice Dance* being filmed next month.'

Joyce beams.

'VIP, all that. I thought you could bring Joanna.'

'Not Joanna,' says Joyce. 'It's ITV, and she won't have that on.'

'And Elizabeth,' says Jason, with nothing in his hand but his phone. 'My gift to you is this.'

Jason holds up his phone and, very deliberately, swipes his finger across the screen and then puts it back in his pocket. He looks to Elizabeth, who isn't sure how to react.

'Well, thank you, Jason, although I was rather hoping for some Coco by Chanel,' says Elizabeth.

'I think I know what you'd like more than that though,' says Jason. 'To catch whoever killed Ian Ventham?'

'Is that in your gift, Jason?' asks Elizabeth.

'I reckon it is. Dad and I worked it out. Didn't we, Dad?'

Ron nods. 'We did, Son.'

'And, without wanting to sound cocky,' says Jason, 'I reckon that one little swipe will confirm it.'

103

Joyce

I wonder if you know about Tinder?

I had heard about it on the radio, heard jokes about it, but I had never seen it before Jason showed me.

If you know what it is then you can skip through this bit.

So Tinder is for dating. You post pictures of yourself on an app. An app is like the internet, but only on your phone. Jason showed me some of the pictures. The pictures of the men are usually on a mountain, or chopping down a tree. Sometimes the pictures have been cropped down the middle to cut out a former partner. Thanks to my picture in *Cut to the Chase* I know how they do that now.

The pictures of the women are often on boats, or with groups of other women, and you're not sure which one you're supposed to be looking at, so I suppose you take pot luck.

I asked him if people use it for 'one-night stands' and he says that, by and large, people use it for little else. Well, that's a bit of fun, you could say, but the whole thing felt unhappy to me. And the more smiles I saw, the unhappier I felt.

Perhaps that's just me. I met Gerry at a dance I had decided to go to at the last minute to spite my mother. If I hadn't gone then we never would have met. So I know that's an inefficient way of finding true love, but it worked for us. From the moment I laid my eyes on him, he didn't stand a chance. The lucky thing.

So, on Tinder you scroll through photographs of single people who live nearby. Or sometimes married people who live nearby. There is a picture of Ian Ventham on Tinder, in a karate suit, even though he's dead.

Every time you like the look of someone you swipe their picture to the right (or to the left, I can't remember). Meanwhile, somewhere nearby they are scrolling through pictures too and if they like the look of you they also swipe to the right (or left) and the two of you are a match.

Honestly, it breaks your heart to scroll through. It's reminded me of those photos of lost cats you see on lamp posts. It's all that hope, I think.

Anyway, when Jason swiped left or right he was confident of a match. And he was confident that match would be the killer. I trust his confidence on the first matter, I am more dubious about the second.

There is another dating app for gay men called Grindr. Perhaps it's for gay women too? I don't know, I didn't ask. Would they use the same one? That would be nice I think.

So Jason imagines he has solved the case. And perhaps he has, though I doubt it very much. He says it's obvious, but often, in these matters, the answer isn't obvious at all.

At least I have discovered that online dating is not for me. You can have too much choice in this world. And when everyone has too much choice, it is also much harder to get chosen. And we all want to be chosen.

Goodnight all. Goodnight Bernard. And goodnight Gerry, my love.

104

Having spent a very happy morning preparing, changing outfits and texting friends, Karen Playfair is now alone for a moment, sitting in an unfamiliar armchair. She is shaking her head, thinking about the optimism of this morning and then the reality of the lunch she's just had.

Karen has had some bad dates on Tinder. But this was the first time that someone had accused her of murder.

The match had pinged onto her phone yesterday evening. Jason Ritchie. Well, I don't mind if I do, she had thought. This is a cut above your average. He'd messaged, she'd messaged, and before you knew it, there they were in Le Pont Noir, ordering a crayfish salad with radicchio. A whirlwind romance in the offing.

Karen shifts in her armchair and idly picks up a magazine from a pile on the coffee table. It's more of a newsletter really. *Cut to the Chase.*

Back to the date. There had been some small talk, not too much, Karen knew very little about boxing and Jason knew very little about IT. Lightly sparkling water arrived, and that's when Jason mentioned Ian Ventham. Karen immediately realized that this wasn't a date, and felt foolish. But worse was to come.

She can hear Ron Ritchie in his kitchen now, he's opening a bottle of wine. Jason's nipped to the loo. She starts flicking through *Cut to the Chase*, but her mind keeps going back to Le Pont Noir.

All those questions Jason had fired at her. Hadn't she been

there the morning Ian Ventham was killed? Yes she had. Wasn't her dad refusing to sell his land to Ian Ventham? Well, yes he was, but, look, here comes our crayfish. Didn't she want her dad to sell the land, to take the money? That was her advice, yes, but it was her dad's business. Surely if he sold, then some of that money would be coming to her? Well, you could certainly assume that, Jason, but why not just come out with it and say what you want to say?

And so he did. It was almost funny, thinks Karen, reliving it. She hears the loo flush. What was it he had said?

Jason had leaned forward, very sure – certain, in fact. You see, the police had been looking for someone who was there in the 1970s and was still there now, and they had been right in a way. They'd found bones and maybe someone had been murdered, all those years ago. But forget the bones, they were missing the simplest trick in the book: greed. Ventham was in the way of Karen making her millions. Her dad wasn't budging, and so Ventham had to go. Jason mentioned some drugs you could only get on the dark web and didn't Karen work in IT? Wasn't that convenient? Jason had solved the case and felt sure he was about to get a confession. Honestly, some men!

He hadn't expected Karen to laugh in his face and explain that she was a database administrator for a secondary school, who could no more access the dark web than fly to the moon. That she had misheard Jason's mention of fentanyl as Ventolin and had wondered what he was on about. That she lived in one of the most beautiful places in England, and while she would certainly swap that for a million pounds, she would rather be there with her dad happy, than in some executive new-build in Hove, with her dad miserable. Jason looked like he was going to come back with a clever response but, when he tried, none came.

Jason walks back into the room and Karen remembers how crestfallen he had looked. He knew she was telling him the truth. That his little theory was wrong. He had apologized and offered to leave, but Karen had wondered if they shouldn't make the best out of a bad deal and enjoy the rest of their lunch. What if they ended up together? Wouldn't this be the greatest 'and how did you two meet?' story of all time? Which set them both laughing and set them both talking and turned the whole thing into a lovely, long, boozy lunch.

Which is why Jason had asked her back here for another drink and to do a bit of explaining to his dad.

Right on cue, Ron Ritchie walks in with a nice bottle of white and three glasses.

Jason sits down next to her and takes the glasses from his dad. He really has been charm itself since he accused her of murder.

Karen Playfair puts her copy of *Cut to the Chase* back down on the pile. And as she does, she sees the photograph. Halfway down the page. She picks the newsletter up again and stares closely. Just to make sure.

'You all right, Karen?' asks Jason, as Ron pours the wine.

'The police wanted someone who was here in the seventies, who's still here now?' asks Karen, slowly and carefully.

'That's what they reckon,' says Jason. 'Obviously, I thought they were wrong, but we saw how that played out.'

Jason laughs, but Karen does not. She looks at Ron and points to the face in the photograph. 'Someone who was here in the seventies and is still here now.'

Ron looks, but his brain won't take it in.

'You're sure?' he manages to ask.

'It was a long time ago, but I'm sure.'

Ron's mind is travelling at speed. This can't be. He's searching for reasons why this must be wrong, but can find none. He puts the wine down on the coffee table and picks up *Cut to the Chase*.

'I need to go and talk to Elizabeth.'

105

Steve's Gym looks a lot like its owner. A squat, brick building, intimidating at first sight, but with the door always open and everyone always welcome.

Chris and Donna step over the threshold.

After the excitement in the graveyard yesterday, Chris and Donna had gone back to Fairhaven and checked on Joe Kyprianou's hunch about the original investigation. No one from Kent Police had ventured into Northern Cyprus. There was no mention of Johnny's family connections. There had been no meaningful investigation at all. Chris had seen the names of the two officers who had been sent to Nicosia. No surprises. They'd have come back with tans and hangovers and nothing else.

He and Donna had then been having another look at all those passenger lists, coming in from Larnaca to Heathrow and Gatwick in the week before the murder. Nearly three thousand names, mainly men and mainly Cypriots.

Looking through list after list of names, Chris remembered something else that Joe Kyprianou had said. If Johnny had come to the UK, he would have needed help. A fellow Cypriot would be the obvious choice. Did Chris know any?

As the names flashed before his eyes, he realized that he did.

They had then gone back to the original Tony Curran file. There was no doubt that, in the early days, Steve Ercan had been in and around the Tony Curran crew. Mentioned in dispatches, but never anything to bring him in for. And whatever he had been doing for Tony hadn't lasted long. He'd opened Steve's Gym ages ago and it had gone from strength to strength, as it were. Chris and Donna both knew officers who trained there. Decent officers too, not fools. The place had a good reputation, and that wasn't the case with all gyms.

Even today the gym was packed. A Wednesday afternoon, an atmosphere of quiet hard work, no preening and posturing. Chris has been meaning to join a gym, but at the moment he was waiting for his knee to stop hurting. No point aggravating it. As soon as it has settled down, he'll join. Take the bull by the horns. He had felt a sharp, stabbing pain in his arm after the run up the hill to the graveyard to save Elizabeth. Almost certainly nothing, but even so.

Steve had been expecting them and met them by the door with a crushing handshake and a huge smile. They are now in his office. Steve is sitting on a yoga ball and chatting happily.

'Listen, you know as well as anyone, we don't have trouble here, and we don't cause trouble here,' says Steve Ercan.

'I do know that,' agrees Chris.

'The opposite, innit? You know that. We take people in, we turn them around. No secrets, you just ask whatever, yeah?'

'I was in Cyprus recently, Steve.'

Steve stops smiling and bounces a little. 'OK . . .'

'I didn't really know much about it before I went, I just thought holidays, you know.'

'It's very beautiful,' says Steve Ercan. 'Are we just gossiping or what?'

'What are you, Steve? Greek Cypriot or Turkish Cypriot?' asks Donna.

There's a beat, very short, but very telling to a good

copper. Steve shakes his head. 'I don't get involved in all that, not for me. People are people.'

'We're agreed on that, Steve,' says Chris. 'But even so. What side of the line were you? We can probably find out another way, but since we're here . . .'

'Turkish,' says Steve Ercan. 'Turkish Cypriot.' He shrugs; it's of no concern.

Chris nods his head and writes something down, just keeping Steve waiting for a moment. 'Like Johnny Gunduz?'

Steve Ercan tilts his head to the side and looks at Chris anew. 'That's a name from a long time ago.'

'Isn't it, though?' says Chris. 'Anyway, that's why I was in Cyprus. Trying to track him down.'

Steve Ercan smiles. 'He's long gone. Johnny was crazy. Good luck to the guy, but someone would have killed him by now. Guaranteed.'

'Well, that would explain why we can't find him. But, you know, Steve, I'm a police officer, and sometimes something doesn't seem right.'

'That's the job, innit?' says Steve Ercan.

'I want to suggest a story,' says Chris. 'Just something we've been thinking about. And you don't have to say anything. You don't have to react, just listen. Can you do that?'

'I've got to be honest with you, I've got a gym to run and I still don't know what you're doing here.'

Donna holds up a hand and concedes the point. 'You're right. But just hear us out. Two minutes and you'll be back out there.'

'Two minutes,' accepts Steve.

'You're one of the good guys, Steve,' says Chris. 'I know that, I don't hear a bad word about you.'

'I appreciate that, thank you,' says Steve.

'But here's what I worry has happened,' continues Chris.

337

'I think a few weeks ago you get a message, or maybe it's just a knock at the door, I don't know. Either way, it's Johnny Gunduz.'

'Nope,' says Steve Ercan, shaking his head.

'And Johnny needs help. He's back in town for something. Maybe he doesn't say what, maybe he does. And he turns to you, a little favour, for old times' sake. Somewhere to stay? Maybe just that. He doesn't want a record of whatever his new name is anywhere in town. And no one's to know?'

'I haven't seen Johnny Gunduz in twenty years. He's dead, or he's in prison, or he's in Turkey,' says Steve Ercan.

'Maybe,' says Chris. 'But Johnny could be trouble if he doesn't get what he wants. He could burn this place down pretty easily, I'd have thought. He's the type to do it too, so maybe you had no choice? And it's only a couple of days. He's just got to deliver a couple of things, then tie up a loose end. Then he'd be gone. How does that sound to you, Steve?'

Steve Ercan shrugs. 'Like a pretty dangerous story.'

'You've got a flat above the gym?' asks Donna.

Steve nods.

'Who stays there?'

'Anyone who needs to. Not everyone who comes in here is from a stable background. A kid tells me he can't go home, I don't ask the reason, I just hand him the keys. It's a safe place.'

'Who was staying in the flat on June the seventeenth?' asks Chris.

'No idea, I'm not the Hilton. Maybe some kid, maybe me.'

'Maybe no one?' asks Donna.

Steve Ercan shrugs.

'But you think maybe someone?' says Chris.

'Maybe.'

'Johnny is very well connected, Steve. In Cyprus?' says Chris.

'Not my world.'

'You've still got family over there?' asks Donna.

'Yes,' says Steve Ercan. 'Lot of family.'

'Steve, if Johnny Gunduz had come here and asked if he could stay,' begins Chris. 'If he put pressure on you of any kind. Or maybe he paid you? If you agreed. If he slept upstairs on June seventeenth. There's no way you would tell me?'

'No.'

'Consequences too great? Consequences for family in Cyprus?'

'I think that's been two minutes, if we're honest.'

'Agreed,' says Chris. 'Thank you, Steve.'

'Any time. You're always welcome here. I mean that. We could sort that gut out in a heartbeat.'

Chris smiles. 'It had crossed my mind, Steve. I don't suppose there's any way I could take a look upstairs before I go? Just see if Johnny left anything?'

Steve Ercan shakes his head. 'You could do me a favour though.'

'Go on,' says Chris.

'Could you stick this in Lost Property? Someone dropped it a couple of weeks ago and I've asked and asked, but I don't know who it belongs to.' Steve reaches into a drawer and pulls out a clear plastic wallet, filled with cash, and hands it to Chris. 'Five thousand euros. Some tourist must be kicking themselves.'

Chris looks at the cash, looks at Donna, then back at Steve. Would this have prints on it? Doubtful, but at least Steve is letting him know he's right. 'You don't want to keep it?'

Steve Ercan shakes his head. 'Nope, I know where it's been.'

Chris hands the envelope to Donna and she puts it in an evidence bag. They both know that Steve Ercan has just been very brave. Chris stands and shakes him by the hand.

'I know Tony Curran was a bastard,' says Steve Ercan. 'But he didn't deserve that.'

'Agreed,' says Chris. 'Up to a point. Anyway. Me and my gut will be back here soon.'

'Good lad.'

106

Elizabeth leaves Stephen sleeping. Bogdan will be around after work for a game of chess. She hopes they will both be there when she gets back. She'll need the company.

The knob has come off the bedroom wardrobe door and Elizabeth casually leaves it on the kitchen table. She bets that Bogdan won't be able to resist fixing it.

Ron had come to her with the photograph that Karen Playfair had seen. Karen would have been young at the time, but she was sure. Elizabeth had tried to piece it all together in her head. It seemed impossible at first. But the more she thought about it, it began to seem horribly true. She worked out the steps, one by one. Ibrahim had come back an hour ago, with the final piece of the jigsaw, so now is the time. The case is solved and only justice remains.

Elizabeth walks out into the cold evening air, not turning back now. The skies are getting darker earlier and the scarves are coming out of the wardrobes. Summer is still keeping a lid on autumn, but it won't be long. How many more autumns for Elizabeth? How many more years of slipping on a pair of comfortable boots and walking through the leaves? One day, spring will come without her. The daffodils will always come up by the lake, but you won't always be there to see them. So it goes; enjoy them while you can.

But right now, with the job at hand, Elizabeth feels an affinity with the late summer. The leaves clinging gamely on, the last hurrah of the heat, the odd trick still up its sleeve.

She sees Ron making his way over, grim-faced, but ready.

Hiding his limp, keeping his pain to himself. What a fine friend Ron is, she thinks. What a heart he has. Long may it go on beating.

As she turns the corner she sees Ibrahim waiting by the door, folder in hand. The last piece of the jigsaw. How handsome he looks, dressed for the occasion, ready to do whatever's necessary. That Ibrahim might ever die seems absurd to Elizabeth. He will certainly be the last of them. The last oak in the forest, standing still and true, as the aeroplanes whizz overhead.

How to begin? thinks Elizabeth. How to even begin?

107

Chris gets the nod. An international warrant has been issued for the arrest of Johnny Gunduz for questioning over the murder of Tony Curran. A good end to the day. The euros Steve Ercan gave them had no prints, but had been taken out at a bureau de change in Northern Cyprus three days before Tony Curran's murder. He'd given Joe Kyprianou the address of the bureau, in case of CCTV, but Joe had taken one look at the address and laughed. No chance.

Would the Cypriot authorities ever find him? Who knew? You'd think so, but after the initial rush, how hard is anyone really going to look? Maybe Chris will even get another trip over to Cyprus. That would be nice. Either way, he's done all he can and it's up to the Cypriots now, if they fancy their chances. Whatever happens, Chris will look good.

It is a cause for celebration, but Chris has had too many nights in the pub with too many coppers over the years. What he'd really wanted was a curry at home, get Donna round, watch something on TV, bottle of wine and send her home at ten. Maybe talk a bit about Ventham. What have they missed?

Chris had a worrying thought earlier. A stupid one, really. Only, hadn't the convent had a hospital, all those years ago? Wasn't Joyce an ex-nurse? Run the name Joyce Meadowcroft through the computer? Could he talk to Donna about it?

But Donna had a mystery date tonight. Casually dropped it into the conversation on the way back from Steve's Gym. So, he would go home and have a night in by himself, with a curry. Chris knew that was where this was heading. The darts was on Sky.

Chris wondered whether this was a tragic plan, or simply the sort of plan that people would think was tragic. Was he a content man, doing the things he liked alone? Or was he a lonely man, making the best out of what he had? Alone, or lonely? This question cropped up so often these days, Chris could no longer be confident of his answer. Though if he were a betting man, his money would be on lonely.

Where was his date?

If he leaves right now, it will be rush hour. So Chris closes the Tony Curran file and opens up the Ventham file. If he can solve one murder, he can surely solve two more? What has he missed? Who has he missed?

108

They make their way along the corridor, Elizabeth and Ibrahim, with Ron carrying a couple of extra chairs. A job to do.

Behind them, double doors swing open and Joyce hurries after her friends.

'Sorry I'm late. The beeper was going off on my oven and I couldn't work out why.'

'Sometimes it can be a very brief power outage. Then the clock tries to reset itself,' says Ibrahim.

Joyce nods. Without thinking, she takes Ibrahim's hand. Ahead of them Elizabeth has taken Ron's hand too and they walk in silence until they reach the door.

Despite the circumstances, Elizabeth knocks. As she always does.

She opens the door and there he is. The man Karen Playfair had recognized after all those years. His picture next to Ron, holding the fox that he had saved.

The same old book is open at the same old page. He looks up and seems unsurprised to see the four of them.

'Ah, the gang's all here.'

'The gang's all here, John,' confirms Elizabeth. 'Do you mind if we sit?'

John gestures for them to do exactly that. He puts down his book and pinches the bridge of his nose. Ron looks over at Penny, comatose on the bed. Nothing left of her, really, he thinks. Gone. Why hasn't he been to see her? Why had it taken this?

'How shall we do this, John?' asks Elizabeth.

'Up to you, Elizabeth,' replies John. 'I've been waiting for that knock since the moment I did it. Just took each day as a bonus. I do wish you'd taken a bit longer, though. What was it, in the end?'

'Karen Playfair recognized you,' said Ibrahim.

John nods and smiles to himself. 'Did she? Little Karen. Goodness!'

'You put her dog to sleep when she was six, John,' says Joyce. 'She says she would never forget your kind eyes.'

Elizabeth is in her customary seat at the foot of Penny's bed. 'Do you want to start, John? Or shall we?'

'Shall I?' says John, and shuts his eyes. 'I've been over it so many times in my head.'

'Who is in the grave, John? Whose bones are they?'

Eyes still shut, John looks up to the heavens, lets out a sigh from the ages and begins.

'It would have been the early seventies, maybe ten miles from here. Greyscott, one of the sheep farms. There used to be any number around here, you know? Long time ago now. I think I'd started in 1967, Penny would remember for sure, but around then anyway. The farmer was an old boy called Matheson and I knew him well enough by that point. I'd go out there every now and again. You know, something would happen. This time around, he'd had a mare just given birth. The foal had died and the mare was in distress. She was in such pain, screaming, and he hadn't wanted to shoot her, which I understood, so I gave her an injection and that was that. Done it many times, before and since. Some farmers will just shoot them, some vets will too, but not Matheson and not me. Anyway, he made me a cup of tea and we got chatting. I was always in a hurry, but I think he was a very lonely man. There was no family, no one to help him on the farm, money running out, so I think he welcomed the company. It was very bleak up there, that's how it seemed to me that day. I had to be on my way, but he didn't want me to leave. You will judge me, I know, or perhaps you won't, but suddenly something seemed clear as day to me. He was in distress, great distress. If Matheson had been an animal he would have been screaming. You have to believe that. And so I reached into my bag and I offered him a flu shot, you know, see him through the winter and all that. He was glad of the offer. He rolled up his sleeve and I gave him his shot. The same shot I'd just given the mare. And that was the end of the screaming and the end of the pain.'

'You put him out of his misery, John?' asks Joyce.

'That's how I saw it. Then and now. If I'd had my wits about me I would have conjured up some clever little con coction, something that wouldn't show up in a post-mortem, and left him there to be found by the postman, or the milk van, or whoever knocked there next. But it was spur of the moment, so there he was, pumped full of pentobarbital and I couldn't take the risk that someone might look into it.'

'So you had to bury him? This Matheson?' asks Elizabeth.

'Quite so. I would have buried him there and then, but you'll remember they were buying up farmland left, right and centre those days, building houses everywhere, and I thought it'd be just my luck to bury him, then have him dug up by builders a month later. And that's when I remembered.'

'The graveyard,' says Ron.

'It was perfect. I knew it from visiting Gordon Playfair. It wasn't on farmland, and no one was going to be buying a convent, for heaven's sake. I knew how quiet it was, I knew no one visited. So I drove up one night, a couple of days later, lights off. Picked up my spade and did the deed. And that was that, until one day, forty years later, I saw an advert for this place.'

'And here we all are,' says Elizabeth.

'And here we all are. I persuaded Penny it would be a lovely place to retire to, and I wasn't wrong there. I just wanted to keep an eye on things. You think they won't dig up a graveyard, but you never know these days, and I wanted to be close by in case the worst happened.'

'Which it did, John,' says Joyce.

'I couldn't dig the body back up; too old, too feeble. And I couldn't risk the grave being dug up and the body being found. So in the panic of that morning, in all the chaos while we were holding him back, I slid a syringe into Ventham's arm and seconds later he was dead. Which is unforgivable in every way. Unforgivable. And from that moment I've been waiting for you to come, and I've been waiting to face the consequences of what I've done.'

'How did you magically have a syringe filled with fentanyl, John?' asks Elizabeth.

John smiles. 'I've had it for a long time. In case I ever needed it here. If they ever wanted to move Penny.'

John looks at Elizabeth, through clear eyes.

'I'm glad it was you at least, Elizabeth and not the police. I'm glad you solved it. I knew you would.'

'I'm glad too, John,' says Elizabeth. 'And thank you for telling your story. You know we will have to tell the police?'

'I know.'

'We don't need to do it this very second though. While it's just us, can I clarify two little things?'

'Of course. It was a long time ago, but I'll help if I can.'

'I think you and I agree, John, that Penny probably doesn't hear what goes on in this room? Whatever silly nonsense we say to her? That we're kidding ourselves, really?'

John nods.

'But I think we're also agreed that maybe she can? Just maybe? Maybe she hears it all?'

'Maybe,' agrees John.

'In which case, John, perhaps she can hear us now?'

'Perhaps.'

'Even if there's the slightest chance, John. The slightest chance that Penny heard what you just said. Why would you do that to her? Why put her through that?'

'Well, I . . .'

'You wouldn't, John, that's the truth. That would have been torture,' says Elizabeth.

Ibrahim sits forward. 'John, you said that killing Ian Ventham was unforgivable. And I believe, truly, that you mean that. It was an act beyond your imagining. And yet you ask us to believe that you committed that act simply to save your own skin? That doesn't ring true, I'm afraid. You committed an act you knew to be unforgivable. And I'm afraid we see only one reason for that.'

'Love, John,' says Joyce. 'Always love.'

John looks at the four of them. Each implacable.

'I sent Ibrahim to have a look at one of Penny's files this morning,' says Elizabeth. 'Ibrahim?'

Ibrahim takes a small manila file from his shopping bag and hands it to Elizabeth. She opens the file on her lap.

'Shall we get to the truth?'

Chris is alone. The remains of a takeaway curry are in front of him. Michael van Gerwen dispatched Peter Wright by six sets to love, finishing the darts early. So now there is nothing on TV and no one to watch it with. He is wondering whether he should go to the twenty-four-hour garage for some crisps. Just to take the edge off.

His phone buzzes. That's something, at least. It's Donna.

> Might watch Jason Ritchie's Famous Family Trees on catch-up. You fancy?

Chris looks at his watch, it's nearly ten. Why not? Another buzz.

> And wear your dark blue shirt, please. The one with the buttons.

Chris is used to Donna by now, so does as he is told. As always, he gets changed without looking in a mirror, because who wants to see that? He texts back.

> Yes ma'am, anything for a bit of Jason Ritchie. On my way.

Donna's date had clearly not been a roaring success.

'She keeps them in storage, John,' says Elizabeth, holding the manila file. 'I don't know if you've ever been? It's files of all her old cases. You're not supposed to keep them, but you know Penny. She made copies of everything, just in case.'

'In case they might help catch a killer many years later,' says Joyce.

'Anyway, John, after Karen Playfair recognized you, it got me thinking, and I just needed one final thing checking in one of the files.'

'Would you like some water, John?' asks Joyce.

John shakes his head. His eyes are on Elizabeth as she begins to read from the file.

'There was a case in Rye, in 1973. Penny must have been very junior. I can't imagine Penny ever having been junior, but you must remember it very clearly. Probably seems like yesterday. The case concerned a girl named Annie Madeley. You remember Annie Madeley, Penny?'

Elizabeth looks over to where her friend is lying. Listening? Not listening?

'Stabbed during a burglary and bled to death in the arms of her boyfriend. Around came the police, including Penny, that's in the file. Found broken glass on the floor, where our burglar had got in, but nothing stolen. The burglar had been surprised by Annie Madeley, panicked, picked up a kitchen knife, stabbed her and fled. That's the official account if you want to read it. Case closed. But Ron was the first to sniff it out; he didn't like it one bit.'

'It stunk, Johnny,' says Ron. 'A burglar in the middle of the day, on a busy estate? With people at home? You might burgle on a Sunday morning, while everyone is at church, but not Sunday afternoon, not the done thing.'

Elizabeth looks over to her friend. 'You must have thought that too, Penny? You must have known the boyfriend had stabbed her, waited for her to die, then called the police.'

She dabs Penny's dry lips.

'We started looking into it months ago, John. The Thursday Murder Club. No Penny, but we carried on. I was surprised we'd never looked at the case before, surprised Penny had never brought it in. We started looking at it, John, seeing if the police had got it wrong all those years ago. I read the report on the knife wound and it didn't seem right to me, so I asked Joyce about it. In fact, it might have been the first thing I ever asked you, Joyce?'

'It was,' remembers Joyce.

'I described the wound and asked her how long it would take to die, and she said around forty-five minutes or so, which didn't fit the boyfriend's account at all. He had chased the burglar – no one saw this, John – rushed back to the kitchen, held Annie Madeley in his arms and rang the police immediately. I then asked Joyce if someone with any medical training could have saved her and what did you say, Joyce?'

'I was certain, it would have been easy. You'll know that too, John, with your training.'

'Now the boyfriend had been a soldier, John, invalided out a few years before. So he could have saved her, no question. But that's not the way the investigation went. I'd like to say that things were different in these cases back then, but no doubt he'd get away with it today too. They searched for the burglar, but with no luck. Poor Annie Madeley was buried and the world kept turning. The boyfriend disappeared shortly afterwards, in the middle of the night, with rent owing and we come to the end of the file.'

'So we were looking into all of this, but then events took over, of course,' says Ibrahim. 'Mr Curran, Mr Ventham, the body in the graveyard. We put the case to one side while we had a real murder right in front of us.'

'But we all know we don't come to the end of the story, don't we, John?' says Ron.

Elizabeth taps the manila file.

'And so I sent Ibrahim off to look at the file, with one question. Can you guess what it was, John?'

John stares at her. Elizabeth looks at Penny.

'Penny, if you can hear, I bet you know the question. Peter Mercer, that was the name of the boyfriend, Peter Mercer. I asked Ibrahim to find out why Peter Mercer had been invalided from the army. And if you hadn't guessed the question, I bet you can guess the answer, John. Have a go, it's all too late anyway.'

John buries his head in his hands, drags them down his face and looks up. 'I assume, Elizabeth, it was a gunshot wound to the lower leg?'

'It was just that, John.'

Elizabeth pulls her chair nearer to Penny, takes her hand and speaks to her quietly and directly. 'Nearly fifty years ago Peter Mercer murdered his girlfriend, then vanished into thin air. And everyone thought he'd got away with it. But it's really not all that easy to get away with murder, is it, Penny? Sometimes justice is waiting just around the corner, as it was for Peter Mercer one dark night when you paid him a visit. And sometimes justice waits fifty years and sits beside a hospital bed holding the hand of a friend. Had you just seen one too many of these cases, Penny? Tired of it? And tired of no one listening?'

'When did she tell you, John?' asks Joyce.

John starts to cry.

'When she was first ill?'

John nods slowly. 'She didn't mean to tell me. You remember how she was, Elizabeth? The mini-strokes?'

'Yes,' remembers Elizabeth. They were very gentle at first. Nothing too alarming, unless you knew what they were. But poor John had known exactly what they were.

'She would say all sorts of things. See all sorts of things. Plenty of make-believe, and then the present sort of disappeared and her mind would go further and further back. Kept spooling back until it found something familiar I suppose. Just looking for something that made sense, because the world around her had stopped making sense. So she'd tell me stories, sometimes from her childhood, sometimes from when we first met.'

'And sometimes from her early days in the police?' prompts Elizabeth.

'All things I'd heard before at first. Things I remember from the time, old bosses, little scams they'd pull, fiddling expenses, pub instead of court, the sorts of things we'd always laughed about. I knew she was adrift and I wanted to hold on to her as long as I could. Do you understand?'

'We all do, John,' says Ron. And they do.

'So I would keep her talking. The same stories over and over again sometimes. One reminding her of another, reminding her of another, reminding her of the first one again, and round we'd go. But then . . .'

John pauses and looks at his wife.

'You say you don't really think Penny can hear you, John?' says Elizabeth.

John shakes his head, slowly. 'No.'

'And yet every day, you come here. You sit with her. You talk to her.'

'What else is there for me to do, Elizabeth?'

Elizabeth understands. 'So, she was telling you stories. Stories you knew. And then one day . . . ?'

'Yes, and then one day it was stories I didn't know.'

'Secrets,' says Ron.

'Secrets. Nothing awful, only little things. She'd taken money once. A bribe. Everyone else had taken it and she felt she'd had to. She told me that as if she had told me many times before, but she hadn't. We all have secrets, don't we?'

'We do, John,' agrees Elizabeth.

'She'd forgotten what was a funny story and what was a secret. But there must have been something still working, a final lock on a final gate. The last thing to give.'

'The worst secret of all?'

John nods. 'By God she held on to it. She was already in here. You remember when they moved her in?'

Elizabeth remembers. Penny had gone by this time. Conversations were snippets, incoherent, sometimes angry. When would Stephen come in here? She needed to get back to him. Just get this done and go home and kiss her beautiful husband.

'She didn't even recognize me by then. Well, she recognized me, but she couldn't place me. I came in one morning. About two months ago, you know, and she was sitting up. It was the last time I remember her sitting up. And she saw me, and she knew me. She asked me what we were going to do and I didn't understand the question, so I asked her, "Do about what?"'

Elizabeth nods.

'And she started to tell me, and she was very matter of fact. As if there was something in the loft and she needed me to get it down. Nothing more than that. Nothing more than that. You know I couldn't let people find out what she'd done, Elizabeth? You know that? I had to try something.'

Elizabeth nods.

'We'd picnicked up on the hill a few times,' John continues. 'It really was very beautiful. I'd always wondered why we stopped.'

They sit in silence. Broken only by the quiet electronic beeps by Penny's bedside. All that remained of her, like a lighthouse blinking far out to sea.

Elizabeth gently breaks the silence. 'Here's what I think we should do, John. I'm going to get the others to take you home. It's late, have a sleep in your own bed. If you have letters to write, then write them. I'll come with the police in the morning. I know you'll be there. We'll step outside for a moment so you can say goodbye to Penny.'

The four friends step outside and Elizabeth watches through the clear border of the frosted window in Penny's door as John holds his wife in his arms. She looks away.

'You'll see John back safely, won't you? If I stay with Penny for a moment?' she asks the others, and gets nods in return. She opens the door again. John is putting on his coat.

'Time to go, John.'

111

The lights in Donna's flat are low and Stevie Wonder is working his magic from the speakers. Chris is happy and relaxed, shoes off, feet up. Donna pours him a glass of wine.

'Thanks, Donna.'

'Pleasure. Nice shirt by the way.'

'Why thank you. It's just something I threw on.'

Chris smiles at Donna and Donna smiles back. Donna can sense what is about to happen and it makes her very happy.

'Mum?' inquires Donna, holding the bottle towards her mother.

'Thank you, darling, I will.'

Donna then pours a glass of wine for her mother, currently sitting beside Chris on the sofa.

'Honestly, you could be her sister, Patrice,' says Chris. 'And I'm not just saying that because Donna is ageing so badly.'

Donna mimes throwing up while Patrice laughs.

'Madonna told me you were charming.'

Chris puts down his wine, a look of delight creeping onto his face. 'Sorry? Who told you I was charming?'

'Madonna,' she tilts her head towards her daughter.

Chris looks at Donna. 'Your full name is Madonna?'

'If you ever call me that I will taser you,' says Donna.

'It would be worth it,' says Chris. 'Patrice, I think I love you.'

Donna rolls her eyes and picks up the remote. 'Shall we watch Jason Ritchie?'

'Sure, sure,' says Chris, distracted. 'So what do you do for a living, Patrice?'

'I teach. Primary,' says Patrice.

'Do you?' says Chris. Teacher, sings in a choir, loves dogs, that's his fantasy checklist.

Donna looks Chris straight in the eye. 'And she sings in the choir on a Sunday.'

Chris refuses to hold Donna's gaze and turns back to Patrice.

'This is going to sound like a ridiculous question, Patrice, but do you like dogs?'

Patrice takes a sip of her wine. 'Allergic, I'm afraid.'

Chris nods, and sips, then gives his glass an almost imperceptible raise towards Donna. Two out of three ain't bad. He is glad he is wearing his blue shirt with the buttons.

'What happened to your date?' Chris asks Donna.

'I just said I had a date. I didn't say it was my date,' replies Donna.

Donna's phone buzzes. She looks at the screen.

'It's Elizabeth. She wonders if we're free tomorrow morning? Nothing urgent.'

'Solved the case no doubt.'

Donna laughs. She hopes everything is OK with her friend.

112

Penny's bedside lamp is turned as low as it can go, just enough light for two old friends with familiar faces. Elizabeth has Penny's hand in hers.

'So, did anyone get away with anything, darling? Tony Curran didn't, did he? Someone did for him. Johnny, so everyone seems to think, though I have a theory about that I must discuss with Joyce. No loss there, anyway. And Ventham? Well, you know John has to pay for that. I'll take the police there in the morning and they'll find his body, we both know that. The moment he's home, a little nightcap and that's that. He knows enough to make it peaceful at least, doesn't he?'

Elizabeth strokes Penny's hair.

'And what about you, darling? You clever girl. Did you get away with it? I know why you did what you did, Penny; I see the choice you made, to deliver your own justice. I don't agree with it, but I see it. I wasn't there. I wasn't facing what you were facing. But did you get away with it?'

Elizabeth places Penny's hand back on the bed and stands.

'It all rather depends, doesn't it? On whether you can hear me or not? If you can hear, Penny, you'll know that the man you love has just walked off into the night to die. All because he wanted to protect you. And that all comes down to the choice you made all those years ago. And I think that's punishment enough, Penny.'

Elizabeth starts to put on her coat.

'And if you can't hear me, then you got away with it, dear. Bravo!'

Elizabeth's coat is now on and she places a hand on her friend's cheek.

'I know what John did while he was holding you, Penny, I saw the syringe. So I know you're off too, and that this is goodbye. Darling, I haven't really spoken about Stephen recently. He's not at all well and I'm trying my best, but I'm losing him bit by bit. So I have my secrets too.'

She kisses Penny's cheek.

'Dear God I will miss you, you fool. Sweet dreams, darling. What a chase!'

Elizabeth leaves Willows and walks out into the darkness. A quiet, cloudless night. A night so dark you think you might never see morning again.

113

Chris takes a taxi home and walks the long walk up to his flat. Is it the booze, or is he a little lighter on his feet?

He opens his front door and surveys the scene. A few things would need to be tidied away for sure, take the recycling out, maybe buy some cushions and a candle? The bathroom door still stuck whenever it was opened, but nothing that a bit of sandpaper and hard work wouldn't fix. Go to Tesco's, buy some fruit, put it in a bowl on the dining table. Of course, also buy a fruit bowl. Clean the bedding. Replace toothbrush. Buy towels?

That should do it. Just enough to convince Patrice that he was a regular human being and not a man who had given up on life. It didn't take much. Then he could send her a text, invite her round for dinner while she was in Fairhaven.

Flowers? Why not? Go crazy.

Chris switches on his computer and waits for his emails to load. A bad habit, checking in before bedtime. Delaying bedtime, usually. Three new emails, nothing that looked like it would detain him. One of his sergeants was doing a triathlon, a cry for help, for which he expected to be sponsored. An invitation to the Kent Police Community Awards night, bring a guest. Would that count as a date? Probably not; he would check with Donna. Then an email from an account Chris didn't recognize. Didn't happen often; Chris kept his personal account as private as one could these days. From 'KypriosLegal', subject, 'Strictly Private and Confidential'.

From Cyprus? Had they found Johnny? Were solicitors warning the police off? But why would it come to his personal account? No one in Cyprus had this email address.

Chris clicks on the email.

Dear Sir,

Our client, Mr Demir Gunduz, has asked us to forward this correspondence to you. Please be advised that all and any information included in this correspondence is to be treated as confidential. Please direct any reply to our offices.

Your faithful servant,
Gregory Ioannidis
Kyprios Associates

Demir Gunduz? Demir who had laughed when Chris had handed him his card? Well, wasn't this turning into quite the evening? Chris clicks on the attachment.

Mr Hudson,

You say my son came back to Cyprus in 2000. You have proof of this. I need to tell you that I did not see him then and have not seen him since. Not once. I have not seen my son, I have had no letter or no call from my son.

Mr Hudson, I am old, you have seen this with your own eyes. As you look for Johnny, you must know that I too look for him.

I will never speak to a police officer, you understand, but I ask for help today. If you can find Johnny, if you have information of any type, there is great, great reward for you. I fear Johnny is dead.

He is my son and I want to see him before I die, or to know this is impossible and be allowed to grieve. I hope you accept this with compassion. I am asking you please.

Greetings,
Demir Gunduz

Chris reads it through a couple more times. Nice try, Demir. Is he expecting Chris to share this with the Cypriot police? With Joe Kyprianou? Surely he is. Does this mean the Cypriot police are getting close to Johnny? One last effort to throw them off the scent?

Or is it what it says it is? A plea from an old man to find his missing son. In his younger days, Chris might have believed this. But he's seen too much, heard too much from people saving their own skins. Any story. And he knows where Johnny Gunduz was on 17 June.

Johnny is not dead. Johnny went home, with Tony Curran's money. He changed his name, got a nose job and whatever else his dad's money would pay for and has been living it up ever since. Johnny is sunning himself somewhere in Cyprus, happy with his lot. Without an enemy in the world, now that Tony Curran has been dealt with.

Demir Gunduz will not be getting a reply.

Chris shuts down his computer. He really wishes people would stop doing triathlons.

114

Elizabeth is out late, but Bogdan and Stephen have not noticed.

Bogdan has his lower lip jutting out to one side as he thinks. He taps on the table, thinking about the right move. He stares across at Stephen, then back down at the board. How does this man play like this? If Bogdan isn't very, very careful he is going to lose. And Bogdan doesn't remember the last time he lost.

'Bogdan, can I ask you a question?' says Stephen.

'Always,' says Bogdan. 'We are friends.'

'It won't put you off? I have you in a bind here. I wonder if you need to concentrate?'

'Stephen, we play, we talk. They are both special to me.' Bogdan moves his bishop. He looks up at Stephen, who is surprised at the move, but not yet concerned.

'Thank you, Bogdan, they are both special to me too.'

'So, ask me a good question.'

'It's only this. Well, firstly, what was the name of the chap?' Stephen attacks Bogdan's bishop, but senses he is being lured into something.

'Which chap, Stephen?' asks Bogdan, looking down at the board, grateful for the chink of light which has just appeared.

'The first one who was killed? The builder?'

'Tony,' says Bogdan. 'Tony Curran.'

'That's the one,' says Stephen. He rubs his chin as Bogdan protects his bishop and opens the board at the same time.

'What's the question?' asks Bogdan.

'Well, it's just this, and forgive me if I'm speaking out of turn, but from everything I hear about it, I think you killed him. Elizabeth talks to me, you know.' Stephen moves a pawn, but can see there's nothing much doing.

Bogdan looks around the room for a moment, then back at Stephen.

'Sure, I killed him. It's a secret though, only one other person knows.'

'Oh mum's the word, old boy, no one will hear it from me. But I don't really understand why. Not money, surely, that doesn't seem your style at all?'

'No, not money. You got to be careful with money. Don't let it be in charge.' Bogdan advances a knight and Stephen sees what he's up to at last. Delightful, really.

'What was it then?'

'It was simple, honestly. I had a friend, my best friend when I arrived in England and he drove a taxi. One day he saw Tony do something he shouldn't.'

'What did he see?' Stephen surprises Bogdan by moving his rook. Bogdan smiles a little. He loves this crafty old man.

'He saw Tony shoot a boy, a young boy from London. About something, I don't know, I never found out. A drug thing.'

'So Tony killed your friend?'

'Well, the taxi company is run by a man named Johnny. They called him Turkish Johnny, but he was Cypriot. Johnny and Tony were in business, but Tony was the boss.' Bogdan stares down at the board, taking his time.

'So Johnny killed your friend?'

'Johnny killed my friend, but Tony told him to. I don't care, is same thing.'

'It is. We're agreed there. And whatever happened to Johnny?'

Bogdan feels the need to withdraw his knight. A waste of a move, but never mind, these things happen.

'I kill him too. Straight away, pretty much.'

Stephen nods. He stares at the board in silence for a while. Bogdan thinks he may have lost him, but he has learned you have to be patient with Stephen sometimes. And sure enough.

'What was your friend's name?' Stephen keeps looking at the board, trying to conjure something from nothing.

'Kaz. Kazimir,' says Bogdan. 'Johnny, he ask Kaz to drive him to the woods, he has to bury something and he needs help. They walk into the woods, they dig and dig, for whatever Johnny needs to bury. He was a hard worker, Kaz, and nice, you would like him very much. So then Johnny shoot Kaz, pop, one shot and buries him in the hole.'

Stephen further advances his pawn. Bogdan glances up at him and gives him a little nod and a smile. He scrunches his nose for a moment as he looks back at the board.

'I thought Kaz had run away, maybe home, keep his head down, OK? But Johnny is stupid, not like Tony, and he speaks with his friends and says he shot this guy in the woods and the guy did all the digging, and isn't this funny? And I hear about this.'

'So you go into action?' asks Stephen.

Bogdan nods, and wonders about his bishop and whether Stephen might just have something up his sleeve. 'I tell Johnny I need to speak to him. Don't tell Tony, don't tell the others. I say a friend works in Newhaven, at the port, and there might be some money for him, and is he interested? And he's interested, so we meet at the port, about two a.m.'

'And there's no security?'

'There's security, but the security man is a cousin of my friend, Steve Ercan. A good guy. He really does work at the port. Is easier to lie with the truth. So Steve comes along too.

Steve knew Kaz. Steve liked Kaz like I did. So we walk across to harbour steps and get in a little boat and Johnny, he is stupid, he just think about money, and we chug, chug, chug, and it's choppy and I'm telling him the plan and we use this boat to smuggle people and Steve's cousin will turn a blind eye and think of all the money. Then I take out a gun and I tell him kneel down, which Johnny thinks is a joke, and I say you killed Kazimir, just so he knows why he's there, so suddenly he thinks it's not joke, and I shoot him.'

Bogdan finally moves his bishop and it is Stephen's turn to scrunch his nose.

'I take his keys and his cards. We weigh him down with bricks and throw him over, never to be seen. Back we go to Newhaven, we say thank you to Steve's cousin, let's not speak of this. Then me and Steve, we drive to Johnny's house, we let ourselves in, we take his passport, we pack suitcase full of clothes, there is piles of money, you know, drugs money, and we take this too, and anything valuable we find. Some of the money is Tony's, like a lot, so I was glad to take it.'

'How much money?' asks Stephen.

'It was like hundred grand. I send fifty grand to Kazimir's family.'

'Good lad.'

'The rest I give to Steve. He wanted to open a gym and I thought was good investment. He's a good guy, no nonsense with him. Then I drive Steve to Gatwick, he take flight to Cyprus on Johnny's passport, no one looks. Easy. Then Steve fly straight back to England on his own passport. I call the police, anonymous, but I know enough that they take me serious. I tell them Johnny killed Kaz, and they raid his house.'

'And they find his passport gone and his clothes gone?'

'Exactly.'

'So they check the ports and airports and find he's scarpered off to Cyprus?' Stephen attacks Bogdan's bishop with a pawn. Just as Bogdan had hoped.

'And so they check and check for Johnny for a bit in Cyprus, but he's disappeared, and they just leave to Cypriot police in the end. No evidence that Johnny killed anyone, no drug money in his house, so everyone just forget in the end. Just move on.'

'Took your time with Curran though, eh?'

'Always just waiting for the best time. Just planning. I didn't want to get caught, you know?'

'I should think that would be the last thing you'd want, yes,' says Stephen.

'Anyway, couple of months ago I installed his surveillance system, the cameras, the alarm system, all of this. And I fitted the whole thing wrong pretty much. Nothing recording.'

'I see.'

'And I thought, so, now is the time. I can get in house, I got keys made, no one can see me.' Bogdan attacks Stephen's pawn, opening up a front that Stephen does not want opened up.

Stephen nods. 'Clever.'

'Just after I did it there's a ring, ring, ring at the door, but I stayed pretty calm, no worry.'

Stephen nods again and moves a pawn in quiet desperation. 'Good for you. What if they catch you?'

Bogdan shrugs. 'I don't know. I don't think they will.'

'Elizabeth will work it out, old boy. If she hasn't already.'

'I know, but I think she will understand.'

'I do too,' agrees Stephen. 'But the police would be a different matter. They are less easy to charm than Elizabeth.'

Bogdan nods. 'If they catch me, they catch me. But I laid a pretty good false trail, I think.'

'A false trail? And how did you do that?'

'Well, when we went to Johnny's house on that night, one of the things we took was a camera, so –'

Bogdan breaks off as they hear a key turn in the door. Elizabeth back late from something or other. Bogdan puts a finger to his lips and Stephen does the same in response. She walks in.

'Hello, boys.' She kisses Bogdan on the cheek and then holds Stephen in a tight embrace. As she does, Bogdan moves his queen and closes his trap.

'Checkmate.'

Elizabeth lets Stephen go and he smiles at the board and at Bogdan. He reaches out and shakes his hand.

'He's a crafty bugger, this one, Elizabeth. A grade-A crafty bugger.'

Elizabeth looks down at the board. 'Well played, Bogdan.'

'Thank you,' says Bogdan, and starts to set the pieces back up again.

'Well, I have quite a story for you both,' says Elizabeth. 'Can I make you a cup of tea, Bogdan?'

'Yes please,' says Bogdan. 'Milk, six sugars.'

'A coffee for me, love,' says Stephen. 'If it's not too much trouble?'

Elizabeth walks into the kitchen. She thinks about Penny, surely dead by now? That was how it ended, in an act of love. Then she thinks about John, settling down to a final sleep. He had taken care of Penny, but at what cost? Is he at peace? Is he out of his misery? She thinks of Annie Madeley and everything she has missed. Everyone has to leave the game. Once you're in, there is no other door but the exit. She reaches for Stephen's temazepam, then pauses and puts them back in the cupboard.

Elizabeth walks back to her husband. She takes his hand

in hers and kisses him on the lips. 'I think it might be time to cut down on the coffee, Stephen. All that caffeine. It can't be good for you.'

'Quite so,' says Stephen. 'Whatever you think is for the best.'

Stephen and Bogdan begin another game. Elizabeth turns back to the kitchen and neither man sees her tears.

115

Joyce

Sorry I haven't written for a while, it's been very busy around here. But I have a gooseberry crumble on the go and I thought there might be a few things you'd want to know.

They buried Penny and John the Tuesday before last. It was quite a quiet one, and it rained, which seemed about right. There were a few old colleagues of Penny's there. In fact, more than you would think, considering. It had been in the papers, Penny and John. They hadn't got the whole story straight, but they were near enough. The news had got wind that Penny was a friend of Ron, too. He was interviewed on *Kent Today* and they even showed it on the normal news later. Someone came down from the *Sun* to talk to him, but Ron was having none of that. He told them to park outside Larkin Court and then had them clamped.

Elizabeth wasn't at the funeral. We haven't discussed it, so that's that, I'm afraid. I wonder if she had already said her goodbyes? She must have, mustn't she?

I don't even know if Elizabeth has forgiven Penny. I'm afraid I take the Old Testament view that what Penny did was right. That's just me, and it's not something I would say out loud, but I'm glad she did what she did. I hope Peter Mercer was alive long enough to know what was happening to him.

Elizabeth is a good deal cleverer than me, and will have thought about it more, but I can't see that she could really blame Penny for what she did. Would Elizabeth have done the same? I think so. I think Elizabeth would have got away with it though.

But I do think Elizabeth must be sad at the secret. There were the two girls, Elizabeth and Penny, and their mysteries, and all the while Penny was the biggest mystery of all. That must hurt Elizabeth. Perhaps one day we'll talk about it.

Penny killed Peter Mercer and she kept it from John all her life. Until dementia broke her. And once John knew, he had to protect her. That's love, isn't it? That's what Gerry would have done for me. Because Peter Mercer murdered Annie Madeley, Penny murdered Peter Mercer. Because Penny murdered Peter Mercer, John murdered Ian Ventham. So it goes, I suppose. And at least now it's done. I wish peace on Penny and John, and I wish peace on poor Annie Madeley. For Peter Mercer, and for everything he caused, I wish nothing but torment.

The police have yet to find Turkish Johnny by the way, but they're looking. Chris and Donna have popped over here a couple of times. Chris has a new lady friend, but is being coy about it for now, and we can't get Donna to talk. Chris says they'll catch up with Johnny eventually, but Bogdan was round to fix my power shower the other day and he says Johnny is too smart for that.

If you really want my view, Johnny is far too convenient. Johnny came over and killed Tony for informing on him all those years ago? Why would Tony have informed on him? For his part in clearing up a murder that Tony committed? That makes no sense to me.

No, the only person too smart to be caught around here is Bogdan.

Don't you think he killed Tony Curran? I do. I'm sure he had a good reason, and I look forward to asking him. But not until he's fitted my new replacement window, because what if he takes offence? I wonder if Elizabeth suspects him too? She certainly hasn't mentioned chasing down Johnny recently, so perhaps she does.

I will have to check the crumble in a bit. Shall we get on to more pleasant tidings?

Hillcrest is already up and running, there are cranes and diggers up on the hill. They say Gordon Playfair got £4.2m for his land, and by 'they' I mean Elizabeth, so you can take it as gospel. He said goodbye to the house he'd lived in for seventy years and packed his belongings into a Land Rover and trailer. Then he drove the 400-odd yards down the hill and unpacked it all at a nice two-bed in Larkin Court.

Bramley Holdings gave him the flat as part of the deal. Which brings us on to another bit of news.

'Bramley Holdings'? It wasn't about apples, after all. I told you, though, that the name had rung a bell? Well, here's why.

When she was very small, Joanna had a little toy elephant, pink with white ears, and she would never let me wash it. I can't imagine the germs it carried, but I think that's not necessarily a bad thing with children. And the name of that elephant? Bramley. I had quite forgotten. She had so many toys and I'm a terrible mother.

Perhaps you see where this is going, though?

You remember we had taken Ventham's accounts to Joanna, of course, back when Elizabeth wondered if Ian Ventham had murdered Tony Curran?

Anyway, Joanna and Cornelius had looked through the accounts for us and they'd reported back, and that was the end of the matter.

But for Joanna it hadn't been the end of the matter at all. Not a bit of it.

Joanna and Cornelius had liked what they saw in the accounts. And they had liked what they read about Hillcrest. So Joanna had made a presentation to the other board members – this scene, in my head, is around the aeroplane-wing table – and then they bought the company. She was planning to buy it from Ian Ventham, but, of course, ended up buying it from Gemma Ventham. So isn't that a turn-up?

Joanna owns the whole place. Or Joanna's company, but that's the same thing, isn't it?

Now, this leads me on to Bernard, and you'll see why.

Joanna and I had never talked about Bernard, but she came down to be with me at the funeral, so had Elizabeth told her perhaps? Or did she just know? I think she just knew. So she came down and she held my hand, and in a weaker moment I put my head on her shoulder and that was nice. After the funeral she told me about Bramley Holdings. I pretended I had known all along, because I felt guilty about forgetting the elephant, but Joanna sees straight through me.

But we talked, and I told her I didn't think this was the sort of business they bought, and she agreed, but said it was 'a sector we have been keen to get into', but I see straight through her too and she admitted that was a lie. She did say there was plenty of money to be made, but she told me she had another reason too. Which I'll tell you now.

She sat on the lounger that she bought me, that would have been a tenth the price in IKEA, right beside the laptop she bought me that will never be carried anywhere, and here is what she said.

'Remember when you moved in here, and I told you it was a mistake? I told you it would be the end of you? Sitting in your chair, surrounded by other people just waiting out their days? I was wrong. It was the beginning of you, Mum. I thought I would never see you happy again after Dad died.'

(We had never talked about this. Both our faults.)

'Your eyes are alive, your laugh is back and it's thanks to

Coopers Chase and to Elizabeth and to Ron and Ibrahim and to Bernard, God rest his soul. And so I bought it, the company, the land, the whole development. And I bought it to say thank you, Mum. Though I know what you're going to say next, and I promise I will also make millions out of it, so don't panic.'

Well, I wasn't panicking, but that was what I was going to say next.

And so a couple of things you will want to know. The Garden of Eternal Rest is staying exactly where it is. Joanna says they'll make quite enough money out of Hillcrest, so The Woodlands has been quietly shelved. The graveyard is now protected, even if Coopers Chase is sold again (Joanna says they will sell it again one day, that's their job). But just you try and buy it, you'll see there are all sorts of covenants in place. It's going nowhere.

By the way. Just now, when I said it was both our faults that we hadn't talked about Gerry? Of course it wasn't both our faults. It was my fault. Sorry, Joanna.

We had a ceremony the other day. Elizabeth invited Matthew Mackie for lunch and along he came, no dog collar this time. We broke the news to him that Maggie was safe and I thought he would cry, but he didn't, he just asked to visit the grave. We walked up the hill with him, then we sat on Bernard and Asima's bench while he pushed open the iron gates and knelt beside the grave. This is when the tears came, as we knew they would when he saw the headstone.

I had watched a couple of days ago as Bogdan had spent the best part of the morning gently cleaning up the inscription 'Margaret Farrell, 1948–1971', before carving underneath, 'Patrick, 1971'. There really is nothing Bogdan can't do.

When Father Mackie broke down at this, we sent Ron to hold him and the two of them stayed there quite some while. Elizabeth, Ibrahim and I stayed on the bench and took in the view. I like it when men cry. Not too much, but this was just right.

There are always plenty of flowers on Maggie's grave now. I have added some of my own, and I'm sure you can guess where I got them from.

You'll want to know about the bench, too. Well, busy Bogdan took to the concrete with a pneumatic drill, then dug down until he found the tiger tea caddy, which he gave to me.

In Bernard's final letter there was rather a moving post-script, in which he had asked that his ashes be scattered off the pier in Fairhaven. I have it here.

'Part of me and part of Asima will always be together, right here. But she is floating free in holy waters, so let me drift on the tide until one day I find her again,' he had said. Very poetic Bernard, I'm sure.

Too poetic.

You and I know Bernard well enough to know that this was sentimental bunk. It was a message to me and it wasn't exactly the Enigma code. I wonder if Bernard might have thought I was a little thick, but I suppose he wanted it spelled out, just in case. Anyway, I knew Bernard had given me my instructions.

Sudhi and Majid had stayed at an airport hotel after the funeral, because that's their way, and I had offered to keep Bernard's ashes safe until they headed down to Fairhaven. When will these two learn?

I had Asima's ashes in the tea caddy and I had Bernard's ashes in a simple wooden urn. I took out my scales. Proper ones, because I don't trust the electronic ones.

I was very careful tipping out the ashes, because, much as I liked Bernard, I didn't want him all over my worktop. Within minutes, and with the help of a couple of intermediary bits of Tupperware (I felt a bit guilty about that) the deed was done.

In the tiger tea caddy that they had both wanted to buy the other for Christmas was half Bernard and half Asima. The next day we buried the tea caddy back under the bench where it belonged. We asked Matthew Mackie to bless the site and I think he was touched to be asked and did a lovely job.

And in the urn, half Asima and half Bernard. And, unbeknownst to them, that's what Sudhi and Majid took to Fairhaven the following day, so Asima could finally float free, but still in the embrace of the man she loved. We didn't join them, as we didn't really want to interfere.

I honestly don't know what to do with the Tupperware I used. If you've used two Tupperware containers to help mix the ashes of a dear friend and a woman he loved, without letting their children know, is it more disrespectful to keep them, or to throw them away? This is honestly not the sort of thing I had to worry about before I moved to Coopers Chase. Elizabeth will know what to do.

Talking of Elizabeth, she rang me earlier to tell me that someone had slid a very interesting note under her door. She wouldn't say what it was, but she said she'd have to pay someone a little visit and then she could tell me. What a tease!

Well, it is Thursday, so I must be on my way. I worried that, after Penny, we might stop meeting, or perhaps it would feel different. But that's not really how things work around here. Life goes on, until it doesn't. The Thursday Murder Club goes on meeting, mysterious notes are pushed under doors and murderers fit replacement windows. Long may it continue.

After the meeting I will pop over and see how Gordon Playfair is settling in. Just being a good neighbour, before you ask.

And, right on time, there's my crumble. I will let you know how everything goes.

Acknowledgements

Thank you so much for reading *The Thursday Murder Club*. Unless you haven't read it yet, and have just turned straight to the acknowledgements, which I accept is a possibility. You must live your life as you choose.

I first had the idea for *The Thursday Murder Club* a few years ago, when I was fortunate enough to visit a retirement community, full of extraordinary people with extraordinary stories, and even its very own 'contemporary upscale restaurant'. The residents of that retirement village know who they are, and I thank them for their support. Don't get ideas and start murdering each other though, please.

It is hard work writing a novel. I'm assuming that's the case for everyone, although who knows? Perhaps Salman Rushdie finds it easy? Either way, many people have helped me, knowingly or unknowingly, along the way. It is lovely to be able to thank them publicly here.

I want, first of all, to thank Mark Billingham. I had wanted to write a novel for a long time, and over a very nice lunch at Skewd Turkish restaurant in Barnet (delicious, great value for money, try the chicken wings) Mark gave me exactly the encouragement I needed, at exactly the right time. He also told me there were no rules to writing a crime novel, and then proceeded to tell me two great rules which I kept in mind throughout the writing of this book. Anyway, Mark, I will be forever grateful.

I was secretly squirrelled away for a long time writing *The Thursday Murder Club* and I want to thank a number of people for encouraging me to not give up during this time. Thank you to Ramita Navai, the best friend I could ever wish for, to Sarah Pinborough for telling me that, yes, it is supposed to be this difficult, to Lucy Prebble for always reminding me to 'get it done, and then get it good', to Bruce Lloyd for keeping the train on the tracks, and to Marian Keyes for the kindness and for the candle.

Also, special thanks to Sumudu Jayatilaka for being my first reader. It will always mean the world to me.

There comes a point when a book more or less exists, and that's when you need wise and brilliant people around you to make it better. The few people who saw early drafts of this book, and are forever sworn to secrecy, include my wonderfully talented brother, Mat Osman (author of the brilliant *The Ruins*, also out now), and my friend Annabel Jones, who took time out of her ridiculously busy *Black Mirror* schedule to read the book and provide so many answers I was missing. Thank you so much, Annabel; you should do this for a living.

I want to thank the brilliant team at Viking, most particularly my editor Katy Loftus, for backing me and supporting me, and for coming up with so many different, kind, ways of saying, 'I'm not sure this bit really works.' And behind every great editor is a great assistant editor, so thank you from us both to Vikki Moynes.

Thank you also to the rest of the team at Viking: editorial manager Natalie Wall, the comms team Georgia Taylor, Ellie Hudson, Amelia Fairney, Chloe Davies and Olivia Mead, who have heard me say 'well, maybe' so many times. Thank you too to the amazing sales team – Sam Fanaken, Tineke Mollemans, Ruth Johnstone, Kyla Dean, Eleanor Rhodes Davies, Rachel Myers and Natasha Lanigan – and to Eleanor Beckford, Annie Underwood and Ruppa Patel who took on the Herculanean task of keeping *The Thursday Murder Club* in stock and were victorious. To

Richard Bravery for creating the cover of my dreams and the DeadGood online team, and Indira Birnie from the Penguin UK website for spreading the message far and wide. A book is such a team effort, and I couldn't wish for a better team.

I would also like to thank my US editor, Pamela Dorman, and her wonderful assistant editor, Jeramie Orton, and I apologize once again for making you have to google Ryman's, Holland & Barrett and Sainsbury's 'Taste the Difference'. I am also indebted to the thoroughness and forensic creativity of my copy-editor, Trevor Horwood, without who I would never know what the days of the week certain dates were in 1971. Or, as Trevor would immediately point out, 'without whom'.

Writing a book is its own reward, and I was very ready to chalk this whole project up to experience before sending the very first draft to my agent, Juliet Mushens. From her very first reply, however, things changed and, thanks to Juliet, I realized that *The Thursday Murder Club* might be an actual book, which actual people might actually read. Juliet has been a force of nature from the start – brilliant, creative, funny and refreshingly unconventional. I couldn't have done any of this without her. Thank you so much, Juliet. She is ably supported by the wonderful Liza DeBlock, who, given she has to deal with so many important contracts, is, refreshingly, slightly more conventional.

I'll end, if I may, with the big guns.

Thank you to my mum, Brenda Osman. I hope that, amongst other things, there is a sense of kindness and justice, running through *The Thursday Murder Club*, and that comes from you. It comes as well, of course, from your parents, my grandparents, Fred and Jessie Wright, much missed but, I hope, very present within these pages. Thank you too to my wonderful auntie, Jan Wright. We are a small family, but I think we pack a punch.

And thank you, finally, to my children, Ruby and Sonny.

I have no intention of embarrassing you too much, so I will just tell you how much I love you.

Read on for a preview of the next book in the Thursday Murder Club series . . .

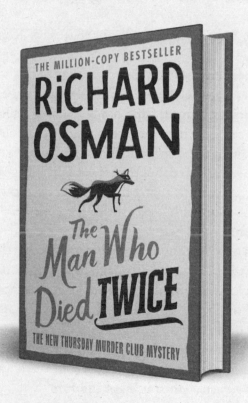

PRE-ORDER NOW

1

THE FOLLOWING THURSDAY . . .

'I was talking to a woman in Ruskin Court and she said she's on a diet,' says Joyce, finishing her glass of wine. 'She's eighty-two!'

'Zimmer frames make you look fat,' says Ron. 'It's the thin legs.'

'Why diet at eighty-two?' says Joyce. 'What's a sausage roll going to do to you? Kill you? Well, join the queue.'

The Thursday Murder Club has concluded its latest meeting. This week they have been looking at the cold case of a Hastings newsagent who murdered an intruder with a crossbow. He'd been arrested, but then the media had got involved, and the consensus was that a man should be allowed to protect his own shop with a crossbow, for goodness' sake, and he walked free, head held high.

A month or so later police had discovered that the intruder was dating the newsagent's teenage daughter, and the newsagent had a long record of GBH, but at that point everybody had moved on. It was 1975, after all. No CCTV, and no one wanting to make a fuss.

'Do you think a dog might be good company?' asks Joyce. 'I thought I might either get a dog or join Instagram.'

'I would advise against it,' says Ibrahim.

'Oh, you'd advise against everything,' says Ron.

'Broadly, yes,' agrees Ibrahim.

'Not a big dog, of course,' says Joyce. 'I haven't got the hoover for a big dog.'

Joyce, Ron, Ibrahim and Elizabeth are enjoying lunch at the restaurant that sits at the heart of the Coopers Chase community. There is a bottle of red and a bottle of white on their table. It is around a quarter to twelve.

'Don't get a small dog though, Joyce,' says Ron. 'Small dogs are like small men: always got a point to prove. Yapping it up, barking at cars.'

Joyce nods. 'Perhaps a medium dog, then? Elizabeth?'

'Mmm, good idea,' replies Elizabeth, though she is not really listening. How could she be, after the letter she received last night?

She's picking up the main points, of course. Elizabeth always stays alert, because you never know what might fall into your lap. She has heard all sorts over the years. A snippet of conversation in a Berlin bar, a loose-lipped Russian sailor on shore leave in Tripoli. In this instance, on a Thursday lunchtime in a sleepy Kent retirement village, it seems that Joyce wants a dog, there is a discussion about sizes, and Ibrahim has doubts. But her mind is elsewhere.

The letter was slipped under Elizabeth's door last night, by an unseen hand.

Dear Elizabeth,

I wonder if you remember me? Perhaps you don't, but without blowing my own trumpet, I imagine you might.

Life has worked its magic once more, and I discover, upon moving in this week, that we are now neighbours. What company I keep! You must be thinking they let in any old riff-raff these days.

I know it has been some while since you last saw me, but I think it would be wonderful to renew our acquaintance after all these years.

Would you like to join me at 14 Ruskin Court for a drink? A little house-warming? If so, how would 3 p.m. tomorrow suit? No need to reply, I shall await with a bottle of wine regardless.

It really would be lovely to see you. So much to catch up on. An awful lot of water under the bridge and so on.

I do hope you remember me, and I do hope to see you tomorrow.

Your old friend,
Marcus Carmichael

Elizabeth has been mulling it over ever since.

The last time she had seen Marcus Carmichael would have been late November 1981, a very dark, very cold night by Lambeth Bridge, the Thames at low tide, her breath clouding in the freezing air. There had been a team of them, each one a specialist, and Elizabeth was in charge. They arrived in a white Transit van, shabby on the outside, seemingly owned by 'G. Procter – Windows, Gutters, All Jobs Considered', but, on the inside, gleaming, full of buttons and screens. A young constable had cordoned off an area of the foreshore, and the pavement on the Albert Embankment had been closed.

Elizabeth and her team clambered down a flight of stone steps, lethal with slick moss. The low tide had left behind a corpse, propped, almost sitting, against the near parapet of the bridge. Everything had been done properly, Elizabeth had made sure of that. One of her team had examined the clothing and rifled through the pockets of his heavy over-coat, a young woman from Highgate had taken photographs, and the doctor had recorded the death. It was clear the man had jumped into the Thames further upstream, or been pushed. That was for the coroner to decide. It would all be typed into a report by somebody or other, and Elizabeth would simply add her initials at the bottom. Neat and tidy.

The journey back up those slick steps with the corpse on a military stretcher had taken some time. A young constable, thrilled to have been called to help, had fallen and broken an ankle, which was all they needed. They explained they wouldn't be able to call an ambulance for the time being, and he took it in fairly good part. He received an unwarranted promotion several months later, so no lasting harm was done.

Her little unit eventually reached the Embankment, and the body was loaded into the white Transit van. 'All Jobs Considered'.

The team dispersed, save for Elizabeth and the doctor, who stayed in the van with the corpse as it was driven to a morgue in Hampshire. She hadn't worked with this particular doctor before – broad, red-faced, a dark moustache turning grey – but he was interesting enough. A man you would remember. They'd discussed euthanasia and cricket until the doctor had dozed off.

Ibrahim is making a point with his wine glass. 'I'm afraid I would advise against a dog altogether, Joyce, small, medium, or large. At your time in life.'

'Oh, here he comes,' says Ron.

'A medium dog,' says Ibrahim, 'say a terrier, or a Jack Russell perhaps, would have a life expectancy of around fourteen years.'

'Says who?' asks Ron.

'Says the Kennel Club, in case you want to take it up with them, Ron. Would you like to take it up with them?'

'No, you're all right.'

'Now, Joyce,' Ibrahim continues, 'you are seventy-seven years old?'

Joyce nods, 'Seventy-eight next year.'

'Well, that goes without saying, yes,' agrees Ibrahim. 'So,

at seventy-seven years old, we have to take a look at your life expectancy.'

'Ooh yes?' says Joyce. 'I love this sort of thing. I had my Tarot done on the pier once. She said I was going to come into money.'

'Specifically, we have to look at the chances of your life expectancy exceeding the life expectancy of a medium dog.'

'It's a mystery to me why you never got married, old son,' says Ron to Ibrahim, and takes the bottle of white wine from the cooler on the table. 'With that silver tongue of yours. Top-up, anyone?'

'Thank you, Ron,' says Joyce. 'Fill it to the brim to save having to do it again.'

Ibrahim continues. 'A woman of seventy-seven has a fifty-one per cent chance of living for another fifteen years.'

'This is jolly,' says Joyce. 'I didn't come into money, by the way.'

'So if you were to get a dog now, Joyce, would you outlive it? That's the question.'

'I'd outlive a dog through pure spite,' says Ron. 'We'd just sit in opposite corners of the room, staring each other out, and see who went first. Not me. It's like when we were negotiating with British Leyland in 'seventy-eight. The moment one of their lot went to the loo first, I knew we had 'em.' Ron knocks back more wine. 'Never go to the loo first. Tie a knot in it if you have to.'

'The truth is, Joyce,' says Ibrahim, 'maybe you would, and maybe you wouldn't. Fifty-one per cent. It's the toss of a coin, and I don't believe that is a risk worth taking. You must never die before your dog.'

'And is that an old Egyptian saying, or an old psych-iatrist's saying?' asks Joyce. 'Or something you just made up?'

Ibrahim tips his glass towards Joyce again, an indication

of more wisdom to come. 'You must die before your children, of course, because you have taught them to live without you. But not your dog. You teach your dog only to live *with* you.'

'Well, that is certainly food for thought, Ibrahim; thank you,' says Joyce. 'A bit soulless, perhaps. Don't you think, Elizabeth?'

Elizabeth hears, but her mind is still in the back of the speeding Transit van, with the corpse and the doctor with the moustache. Not the only such occasion in Elizabeth's career, but unusual enough to be memorable – anyone who knew Marcus Carmichael would have known that.

'Get a dog that's old already; beat Ibrahim's system,' Elizabeth says.

And here was Carmichael again, years later. Looking for what? A friendly chat? Cosy reminiscence by an open fire? Who knew?

Their bill is brought to the table by a new member of the serving staff. Her name is Poppy, and she has a tattoo of a daisy on her forearm. Poppy has been at the restaurant for nearly two weeks now and, thus far, the reviews have not been good.

'You've brought us table twelve, Poppy,' says Ron.

Poppy nods. 'Oh, yes, that's . . . silly me . . . what table is this?'

'Fifteen,' says Ron. 'You can tell because of the big number fifteen written on the candle.'

'Sorry,' says Poppy. 'It's just remembering the food, and carrying it, and then the numbers. I'll get the hang of it eventually.' She walks back to the kitchens.

'She is very well meaning,' says Ibrahim. 'But ill-suited to this role.'

'She has lovely nails though,' says Joyce. 'Immaculate. Immaculate, aren't they, Elizabeth?'

Elizabeth nods. 'Immaculate.' Not the only thing she has

noticed about Poppy, who seems to have sprung from nowhere, with her nails and her incompetence. But she has other things on her mind for now, and the mystery of Poppy can wait for another day.

She is going through the text of the letter again in her head. *'I wonder if you remember me?'* *'An awful lot of water under the bridge since then.'*

Did Elizabeth remember Marcus Carmichael? What a ridiculous question. She had found Marcus Carmichael's dead body slumped against a Thames bridge at low tide. She had helped to carry his dead body up those slick stone steps in the dead of night. She had sat feet away from his corpse in a white Transit van advertising window cleaning services. She had broken the news of his death to his young wife and she had stood beside the grave at his funeral, as an appropriate mark of respect.

So, yes, Elizabeth remembers Marcus Carmichael very well indeed. Time to be back in the room though. One thing at a time.

Elizabeth reaches for the white wine. 'Ibrahim, not everything is about numbers. Ron, you would die long before the dog, male life expectancy is far lower than female life expectancy, and you know what your GP has said about your blood sugar. And Joyce, we both know you've already made up your mind. You'll get a rescue dog. It'll be sitting somewhere right now, all alone with big eyes, just waiting for you. You will be powerless, and, besides, it'll be fun for all of us, so let's stop even discussing it.'

Job done.

'And how about Instagram?' says Joyce.

'I don't even know what that is, so feel free,' says Elizabeth, and finishes her wine.

An invitation from a dead man? On reflection, she will be accepting.

FOR EXCLUSIVE GIVEAWAYS, QUIZZES AND THE LATEST UPDATES

The Thursday MURDER Club

NEWSLETTER